Awakening

Book One in the Fire & Ice Series

By

Karen Payton Holt

AF472652

Copyright - Karen Payton Holt: 2018

All rights reserved.

No part of this publication may be reproduced, stored in a retrieval system, or transmitted, in any form or by any means without prior written permission of the author, except for 'brief quotations' as part of articles of critique or review.

No part of this publication may be circulated in any form of binding or cover other than that in which it is published.

The story is a work of fiction.
All characters in this book are fictitious and any resemblance to real persons, living or dead, is purely coincidental.

If you are here, you are about to read my book and to start out on an adventure.

Think 'Twilight' meets 'Game of Thrones', with a dark twist, and you are in the right mindset to enter the world of Fire & Ice.

This is BOOK ONE in the Fire & Ice Series:
Awakening.

Five more upcoming releases are:

BOOK TWO: Survival
BOOK THREE: Earth Walker
BOOK FOUR: Heart of Stone
BOOK FIVE: Invasion

Fire & Ice Prequel: Death of Connor Sanderson.

For the latest news on the publishing dates visit my websites:

karenpaytonholt.com
Karen Payton Holt on Facebook.
@karenpaytonholt on TWITTER.

This is the start of our epic journey, and I hope you enjoy the book. Please share your thoughts and feelings in reviews – this is my first novel and I welcome your support!

I dedicate this novel to the two people who believed in me, drove me forward, and, at times, gave me a much needed kick up the posterior.

This is for my mum, Sylvia, and my friend of forty years, Steve.

Chapter 1

Survival rule number one, don't get caught.

Rebekah headed out along Half Moon Street and turned left into Piccadilly. Long strides drove her forward, but she kept her footfalls light. Silence was an ingrained habit.

This part of London – The City of Westminster - showed signs of an affluent past. A brisk walk across Green Park would take her to Buckingham Palace, its weathered façade presenting a brave face to an empty world. At the end of the road, Rebekah could just make out the somber landmark of the legendary Piccadilly Circus. Soot-black tracks left by broken neon lights snaked across the stained walls of the buildings. She found it hard to imagine how it would feel to push her way along this street through a crush of eager tourists. She dimly remembered, from her six-year-old perspective, city traffic rushing by as she was guided along by her mother's hand. At that time, being so small, the petrol fumes from the rumbling growling engines were overpowering. *Was it really fifteen years ago?*

A sudden staccato of bird song broke the silence, and the rustling leaves whipping along the street focused her attention. *It's getting late.* The tightening of her skin had nothing to do with the cold. She scanned the grime-encrusted glass of the shop front windows, checking for signs of movement. The object of the mission was simple. With a grim smile, she recalled Harry's gruff instructions: *Get in, raid the drugstore, and get out.*

Outside the store, keeping her movements small and contained, she pulled a cut-down crowbar from her backpack.

The exposed wood of the door frame looked solid, but Rebekah had no concerns about her skills; practice had made perfect. She might look light and feminine, but her frame was entirely honed muscle. Fitting the blade in-between the door and the lock, it took seconds for the wood to crack and the door to spring open.

Rebekah stepped from the sidewalk into the gloomy interior of the derelict store, hesitating only long enough for her eyes to adjust. She took a deep breath, set her jaw, and strode forward. Her sneakers made barely a whisper as they skimmed the marble tiled floor, disturbing the layer of dust. *No one has been here in ages. 'They' don't need medicine.* Despite the evidence of abandonment, a prickling of unease drove her on. *Let's get this done.*

In the pharmacy section, she opened her backpack, pulled out a wad of cotton gauze, and scanned the bottles which filled the shelves. She zeroed in on 'antibiotics' and 'painkillers'. Expiration dates no longer mattered. *No one has died from swallowing old pills, not yet, anyhow.* Working methodically, she opened each container, stuffed wadding inside, and, if the pills didn't rattle when she shook the bottle, it went in her bag.

Checking her watch, she grimaced. *Nearly three o'clock. It'll be dusk soon.* She abandoned the remaining dozen bottles or so, hoisted the backpack up onto a shoulder and headed for the exit doors. The light blue decal emblazoned across the window told her the drugstore was an outlet of 'Boots the Chemist', and she made a mental note to tell Uncle Harry to change the foraging status here to 'amber', designating it almost empty.

Rebekah paused with a foot over the threshold. She resisted the urge to rub the goosebumps on her bare arms. Autumn in England was harsh, and chilled flesh was a useful survival tool. She shot a look up at the clouds stampeding across the sky. The clumps of gray blotting out the weak sunshine was the last thing she needed; darkness meant danger. Her stomach churned.

She glanced left, then right, and set her sights on Green Park. In the eco-town library books, she had seen pictures of the Royal processions and spectacular firework displays once held there. This ghostly quiet and expressionless London made her feel cheated. *'They' have a lot to answer for.* Through the park, a straight run down to Vauxhall Bridge Road, over the River Thames, and she'd be back at the safe house. *Okay, let's get moving.*

Taking a deep breath, Rebekah darted forward into the street. But, without warning, the wind picked up. The sudden chilling blast whipped feathered strands of blond hair across her face. *Shit, they're coming. How many?* Even though her brain screamed 'go back', she hurried on across the asphalt. She leapt up onto the opposite sidewalk, vaulted over the top rung of the iron railings, and into the overgrown parkland on the other side. She landed heavily on the potholed ground, struggling for balance as the shrieking gale plastered her shirt to her body. Rebekah stood stone still. *Too late.* The cover of some sturdy oak trees was tantalizing, but they were too far away. *Don't move. That's Greg's theory: Don't run, don't move.*

She shrugged the backpack from her shoulder, dangling it from her fingertips before letting it fall into the knee-high grass. She wanted to follow it, sink down onto her knees, lie flat even, but he was already here.

She prayed as the scream of rushing air filled her ears.

The dark mass streaked across her vision like the trailing blur of a comet. As the air pressure dropped in its wake, and the fear aching in Rebekah's chest began to ease, the shockwave hit, tossing her into the air like an under stuffed rag doll. Landing with a thud, twenty feet away, winded and unable to breathe, she lay gazing skyward. Dirty gray clouds retreated behind a black velvet curtain, and, as her lips formed the word 'ouch', she lost consciousness.

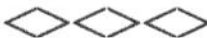

Rebekah awoke with every muscle locked tight. Awareness had arrived with a jolt and she felt sick. *I'm in their hospital.* Every body part screamed with tension, but 'they' didn't fidget, and so, neither must she.

When she rocked her head, it pressed on a bruise, bringing tears to her eyes. A memory broke the surface like an iceberg wallowing in murky depths. *I'm still alive, so I didn't bleed.* Taking a careful breath made her ribs ache and she remembered the hard landing on cold ground, and then the littering of stars which filled her head. *Lights out.*

Her fingertips explored the padded edges of the narrow bed. Her heart sank. *An examination table.* The thin foam mattress compressed beneath her shoulder blades made lying still hurt as pins and needles numbed her buttocks. She dropped her head to one side, prepared for the soreness this time, and assessed the cold sparse examining room. There were no monitors for reading the vital signs of life, no resuscitation aids, and no oxygen tanks. There was not even a trolley of dressings for wounds. However, a frightening array of Mole grips and pliers winked in the light.

Her cramped muscles burning from staying still, she gave herself another survival lecture. *Get out. Now.* It took only a few deep breaths to calm her pulse rate, proving that the enhanced beta-blockers coursing through her system were still working. *The pheromone suppressant spray is good for eight hours.* She swallowed noisily. The room was cold, and wearing summer clothes in autumn had chilled her skin. *But for how long?*

Registering for the first time that the room had no windows, she calculated the number of steps needed to reach the door and began the countdown in her head. *Three, two-*

At a blur of movement, her thoughts hit a brick wall. *Someone's in here.*

The door clicked as it swung closed and a puff of air brushed across her skin.

Through hooded lashes, Rebekah gathered a fleeting impression of a square jaw and black glossy hair. Fear killed the urge to leap from the table. She could not move.

"I'm Doctor Connor," he said as he glanced around the room. "Your escort has stepped out?"

Rebekah nodded. *Escort?* She knew a minefield when she saw one. To say as little as possible was all she had left.

His expression became fixed. "Unconscious for two minutes. That's not enough time to rehydrate. Let's take a look at you."

Only two minutes? Shit. Dredging up knowledge of predators and prey from when natural history still had meaning, Rebekah stayed frozen.

The doctor's eyes glittered as he swept a glance over her face, before traveling down the length of her body. He absently brushed hair back from his brow. Rebekah struggled with the tightness in her chest at the thought of those long, white fingers wrapped around a set of Mole grips.

In silence, he leaned forward and placed a hand on her ankle. His touch was cold, but not icy. *Maybe, he has just fed?*

When his assessment reached her hips and his hands spanned her pelvis, she suppressed a flinch at the pressure.

His detachment felt encouraging. Rebekah concentrated hard on directing an unblinking stare at the ceiling while his fingertips moved upward and probed her stomach. With a jolt, as if he'd been stung, the tendons in his neck became corded, and his white coat tightened over his shoulders. In a blur of agitation, he whipped his cold fingertips away.

Gripping the edges of the mattress, Rebekah kept the doctor in her sights.

"Your feeding network appears to be intact," he said gruffly. He cleared the gravel from his throat and looked her in the eye. "When did you last feed?"

"An hour ago," she whispered.

A frown chiseled into his brow as he fired off a series of questions which set Rebekah's mind reeling.

"Have you suffered infrared exposure?"

"Any tendon sheath grating?"

"Lubrication dead spots?"

"Problems swallowing or stiffening of the jaw?"

She shot back the answers, hoping 'no' was the correct option.

He plowed on as though working through a tick list inside his head. His gray eyes clouded with preoccupation, like warm breath on cold glass.

Is that a good sign? Is he bored?

Searching for clues, she noticed his chest moved when he expelled air through his throat to speak. *Can I disguise my breathing that way? And for how long?* Uncle Harry's modified beta-blockers worked, but she knew her depressed heart rate might be detectable at close quarters. *He's getting too close.*

"Can I go now?" she asked in a monotone she hoped fit in with a just-fed persona.

The doctor met her stare, and after what seemed an age of deliberation, his broad shoulders shifted. "Sure, you seem fine. But, if you get any hardening, come back. Once your flesh becomes desiccated, I can't help you." He paused, looked more closely into her eyes, and added, "Get some sleep. Your stress levels are high, and you know what that does."

The door swung shut. Her brain barely detected the white blur of movement which her eyes missed altogether. *He's gone.*

Her still-clenched muscles burned as a jack-in-the-box of chaotic words taunted her. Hardening, rehydrating, tendon sheath grating, and dead spots was an information explosion of concepts; but one stood out, like the flare of a match head struck in the dark; 'sleep'. *The streets are never empty. We thought they didn't sleep.*

"And what about stress levels?" she whispered.

Before she could persuade her frozen muscles that movement was a good thing, a breeze fanned her hair and a shadow dimmed her vision again. The doctor was back. Even her brain had not registered the movement this time.

"When were you turned?" he asked sharply.

Rebekah suppressed her start of surprise, cursing the missed opportunity of escape. *Did he hear me?* A flutter of panic fought to engulf her.

His nostrils flared as he repeated, "When were you turned?"

How old am I? She studied the doctor's smooth twenty-something looking face and tried to think in immortal years.

"Just decades will do," he pressed.

"Two." Rasping through a dry throat, she plucked the figure out of midair and mentally crossed her fingers.

"Two decades? *Maybe* that explains the smell, the residue of congealed human blood..." His voice trailed off as he sank into thought.

The tense expression on his face scared her. *Is this it? Game over?*

In a heart-stopping change of direction, he shrugged off his distraction and said firmly, "You need revival sleep."

At her blank look, he muttered, "Oh for heaven's sake. Brain tissue is thirsty, but you've just fed, right?" Clearly impatient, his glance moved down over her exposed neck to the bow of her clavicle. “Your color is-”

“Yes,” she cut in, almost choking when his attention darted back to her face. “I’ve just fed.”

“Good. Dead bone marrow no longer makes blood, so you have to be well-fed for this. Body tissue rehydrates spontaneously, but not the brain. You have to work at that.”

Rebekah risked a nod.

“Relax, clear your mind and visualize opening the door to the dehydrated control center in your brain. In this case your stress center. Your reflexes should take care of the rest. It will get easier to master, but be sure to practice in a safe place.” The doctor stared at her, looking for some sign she understood.

Rebekah nodded again, hanging onto a neutral expression. Even if she could have forced the words out, she dared not ask questions. She hoped silence would encourage him to continue.

His tone was condescending as he said, “And do it soon, before you get too agitated. If you don’t feed, your tissue will harden, your throat will shrivel, and then, it’s too late.” He ticked the list off on long pale fingers. “Locked-in syndrome; a conscious brain trapped inside a granite body.”

He spoke slowly, and she guessed he thought she was stupid. But she wasn’t complaining.

“Revival sleep,” she muttered, “Okay.”

A scowl etched deep lines into his firm skin. “When your escort gets here, go straight back to your cluster house. You should know all this. And rehydrate only *one* control center at a time, or your brain will shut down.” His gaze sharpened. “Is that what happened today? When they found you lying outside? For goodness’ sake, this is survival one-oh-one,” he muttered, and then he vanished again.

Rebekah counted to five. *It’s now or never.* She swung her legs over the side of the bed and shoved her feet into her sneakers. The room swam, and her feet felt numb, but she drove the sensations to the back of her mind. Gritting her teeth, she crossed the room and steadied herself with a hand on the wall. She eased open the door and emerged cautiously into a silent hallway. The green emergency exit sign was no longer illuminated, but the sight of a gray man running on a black background still galvanized her into action. Keeping her movement smooth and fast, she headed out along the deserted expanse of waxed floor. Her heart clattered as she pushed open the exit door and welcomed the chilled damp air on her skin.

Outside on the street, she pressed back into the cold marble stone wall of the hospital and a shudder rattled through her body. Relief made breathing hard as she tried not to think about the doctor. *They still pretend to be human, like a veneer of civility over an empty shell.* She found the echoes of human behavior creepy.

The doctor had looked so normal. It was not what she wanted to see, slate-grey eyes sharp with intelligence. His breath had fanned her face with a clean sharp scent and not the stench of rotting flesh she expected.

Her heart thumped and her tongue glued itself to the roof of her mouth as she glanced back at the closed exit door. *Did I fool him or is he raising the alarm? Calling to have me taken to the farm.* Her chest hurt as she took a deep breath and shoved away from the wall.

Doctor Connor strode along the corridor, his coat flaring out behind as he found relief in acceleration. Agitation was not a familiar sensation, and he didn't like it.

Broken bones in immortals were rare, so his inspection of the girl had been cursory, although essential. He knew displaced bones could interrupt the blood flow through the tissue and the dead spots would harden to a leaden weight. *Removal's not always possible and no one enjoys dragging a lump of granite around, so it's best to catch it early.*

Still replaying the consultation, he whisked down the hallway, his fingers flexing at his sides as if he relived the jolt which shot up his arm when he touched the chilled flesh of her stomach. His jaw snapped shut. He huffed in irritation, and the same odor which burned his sinuses when in the examination room stung his nasal lining again.

What was *the singeing aroma?* He groped around in his mental filing system. *It was more than the metallic blood fumes detectable after feeding. Somewhere in the last hundred years I've had this feeling, but when?* His throat felt raw, and the urge to feed flooded his mouth with a venom and anticoagulant cocktail. The girl's scent clung like syrup, and it was as though someone had rung his dinner bell. *I'm missing something.*

His frustration grew as he chased down and discarded possibilities.

Perhaps I *need revival sleep.* He found putting in forty hours at the hospital easy. He preferred dealing with those he could read. *Most of the patients I see are as challenging as a comic book. Take that female, her mistakes are tragically predictable.*

Connor grinned. *Now, if Julian had his way and forced me to join the hive council, I'd* expect *my stress levels to be through the roof. Dealing with manufactured smiles and cloaked intentions of councilors may have suited Julian for the past few decades, but I favor the direct approach.*

Thankfully, Connor found the familiar surroundings of his hospital made handling his sleep requirements an effortless routine. *Until today.*

It amused him knowing humans thought the undead didn't sleep'. *If only they knew.* Sleep was the dangerous balancing act of relinquishing control and letting the inner demons out to play. The *difficulty* came in choosing *when* to sleep.

And the girl won't survive long if she doesn't get to grips with that. Connor's thoughts settled a hard smile on his face as he muttered aloud, "I don't have time to babysit her, and she should have learned this stuff by now. It's not that hard."

He wondered if he should have talked her through the anger management of rap-sleep and the psychosis of grave sleep, then grimaced.

I feel like a glorified nursemaid. But the girl was gnawing at instincts which stretched beyond those of parenting. Her scent had gotten past his throat. His lungs stung, even now. His ribcage bellowed to expel her taste and he began to pant uncontrollably;

this was not a normal undead function. *The last time I felt like this, I was on the human farm and overdue for rap-sleep. Their damp odor played havoc-*

Connor stopped dead as realization hit.

He retraced his steps, sweeping through the empty examination room, then raced along the hospital corridors. He burst out through the solid glass doors, stopped at the top of the flight of stone steps, and scanned the sidewalk. He glanced at his watch. *Fourteen seconds. She can't have got far.* He descended the steps and made his way to the side exit. When he saw the girl, he surged forward, gripped her arm and moved her into a shaded alcove. He stood so close she couldn't look up without colliding with his chin.

"You're human," he said, pushing the words through clamped teeth. He turned his head to watch the street, the muscle ticking in his jaw betraying his air of calm.

Looking down, Connor met her gaze and, even though she was trembling, he found gritty determination in her brown eyes. Her chin lifted to a defiant angle, and he almost smiled. *What did it take to brazen this out?* He cocked his head as the rushing tide of her pulse throbbing against his cold palm stirred the silt of his own human memories. Things were suddenly not as clear as he expected.

She swallowed noisily.

"Where is your hideaway?" he asked. "And don't waste time lying, you need to get back before others notice you." He glanced down at her set features. "You'll be safer with me."

"I can get back alone."

"Mmm. Our females are outnumbered," he said quietly.

"What are you?" she whispered.

"Folklore labelled us vampires." Connor smiled. "It's as good a name as any."

The girl frowned.

Connor rocked his weight from one foot to the other, impatient to get moving. "Enough talking, we need to move. You'll stand out like a sore thumb without an escort. Human men were no match for our females, however, when up against our own kind, you- I mean *they* are still the weaker sex. You *need* me." Skepticism coated the words as he added, "And, do you know what time it is?"

Despite his white-coated torso obscuring her view, Connor sensed that she understood. Beneath his grasp, he felt a shudder rattle through her body. He shifted slightly, allowing her sight of the eerily silent procession of bodies flowing past, each one had peacefully rapt expressions molded to their faces. By early evening, the streets would be crowded with immortals out walking.

"It's called 'promenade'. You'll just have to trust me," he said. Raising a brow, he added, "So, where are we going?"

The slump of her shoulders was the sign Connor needed. She had barely acknowledged defeat when he slipped his cold hand around her waist and spanned her ribcage. The girl's feet lightly skimmed the sidewalk as he disguised her cumbersome human gait. Using the flowing tide of promenade, they glided along until he peeled away from the throng and accelerated rapidly through the deserted side streets.

Shooting a penetrating glance down at her dazed profile, he asked, "Which street?"

He interpreted her hand signals with unerring accuracy until at the opportune moment, he reduced their speed to that of a cruising car and looked down into her closed features.

"This is it." She grudgingly flared out an arm.

Bringing them to a standstill, Connor slowly released her. A feeling of reluctance took him by surprise and, for a moment, time stood still, until he stirred and broke the spell. Jerking his chin up, being abrupt to the point of rudeness, he said, "Goodbye, and be more careful." In a gusting vortex which kicked dirt up from the sidewalk, he vanished.

Chapter 2

Fighting the prickling resentment, Rebekah almost muttered 'overbearing leech', but thought better of it. It irritated her that he gave so little away. *He called the evening invasion 'promenade'.* The group had worked out that sunset was a siren call to them – cold ones, immortals, undead, nightwalkers, vampires – call them whatever worked, but she had hoped to find out more. *But, maybe there is no more.*

The numbing cold of wind-chill had left her arms feeling leaden. Her head still spun from the fast-forward propulsion which had blended the images of London into the whisking colors of a spinning top. Even though the biting breeze buffeting her body numbed her thoughts, it hadn't scattered all her senses. Rebekah looked up and down the deserted street, listening for anything out of place. The anxious moment of standing on the uneven paving slabs stretched into one of full-blown, immobilizing fear. *What happens now? Has he really gone?*

Wrapping her arms around her ribcage, she tucked her chin down and powered her way down the street. The thirty minutes it took her to scurry along the sidewalk, hugging the straggling hedge boundaries of the front gardens and listening, left her lungs burning from sucking in cold air. Like a rabbit caught out in the open, she stopped suddenly, held her breath and scanned the shadows.

She swallowed the lump in her throat, and darted sideways up the steps of a Victorian terraced house.

Built in an era when houses were constructed entirely of brick, the thick walls of the safe house provided a feeling of protection. The grime on the windows and peeling paintwork fostered an air of neglect, and overgrown paving slabs out front made it appear as deserted as every other house in the terrace. The dwelling represented a place to sleep and store supplies ready for transportation to the eco-town. Situated south of the River Thames, and away from the hub of the vampire community, it served as a refuge for humans, provided they kept quiet. *Until now.*

Once inside, she welcomed the cool embrace of the dark hallway. When the heavy door closed, it felt like diving underwater; it dampened all sound except for the palpitations inside her chest. She stood motionless while her eyes adjusted to the gloom, holding her breath and listening until the tendrils of hope evaporated on a sigh. *I'm alone.*

Panic clawed at her chest, and she refused to let it win. *Keep calm, it's not as though I don't know what to do.* Handling an 'emergency' formed a big part of 'forage' training. *I have to prove I can be trusted if I want to visit London again.* Using slow steadying breaths, she took back control of her body and walked forward.

Cobwebs hung from the high ceilings and the empty lightbulb socket dangling from the elaborate Victorian plaster rose taunted her. Along one wall, a succession of brass-framed mirrors captured any stray beams of early evening light and nurtured them. *It's a pathetic attempt at an early warning system, but they* do *have reflections, and we'll take anything we can get.* Trying to gather intelligence about the enemy felt like an impossible task. Some of them moved faster than others, some appeared stronger, and they were out there twenty-four seven. *We don't have much to go on.*

Her own gray reflection was a wraithlike companion which, strangely, offered comfort.

At this moment, she should have been hanging on to Uncle Harry as they hurtled through the streets on a motorcycle. It was not the most practical option, but riding a fast motorcycle drew less attention than driving a car. Although vampires could move faster than any motorized vehicle, they had been seen riding motorcycles, apparently for amusement.

What a mess. Careful not to stray from the thick carpet which ran up the middle of the polished wooden floor like the stripe along a badger's back, she made her way along the hallway and through to the gloomy kitchen. A footfall on bare boards would echo through the house. *I think today's list of stupid mistakes is quite long enough.*

Rebekah took a plastic cup from the silicone mat covering the stainless-steel drainer and dipped it into a basin filled with water. She drank it down in one, grateful to wash away the sandpaper dryness from her throat, at last. A length of plastic tubing snaked from the faucet, lying like a serpent in the bottom of the basin. She turned the faucet on, and watched the current tumble in lazy rolling waves, barely stirring the surface as the water level replenished. *No splashing allowed.*

Automatically, she washed down two vitamin D tablets, and chewed on a glazed, odor-free spinach and sesame seed energy bar. She moved slowly through to the large sitting room where neglected upholstered chairs and a couch sulked in the cold shadows. Whispering and hiding in the dark spaces below the house were the harsh realities of life for humans out in the field. But, having tasted freedom of a sort, she would find it hard to bear the confinement of their subterranean eco-town, if that was the consequence of her foolishness today.

A wave of irritation hit her, and recalling the doctor's probing gray stare filled her with anxiety.

Will Uncle Harry ever trust me again? At least I'm safe, for now. She pulled open the hinged hatch-door in the floor and gripped the warm wood. As she descended the steps into the basement the cool air chilled the sweat on her brow. She grimaced. *Not as calm as I thought.*

Passing her hormone test had been as liberating as getting her driver's license in the old world might have been. Waiting for her estrogen levels to stabilize to enable her to visit London, and to feel like a grown-up at last, had been a big deal. *Harry was good, but even he couldn't invent a spray which suppressed the stink of rampant teenage pheromones.*

The heavy weight of dread settled in her stomach as she pulled the hatch closed behind her, wincing at the squeak of the rubber edges. Leaving the eco-town also put distance between her and Douglas, Uncle Harry's right hand man. He was fifteen years older than she was, and the glint in his eyes when he looked at her chilled her to the core. Douglas, wearing an avid expression on his pale flaccid features, seemed to lurk in the corners of the communal caverns every time she walked in. She was being stalked, and her turning twenty-one was the reason.

Rebekah frowned and tried to push him from her mind. *Douglas can't force me to marry him; this isn't the Dark Ages.* She ignored the little voice inside which disagreed. In many ways, that's exactly what it was. With every passing day, he inhabited her nightmares more and more. She knew the theory of how men and women made love, and had even, as those desires emerged, come to know her own body, but just the *thought* of his hands on her made her shudder.

Crossing to a sagging canvas bed, she laid out flat and stared at the foam-padded underside of the thick oak floorboards overhead. Getting home remained her only option.

Her spine stiffened with determination. *All I have to do is follow protocol.* If she lowered her chin, she could make out the dark smudge of the pane of dirty glass in the sidewalk level skylight. *As soon as dawn arrives, I'll make my own way to Station Four.*

The humans called their habitat 'Station Four' out of bravado, not wanting to believe they were alone in those early post-pandemic days. The collapse of human communications systems plunged them back to Prehistoric times, in terms of making contact with others. Their scouting parties had turned up only one other eco-community, about thirty miles away and, after so long, it seemed unlikely any future discoveries would make four an appropriate number.

The eco-town had been excavated beneath the North Downs in Kent, but it was close enough to London to make the city accessible. The entrance to the labyrinth of subterranean caverns was by way of a tunnel dug into the undulations of a Kentish hillside. Disguised as an eroded fissure, the opening was practically invisible. *Unless they do a grid search. The last one of those was about five years ago. We were feeling safe, until I messed up.*

So, her plan was to move out, using the emergency route which skirted around the vampire clusters, and pray. *The beta-blocker should work long enough to get me through the worst.* But, it was all down to fate. *Okay girl, but first, sleep. No telling when I'll get to do that again.*

She closed her eyes and when fitful sleep rolled in, Douglas' face emerged through the tumbling black clouds. Her features pinched tight as the nightmare unfolded and she surrendered to its embrace. Douglas' small eyes burned in a bullish face, the sneer on his mouth slack with an expression she had glimpsed only the other day. A flush stained his cheeks, and she shivered, knowing it was arousal.

As Douglas' face closed in, and she turned her head away on the thin pillow, the heavy blanket felt like lead weights holding her body down. But then, the eyes staring at her melted to cool gray, and the chiseled features became those of the vampire doctor. She shivered again, but the tingle drifting over her skin felt like an awakening.

Rebekah woke with a jolt, struggling to breathe in the dark. Her first thought was of the doctor and the urge to escape was overwhelming. Damp heat chilled her flesh and her pulse throbbed in time with her sluggish heartbeat. She felt different, and it scared her.

Pushing back the blanket and dropping her hand down, she brushed her fingers across the floor, closing them around the small plastic bottle containing her last beta-blocker. It was meant for the morning, but her heartbeat pounding in her ears sounded so loud she feared the worst. *If I save it, I might not be alive in the morning.* She felt as though every vampire on the planet must be able to hear her thundering pulse. Swallowing the tablet down with a mouthful of water, she lay back on the mattress. After staring into the blackness for endless seconds, she forced her eyes to close once more, and, this time, Douglas stayed away.

Chapter 3

After Doctor Connor left the girl standing open-mouthed on the sidewalk, he headed out across West London. The autumn sky darkened as rapidly as his mood. This time of year, dusk did not so much creep up upon you as crash down like a blackout curtain. He did the same inside his own mind. *Forget you found her.* Having a human pet was forbidden in these times of shortage, and Connor had never wanted to indulge the urge, even when humans were plentiful.

He set a course for the distant sweeping arc of floodlights; a glittering halo around the complex of Human Farm Factory Eight. The blood yield fed the members of the London Hive, also numbered eight of the ten hives spread throughout England.

How many hives, with their human farm factories, crop production programs, and hospitals, were scattered throughout Europe, America, and the rest of the world, Connor could not even begin to guess at. He had experienced over eighty years of feeding only on humans who, in his view, deserved their fate. The last fifteen years of human factory farming since the 'rise', still made him uncomfortable.

A human didn't stand a chance when pitched against a vampire; the label given to their distant cousins still remained the best fit.

Connor's stride faltered.

At least, before the balance of power shifted, *most* of mankind lived life blissfully ignorant of the horror lurking in the shadows. Now, each and every one suffered the same fate. *Reducing humans to a state where they see death as a release is wrong.*

He gritted his teeth and moved rapidly on until the buildings of London gave way to an impressive expanse of rolling green pasture. The lush water-soaked grass appeared oily and black in the moonlight, but Connor knew that on sunny days the view would be picture-postcard perfect, were it not for the hulking gray rectangles of the rows of human siphoning sheds.

His appraising glance took in the vista of the complex and its regimented construction of three perimeter fences with dead spaces of containment in between. Each chain-linked metal barrier was over a dozen feet tall. Razor wire threaded its way along the top edge, its teeth glinting with malice even in the subdued moonlight. Connor knew its bite looked even more spiteful when the sunlight picked out the barbs and they said, 'Try me'.

The hive had erected the compound with haste and little imagination when Mother Nature had redefined 'eternity' and given it an expiration date. In a bitter irony, the humans housed here were the genetically strong specimens who survived a pandemic which killed eighty percent of their fellows. Their *only* obligation now was to live, continue to stay healthy, and feed the undead community of the City of London.

Connor made the final approach to the human farm, crossing the last mile of potholed grass at speed. He focused on his reason for being here and hoped his medical students would pass the test. The grade was black or white. *Flying colors, or crash and burn.*

The first perimeter fence loomed as a time-wasting obstacle. Connor sprinted forward. Leaping more than ten feet in the air, he grabbed hold of the meshed-wire fence and hung on. As the metal links rattled, he swung his legs upwards and vaulted over the top. Landing soundlessly on the soft earth, he loped the twelve yards to the foot of the next fence.

He waited this time, because the compound guard appeared at the same moment.

"Doctor Connor." The guard nodded as he opened the gate and stepped back in one fluid motion. "I trust you have clearance."

Connor delivered his familiar dead-pan refrain. "About two inches, I think."

The guard shook his head slowly and smiled. "The students are ready and waiting for you."

"Excellent," said Connor as he walked away.

The guard fell into step beside him. "Do you think this class will pass the final test?"

Connor studied his companion's sixty-something year old face. Drawing in his scent, he reminded himself that the gatekeeper was young, in vampire terms. *Forty immortal years to my one hundred.*

He smiled. "Honestly? I think maybe two will make the grade. Resisting a human when they bleed is not something we're designed to do."

"You seem to manage it easily enough."

"Ah well, I was a surgeon when I was alive and there is not a squeamish bone in my body. Maybe that's the secret."

But Connor knew it was more than that. He had quickly learned that by flexing his diaphragm, he could slam his vocal chords shut and create an airlock which kept human scents at bay. Sadly, like the ability to be a world-class athlete, it was a natural talent which could be honed, but not one he could teach.

Out of curiosity, Connor asked, "Have you thought of enrolling? See if you can pass the grade as an intern? Work in the siphoning sheds would be more rewarding than walking the perimeters night after night."

The guard laughed gently and mimicked Connor's words. "Ah well, *I* was a mailman when I was alive, and there are a number of squeamish bones in my body."

Connor laughed too. "Fair enough." Passing through the final gate and into the compound, he waved a hand in farewell.

The brushed steel exteriors of the siphoning annexes burnished in the glare of the floodlights, bathing the clearing between the human barracks and the siphoning sheds in an illusion of daylight.

The atmosphere reminded Connor of the Nazi concentration camps where he passed time during the Second World War. They were invaluable training grounds, and he still found comfort in chaos, and in maintaining control while those around him lost it. The decades when the undead were in hiding, he remembered as a gift of gluttony. *I fed on humans with breath-taking frequency, going unnoticed because men were hell bent on fighting each other.*

He hadn't known then, that the human form you possessed when you were turned became your raw material, to be enhanced or wasted. Having a quick mind and a towering muscular frame upon which to build, Connor's thirst acted as a survival tool, instinctively honing his daunting acuity and lethal strength.

Posing as a surgeon, and operating on humans in the makeshift hospitals on the battlefields in France during the First World War, he became adept at resisting the thick scent of human blood and could choose when to kill. It was not until eight decades later, when the hive emerged to round up the dwindling human population and herd them onto the farms, that he discovered his control was exceptional.

Tapping into that control now, Connor set his sights on the loading bay doors of the nearest siphoning shed and moved quickly down the wet concrete path.

As he stepped inside, the subdued lighting draped his shadow over the polished floor. The frequent passage of trolleys used to transport the less cooperative humans had worn tire tracks into the ramp running up into the building; it was a reminder that there were still some who thought giving blood was a choice and fought to keep their nine pints to themselves.

The human spirit never fails to amaze me. Connor shook his head, walked into the large storeroom which served as a training area, and greeted his students.

"Good evening, gentlemen. So, this is it, your final test. The patient today needs a new siphoning tube. I removed the valve from the collapsed vein yesterday. Today, we will insert a new catheter and glue it in place until it heals over. You will then take samples of blood from the human, as a test." Connor took in the three determined faces. "The best piece of advice I can give is, use your sleep centers."

Over the centuries, vampires had evolved a way to rehydrate the brain after feeding without the need to lose consciousness, taking them further away from the age old urban myth. Connor reminded the group it was a mixed blessing. "If you are to work here on the farm, it's critical you become expert in controlling your impulses, and the way to do that is through revival sleep."

Connor referred back to his favored analogy of a multiple personality disorder. "Think of it as having three locked compartments inside your head. You have one key and only one door can be opened at a time." He visualized his own compartments, and each of the inmates which vied for attention. One enjoyed killing, the other resembled a volatile drunkard, and the third, and the one they needed to tap into when near humans, was chilled-out and mellow.

As part of their training, the students practiced unlocking their sleep centers daily, until it became instinctive. Of the twenty who had enrolled, hoping to become interns on the farm, Connor was inclined to trust only these three. Even for himself, preparation was everything and after his encounter today, his lecture was tinged with irony. *I messed up today.* The uneasy feeling of having a hole punched in his own armor mocked him.

"You all know how to unlock the door to the relaxation of revival sleep. Put your masks on and do it now," he said mildly. Satisfied, as glazed gazes softened their expressions, Connor stopped breathing and slipped on his own flexible transparent plastic mask.

The door to the room sprang open, and a porter entered, wheeling in a middle-aged human male laid out on a metal examination table. The man's eyelids were half-closed in drug-induced sleep. His blood sample would be tainted and undrinkable, but in Connor's book, easing suffering was more important.

Connor selected a catheter tube from a metal tray and offered it to the student who stepped forward.

Taking hold of the thin tube, the student inspected the man's arms and considered the marks which tracked the path of collapsed veins. With a deft sweep of his cold fingertips, he located an unscarred vein and steadily pushed the catheter underneath the skin until it flooded with blood.

"Careful, you must advance it enough so that he cannot pull it out once it has knitted in place, but we want him as comfortable as possible," Connor said quietly.

The student nodded, fed more of the tube into the vein, and then applied the surgical glue to fix the valve in place. He stepped back with a grimly satisfied smile.

Connor nodded his approval and gestured to the next student.

The tall wiry vampire retrieved an I.V. bag from a crate, slipped it over a hook where it hung below the level of the patient on the trolley, and then he connected a coil of thin transparent tube to the catheter valve in the patient's arm. Twisting the tap open, he flicked the tube until blood snaked lazily along its length, before attaching it to the I.V. bag.

A thick sweet scent plumed to fill the room, and every eye, apart from Connor's, was fixed onto the meandering path of oozing warm blood.

As the wiry student shifted his weight to withdraw, Connor surged forward and shoved him aside. In two seconds, Connor had the remaining student pinned to the wall by the throat. The vampire's panting breath misted up his mask until Connor's firm grip strangled the growl rattling in his throat and cut off his windpipe.

Connor stripped away his own mask with his free hand and said, "It's okay. Relax, and I'll take you outside."

The student slumped in his mentor's grasp, and Connor lifted him bodily out through the door.

Returning to the room alone, Connor dismissed the remaining pair with a tight smile. "He will be okay now. I'll tell Supervisor Matthew you are both ready to work in the siphoning sheds. Well done."

When the porter collected the sleeping patient, Connor followed him out, walked along the hallway, and made his way outside into the glare of the floodlights to where the supervisor waited for him.

"Doctor Connor," he said, "did they pass?"

"Sad to say, only two. Walk with me, Matthew," said Connor casually, settling into a relaxed stride. "So, Charles, in the blood dispensary, tells me that there are clots in some of the blood bags you are sending out."

Connor grinned when the supervisor bristled.

"Let's go and take a look, shall we?"

They moved in silence between the sheds, which were numbered like hospital wards, but there the similarity ended. Inside, instead of beds, rows of steel tables, each with a drainage gully running around the outer edges, performed only one function. *We don't want to waste a drop.* Humans provided blood, and restraining straps made it clear they had no choice. Connor grimly wished his synthesized blood trials had succeeded this time around, and that he could see an end to this.

True, humans were fed, clothed, provided with reading materials, and their hobbies indulged, although most were too tired to rouse themselves to do more than just sit. Connor remembered the spark of life in the human girl's eyes when he had laid his hand on her outside the hospital, and he found admiration sneaking in through that hole in his armor. *To reduce her to this would be tragic.*

Inside siphoning shed number two, Connor pushed his mask into place, but even through the plastic, the full-bodied aroma of stored blood swelled the capillaries inside his nasal passages and the scent wafted into his brain. His nose wrinkled at the disconcerting marriage of distaste and excitement.

Frowning with renewed purpose, he burst through the doorway into the ward.

As he expected, row upon row of human donors greeted him, each one laid out and strapped to the stainless-steel beds in a parody of the living dead.

"Well, Matthew." Connor's grin was empty. "Nice place you have here. The bad news is, in one day, Charles reported that two of the hive suffered seizures due to blood clots. I'm thinking deep vein thrombosis or a platelet clotting disorder. So, we just need to find the human and treat him."

The supervisor was indignant. "Why did they drink it?"

Connor laughed harshly. "You know better than that. If the blood was warm and beneath human skin, they would have detected disease. But, cold and in a vial? They just downed it and suffered the consequences." He flexed his lungs, filling them with the heavy aroma of human bone marrow being pushed to its replenishment limit. "I must say, I prefer the more optimistic setting of my hospital." He pinned the supervisor in his gaze. "One that I control."

The supervisor stared back with resentment printed upon his face.

"Let's get started." Connor shot a glance at his watch. "I want to be back at the hospital before the eleven p.m. blood delivery comes in."

"What do you suggest?" Matthew waved his arm to indicate the sea of reclined bodies. "Help yourself."

Connor pulled off his mask and grabbed a clutch of pinprick tests from a nearby storage chest. He made his way down the line of humans, moving quickly, gripping each wrist, pricking the skin and collecting a smear of blood. He spent but a moment rubbing it between his fingertips, checking for the gritty texture which would reveal blood clots to his heightened sense of touch, before moving on to the next.

Panic rippled through the ward like a stiff breeze flattening the grass in a meadow. Connor's attentions were like a bird strike. With their inferior senses, the humans didn't see him coming. They felt the unexpected shock of his icy grip, but the examination was over before they registered it.

The twenty-third patient halted Connor in his tracks.

"This one." Connor detached the three-quarters full bag of blood and turned the tap to seal the end of the catheter, wasting only two drops onto the floor. "Tag him, and cease siphoning until we run a full blood work-up and begin treatment," he barked.

Behind his own plastic face shield, Matthew's features tightened with reluctant respect.

Connor returned to the supervisor's side, after having found two more patients with clots floating in their bloodstreams. His jaw clenched. "You are failing in your duty here, Matthew. The vampires' suffering is not the issue, losing one of our humans is a far more serious price," said Connor, sternly. "Don't get complacent. If these humans have deep vein thrombosis, then it's because they are immobile for too many hours. I want you to make sure the humans exercise, and pay more attention to their health, do you understand?"

Supervisor Matthew nodded. "Yes, Doctor Connor."

Connor met his defiant stare. "Let's make this clear, if *one* of them dies, then you will face the consequences. I will see to it." His icy tone left no room for doubt. "I'll drop by in a few days with the blood test results. For now, I have to get back to the hospital. Goodnight." He turned on his heel and disappeared from the shed before he gave in to the temptation to shake some sense into the supervisor.

With the scent of human desperation and defeat still fresh in his mind, arguments raged inside Connor's head as he made the return journey to the hospital. He almost headed south over the River Thames and followed the same route along which he had carried the human girl.

He felt like an alcoholic being lured into a bar. Vampires had stopped hunting for human survivors of the pandemic a long time ago, smugly assuming that they were all now in captivity. *Humans are nothing more than livestock.* Their siphoned blood was delivered to the hospital daily, like groceries for distribution.

When the human food supply plummeted to critical levels, the hives formed, and rationing began. *The last fifteen years have been a steep learning curve.*

Some vampires refused to bow to a chain of command. *And they did us a favor when they tried to survive on animal blood.* It revealed an inescapable truth; animal blood alone cannot rehydrate the thirsty tissue of an undead brain. *The price is an eternity of dementia. Having once* been *human, we* need *a daily dose of human blood to remain healthy.* So, immortals had accepted their fate. *They come in, collect their quota, and think no further than that.*

The inmates of the human farm supported the London hive numbers for now, but the cloud on the horizon was that humans age and die. *And it will be sooner, rather than later, with Supervisor Matthew in charge.* Breeding humans was tough, especially with the stock comprising of many more men than women. *And the females will do anything not to deliver a baby into our hands.* His smile was bitter.

The last attack by a 'feral' cost the hive four humans. The undead who succumbed to dementia had no concept of fear.

Thought process crumbled and they 'hunted' in the most primitive, mindless sense of the word. Ferals were like wolves circling a chicken coup, but the last sweeps of the overgrown countryside around London had not flushed any out. *It looks like they are dying out at last.*

Connor's efforts to find a synthetic substitute for human blood isotopes had, so far, come to nothing. Any chance to increase the human herd could not be dismissed. *I'm obliged to report this girl for capture and farming, but...* He darted a glance at his watch. *She will have moved out already, if she has any sense, and I'll not see her again.* He stopped short, rubbing the palm of the hand that had gripped her arm along the length of his thigh, as though trying to remove her stain. Distaste flooded him, and he thought, *LIAR*.

Chapter 4

Connor felt relief when he arrived back at the hospital.

Erasing the girl from his mind, he moved along the corridor following the smell of blood as though he could see it. He pushed aside the jellied-plastic doors leading into the human blood dispensary and scanned the dozens of vampires waiting silently in line.

With gray ceiling tiles, pristine white walls, and a slick wet-look linoleum floor, the room appeared bland, until Connor glanced left and took in the wall of tall glass-fronted storage cabinets. Shelves filled with vials of blood in every shade of burgundy and claret were like a siren call, and the room of happy victims all faced that direction as though considering the choices on offer.

Connor purposefully threaded a path between the rows of vampires. Arriving at the front of the queue, he slipped behind the dispensing desk and stopped beside the slight frame of Charles, the dispensary clerk.

Unfazed by the sudden intrusion, Charles silently watched Connor open up a cooler box and drop the I.V. bags from the farm patients inside.

"Run coagulant tests on these samples, Charles. I gave Supervisor Matthew a rocket. He should up his game, now."

"Good," said Charles. "I'd like to get my hands on him."

Connor smiled. The clerk was a small terrier of a vampire. His sandy hair refused to lie down and his brown eyes gleamed with a sharp intellect.

"How's it going?" said Connor, gazing out over the sea of faces.

"All under control. Should be about another hour."

"You'll have two hours then, to unload the blood delivery from the farm and test it before the next cluster arrives. Is that enough time?"

Charles jerked his head towards the waiting vampires. "This is the last working party. They're going out to service a fleet of trucks tonight. After that I only expect to see the ones dropping by before they go down to Exeter to hunt on Dartmoor."

"All work and no play, hmm?" Connor murmured.

"Wishing you had time to hunt tonight?" Charles asked idly.

"Something like that." Connor laid a hand on Charles' shoulder. "Well, I'll leave you to it," he said and moved away feeling more uneasy.

Even civilized vampires still enjoyed the thrill of the hunt, and the jaunt down to Exeter was a mere two hundred miles. It marked the closest boundary of the three hundred and fifty square miles of Dartmoor scrubland; the enclosure which was now home to the big cats moved out of the human zoos of the 90's.

Connor visited the hunting grounds regularly, and the excitement that sang through him at the prospect of the journey was hard to beat.

Will the girl be wandering about when the hunting parties set off tonight? Connor's walk slowed, becoming an aimless circle as anxiety took hold. With a harsh laugh, he faced his own stupidity. He had not prepared for a human examination. *Putting on my mask and using revival sleep didn't occur to me. Idiot.* The cloying residue of her sweet smell coated his throat again and lay as a creamy pool in the pit of his stomach. He had no memory of food, but he felt full.

Her fierce stubbornness had winded him, and he shook his head in disbelief. *Somehow, she survived out there fifteen years.* The heart of a lion inside a sacrificial lamb. *She'd almost be worth the risk, to keep her as a pet and get inside that head of hers.*

Suddenly whipping around and peeling the white coat from his powerful shoulders, he decided it was not a crime to make sure she had gone.

The walls of the hospital corridors melted to a chalk-white blur as he gathered speed. With a flick of the wrist, he delivered the coat into the open mouth of a laundry basket without breaking stride. Taking a shortcut through a deserted loading bay, he pushed on the emergency exit and the inch-thick metal door flew open as though it was made of cardboard. He hit the sidewalk running and retraced his steps to the house he had taken her to only a few hours before, and then kept going. *I just needed to make sure she was safe*. He guessed she would lie, and she didn't disappoint him. Tracking her to the *real* hideout was child's play.

Stopping on the sidewalk outside the rundown Victorian house, Connor surveyed the shabby facade. A grim smile creased his cheeks, giving fleeting expression to the smooth skin. *So, I'm risking becoming an immortally conscious brain, trapped inside a granite body. Forever. Nice.* Humans were community cattle. If a vampire kept one hidden, or was foolish enough to kill one, he was guilty of threatening the food supply and sentenced to an eternity of locked-in syndrome.

As a doctor, Connor had seen vampires condemned to this state when, by their own stupidity, they neglected revival sleep. Escalated stress levels prevented feeding, allowing dehydration to progress to the point of no return. *That 'point' is a call I've had to make more often than I would like. It's definitely not a picnic.*

His fingers twitched. Thinking of stress levels brought the texture of her smooth stomach to mind.

Okay, the house is in darkness, but what does that mean? Nothing, he decided as he ascended the wide stone stairway. At the front door, he turned the handle and kept turning until the metal inside twisted and gave way with a crack that rang out like a gunshot to his sensitive ear.

He passed through the house in a breeze of movement. There were eight rooms in all. *No one is here*. Stopping in the hallway of mirrors, where the reflection of his starkly white face floated in the gloom like a macabre magician's illusion, he could not help but be intrigued. The foam padded rack of rubber flashlights and the collection of soft moccasin shoes positioned just inside the door proved the humans had some understanding of the dangers they faced.

The largest room on the ground floor revealed much more than Connor bargained for. A mosaic of cork tiles covered the longest wall, and an array of woolen-legged spiders crawled over a map which recorded the girl's activities of the last decade. His lip curled in derision. *Or rather, the activities of her group.* Upon closer inspection, the head of each tack forming the body of each spider was color-coded, and indicated the location of resources the humans considered important, such as hardware stores, large food outlets of canned and dried goods, textile warehouses, and pharmaceutical chains.

The foraging map also recorded the stock reserves. A black pin declared a neighborhood as empty, a red pin warned the area carried a high risk, with a variety of other colors relaying other useful information.

Connor ran his fingertips over the yellowed pin-pricked parchment as though he could somehow absorb their thoughts. He cast a glance around at the meager furnishings hoping to see a pile of wooden stakes, or a few strings of garlic bulbs he could laugh at. *So, not superstitious vampire hunters then. Survivors.*

Lurking in the darkest corner, a black rectangle arrested his attention. Although the sweeping strokes of a blackboard rubber had wiped it clean, his preternatural sight read the erased words as though they had been engraved – 'Rebekah, meet at Station Four, Uncle Harry'. *Rebekah.* As he digested this, chaotic thoughts wrestled for supremacy. Doing-the-right-thing is taking a beating, he thought dryly.

Occasionally, the discovery of an emaciated human straggler caused a ripple in the pond of vampire boredom. They were quickly introduced to life on the farm and just as quickly forgotten. *But, this 'Station Four' is not one straggler.* It suggested there were organized groups of free humans, a society, even. *What the hell should I do with that? My status as a doctor makes this an easy choice, and setting a trap is a piece of cake. So, what am I still doing here?*

He retraced his steps back along the hallway. *She's gone. I could leave it at that.* He sighed in exasperation, and as her scent clawed at him, he found some release from frustration by giving free rein to his feeding instinct.

Venom flooded his mouth, his shoulder muscles knotted, and his gut twisted as his body prepared to release the tension which, if she was within his grasp, would have snapped his jaw closed as it locked onto her flesh and drenched him in her fragrance.

He pulled himself up short. It was not only his gut which tightened, and conflict raged again. With a wry smile, he considered staying to take rap-sleep. *Okay,* that *control center needs refreshment.* He glanced back along the passageway. The house provided the seclusion he needed. *But definitely not here.* Her pervasive smell was too distracting.

Relieved that he could now pretend she had never existed, he left the house. As he moved away, almost off the bottom step and onto the sidewalk outside, he heard it. *A sigh.* His muscles, with the tensile strength of steel, locked in an effortless comical mid-step posture.

Three seconds saw him back inside the house, standing with his ear cocked towards the wooden floorboards. *Stupid. Of course she would hide.* He could hear the whisper of the air moving through her lungs, and a full feeling weighed him down again as he tuned into a sluggish syrup-thick heartbeat, so slow it was a lullaby.

Within the space of one of those heartbeats, he was down inside the basement with the trap door back in place. He lowered himself down on to a wooden bench near her bed and watched her sleep. An empty bottle of beta-blockers gave him another moment of revelation. *Ah, not losing my marbles then, suppressed physiology.* A frown creased the porcelain perfection of his skin.

He studied her relaxed features. Flexing the bellows of his ribcage, he filled his lungs with the air inside the musty space and infused his nasal lining with the cloying scent her warm body percolated. His cheekbones bleached to bone-white as he prevented the sneer molded to his lip from baring his teeth.

His penetrating gaze clung to Rebekah's face. Her lashes fluttered, and then, her eyes snapped open.

She shot out of the bed and made it to the bottom step before he surged to his feet and caught her in a vise-like embrace. His arms encircled her, holding her pinned to his chest as her heart shunted blood into her brain so fast Connor could smell the waves of adrenalin.

"Don't struggle," he muttered.

Holding her still, Connor crumbled the handful of wood he had gouged from the bench into sawdust; instinct had kicked in, and he had forgotten to release his grip when he leapt after her. His lips brushed her hair as he spoke again. "Don't move. I *will* hurt you." He paused to gulp down the acrid concoction that had oozed into his mouth in expectation of a meal. "And I don't want to," he finished on a hoarse whisper.

The girl, *Rebekah*, he reminded himself, froze.

And Connor froze too. His braced arms formed a cage, and not pulling her back into him took all his willpower as visions of her sleep-flushed peach skin flashed like strobe lights inside his brain. Without moving, his body took action of its own - his aroused mind shot the signal to his aching groin and his vision clouded alarmingly to red.

Connor cleared his throat. "I'm sorry. I need to sleep." He was deliberately vague. *I've already revealed too much; revival sleep was certainly news to her, and I need rap-sleep. Now. But first, I have to feed.*

Suddenly, every fiber in his body compelled him to steal her heat. He needed to escape the lure of the warm river of blood flushing her skin before his control faltered.

He lowered his arms carefully, intending to step away, but, as Rebekah turned to look at him in alarm, his mind, all three centers of it, scattered. Slipping his fingertips into her hair, he framed her skull in his palm and leaned in to sip the salty, nervous perspiration from her top lip. She gasped, and her hot hands branded him as they settled on his chilled torso.

Connor was captivated by the shockwave of the shiver that knotted her stomach and stole the breath from her chest. As his cool tongue traced over Rebekah's lips to taste her, he drowned in another rush of her adrenalin as she closed around him and pulled him in.

His hunger surged, but before her blood-red vapors could steal his sanity, he tore himself away, snarling in an effort to expel her scent.

In the next moment, the damp night air filled his lungs as he raced away, his tendons and sinews resonating with a low thrum while he found refuge in acceleration, ramping up his speed until the dark streets were a blur.

Like an animal going to ground, self-preservation drove him back to the familiar territory of his hospital, with the solution to his sudden surge of bloodlust there at his fingertips, in vials, and not confusing the hell out of him.

Slowing his pace to a sprint, Connor arrived in the loading bay as the human blood delivery was in progress. He narrowed his gaze, even though the blown pupils of his vampire night vision adjusted to the sudden glare of the fluorescent lighting in less than a nanosecond. Most buildings had no electricity supply anymore, however, the hospital did. *Old habits die hard, and a darkened hospital will always seem wrong.* The array of crimson glass vials winking in the light drew him along the corridor, and when he passed the loaded trolleys, he snagged two vials of blood and slipped them into his pocket.

He powered on around a corner and narrowly avoided colliding with a member of the vampire council. Like a cat whose territory had been invaded, the hackles prickled on Connor's neck. He recoiled, stepping back a pace. His marble face adopted a carefully blank expression as he inclined his head in salute and apology. "Councilor Serge."

Serge's reptilian-yellow eyes glistened while he stared intently up at Connor's impassive features. "Ah, Doctor Connor, who was that young vampire I saw you with earlier? She looked a little... slow." He oozed oily concern. "I do hope you looked after her?"

Already uneasy, Connor's guard went up. *This guy is literally a bloodhound, and if he suspects she's human, he will track her down. Even beta-blockers won't help if the hunt is on.* Connor ruefully admitted *he* should have known immediately. Her smell alone was enough, but he had been distracted by his own responses.

Connor shrugged. "Just a dehydrated youngling. It slowed her down some, and her escort had to leave, so I returned her safely to her cluster." He forced a callous laugh. "Graveling has set in. She'll not be much use for anything other than kitchen duty on the farm." Looking past the councilor, he adopted a distracted doctor-on-a-mission air, and began to move away.

Serge's voice stopped him. "Name?" At Connor's sharp look, he said, "I assume she has a name? I'll look out for her application at the farm."

Connor's hackles rose again as Serge's smile pulled his dried skin tight over angular bones. A knot of tension almost turned Connor into the most stupid vampire on the planet. Attacking a councilor was a death sentence without trial.

Connor eased his shoulders and said, "Annabelle, her name is Annabelle."

Serge inclined his head with a knowing look. "I'll look out for her," he said, before, turning on his heel, he moved away.

Connor watched until Serge was a black smudge in the distance. A low growl escaped Connor's lips. *The guy stinks*. Wondering why the councilor never noticed the decaying blood clot aroma which clung to him, Connor did the breath-on-your-palm date ritual to check his own and was relieved to find it odor free. *But why should it matter?* Rebekah's taste still lingering on his lips suddenly propelled him into action.

He considered every square inch of the hospital his home. Moving through his own terrain, Connor's rap-sleep habits had an ingrained routine which took him the length of the building to the seclusion of his usual spot, examination room 2.

Taking a short cut, he pushed his way through the mortuary door, and the vampire attendant on duty looked up.

"Carry on, Isaac," Connor said, dipping his head in greeting. But, an open cadaver drawer caught his eye and curiosity got the better of him.

The female vampire laid out on the metal bed calmly clasped her hands, rested them on her stomach, and expelled her breath in a long sigh.

"I won't be a moment," Isaac said, "she's nearly there."

Connor watched closely as the attendant turned back to where the vampire, lying motionless, had closed her eyes.

Isaac lifted an eyelid and, nodding in satisfaction, he muttered, "She's asleep now." Quickly, he fastened restraining straps over her body and yanked them tight before gripping the drawer handle. The metal tray shuddered as her body erupted into convulsions, and her eyes snapped open.

Connor recognized the cavernous oil-black sheen of her blown pupils as classic signs of grave sleep. The blood rushed in to hydrate the brain center which housed a bloodthirsty psychopath, the urge to kill burned along her nerve endings.

Unperturbed by the violent rattling of metal, the attendant trundled the drawer in along its rails, pushed it home, and the rubber seal on the door frame muted her murderous rage. Isaac flipped the metal catch, turned the door marker over to display red, and faced Connor.

"It's a busy night for grave sleep," Connor said, indicating the high number of red 'occupied' tags jiggling on the cadaver drawer handles. The pressed-tin discs clattered against the locked brushed-steel doors. With the familiar shrieking sound of vampire nails clawing at the confines of their prisons punctuating their conversation, Connor asked, "Have you let the blood dispensary know you are full?"

"Yes, Doctor Connor."

"Good, I don't want to pronounce deaths we can avoid. It's better if Charles redirects the overflow to the abattoir cold-stores, now."

Some vampires still left the city limits to take grave sleep, and sought out old haunting grounds, literally. Elder vampires, hundreds of years old, laid claim to mausoleums, feeling it was more dignified.

Connor was not concerned where they sought seclusion, as long as they obeyed the law. Confinement for grave sleep was mandatory. The uncomfortable necessity of vampires clustering around their food source made conflict inevitable, and in some cases fatal. *The upside is we now have someone to lock us away.*

"I hear you had another one in today," Isaac said.

"Female?" Connor met the vampire's curious gaze. "I did, yes. I guess two in one day *is* unusual."

"Will they die out altogether, do you think?"

"I hope not, but they are still the weaker species, pound per pound of muscle, that is. They will always come off worse if they go up against a male vampire. Though, there are no winners, not really," said Connor. "Let's face it, wounding a vampire will get you locked up in Storage Facility Eight for decades. No one wins."

The vampire attendant shook his head. "Go back forty years, and I was so tired of killing, I kept a pet. It was before the pandemic, of course," he said hastily, darting a nervous look at Connor.

Connor shrugged. "I'm not about to judge you. That was then."

When food was plentiful, feeding from a human pet was thought of as worse than killing, in the eyes of some. It was an art form of a kind, only taking the amount of blood per day the healthy human body could replace. Now, it was frowned upon as being greedy. Vampires were expected to share.

"Anyhow, Doctor Connor, you must have seen a lot of changes in a hundred years. Losing all the female vampires will be just another nail in our coffin, in my book," he said.

"Nothing stays the same. We are all fighting for survival in one way or another, not just females," said Connor grimly. Realizing that Rebekah's presence may have stirred an interest in other vampires inside the hospital was an uncomfortable thought. *Stick to the story.*

"I took her back to her cluster, so she's safe."

As the vampire attendant drew a breath to answer, the wall of cadaver doors rattled with renewed vigor.

With Rebekah's fight for survival front and center in his mind again, Connor smoothly made his escape. "I have rounds. And I can see you are busy." He tossed the words over his shoulder as he moved away, barely catching Isaac's nod of agreement. The doors swung shut behind him and he headed towards the wing which, in the human era, had been the 'out-patient department'.

When he arrived at the examination room, he didn't miss a beat. Moving fast, he flipped the white disc secured to the door handle over to display disturb-at-your-peril red, disappeared inside, and closed the door with a decisive click.

He retrieved the glass vials from his breast pocket, flipped the lids open and quickly downed the contents. Connor calculated that taking his full quota of human blood would kick-start the chemical reaction and accelerate the refreshment of rap-sleep.

This was not the chilled and mellow inmate of revival sleep to which he was relinquishing control of his mind. In rap-sleep the craving for physical pleasure and aggression went on the rampage, hence the name: *rapacious.*

He could take his rap-sleep in any place or position, even standing. Connor, however, observed the social code which gave fair warning to others. He crossed to the examination couch and in an effortless glide, reclined until he was lying flat. *It's the drunkard rather than the psychopath, but still.* The signal being given to others was 'steer well clear'.

Gazing at the ceiling, he tuned in to what was happening inside his body, taking an inventory of his tight muscles and sinews. Satisfied when hydration tingled through his blood network, he closed his eyes, linked his fingers over his stomach and visualized the opening of the cell door.

The blood vessels in his optic nerve glowed like red threads on a pink background as electrical impulses exploded inside his head. His stomach lining absorbed the blood, and, as it hijacked his arterial network, his pulsing carotid arteries filled his ears with a rushing sound.

Blood cascading into his temporal lobe welcomed Connor to a piece of Hell on earth.

Fiber optic darts of pain hit all his nerve endings at once, his groin flooded, and he grinned at the irony of his last conscious thought. *Would humans be surprised to learn that, rather than the sex-starved beasts of myth, if we find 'the one', we mate for life?*

Without that tie, many vampires took their pleasure whenever and wherever they pleased. Connor chose solitude, but rap-sleep gatherings were common; when the barriers tumbled down, they were driven to slake their thirst for pleasure. The downside was that not every vampire survived it because some were a little *too* enthusiastic.

Connor gave himself over to the searing inferno and his errant mind conjured a face with delicate elfin features, chocolate-colored eyes with long lashes, framed by blonde feathered hair. The erotic images flooded his hardening groin with unbearable pressure and his fantasies took flight.

He imagined touching the velvet texture of her skin. He stained her breasts with love bites, pulling her blood near the surface where he could almost taste it, smell it; *Rebekah.*

Riding the wave of feral desire, he burrowed his hand into his pants, sliding down, and stroking over the tight globes hugging his body as he hissed in anticipation. Closing his fist around the satin-coated steel of his excitement, he pushed into his hand.

The dream Rebekah, who existed only inside his head, stood naked before him. Turning her around, his hands covered her breasts, their heat scalding his palms. Her hair brushed his cheek as her head fell back and she groaned.

His hard arousal pushed between her thighs, the satin length of him caressing, until her slick heat soaked him. She reached down, her fingers brushed his tip, and he growled, swallowing down the venom flooding his mouth as his need for release boiled over. He tugged hard on her nipples, and as her hips jerked back into his, he pressed her forward. Her hands gripped the edges of the examination table, laying the pink wet folds between her thighs open to him, and, in a surging stroke, he thrust up inside her.

Embers of lust burned in his groin as, covering her back, he kneaded her breasts. On a guttural sigh, in deep brutal strokes, he drove into her body until shuddering release rampaged through him. He bit down hard on her shoulder. Every sinew in his body vibrated.

His eyes snapped open. As he eased his grip away from his sated body, his fingers shook. *What the hell?*

Nervous tension skittered through his body. He quickly stood and adjusted his clothing. He had to go and find her, and he knew now, he had no choice.

He had never dreamed of a specific person before, and he had no idea what it meant.

All he could think of now was to get her out of London before Serge caught up with her. *Or take her as a pet. If I feed from her, maybe I will stop obsessing.*

He shook his head as he opened the door. “Damn it,” he muttered softly.

Chapter 5

Dusk fell as the five human men walked in single file along the deserted railway tracks. They wore grime-blackened combat gear and dirty strips of linen wrapped around their boots deadened their footfalls. The dried mud on their faces accentuated the whites of their eyes as they scanned left and right.

The shelter of the steep embankments on either side made them feel safe, but they had all been out on long-range missions into vampire territory too often to trust the feeling.

Greg hung onto the consolation that the forty mile journey to the abandoned Royal Army Armament Depot at Chattenden had not been a wasted effort. *If you don't count the fact that we didn't* actually *find any weapons, the hike has been worthwhile.* They had filled their kitbags with army ration packs they found in the quartermaster's stores.

Away missions meant humping food supplies, which presented problems in terms of smells and the stay-fresh factor. Only a few drops of water was needed to activate these self-heating food pouches. They would taste terrible in comparison to the food Oscar provided, but would be safer.

As for the grenades and hand guns they hoped for, they had come up empty. When the vampire invasion began, the Royal Navy had evacuated with ruthless efficiency.

But, it had been worth a try. Life for the group of humans had settled into a state of mind-numbing monotony. Greg's Royal Marine training left him crying out for combat, and being unarmed and passive was a tough pill to swallow. But swallow it he had, after all, if you fire a gun at an undead, the chances were you'd piss him off and not a lot more.

But land-mines, they might have been a different story. Greg sighed. Claymores and grenades were the stuff his dreams were made of.

The wind picked up suddenly and plastered Greg's combat jacket to his chest. The five men dropped to the ground like stones.

Their black-gloved hands covered the backs of their heads as they pressed their cold faces into the gritty gravel-packed earth.

Lying prone, no one moved until Greg scuffed the ground with his steel-toed boot three times. Climbing up from under the seventy pound heavy duffle bags took a lot more effort than the dive downwards had taken.

Greg's grin said, 'phew, false alarm'. They were hypersensitive to sudden changes in the air pressure as an early warning of vampire activity, but it was better to be safe than sorry.

The men huddled together, and mouthing the words quietly, Greg said, "The woods outside Vigo Village are a mile northwest of here." He jabbed a black-clad thumb in the precise direction. "Base-camp is ten miles on from there." Greg tapped his watch and put up two fingers. "It's 1800hrs. We can be there in two hours if we get a clear run through. Stan?"

The stout man jerked his chin and whispered, "I'm not fucking past it yet, tha knows."

Greg grinned and launched a punch which Stan dodged with the ease of a well-practiced ritual. "C'mon, you old bastard, let's get this done."

Stan hoisted his kitbag higher and pulled his woolen hat lower over his brow, covering the crop of snow white hair which framed a walnut wrinkled face. His hefty bulk boasted more muscle than men half his sixty years, and he beat two of his companions to the top of the embankment as he trudged up the slope without breaking stride.

Crouching low, the five figures ran across the blackened meadow, grateful for the autumn night sky, thick with shadow. Dropping down onto his knee at the edge of the wood, Greg pulled out the only pair of night vision goggles they owned and set them high on his forehead.

"Okay," he hissed. "I'll go first. Use the owl call signal if you lose sight of me."

He set off into the woods, pulling the goggles down into place when the light level dropped to pitch-black. Moving slowly, he listened for the signal, reassured by the faint rustle of canvas kitbags rubbing over combat gear close behind. Vampires usually stayed in the City of London until midnight, at which time they appeared like cockroaches swarming the countryside.

Closer to the eco-town, humans had the vampire movements figured out. They farmed the fields of crops which fed their humans, and the London docklands saw a lot of vampire traffic to and from, as they drove trucks, of all things. But this far northeast of the human settlement, Greg had no idea what to expect.

We'll dig in at base-camp for the night. The twenty-five miles home will take three days, if we're lucky.

A yelp in the darkness behind him chilled his blood. *Shit.*

Spinning around, Greg saw three of the guys circling carefully. *Fuck, where's Stan?*

Retracing his steps, he found Stan sitting on the ground, doubled over his leg. His tight face gave away the swear words being held back by his clamped lips.

Dropping down beside him, Greg lifted a brow. "What?"

"Fucking badger." Rolling onto his back, Seth revealed the blood-soaked stain below the knee of his pants leg. "The fucker bit me."

Greg jerked his chin to the others and they turned away, scanning the woods as far as their unaided human sight could allow.

"Slowing down in your old age, ay mate?" muttered Greg, as he cut away the blood-sodden fabric and disguised his grim expression with a smile.

"Piss off," Stan groaned.

Greg grunted with the effort of tightening a linen tourniquet below his friend's knee. Inspecting his handiwork, he said, "Take more than a badger to finish you off, but you aren't going anywhere tonight, not with seventy pounds on your back."

Ignoring Stan rolling his eyes, Greg poured iodine over the tear in the older man's leg, sprayed antiseptic over the exposed flesh around the wound and, even though it was not meant for deep lacerations, he sprayed plastic field Band-Aid over the area. Three applications created a membrane which held back the bleeding.

"I can carry on."

"Not this time, Stan." Greg wound several layers of Saran-wrap around the limb and a field bandage over that. Satisfied, he reached out and tugged the nylon strap dangling from the backpack of the nearest man. "Hey, Stan's gonna dig in here while we get the supplies back. Dig a hole at the bottom of that oak tree."

Greg handed over the night vision goggles, rested back on his haunches and gripped his friend's arm.

His guy moved off, pulling a metal trowel from his utility belt as he scuffed his boot into the mulched ground, looking for a soft spot.

"I'll come back for you tonight, Stan. It's about two hours to base-camp, and I'll hike back here in an hour. Think I can trust you to keep your gob shut for three hours?"

Stan grinned. "Sure thing, Sarg."

"Here. Take these."

Stan swallowed down the beta-blockers Greg pressed upon him as their man re-emerged beside them and silently handed back the goggles.

"C'mon, let's get you tucked up for the night," said Greg.

Taking some of the old guy's weight, he helped him over the rough ground. Once Stan was settled into the dug out between two tree roots, they covered him over, leaving one hand and his face exposed.

"Back soon. Hang in there, okay?"

Pulling on the night vision goggles once more, Greg took out a knife, and as the four men moved off, he cut a lump of bark out of every sixth tree they passed.

Looking back, Greg saw Stan rest his head against a tree root and close his eyes. He'd been in Stan's place, reduced to breathing quietly and listening to the sound of your men moving off through the woods. *Of course, that was before the bloodsuckers.*

Lifting a fist to halt the others, Greg jogged back to Stan and dropped to his knee. "I'll be back in two and a half hours, got it?"

Stan smiled.

◇◇◇

When Greg returned, the world inside the dense woodland, even viewed through night vision goggles, took on the appearance of air filled with charcoal dust. It almost felt like his eyes were still closed. The confusion of shadows reduced him to counting trees and feeling for the markers gouged into the bark.

Relieved when he reached the trunk of the sturdy English oak where he had left Stan, his strained stare scoured the tumbled clumps of earth around its base, and anxiety closed a cold grip around his chest. He eased the medical kit from his shoulders and smothered the litany of swearwords rattling through his head. *Shit, stubborn old buzzard. Stay here, how bloody hard is that?*

The shallow grave was empty.

Fear for himself, Greg took in his stride, but when it came to his men, the responsibility was crushing at times. How do you train men to hide and *not* fight? Being silent every waking moment shredded their nerves. *We have to stay below the radar and battle the survival instincts of fight or flight. The truth is, we can't do either and win.*

In the movies he watched as a youth, vampires were fierce white-faced creatures who dissolved if you threw holy water at them or rammed a stake through their hearts. The reality was very different, and so was the world he lived in as a man.

In *this* world, where vampires had risen, humans were prisoners on the human farm.

Shit, Stan. At least if they found him, he'll still be alive. Humans were a valuable food source.

Moving in slow motion, aware of every groan and creak of the mud-stained fabric of his combat gear, Greg scanned the woods slowly. Looking for a moving bulk large enough to be a man in the spectrum of gray, Greg crept forward. *I have to be sure.* His flesh crawled. *They could be watching, and I wouldn't know it.* Greg grinned. *Fuck, I'd fight. Death would be a blessing.*

Autumn was tough because dusk came in like a fog bank. Getting back to the eco-town before dark was always the aim, but on a long-range foraging mission, digging in for the night came with the territory.

Why the hell didn't you stay put, Stan?

Greg dry swallowed two more beta-blockers and inhaled deeply through his nose. Keeping his body's responses under control was the only weapon he had.

Stan was no rookie, and he knew Greg would make it back. That thought scared Greg. The plastic membrane sprayed over the wound would only hold for so long, so binding it and staying still was all they were left with. *Stan wouldn't have left, not unless he was forced into it.*

Greg caught a flash of movement through the trees and froze. *Could be a deer-*

The cramped feeling in his neck told him it wasn't. A guttering groan drifted on the breeze and Greg screwed his face up tight. *Shit.*

A shower of splintered wood rained down upon his head as a heavy wet thud shuddered through the tree branches above. The blurred comet trail of a man-sized mass smeared across his vision, the ground shook, and his throat filled with bile as he looked down at the broken body and into Stan's slack face.

Greg froze. Staring at his friend, he prayed the old man was dead already.

Stan's body twitched, and he frothed at the mouth. An oozing slug trail of blood crept down over his face. His head dropped to the side and his eyes looked straight into Greg's soul.

Sorry, buddy. Greg's muscles burned as he locked his knees and fought the urge to fight. Playing dead while standing up was the hardest thing he had ever done.

A shower of debris pelted Greg's face as a fast-moving black shape emerged from the cowering shadows of the woodland.

The white face floating above a crow-like silhouette stopped and a black grin cut the face open. Jet beads glittered in ebony sockets as the creature lowered his chin, and in a chillingly human gesture, nudged Stan's slack body with his boot. A wet growl rumbled in its throat as he bent, grabbed the front of Stan's jacket, and lifted him.

Stan's body swung gently. The grinding sound of broken bones stuttered through the night air. The ligaments of an arm tore and the swaying weight slipped, and began to fall slowly from its sleeve.

Greg glued his eyes front and center. The trick was to breathe slowly, and trust the pheromone suppressants, mud packed skin, and beta-blockers gave him a chance. He heard the arm hit the floor with a dull thud, and the tendons in his neck jerked as he tried not to look.

The creature pulled Stan's sagging body forward and stared into his face.

Shit. He's still alive.

Panic rattled through Stan, his legs jerking in spasm. The grinning white face tilted in bird-like curiosity and as the *thing* smothered Stan's body in an embrace, the slopping sound of wet flesh tearing filled Greg's throat with bile.

His stomach contents lodged in his throat, burning a hole in his chest.

The creature's embrace eased, and Stan's feet stirred the undergrowth in a desperate shuffle of twitching muscles. The stiffened inhuman mask of white caught the moonlight. It hovered over the clump of bleeding flesh clutched in its hand, and then bit down into Stan's heart.

Tossing the bloodied mass aside and pulling the dangling body abruptly forward, the creature shoved Stan's head back, snapped his spine, and tore into his neck.

A moment later, the body dropped to the ground, and the creature looked up.

Greg's flesh crawled as, even knowing he stood buried in dark shadow he felt as if its eyes raked over his skin. The flared nostrils dripped blood down over the stark white features and Greg prayed.

He was terrified that even closing his eyes would make a sound. His thigh muscles burned and his brain screamed 'run'. *And end my frigging life? Crap.* If this was a pissing contest, Greg knew he had already lost. A cloud covered the moon and the world through his night vision goggles became a cluster of coal lumps, again. But which one was the monster?

His face hurt as the darkness seemed to burrow inside his eyeballs.

Fuck. Was it a vampire? Zombie? Zombire? Hysteria bubbled in Greg's throat. All he knew was, in the fifteen years since vampires had risen he had never seen a creature like this. *What the hell. Are they mutating now?*

He closed his eyes, held his position as long as his combat hardened frame would let him, and when his knees buckled and he collapsed, he prayed.

Lying in the dirt, he opened his eyes and he was still alive. *Fuck, what happened to make that vampire more animal than fake human?* Greg wasn't sure he wanted to know. Being captured by the bloodsuckers in London was a picnic compared to being in the hands of that sick bastard. *Poor fucking Stan.*

Chapter 6

Rebekah spent a moment of stunned confusion swaying on her feet after the vampire doctor vanished. Waking up to see his silver-gray gaze boring into hers had sent a shockwave through her system. It was as though her dream summoned him. *He caught me off guard.* And now, all she could think of was running. In the cold light of day, her fantasies of him were easier to rationalize. *I fear Douglas, and he disgusts me, next to him, of course the doctor is attractive, or would have been, if he was a human.*

Her fingers trembled, and tasks which should have been easy became incomprehensible. Giving up on attempts at folding, she rammed her belongings into a backpack. The positive action quelling the storm of foreboding which told her that he would return. *He'll be back with a farmer. He has no reason to help me.* And she couldn't understand why that hurt.

When his arm had closed like a band of steel across her chest, fear short-circuited her brain. And yet, she'd found it hard not to do the mindlessly suicidal thing and press back into him.

"He's a vampire, for Christ sakes," she muttered under her breath. The thought scared her more than she could say, but even the throbbing of the bruises he had left on her flesh did not bring her to her senses.

His citrus scent lingered, and in the same way a flashbulb burst marks retina, when she closed her eyes, his image became more vivid. She ruefully acknowledged she knew nothing of vampires. *This Doctor Connor is not the unfeeling block of ice I expected.* And the warmth in the wake of his cold touch was undeniable.

Her fingertips tingled, as if they remembered the texture of the chilled cotton covering his chest when her palms had molded to his smooth hard muscles. It was to hold him back, she told herself. His kiss, fleeting though it was, played on repeat. She could still taste the strangely tart infusion which slicked her mouth before finally, his snarl had shredded her nerves, and then, he disappeared; he had left her struggling for balance, in every sense.

The fleeting contact plagued her. Her heart thudded loudly. *Too loud.* She checked her watch. *He's been gone more than half an hour, an age for a vampire. Is that good?*

"C'mon Rebekah, get a grip," she muttered, as she shoved the last of her clothes into the bag. Cursing under her breath, she fought with the zipper.

◇◇◇

Connor was tempted to appear at her side and help her with the backpack, but he was not sure her heart could cope with racing any faster. He was grimly amused at the ease with which he had once more entered the house, descended into the basement, replaced the access hatch, and moved across the concrete skimmed floor without her noticing. *Humans are such easy prey.*

Resting back against the wall with his fists tightly clenched, Connor stood for much longer than necessary, watching Rebekah's backside sway as her body flexed and turned in the agitated packing process. He opened his mouth and pulled air into his lungs, tasting the atmosphere and gauging his own resolve. He felt satisfied when the level of chest burn cooled from blast-furnace white to poker-red, although it still pushed at the limits of his one hundred years of control.

Her hips rocked as her weight shifted from one foot to the other, and the shadow between her legs tantalized him. Connor decided most of her five feet and six inches of height appeared to be in those long, lithe limbs. The whisper of her denim-clad thighs brushing together shrieked, not so much in a 'nails down a blackboard' moment, but a 'nails dragging down the tight skin of his back' kind of moment. *Shit. The sooner I get her out of here the better.*

His jaw clenched as fire burned in his groin. His rap-sleep fantasy was so close he could almost taste it, but he knew that unleashing his yearnings would grind her bones to dust. A vampire's touch could never be considered gentle. *God, trench warfare had been easier than this.*

Connor had been a mysteriously lucky surgeon working the battlefront in the First World War, miraculously cheating death and saving countless lives. Smiling grimly, he recalled times when he also helped a few on their way, but he had labeled them mercy killings and filed them away in the clear conscience drawer.

In 1910, the human Connor was a twenty-four-year-old medical student studying in London's Royal Eye Hospital under the tutelage of Sir John Creedy. His mentor specialized in ocular surgery, and, keen to gain experience, it was Connor's misfortune to volunteer to run an errand to the mortuary.

That day had started badly when his horse had thrown a shoe, and the farriery blacksmith said, "Sorry, Guvnor, nothing we can do 'til the morning."

Connor remembered tossing the grain boy three copper pennies to pay for a day's feed and livery, and patting the horse farewell. After walking the remaining four miles to the hospital, he donned his starched white coat and threw himself into his grueling schedule.

Pulling on the gold chain which dropped his pocket watch into his palm, Connor peered at it and grimaced. *That was sixteen hours ago.* It was ten p.m., and his thighs ached as though he'd been wading through molasses. As he made his way to Sir John's study, his body longed for a bath and a bed. *Even the thin mattress of the cot in the students' quarters will feel good tonight, when I finally get to lay my head down.*

Announcing his arrival, Connor rapped on the thick oak paneled door.

"Come in." Sir John's muffled command forced him to move.

Connor leaned against the door like a slowly felled tree, and when the solid support swung away, he pulled hastily back, recovered his balance, and stepped into the room.

Sir John looked up and smiled ruefully. "As I understand it, *you* are going nowhere this evening, Sanderson?" He paused, allowing Connor the grace of agreeing with his assessment, before continuing. "That being the case, I wonder, might I call upon you to perform one last task?"

Brushing his fingertips over his clipped beard, Sir John contemplated the ceiling for a moment before turning his attention back to Connor. "Go to the mortuary and tag two bodies for tomorrow's lecture." Sir John lifted the top sheet from the pile of papers on his desk and peered at the one underneath. "Mr. Donaghue. He had a monocle in his personal effects, so we'll have him. And can you choose the second? See what catches your eye, if you'll excuse the pun."

Connor could still hear Sir John's rumbling appreciation of his own humor when he walked away along the ceramic tiled corridors. His footfalls echoed as he descended into the basement. 'Mr. Donaghue, and one for you' was the metronomic chant which focused his tired mind, and the chill in the air cramped his skin into gooseflesh.

His heart pumped. *I'm being tested.* It was an honor to be asked to choose a specimen. Entering the mortuary, the doors hissed at the disturbance, and as their rubber-lined edges sealed closed behind him, an offended silence thickened.

Shaking off the feeling that eyes were watching him, judging him, Connor walked along the line of rigid bodies, flipping back the linen cloths and angling his head to gaze into their stiff faces, until he found Mr. Donaghue. That part of his task done, he rubbed both hands down over his face, hoping the stimulation would wake him up, and he walked the line again.

He peered into each face more closely this time, gently applying his thumb pad to peel back sticky eyelids.

And, it was then that he discovered what a vampire's eyes look like in the moments before they feed.

The blown pupils of the eyes he stared into, suddenly contracted. He recoiled as a spark of laser-blue awareness made his skin crawl, but too late. The sharp pinch to his neck stole his consciousness in less than three seconds, and when the clouds rolled away again, he was laid out in the vampire's place. His face and shirt were soaked in his own blood, and keen fish-scale blue eyes in a translucent ivory face laughed down at him.

The vampire's voice seemed to reside inside Connor's head when he finally spoke. "There are three things to remember."

Connor became transfixed by the thick brown paste oozing from the open wound on the vampire's forearm. The same congealed paste blocked Connor's throat, and he gagged. He couldn't tear his eyes away as the creature's blood engorged tongue licked over the gash and it closed to barely a scratch.

"Sunlight, sleep, and strength." The blood smeared lips bowed in satisfaction. "The first will kill you. The second will save you, and, with the third, you will live forever."

Connor learned quickly. The war in 1914 saved him from hiding. Although he could not feed in plain sight, no one looked closely at dead bodies in a field hospital. The clearing stations acted as holding areas for patients waiting to be shipped out to a base hospital, and many never survived Connor's triage. He was too young to be a qualified surgeon, but the Army was not about to be picky. It helped him to perfect his control, and, if ever he lost it, there was always someone in need of his 'help'. He could easily detect a failing heart.

But, through all the bloodshed and pain, detachment had never presented a problem, until now-

Connor pulled himself back to the present, zeroing in again on Rebekah's movement, and the mouth-watering symphony of whispering fabric. She mumbled under her breath, although, every word chimed loudly in his ear, like a note struck on crystal. Connor buried his clenched hands in his pockets and admitted to needing all his hard-fought for control, and then some.

"You can't take any of that with you, it stinks," he said quietly.

Rebekah's heart leapt into her throat and cold sweat broke out over her body.

His eyes darkened, silver becoming lead as her fear-slicked aroma enveloped him. About to speak again, he chose caution, slamming his vocal chords shut and staring into her eyes with undisguised hunger. He would not breathe, laugh, or cough again, unless he willed it, and an eerie hush filled the empty space.

Connor allowed her scent to wend its way up into his nostrils before he risked speaking again. “You stink, too,” he said, deliberately provoking her, playing with fire.

Assessing the mutinous expression on her face, and guessing that she was about to tell him to go-to-hell, he said, “The plan is to get out of here, yes? Well, to us, you smell. Fear has a delicious odor, and in you it is thick honey, slightly warmed.” He pulled in a deep lungful. “Very enticing, *exciting*, to me.”

As Rebekah opened her mouth to reply, Connor’s cool lips molded over hers, and he swallowed her words as his cold hands closed on her warm buttocks. His citrus-scented flavor filtered into her mouth as before, and then, as before, he snarled. His fingers flexed, pressing new bruises into her body. His tight expression leeched his face to bone-white and he peeled himself painfully away.

Retreating to a safe distance of ten feet, he smoothed his features to a blank, and adopted a relaxed pose, belied by the panting that vampires shouldn’t do, but which helped dilute the effect she had on him. He said colorlessly, “You’ll need to wash and scrub your skin. Now.”

Connor baldly laid out the plan of escape as he set the bowl of water he had collected from the kitchen sink onto the wooden bench in the basement and dropped a bar of unperfumed soap into her hand.

While Rebekah’s head was still spinning, he said, “You have five minutes to wash up while I find a car and bring it around front.” He glowered at her in the dim light, silver-gray flecks in his eyes glittering with his thoughts as he added starkly, “Five minutes, or I will come in and get you.”

The whirlwind of his departure whipped feathered strands of blond hair across her eyes, and when she brushed them quickly aside, she was alone. She toyed with rebellion for ten seconds before, yanking clothes out of her backpack, she stripped off the ones she wore, and in record time washed, rinsed, and pulled clean garments onto cold damp flesh.

Barely seven minutes later, a grimly satisfied Connor pulled the car away from the curb. A truculent Rebekah slouched low in the seat beside him, *wearing* the only clothes she possessed. When she'd joined him in the room above, he had tossed her rucksack back down through the basement hatch and made it clear that shopping was their first stop. *The new clothes smell will cover my stink, apparently.* Mentally ridiculing his condescending tone failed to improve her mood.

"Feeling cold?" Connor asked, glancing at her stubborn profile.

Rebekah shot a sarcastic glance at her tormentor. "Of course I'm cold." Her skin was still tight from being doused with icy water.

"Good," he said briskly, and then stole her anger by saying, "It will help us get you out of here." His pewter-soft regard absorbed the spark of indignation in her brown eyes, and he added on a sigh, "Thank the Lord its dark, at least."

Her cheeks burned as she muttered, "Where are we going, anyway?"

"Shopping, in London?" Connor laughed quietly. "Why, Oxford Street, of course. Things have not changed that much."

Rebekah folded her arms and slumped lower in her seat. "Well, I wouldn't know. Your lot saw to that."

"I'm sorry."

An awkward silence settled between them while Connor concentrated on driving the five miles from Clapham, north over Vauxhall Bridge, and on to Victoria. The districts of London slipped by, dark and silent, save for the occasional appearance of graceful immortal figures weaving smoothly in and out of the shadows.

Staring out at the streets in dread-filled fascination, and watching the ink-black landscape of Hyde Park trickle past the car window, Rebekah could no longer bear it as she realized they could jog faster than the moving car.

Connor's grip on the steering wheel was sure but static, and she felt certain she could do better, despite having been only seven years old when humans stopped driving cars on the roads.

Greg had made sure Rebekah, Leizle and Thomas learned the skill. In his view, 'if you can drive across fields at dusk then you were ready for anything'. His military precision came into its own out in the field. When vampires took to the roads, driving the delivery trucks taking harvested crops to the human farm, he used the activity as camouflage. The additional sound of one small vehicle to the rumble of tires and growling of engines of the convoys going past went unnoticed, if you timed it right.

Rebekah had the urge to shoulder Connor aside and take the wheel. *Some getaway this is turning out to be.*

"Why are you driving so slowly?" she asked in frustration, wanting the journey out of the way. She was already breaking into a sweat, and waiting for him to comment. *Or kiss me again.* She hoped she'd be ready next time, because living dangerously was not alien to her. *I've had to grow up quickly in this post-pandemic world. So, bring it on. Call it research, curiosity, madness, or all of the above.*

On what sounded suspiciously like a chuckle, Connor said, "I'm driving like a vampire. It's not about getting quickly from a-to-b for us. It's about the curiosity of propelling a metal box along and marveling at how it felt to be human. Well, not marveling, scoffing is probably closer, reminiscing, for some, I guess."

"How about you, are you scoffing or reminiscing?" she asked, letting go of her irritation.

"Ah, fishing, huh? Well, as an apology for saying you stink, neither one. When *I* lived, my preferred mode of transport was a brougham carriage, horse drawn. London was a mad melting pot of trolley buses, cars, and bicycles, but a few of us hung on to our carriages." He glanced at her intrigued expression. "1910."

Studying the moonlit relief of his perfect profile, Rebekah pictured him dressed in a waistcoat and starched shirt with a wing-tipped collar, complete with pocket watch. *Yes, starched and pompous suits him to a T.*

Connor pulled the car over to the curb, shrugged out of his jacket, and handed it to Rebekah. "Here, put this on, it will help hide the stink- er, I mean smell." His lips twitched when she nearly took the bait.

"I'll stay in the car," she grumbled.

"I'm afraid not. Vampires don't sit in cars, we drive cars for fun, remember? You'd draw attention like an adult on a kiddies' merry-go-round sitting here alone, so put it on and let's go."

His stern look withered the words of protest on the tip of her tongue, and Rebekah resigned herself to doing things his way.

Stepping out of the car, Connor walked around the hood and was on the sidewalk opening her door before she had time to think. Her legs felt weak as she joined him, and his eyes glittered in the dim moonlight. He looked down at her and said, "Stay close."

They walked into the cave-like gloom of the unlit department store. *Vampires certainly like to dress.* Every section now held only clothes. *I guess they don't need tableware, silverware, or ornaments, just wall-to-wall clothes and shoes.* Though, Rebekah could not imagine a world where the companionship of sitting together while eating and drinking did not exist.

She focused on the vampires moving around the shop floor. Silhouettes slipped through the shadow like silent apparitions, and she decided with alarm there were far more shoppers than she had expected. Connor suddenly stopped walking, and she guessed he had the same thought.

Panic was about to wring her heart dry, when Connor hissed, "Restroom, now."

Feigning casual, he led the way. When they reached the door with a jaunty female effigy wearing a puffed-out skirt stuck onto it, her throat ached with the hysteria bubbling up inside her. *Salvador Dali would love this.*

Pushing the door open, Connor reached back, closed his fingers in a cold bracelet around her wrist, and propelled Rebekah inside ahead of him. "Okay," he said, "we're in trouble, this won't work. Shit." His chest rumbled in frustration. No dressing it up, no frills, he pinned her in his gaze, and said, "I'm going to bite you."

"What? Oh no, no you're not. You did this on purpose," Rebekah hissed, backing away.

He advanced until she was cornered and pressing her backside against a porcelain basin.

With quiet menace, he said, "Sure I did. I'm going to get the death sentence for this." A derisive wave took in the length of her body. "And all I get out of it is a bite?" he muttered, in a 'give me a break' tone. "Now, all *you* have to decide is where?" he said through clenched teeth.

She gulped. "Why? Bite, I mean, what for?"

The muscle in his jaw ticked as he reeled in his impatience. "The beta-blockers are wearing off. You have no more, and you're nervous as hell so your heart rate is up. I *will* bite you and your heart *will* slow. We like to take our time when feeding and venom calms our victims. Your skin will be less-" Connor reached out a finger and ran it down her cheek. "Pink and warm. Perfect."

Rebekah wasn't sure if he was talking about the plan or her skin.

"And, if we're lucky, we'll get you out of here safely." Concentration creased his brow. "Look, there is a councilor called Serge who will be gathering a hunt, and make no mistake, he's not stupid." Connor's eyes met hers, and the excitement simmering in their depths sent a shiver of exhilaration down her spine. "We can't go back. We have to go forward, and this is the only way. So, the only question is, neck, underarm, or groin?" Connor moved in. "Decide."

Carotid, brachial, or femoral arteries. Rebekah knew her human biology. As she drew in a rattling breath, he said decisively, "Underarm. They'll get the scent of a wound near the neck, so, underarm."

Rebekah nodded, pulled an arm out of her sweater and lifted it up, raising her elbow high. Having decided, she thought, let's get on with it. A small imp whispered, 'wonder what he would do if I said groin'. *But I'm not brave enough to try it, not today.*

"Will it hurt?" she asked.

She was not reassured when a fierce frown scored lines into his face and he was suddenly engrossed in assessing her skin. He pressed his open hand onto her collarbone, stroked down under her arm, and around, coming to rest just below her shoulder blade. He pulled her slowly forward. His tone was distracted as he said, “Yes, but I’ll take only a little.”

Stepping in closer, he slid his other arm around her waist and arched her back. Elation flashed in his eyes and his nostrils flared as he said, “Sorry.” Then, he dipped his head.

Smothering a yelp, Rebekah rested her head on the vanity mirror behind, and her breathing faltered as his strong jaws clamped onto her flesh. Pain was the stab of red-hot needles when he pierced her skin, and then, as he began to massage firmly, a seductive, tingling glow laced around her heart. It warmed her chest and trickled down into her stomach like a lazy flow of burning lava.

Her will surrendered with disconcerting enthusiasm, and he became the center of a universe which shrunk to a pin-prick spark of tunnel vision. Vertigo gripped her and distorted her world, and he was all that remained in focus as she pushed her free hand into his hair and pulled him closer. His thigh pressed into the soft cradle of her pelvis, and her body welcomed him, molding to his hard muscles.

How long it lasted, she had no idea, but as he released her flesh, the long, firm strokes of his tongue passing over the wound drew a deep groan from her throat. He suddenly froze, inhaling a slow deep breath as if her scent was thick sweet honey.

His intense features filled her vision, his fingers slipped into the hair at her nape, and his lips dragged over her relaxed mouth. His tart, citrus kiss had the blistering confusion of freezer burn as tantalizing pleasure waltzed on the threshold of pain.

Finally, swallowing her sigh, he pulled away, his cool touch drifting over bare skin.

His eyes glittered with a mesmerizing frosted-silver cocktail as he held her somnolent gaze. Her bones felt like they had melted as Connor guided her upraised arm slowly back down to her side. Her bra strap slid from her shoulder, and he caught it, saving her modesty.

Rebekah froze. Aching excitement rode a sluggish tide in her fuzzy mind when his hand grazed her breast. A flush trailed beneath his knuckles as he settled the strap back in place and withdrew, his jaw muscle twitching as he whispered, "That's better. We need to go."

Silently, he helped her back into her sweater. He stepped back, extended his hand, and his voice rasped over sandpaper when he said, "Sorry." Tugging briefly on her fingertips, he muttered, "I can't hold your hand, but stay close."

Guiding her swiftly back through the store, Connor pulled clothes from the rails, making random selections without apparent thought. He calmly negotiated the indolent shoppers, and within moments, the evening air cooled her skin and filled Rebekah's lungs.

He moved her compliant body toward the car, and Rebekah's brain wallowed in a lightheaded haze. Not knowing how she had got there, the car seat chilled the back of her thighs, and the soft thump of the car door closing felt like a muffled underwater pulse of pressure. The chassis dipped alarmingly beneath Connor's solid weight when he dropped into the seat beside her. The engine purred as the car rolled forward, and Rebekah's body hummed with the slumberous rhythm.

The anxiety of the shopping trip receded to a dreamlike sequence. With her head gently rocking on the headrest, she knew that at this moment, being here with him, nothing else mattered. She felt safe and contented.

Connor glanced over and asked, "Station Four, which way are we headed?"

Rebekah frowned as his words focused her brain like a dose of smelling salts. Her feeling of contentment evaporated when it dawned on her that if this trip was her salvation, and she was no longer sure of that, it was extremely risky for Connor.

Douglas fancied himself as a vampire hunter. She shivered. Thinking of Douglas tainted the embers of excitement stirred by Connor's touch.

None of Greg's survival lectures ever penetrated with Douglas. Rebekah knew Greg would be livid if he heard some of the theories Douglas spouted in his absence. With him out on a long range mission with Stan and the guys, Douglas could be a real ass. The last thing Rebekah heard, Douglas had been experimenting with Tasers and crossbows. *Thank God, if the munitions mission turns up anything good, Greg'll keep it locked away. Douglas is an asshole, but dangerous to Connor? Maybe.*

"It's down the M20, about thirty miles," she mouthed, knowing he would hear, no matter how quiet her voice.

He looked across, confusion at her tone etching lines into the smooth alabaster of his skin.

A beautiful face, Rebekah decided, assessing him closely, taking in the details of his black hair, eyes that glowed like aluminum foil in the fading light, chiseled cheekbones, and the strong column of his throat. *Thirty miles, and then I'll never see him again.*

Chapter 7

Leaving the city, Connor drove south, back over the River Thames. Passing by the side streets which led to the humans' safe house, the car headed to the M25, the Motorway which circled London. He kept the speed below twenty miles an hour. On full alert, thirty minutes passed before he allowed the car's momentum to creep up to where it would raise a vampire eyebrow.

Connor's muscles buzzed with the adrenalin of human blood. He was high on Rebekah's pheromones. He had kissed her as he had wanted to all along, but with little danger of hurting her. He was full, replete, and her mouth was the refreshing glass of warm mulled wine which washed down his meal. All he had felt when her red-hot tongue molded to his, branding his lips with her candied scent, was satisfaction. But, an ache of longing still tightened the back of his throat. *It was not enough. Can I promise not to do it again?* He thought not.

Her blood flushing through his body sharpened his concentration, so he would torment himself another time, but for now, he was focused on getting out of London.

He followed the M20 for ten miles before taking a detour on to meandering country roads. The narrow ribbons of asphalt hugged the tree-lined boundaries of fields and orchards, and offered better concealment. Connor was reluctant to interrupt their journey, but it was two a.m., and knowing Serge as he did, traveling at night was not an option. *Vampires don't drive cars at night. We work at night.*

Like planets orbiting the life giving sun, vampire existence revolved around the human farm, and darkness, of course. Ironically, with pretense stripped away, for the first time in history, vampires had *responsibilities*.

Harvesting crops to feed humans, and planting new ones, meant working together. Something unprecedented in vampire culture, although farming held a fascination for some. In a society where money means nothing, purposeful activity represented a novelty, and, with endless sleepless hours to fill, a complex barter and volunteer system thrived.

Connor didn't receive a wage. *What for? I'm allocated daily rations of human blood. I can choose to have my animal blood the same way, or hunt on the moors if the mood takes me, as it often does. Excited blood tastes better.* Caring for humans was the only pressing task required of vampires, and every other was indulged on a whim.

With London behind them, Connor drove along the winding roads fast and without headlamps, taking his finely tuned preternatural night vision for granted. The imposing hedgerows and trees slipping by as a landscape of jet-black and darkest charcoal were alive with color for Connor. An angular silhouette caught his eye above the rushing scenery, and the decision was made.

Peeling off the road, he eased off the gas until their pace declined to a gentle rolling walk over the packed earth of an undulating track.

"Why are we stopping?" Rebekah asked, her head rocking on the headrest in time with the swaying of the chassis.

"There's a building behind the trees. Somewhere to hide 'til morning." Connor darted a look at Rebekah's pale face. Her drowsy tone caused him a stab of regret. *She's still lethargic.* The loss of blood was not dangerous, but his venom made sleep compelling. If taken to its ultimate conclusion, the victim never woke again. *It's a humane death, at least.*

Connor had diluted his venom with anticoagulant saliva, the chemical reaction vampires use to vary the toxicity of their bite. But, he had miscalculated. *Excitement made me careless*. He felt relief he was not faced with the decision of turning Rebekah to save her from the permanent slumber of death.

The car rolled to a stop outside the farmhouse, and he studied the black lashes tracing the crescents of her closed eyelids. Her features were delicate: arched brows, small straight nose, and a bottom lip fuller than the top. She looked defenseless. *I would turn her, and spend an eternity begging forgiveness, rather than lose her like this.* His dead heart glowed in his chest like granite warmed by the scorching sun. His twenty-four years of being alive were still lucid dreams, and he would never take away one moment of her human existence to satisfy his own needs.

Getting out of the car, Connor left her alone for the brief moment it took to satisfy himself it was safe inside.

The rooms, gutted of furnishings and with bare flagstone floors, could not be called comfortable, but the granite walled construction pleased Connor. *No one will be coming through these walls, not without causing an avalanche.* The impressive walk-in hearth, even though it was littered with decaying leaves, hinted at quaint charm, and the large kitchen boasted an Aga wood burning stove. Despite the thick layer of gritty dust covering every surface, an air of rustic magnificence persisted.

Collecting Rebekah from the car, Connor supported her stumbling weight, guided her through the doorway and across the dirt-covered floor, and lowered her onto the wooden chair he had brushed clean of most of the dirt.

She sat in silence, weaving gently.

Connor moved around the room sweeping, and clearing away the worst of the grit from an area on the floor where Rebekah would hopefully be able to sleep.

"Where are we? What are you doing? I can't see a damned thing," Rebekah whispered.

Connor chuckled. He'd forgotten her dull human senses would leave her disoriented and blinded by the soot black shadows.

Crossing to the window, where boards tacked across the grimy glass only allowed occasional splinters of moonlight to slice through, Connor forced his fingertips in between the slats and crumbled the edges to dust. He pulled away enough pieces to disperse the shadows every time the moon broke from behind the clouds. Rebekah could now, at least make out the comfort of his face.

Satisfied he had done all it was wise to do, he returned to Rebekah.

"Here, you'll need to change," Connor whispered, placing a pile of clothes on her lap and pressing a zip-lock bag into her hands. "Put the ones you're wearing inside and seal it."

"Telling me I stink again? Ever the gentleman, Doctor Connor," she said dryly.

"Please, just Connor. I think we're past formal introductions." He smiled.

Rebekah blushed.

The sweet scent of blood filled the air as the bite wound under her arm throbbed, and Connor added on a strangled note, "I'll be outside the door."

When he returned, Connor cushioned the hard floor with more of the clothes he had plucked from the department store rails, and they sat side by side with their backs against the wall.

He stared straight ahead, wondering what on earth he had gotten himself in to. Rebekah's new clothes fit like a glove, hugging every curve, and they drove him insane. *Bloody girl would look good dressed in a garbage bag*. It scared him, just how accurately he had assessed her size. *Obviously more obsessed than I knew.*

Suddenly clearing his throat, he pushed up to his feet and said, "You must be hungry, I'll find you something." As he headed for the door, he added, "I'll only be a moment, sit tight."

True to his word, seconds later, Connor returned from a foraging trip of the nearby orchard, fields, and woods, and presented Rebekah with an assortment of fruit, vegetables, and mushrooms.

Lowering himself down, Connor sat silently beside her once more, assessing his own body's needs. Easing out his thigh confirmed the worst; a toxic cocktail gripped at the fibers, cramping the muscles. He could not put off the inevitable. *I need to hunt.* The lubricant he needed was blood, and any blood would do. It was a matter of oiling the gears, but he needed to go now, while he could still move well enough to stalk his prey.

"Hey, I've got to go out for a while," he said.

Rebekah inhaled sharply, but before she could protest, Connor's voice cut through the gloom. "I've got to go now. I will be back, but-" He left the sentence hanging when he saw her nodding.

"Okay. Back soon," he said gently. "I need to hunt."

Rebekah blinked.

Connor stood up and pushed his long fingers through his hair, unveiling eyes which glinted with the steely focus of a hunter.

He left the farmhouse and loped across the fields with the awkward gait of a man who had sat in one position too long. He didn't like leaving her alone. *I'll stay within earshot. Two miles should do it.* Pausing to scent the air, he sighed. *It isn't going to be exciting, all I can smell are cows, sheep, and rabbits.* He rolled his shoulders in an ironic bring-it-on gesture, and took off at an easy run.

I prefer the challenge of mountain lion - being literally a heartbeat away from having sinew torn from bone. He enjoyed the snarling undulation of the fight. Ramming his head under the cat's chin and biting down into the esophagus gave him a rush. He reveled in the metallic taste of the blood at the height of the cat's terror, as he finally crushed the ribcage in an embrace which slicked his face and chest in hot syrupy pleasure and stained him red.

This was as far from that as he had been in one hundred years, and he shook his head. *What is my world coming to?* Connor shrugged before he got too distracted. *But hey, I don't mind herbivores, although it's not so much a hunt as sidling up and knocking them over. But on the plus side, they are quick, and today, I need quick.*

Even though it would be a stroll in the park, Connor still bared his chest. He could at least enjoy the freedom, and the sensual buzz of the dying heartbeat beneath the warm flesh thundering against his skin when he tightened his grip.

"Connor?" In Rebekah's mind, he had simply vanished. *How long has he been gone?* She adjusted her position, easing her numb backside on the mattress of clothing which had become a bundle of hard seams and sharp buttons. She welcomed the discomfort because it helped her fight sleep. Her eyelids fluttered, but she needed to stay awake until Connor returned. She tried to picture him hunting; recalling the intensity in his eyes when he'd bitten into her made her skin tingle. Just his kiss had been like a lava flow through every fiber.

Suddenly, a glimmer in the blackness caught her eye, and she whispered, “Oh, you’re back. I-” Sighing with relief, the words died on her lips and she gagged on the smell of rotting flesh. The hairs on her neck prickled when the thickened shadows heaved a sigh of their own, but did not move.

An adrenalin-charged jolt of panic clenching her heart, she shot to her feet. Fear exploded inside her and the next sixty seconds were a kaleidoscope of overloaded senses.

It’s not him. The thought gripped her in a vise of cold steel.

◇◇◇

Kneeling beside his kill out in the meadow, Connor heard Rebekah’s heartbeat pick up pace before she registered it herself, and ice-cold certainty filled his chest.

Closing in silently on the farmhouse with the devastating accuracy of a heat-seeking missile, he covered the two miles in eighteen seconds. Slipping inside, he whisked around the perimeter of the darkened room until, stepping forward, he appeared behind Rebekah like a shadow solidifying into vampire form. Folding her into his embrace, he confronted the intruders.

His breath fanned her hair, wafting over her goosefleshed skin. Her knees began to buckle. She shook as the iron band of his arm pinned her tightly up against a chilled chest.

He draped one arm across her body with his fingertips grazing her hip, settling his other hand casually on to her shoulder. Connor studied the two vampires. The excited glitter in their eyes betrayed the craving lurking behind the carefully indifferent expressions.

Connor smiled. He estimated he had sixty years of experience, control, and, more importantly, strength over them both.

On a deceptively calm note, he asked, “Can I help you, gentlemen? I do hope you’ve not come to take my meal away.” His features eased into a deliberately feral grin. Raising a sardonic brow, he added, “I’m afraid I don’t share.”

The vampires glanced at each other, and then at the tableau of Connor, his chest bare, and the motionless girl in front of him. Their eyes darted to the visible pulse throbbing in her throat. Her heart clattered with a wet distracting rhythm, and Connor knew he had them.

"We're here to collect her for the farm." The taller vampire jerked his head toward Rebekah, dressing his face in a casual mask.

"And me?" Connor's tone held idle curiosity. He knew their minds better than they did. There was no disguising the slur of bloodlust in their speech. *Rebekah would never have made it to the farm.*

He was not surprised Serge had sent juveniles to deal with him. *But then, I project my caring-doctor persona for good reason.*

"You're free to go. We're here for the girl." The smaller mousy-haired vampire could not meet Connor's eye. If he was still human, he would have fidgeted, but instead, being nervous tightened his muzzle and bared his teeth in a manufactured smile.

Watching their faces, Connor decided the taller one would think he was strong enough to take him out. "It's me," he whispered into Rebekah's ear and pressed the blade of his thumbnail into the swell of her breast. He smirked as the milky flesh molded to it before succumbing to the pressure, and a cut opened up in her skin. Slicking his thumb pad in the oozing flow of blood, he met the fevered gaze of his opponents as he deliberately lifted it to his lips.

With every sinew primed, Connor saw the pupils of their eyes dilate to pebbles of polished jet. Snarls ripped from their throats and their diaphragms flexed in a spasm of ecstasy as the smell of human blood hit them. They launched their attack.

The taller vampire hurtled forward, and Connor cast Rebekah forcefully away, sending her cartwheeling up through the air in a surreal fairground ride which left her stomach behind.

Connor rushed in and grabbed the charging vampire by the throat. Without loosening his hold, he sidestepped and twisted until they were back to back. Reaching behind, securing a two-handed grip on the vampire's neck, he leaned forward in an explosive, wrenching jerk. The vampire's spine crumbled. Connor let go, and, like a puppet with cut strings, his victim dropped to the floor with a dull thud.

The smaller vampire turned his back on Connor, intent on following Rebekah's rag doll tumble across the room. Connor caught him from behind, stopping him dead in his tracks. The vampire's head snapped forward, and Connor's teeth whipped over the vertebra at his nape, slicing through the exposed disc of cartilage like a knife through butter. Grabbing a handful of mousy hair, Connor jerked the vampire's head further forward, crushed his vocal chords, and released the dead weight to drop down onto his chest. Connor's final blow severed the spinal cord and captured an expression of shocked surprise on the vampire's face as his skull hit the ground like a stone.

Without wasting a moment, Connor stepped over the fallen bodies and reached out to guide Rebekah's reckless airborne descent.

He sensed her disorientation solidifying into fear as she tensed, bracing for impact and the agony of broken bones.

Closing his cold hands around her flailing arms, Connor slowed her flight. Her head rocked with the abrupt change in direction. As gently as his battle-pumped muscles would allow, he swung her into his chest. The air rushed from her lungs when she collided heavily with his body, finally coming to rest pulled up against the firm planes of his torso.

He enfolded her in his arms, disconcerted by the alien feeling of intense relief which filled him. Framing her face gently in his hands, Connor breathed, "It's over."

His gray eyes glowed like coal embers in a fierce white face as he demanded Rebekah's attention. His magnetic stare drew her in until he saw her sanity return and her mind slowly find focus. With relief, Connor whispered again, "It's over. You're safe, honey, you're safe."

As recognition dawned, the tension drained from her face and she snaked her arms around his waist. Still shaking, she pressed her cheek to his cold chest.

He smiled tightly and tucked her head under his chin. His hands gently followed her contours, finally settling at her waist, and relief ate a hole in his gut. Locked in his embrace, Rebekah's breathing gradually calmed and her heart rate steadied. She gripped his body as if she could not believe he was really there, and Connor fought the raging thirst urging him to taste more than just one thumb pad of her blood.

When the trembling in her knees had stopped, they settled down to wait for dawn. Rebekah sat on the crumpled jumble of clothes again and gripped her raised knees in a way that made relaxation impossible.

"Get some sleep," Connor said, and moved off towards the door. "I'll stand guard."

"Don't go."

Connor turned back as if the anguish in her voice coiled around his heart and whipped him around.

"Please, stay." The dark pools of desolation in her gaze sucked him into their depths. 'I'm scared' was written there on her face, but she would not beg.

"Of course," he murmured. He crossed the room and in a fluid movement lowered himself down beside her. Reclining, with an arm crooked behind his head, he carefully tucked Rebekah in to his side. He was disconcerted when she relaxed and snuggled into him, resting her cheek on his chilled chest. He stared at the ceiling, counting spiders and fruit flies as a form of distraction, until the heat of her body warming him drove him crazy. "Won't you be cold?" he muttered eventually.

"Maybe, but it feels... safe." She raised her head. "You don't mind?"

"I'll live," he said wryly, and was rewarded by her soft laughter.

"It's so quiet," she said in whispered fascination.

Connor knew she meant the silence of his chest, and he smiled in the dark.

A moment during the night almost ended her life when she ran her hand over his stomach, tracing his abdomen with her fingertips. Connor quickly buried her hand in his, trapping her fingers. He turned his head to look down at her. "Please Rebekah, this is already testing me to my limit," he groaned. "I'm only human... well kind of." His smile was tight and his eyes glittered in the gloom.

His fingertips wandered to the congealed wound marring her breast. Running the cold pads over it, he said, “I’m sorry about that, but with the difficulty I have resisting you, I knew those two mutts would have no chance.” He forced another grin. “Now, get some sleep while you can. I’m not going anywhere.”

Chapter 8

Rebekah awoke to sunshine pouring in through the gaps between the wooden slats on the windows, and found she was alone in the farmhouse. Ignoring the stiff remnants of sleep, she sat up and surveyed the room. Two bodies still lay where they had fallen, but the heads were an accumulation of quarry dust. Connor explained the vampires were still conscious, despite their apparent deaths, and the humane thing to do was to grind their skulls to gravel.

I didn't expect him to do it with his hands. It had shocked her. *But, he's a vampire, much as I wish he wasn't.* She frowned as the fear of last night converged with the sneaking discomfort of this morning. *Where is he, anyhow? He said he wasn't going anywhere.*

Anxiety gnawed away at her common sense. She remembered telling him how Station Four, where twenty humans lived, was only fifteen miles away. *Maybe I gave away too much?* But the relief at being alive dropped her guard, and her mouth had run away with her.

Unease prickled down her spine. *What if he was playing me? Is he planning our capture and dispatch to the farm? If so, he knows a lot more now.*

Looking for comfort, Rebekah clutched at straws. *Well, he'll be out of luck.* Some of the guys are out in the field with Greg. *Smart, Rebekah, it also means the one guy who has a chance of saving us isn't there. Shit.*

She jumped to her feet and got moving, fear and anxiety swilling inside her. *He's a vampire for Christ sakes! He only saved me so he could get the others, too.* Tears stung and she swiped at them angrily. *But, I liked him.* She slammed the lid shut on the thought.

Well, he's not here, so I've got a chance to put this right. Leaving the clothes and grabbing only a few pieces of fruit, she rushed out into the sunshine, strode over to the car, and jumped in. She took a nervous moment to look for him. *He could be hiding from the sunlight?* Even though the trees cast heavy shade over the dirt track, he didn't seem to be near the car.

Taking a calming breath, she started the engine. *What if they hear?*

But, she had no choice, so, once the hunk of metal was moving, she kept the speed down to where the engine note seemed quietest. Letting the car roll as much as possible, she gripped the steering wheel. Part of her hoped it *would* bring Connor back, but as the ribbon of asphalt trickled by beneath the tires, disappointment seeped into her cramped muscles.

The jolt of the car as the engine spluttered and died scared Rebekah to death. In the thickening silence, she sat there bathed in sweat and praying. *Shit, that was stupid.* She calculated she had gained only a few miles before the gas ran out. Gritting her teeth, she silently raged against God and the injustice of being stranded, but eventually, she got out of the car.

A breeze rippled through the trees, rustling the cool green canopy overhead and stirring the shadows on the road. Rebekah peered into the undergrowth and shivered. Turning away, she trudged towards the middle of the field. This far outside London, she felt safer in the sunshine.

If he has gone back and got a hunting party together, they'll travel in the woods. Rebekah glanced up at the sky. Today was a scorcher, so at least something was in her favor. *I just need to get back and sound the alert.* They practiced it often enough. *We will pack-up and disappear.* The evacuation drill of the eco-town was hardwired into their consciousness.

The recent heavy bursts of rainfall made the ground boggy in places, and with the sun beating down, pretty soon Rebekah found the humidity suffocating. Her muscles ached from staying low in the chest high grass, but deep down she knew she was not as invisible as she felt.

It was slow going covering the stony ground and feeling hot didn't help. *The pheromone spray isn't going to cope with sweaty me, darn it.* An hour later, hot and sweaty seemed like a picnic. The heat made her feel sick and her legs decided they couldn't take anymore. And then, lifting her face to a sudden scurrying gust of wind which chilled the sweat on her skin, she gave thanks. The sky lowered, the heavens rumbled as they opened, and a typically-English downpour fell out of the sky. She looked up at the thunderous purple clouds, and closed her eyes as the heavy droplets splattered her hot cheeks and soaked her through.

An hour before dawn, Connor had lain with Rebekah in the dark, listening to the lilting tone of her sleepy voice until even *his* hearing could no longer make the tumble of thick sounds into words. The deep sigh of her regular breathing filtered into his head, and the rise and fall of her chest gently massaged his side as the relaxation of human sleep melted her bones. Easing out of the embrace which held her snuggled into him, Connor battled with the monster inside his head, locking every muscle tight as grave sleep beckoned, and the killer rattled on his cell door, demanding rehydration.

The siren call of her slumberous pulse rolled vicious contractions through his gut, and his fingers itched to close around her neck. He ached to bite into her carotid artery and drown in her dying pulse, but not until he at last, buried his body inside hers.

Rebekah stirred, wriggling closer and shifting her weight onto one hip, and the satin warmth of the thigh she stroked over his stomach almost fractured his control. Desperation to dip into her feminine folds made the length of her leg a tourniquet around his middle, cutting off rational thought from gut instinct. Connor slipped away while he still could.

Poised to run, arguing that the attack of last night would not be repeated any time soon, Connor realized he could not take that chance. The vampires had not been 'passing by', and Serge might have sent out scouting pairs in all directions, playing the numbers. *I can't rule it out.*

On a hunch, he patted down the bodies of his two vampire victims and came up empty. Settling back on his haunches, he frowned. He didn't want to run the risk of going back into London to beg Julian for a vial of human blood, but there was no way to hydrate his brain center without it. *It's a long shot, but if these two were out on a mission, then surely-* They were here to fight. Connor checked the tread patterns on the soles of their boots and retraced their steps out through the door of the farmhouse and across the meadow.

The gouges in the muddy field showed they had come in under full speed, but they both stopped twenty yards out. The pre-dawn light cast a glittering blanket over the dew-laden blades of grass, making it easy for Connor to find the flattened spot where the vampires had settled to plan their attack.

He grinned as he dropped down onto one knee. *Bingo.*

Four empty vials lay on the ground, but had been drained in a hurry, and, it may not be much, but dregs of human blood sat in the bottom of each. Not letting the glass touch his lips, Connor tipped the containers up and waited patiently for the droplets to slide along the glass. *In a drought, anything will do.*

Back at the farmhouse, Connor zeroed in on the car. He opened the trunk, surveyed the space, and swept an ironic glance down his solid bulk. Leaning in, he pounded a fist along the back wall, feeling the upholstered padding of the seats jump in protest.

"That ain't gonna hack it," he muttered. *Damn, can this get any tougher?*

He headed around to the rear of the farmhouse, to the wood heap which he guessed would be there. The Aga wood burning stove in the kitchen needed fuel. He expected the short stumpy blocks to be useless, but he found the ax, picked it up and balanced its solid weight in his palm. It had been a while since he had used an ax as a fake human, but he welcomed the distraction.

He set off through the wood, cut three thick tree limbs to length and carried them back to the car.

After packing them into the trunk to strengthen the back wall, Connor rolled himself down inside. He wriggled his shoulders into place, grinding away some of the bark. He pulled the lid down and the lock clicked shut, but he was taking no chances. Twisting in the tight space, he gripped the metal box covering the catch and crushed the mechanism into an ingot of steel.

With a grating sigh, he surrendered to the psychopath ricocheting around inside his brain center, and sank urgently into grave sleep. Convulsions rippled through his body, rocking the car chassis violently until he slowly wound each sinew tight and locked his cramped limbs in place.

His confinement was imperative for Rebekah's safety. *And for my own sanity. Even if I left, I would know where to find her. Bloodlust would drag me back, and I* would *tear out her throat.* For reasons he preferred not to inspect too closely, his mind shied away from the thought of ending her life.

Lying in his less than perfect prison, knowing he had taken every precaution, Connor prayed. His one hundred years of experience was a blessing. Every time the hot tongue of hunger licked over his brain and threatened to overpower him, he came back, gathered his control, and then slipped under again. *It was all part of not spooking the herd when I was a field surgeon in the casualty clearing stations. When I was Sergeant Connor Sanderson of the Royal Army Medical Corps; pretend human.*

But he never expected Rebekah to get in and drive the damn car. The smell of her candied sweat, the memory of her blood staining her breast, and the taste of it on his thumb, clawed at his throat and almost destroyed his sanity. It took every ounce of his iron will to stay still.

Thankfully, the car traveled only a short distance before her compelling presence faded.

Once fully refreshed, he braced his shoulders against the inside of the trunk lid, steadily increasing the pressure until the distorting metal screamed, and, with a final shriek, the mangled lock burst open.

Standing on the side of the road, brushing the sawdust from his shirt, he raised his head and scented the breeze. He set off to find her. *I thought she would sleep longer after the shock of last night, but clearly, she's made of sterner stuff.*

When he *did* find her, red-hot anger sizzled along a fuse wire of frustration.

She was bathed in sunshine, struggling through long grass, and exuding a pheromone cloud that instantly tightened his groin. The constriction of his pants bit into him, and visions of her thighs locked around his hips almost seared a hole in his brain.

Damn it, frigging cocktail of sex and stupidity. Connor concentrated fiercely on tracking her from the dank shade of the tree line, scanning for approaching danger. When the woodlands to his left abruptly fell silent, he swiveled sharply around and listened. Tracing an arc, he moved briskly through the trees, oblivious to the rough bark tearing his clothes as he threaded his way between them, hugging their shadows.

He froze when he saw a vampire moving through the undergrowth.

The vampire's head rotated in a constantly scanning motion, like a radar sweeping the woods. *Looking for roe deer, badgers, what?* There was nothing bigger than that to hunt. *Except... her.*

Turning his face to the breeze, Connor flexed his chest. *I can smell her, but is it because I'm tuned in to her scent?*

Looking back, he stiffened when he caught sight of the vampire's face. A river of dry blood ran down from its slack mouth, ingrained into the folds of his neck. Breathing in gently, Connor passed the odor cloud drifting in the woods over his palate and tasted four-day-old rotted blood. The front of the vampire's black coat glistened like oil and was stiff with veined clots and fragments of dried flesh. *Damn, a feral.*

The constant swinging of the feral's head ceased abruptly and, swallowing the pool of thin bloodied saliva gathered in his throat, he lifted his chin and glared through the trees.

Shit, he's got her scent.

The vampire took off, his mouth gaping and his face folded into a silent snarl.

Connor accelerated, keeping the feral in his sights and tracking the black mass as it oozed in and out of the shadows.

Desperation cramped Connor's chest. *I need to buy her some time.* With a grim smile, he honed his senses and chose his own prey.

Veering left, he closed in on four roe deer in the dappled gloom of a copse. He shot forward, gripped the nearest animal around its ribcage and closed a fist around an antler, easing back on the pressure when it creaked in his palm. Holding tightly enough to restrain the animal, he launched himself back in the direction from which he came.

The deer thrashed, fighting against Connor's unyielding embrace, and the heartbeat cantered loudly inside its chest. *Will it distract him?*

When Connor caught sight of the vampire still traveling through the woods, he released the agitated buck, letting it spring from his arms. As the deer catapulted forward, Connor gripped the animal's hide in his fist, and with a sharp jerk, he tore a hole in the pelt.

The deer bellowed and blood splattered loudly onto the broad leaves of the undergrowth.

Will it work?

Connor circled away as the deer's legs folded and flailed. The terrified buck tried to regain its feet, its brain shouting 'run'.

The scent of gushing blood filled Connor's mouth with saliva, and while he raced forward on a collision course with the feral, he prayed.

When the crazed vampire's wide open mouth suddenly snapped shut and his head shot around, Connor froze. The blown black pupils glittered as he whipped about, tilting his head. The deer bellowed more quietly this time, and the feral set a course for the bleeding animal.

Connor followed on behind.

The vampire smashed into the animal at speed, the impact plowing its body through the undergrowth. He fell to his knees and gripped the deer's head, one clawed finger imploding the animal's eyeball as it burrowed into the skull. His other hand punched through the shuddering body, shattering the sternum as he grappled inside the chest cavity. Pulling out a lump of bleeding flesh, he squeezed it in a fist and a river of blood ran down his arm.

Pushing the warm, bloodied organ into his mouth, the feral shoved his hand back inside the deer. His jaws worked until meat fell from his overfilled mouth, and his hands massaged the offal, trying to force it back in even though it flooded out again.

Connor spared barely a second to swallow his disgust before he drove forward at a full run into the feral's side; more blood splattered out of the gaping mouth. The deviant creature's clawed grip dragged the deer carcass with him for a few yards, until it fell away and hit the floor in a moist thump. Locking an arm around the feral's neck, Connor barreled on through the woods, the vampire's face bearing the brunt of collisions with the trees.

The woodland thinned and Connor looked for sunshine. A dappled yellow glow disappeared as soon as he stepped into it. *Shit, autumn's a bitch.* The feral reached back and dug his nails into Connor's neck, his blood-soaked fingers slipping over Connor's granite skin.

Another golden coin of sunlight appeared on the ground, its slanting rays cutting through the air. Ducking his head and turning his face into the solid back of the vampire, Connor pushed forward into the bright funnel of light.

The feral pressed back into Connor's braced body, scrabbling as his heels slipped on the packed mud. Connor locked every muscle tight and, feeling heat through the coat sleeve on the arm wrapped around the feral's gargling throat, he held fast.

The sizzling of shriveling flesh crackled in the air and the vampire's protests faded. Lumps of deer meat fell from his convulsing throat, sliding down his chest. When the smell of charring skin became overpowering, Connor uncoiled from his cowering position. Stepping back, he shoved the vampire forward. The feral hit the ground and rolled over. Smoke curled into the air, wreathing the scorched head in a billowing halo.

Connor watched with macabre curiosity as the shriveling eyelids peeled back and the fluid of ruptured eyeballs wept from the eye sockets. Lying in the repose of a sunbather, the vampire's smoldering skull contained the heat until the brain itself combusted.

One less feral in the world to worry about. Connor took the scenic route back to Rebekah, satisfying himself that there were no other ferals in the woods.

Arriving back at the tree line, when Rebekah came into sight again, he ground his jaw in frustration. His joints ached as tension stretched every sinew, and he discovered that vampires can indeed have headaches. Recklessness was hard to contain, but he discarded thoughts of calling out her name. Human hearing was dull, and any vampires within a twenty-mile radius would hear him before she did. *My day, so far, is not going great. I sure as hell don't need any* more *complications.* He was not taking any chances.

And then, thank the Lord, it looked like rain. The thunderclouds rolled in, and he watched thick shadows tumbling across the field towards where Rebekah walked, waiting until the wind picked up heralding a rain shower.

Rebekah didn't care that she was drenched, even though the blond, feathered strands of her hair hung in mud-colored rat tails and dripped down her neck. She was tired and dusty, her throat was parched, and nothing mattered but the refreshing rain on her face.

A reverberating thud through her ribcage swept her sideways. The rushing scenery and a cold, hard embrace registered at the same time as fear, which felt like a rodent clawing at her insides.

Coming to an abrupt halt, she was bumped roughly back against a tree and she strangled a yelp of pain as the bark bit into her shoulder blades. In the dappled shade of the woods, she stared up into the eerily-white, smooth face of Connor, and panic upgraded to terror. His beautiful preternatural features wore an expression of blank composure, but the sparks glittering in his flint-hardened gaze mesmerized and scared her. The tendons in his neck twitched as he hung on to his temper by the most tenuous of threads.

Ignoring the bark grazing her skin, Rebekah froze. His frustration uncoiled in slow deliberate movements. Leaning in to form an arch around her, placing his hands on the tree trunk on either side of her head, his lips distorted with a sneer as he said, "What the frigging hell are you doing? Do you want to die? You don't damn well know *what's* out there."

"I thought you'd gone," she muttered. Her gaze skittered around the woods. "Are you alone?"

"Hell, Rebekah." His tension eased when her nervous energy pulsed through him. "Of course I'm alone," he said huskily. "What, did you think-?"

Pinned by his intent glare, Rebekah had no words, only fascination as the silver glimmer in his eyes darkened to lead. The frantic pulse in her neck drew his gaze, and he released the clawed grip of one hand. Absently brushing his fingertips over his thigh, he dusted them free of gouged lumps of tree bark. Entranced, he extended a cool index finger, tracing it over the contours of her clavicle and coming to rest in the V at the base of her throat. He strangled a groan as lust sharpened the planes of his face. Rebekah didn't feel the disgust she always felt when it was Douglas. Her breath caught in her throat and pinpricks of heat scattered over her body.

Connor's eyes stroked over her rain-soaked skin, and his fingertip followed the droplets of water downward, dipping into her damp cleavage.

Rebekah pressed back into the tree, not wanting to break his concentration. Her pounding heart tried to break a few ribs, and anticipation hijacked fear as her mind mapped ahead to where she wanted his hands to go.

She sensed the moment when he reined himself in, and her aroused body shrieked with the agony of frustration. As he shifted his weight, easing the pressure of his fingertips and preparing to withdraw his hand, she covered it with her own.

"I want this," she whispered. "Please, Connor. I want this... I want you." Her voice broke. She pressed his hand firmly to her flesh, and time stood still as her pride hung its head, waiting for the iodine sting of his rejection to stain her cheeks crimson.

Her eyes, dark pools of desperation framed with damp lashes, clouded with a kaleidoscope of all her imaginings. Hunger licked over her tingling skin and she held her breath, suspended between embarrassment, yearning, and paralyzing fear.

A breeze ruffled Connor's hair and her fingers itched to brush it back from his stern brow. His rasping breathing through flared nostrils etched white lines around his mouth.

"Well, you can't have *this*," he breathed, although his hand didn't move away, and his fingers stroked the swell of her breast. His eyes settled on her damp upper lip as he licked his own.

"Maybe... a sip," he murmured. Inching nearer, he finally closed the space. Pieces of tree bark cracked, crumbling beneath his fingers as he fought for restraint. He dipped into her warmth, snaking his tongue in to draw her heated flesh into his mouth, and molding himself carefully to it.

Her excitement buffeted his senses when Rebekah grabbed a handful of his hair in a tight fist, pulling him closer as pleasure surged inside her, and her galloping heartbeat thundered through him.

Connor groaned gently, his spiced citrus saliva coating her mouth as he deepened the kiss, and his questing fingers at last bared her breast. Another shower of sawdust rained down when he ground a fistful of tree bark to powder, and his lips hardened as he lost the struggle to hang on to his civilized veneer. "Oh God, I can't do this," he sighed sharply into her mouth, anguish shredding his tone, but he clung to her kiss for a moment longer.

He left quickly.

Rebekah shivered at the sudden vortex gusting over her damp body. The support of his solid bulk was snatched away, and her hands dropped to her sides.

Connor stood six yards away, torment biting into his features as he stared across the divide. "Believe me, if there was a way-" A snarl hung in the air as the thick undergrowth swallowed him whole, and the snapping of branches were an echo of his agitated retreat. He vanished.

Rebekah sank down onto the soft grass with a shuddering sigh.

Dusk fell while she went through every word Connor had uttered and every expression which had battled for control of his face. *He won't abandon me. I'll wait until he comes back.*

When he finally re-entered the glade as a silent apparition, early evening shadows dappled the wraithlike glow of his skin. He was bare to the waist, and the pink stain on his hand told her he had hunted.

Without speaking, he walked over and lowered himself gracefully onto the ground beside her. His hands molded to her waist as, in one fluid movement, he pulled her gently towards him.

Lying back on the grass, he rolled her body over to cover his own until her knees framed his hips. His hands stroked up over her curves. He caressed her face and his kiss plunged sensually into her mouth.

Rebekah had no idea what had changed, but, like a match to a tinderbox, the spark of pleasure she felt at seeing him burst into flame when her lips met his. Her questions forgotten, she sensed a purpose in him, a determination that swelled her heart with an answering commitment.

"I don't care how this turns out, just make love to me," she whispered.

His sigh melting into a growl, he stroked his fingers into her hair, his other hand smoothing over her buttocks as his hips rocked into hers.

He settled a tantalizing kiss on the frantic pulse in her neck and an adrenalin rush forged a white-hot path through her. He savored the tingle on his cool lips when her cheeks flooded with delightful heat.

Connor's cool caress was a shock of exhilaration on her flushed skin as he rolled her carefully onto her back, and murmured, "I'm not a fan of the missionary position, but this is new ground for me. I need to know I can leave if things get-" He left the thought hanging, looking down into her face.

He went to speak again, but she put a finger to his lips and smiled. "Shh... I know."

His mouth twitched in faltering bravado as he said softly, "Trust me, I'm a doctor."

His eyes searched hers, and finding the reassurances he yearned for, his pupils ate the gray away to glistening threads of silver, and he kissed her again.

Fierce concentration folded his brow as he drifted his fingers down over her skin, undoing the buttons of her shirt. He sighed when he pushed the fabric slowly aside, and beneath his hungry gaze her breasts strained against their confinement.

He tore away the silky fabric of her bra. Fascination painted tension across his features as the hard peaks flooded with heat, warming his questing fingertips. He tugged gently on the pink buds, sighing when she groaned, a feline stretch pushing the soft mounds into his hands.

"Beautiful," he murmured, lowering his head and daring to flick his tongue over one hot tingling tip.

A shiver trembled through her as suddenly, he left.

Pushing back the clouds of excitement Rebekah moaned softly, "No..."

Her breath caught in her throat when she saw him. Resting between her knees, he was naked. Her eyes dragged down over the hard wall of his abdomen to where the ivory tone of his skin darkened in the shadow of his arousal, twitching against his stomach.

"Tell me to stop," he begged, slowly removing the denim barrier of her jeans. He stroked his hand up the inside of her thigh, a snarl molding to his lips as his fingers teased over the pool of damp heat. Desire curled in her belly. He slipped his fingers inside her, his eyes burning with intensity as he groaned, "I don't want to hurt you."

"Love me." She arched her back and took him in deeper. Somewhere inside, she feared this may be her only chance to feel like this.

A growl rumbled in his throat as, slowly uncoiling his shuddering body, his chest brushed her tingling nipples and he kissed her, his tongue echoing the sensual rhythm of his fingers stirring the lava flow of heat in her belly.

He hissed against her lips as aching frustration rippled through her.

"God, Rebekah," he growled, his manhood pushing tentatively at the slick heat between her thighs. "Okay?"

She ran her hands over his solid shoulders. "Please. Now, please."

He eased closer. Settling his stomach over hers, he filled her slowly, and moving in a tentative rhythm, he stole her breath as she clung to him. Little by little, he immersed himself in her heat until fire melted ice in a collision of senses.

Building intoxicating sensations, he traced his fingertips over the contours of her breasts. His tongue playing over her nipple tugged desire through her center and set her senses alight. Hearing, seeing and feeling became a tangled glow of heat trickling along her clamoring nerve endings.

Connor's touch was painfully deliberate, and each time his fingers laid a blush across her skin, his eyes followed the trail. A frown visited his features as he hung on to every sigh shuddering through her.

She was where she wanted to be, and every sinuous movement made her heart race harder as she surrendered to his will.

"Okay?" he breathed again. His gray eyes, glowing like molten steel in the dappled light, raked over her flushed cheeks and finally locked onto hers.

His features hardened as he fought to stay until her simmering rapture exploded in a starburst of unbearable pleasure, leaving her breathless. The tremors sweeping her, rippled through him too, tugging persuasively at him, begging him to join her and to flood her with his infatuation, but he eased reluctantly away. His fingertips dipped inside her, and he delighted in the heat which flared at his touch. Pressing his lips to her slender throat, and smothering a growl of satisfaction, his own release shuddered through him as her body clutching at his hand was enough to take him there with her.

She floated back to earth; heaven descended like a cotton-candy blanket, clouding her thoughts while her heartbeat steadied, and relaxation stole her will to move.

Connor closed his eyes for a moment, enjoying the dull thud of her sated pulse. Holding her gently, he said, "I couldn't stay away, I tried to. But I had to find a way I could be here, with you."

Rebekah lifted her chin to look into his face. Anger and ferocity had been replaced by an expression she could not read. "How...?" She searched for words which would not make her blush.

"Let's just say, I found a more creative way to enjoy revival sleep." He laughed gently and said, "Although strictly speaking, it's an awakening. A waking up of the gentle side, while the beast stays locked away."

The relaxation of revival sleep resembled an out-of-body experience for Connor, where every movement felt like pushing his limbs through water. It allowed him time to fully experience the pleasures tingling through his body, *and* temper his responses.

The depressed senses dulled Connor's lust for blood, at least, that had been his hope. Of course, he knew he couldn't have all of her. *The danger in that is too great.* But he could be with her until his will crumbled. *I never expected to hold back forever. I'm a vampire, not a saint.*

Her energy field, the electrical activity inside her, was a symphony to him. She drenched him in sensations, delicious odors, and static sparks tingled over his skin, imprinting him with her essence. *How could I not be overwhelmed by that?*

Connor could remember the human sensation of burying himself inside soft, heated flesh, and of clinging to a woman's body as his own became a bow of tension. He knew how it felt to let go when every nerve ending seared with desire, release boiling up inside him to infuse her with his love and need in the final expression of his spent body. The thudding heartbeats which slowly came down as two bodies melted into a tangle of damp skin and the pins and needles of trapped limbs.

He wanted that with Rebekah. *But no, that was another life, another man.*

But he *had* discovered the control of revival sleep. Even though scorching hunger abraded his throat and burned like lava inside his chest, he at least had a taste of the passion he dreamed of... *but now.*

Connor rested on his elbow, a serious expression of regret on his face as he gently fitted his fingers to the pattern of dusky pink prints, some already blossoming to lilac bruises, on Rebekah's body.

"Hey you." She called him back from his reverie. She smiled when his eyes met hers, but he saw concern lurking in their depths.

"Hey you, back," he said, but his eyes wandered again, this time to the necklace of love bites staining her skin. None of them had broken the surface. He had not bitten, even though he wanted to. "Not a great start, you look like you've been in a prize-fight."

"Tell me you're not regretting it?" Rebekah's tone was challenging, but her dread was hard to disguise.

She must know I love her, but the depth of my guilt? She cannot possibly understand. "What? You can't think that." He looked at her mutinous face. "I just regret the damage. I thought I'd been so careful."

"Please, Connor, don't spoil it. It was wonderful." Rebekah waited, her eyes begging him to share her joy.

He finally grinned. "You're right, I did okay; after all, you're still in one piece." But she could not know the effort that had taken.

He rolled back onto the grass and took her with him.

As the clouds of sated relief thinned, Connor said slowly, "Rebekah, once I get you home, you have to stay there, for a while, at least. Okay? There are other vampires out there who are not the same as me."

"What do you mean?"

Connor ground his teeth. "Crazed vampires, for want of a better word. Feral, whatever you want to call it." He looked uncomfortable. "They tried to live on animal blood alone. It didn't work."

"So, they are demented?"

He nodded. "They don't often come close to the hives, but I saw one today, so you, *all* of you, need to be careful."

"Okay. I understand."

They both struggled to hold onto the feeling of contentment. They were in their own separate hells as they faced the fact that Station Four was just around the corner, and it signaled the end of their road together.

I have to leave her where she'll be safe. He was determined to do that. *I've Serge to deal with, and I'll need to do some fast talking to escape being charged with 'threatening the food supply'.*

Councilor Serge was riddled with resentment and jealousy, and his raw material was clearly flawed. Because he was old in *mortal* years, for him, vampirism loomed as an eternity of old age. Connor guessed at seven decades. Serge long ago latched onto Connor as a vampire he envied to the point of obsession. This might have been amusing, except that the man had secured a place on the vampire council, and, as a councilor, his petty vendetta caused Connor more problems than it should.

Connor hugged Rebekah closer, disturbing her scent, and sighed. He had no fear for himself, although, until this moment, he had never cared enough about anything to flout vampire lore. *Serge may have suspicion, but he needs proof, and once I leave her here, there will be none. Rebekah will be safe and I'll gladly take whatever comes.*

Rebekah's hell was the dread of arriving at Station Four. *I can't let Douglas discover Connor. He glues himself to Uncle Harry, and he's sure to be there to greet me.*

She shifted in Connor's arms at that thought. *I'm different now, and even Douglas can't take that away.* Douglas' glowering presence would be inescapable once she said goodbye to Connor. There were so few women of marriageable age in the eco-town. He knew he repulsed her, but he would not relinquish his claim easily. *I know that. He might even enjoy the thought.* Rebekah was only now beginning to realize what he was capable of. But she continued to hope. The last time she tried to talk to Uncle Harry, the desolation on his face made ice run through her veins. Douglas insisted their betrothal was a long-standing commitment and refused to budge.

I could *run away. If there was only me to think of.* She had never been afraid of taking on the harsh world in which they lived. She could forage for food and knew of dugouts where she could sleep. She could disappear and try going it alone, but it came back to being a close-knit community. *Finding out about feral vampires makes getting away from Douglas impossible, for now, at least.*

She couldn't blame Harry. *Uncle Harry's a good man, and having a six-year-old to consider must have been a 'damned if you do, damned if you don't' moment. He must have wished for an easier route to salvation.* It had not been easy for any of them to leave everything behind and find a way to survive, and it had to be said, Douglas had been their savior. *And then, there's Leizle. Douglas will turn his attention to her if I reject him.* She was seventeen, and the closest thing to a sister Rebekah would ever have. *I can't let that happen.*

Douglas was a predator driven by greed. *I've managed to keep him at arm's length so far, I'll just have to keep on doing that.* He would not handle rejection well. *I'll find a way out, somehow.* A lump lodged in her throat. *Even if I never see Connor again, Douglas is not going to touch me.*

She closed her eyes and summoned Connor's face, focusing on the details she wanted to store inside. *I don't even know his full name.* Suddenly, it seemed important, a thread of intimacy to hang on to. "What's your name?" she whispered. At his quizzical glance, she said, "Not Connor, the rest, Connor *who*?"

His shoulder shrugged beneath her cheek. "My name was Sanderson. But, of course, *we* don't use surnames, they are for families." He turned to look at her, his smile soft. "We don't have families, only the one who binds us." His hand pressed on her hip, and she suppressed the '*ouch'* inside her head.

Rebekah digested this silently. *Would I have to be a vampire to be his 'one'?* Too embarrassed and fearful of the answer to ask, she sighed.

Misunderstanding, he said, "I don't mind being just Connor. What's *your* name, Rebekah...?"

She grinned against his chest. "Rebekah Wylde, with a Y."

"Rebekah Wylde. How fitting." He chuckled. "Certainly wild, in the reckless sense, hmm?" He sighed in his turn. "There's every chance, if I weren't dead already, you'd be the death of me."

Chapter 9

The late afternoon sun warmed her shoulders as Rebekah picked her way across the rough meadow. Concentrating on lifting her knees to avoid tripping over thick clumps of grass kept the regrets crowding her thoughts at bay, but tears still blurred her vision. *Home.* But it didn't feel that way, not any more.

Two familiar figures appeared, as if by magic, emerging from a blackened fissure in the hillside. Walking forward, they closed the distance, and she shaded her eyes in a pretended squint, quickly wiping the tears away.

"Rebekah, thank goodness. We had a search party set to leave in the morning." Uncle Harry embraced her, and Rebekah swallowed hard. "I'm *so* glad you're home."

She wanted to be glad too, but she had left her heart behind in the shaded woods, and her chest felt hollow. Looking over Harry's shoulder as he released her, a chasm of dread cracked open, and she scrabbled for a foothold on the edge when Douglas approached.

"Harry was getting worried." At a sharp look from Harry, Douglas smiled coldly. "But it's done now, and you're safe."

"What happened?" asked Harry. "We waited at the safe house as long as we could."

"I know, I'm sorry." Ignoring Douglas, Rebekah rubbed the tender spot on the back of her head. "But the good news is, you were right. The beta blockers work, Uncle Harry, although I wouldn't recommend we try it again. I got caught out leaving the drugstore, but I managed to get into the park and stay still. The vampire passed me by."

Douglas snorted, his expression judgemental as he said, "So, where were you? You had time to get back. We have enough to worry about."

"Uncle Harry?" Rebekah noticed the ashen cast to his complexion for the first time.

"Only half the away team have returned. Stan got bitten by a badger and they had to leave him. Greg went back while the rest headed for home. With Stan being injured, it could be a week before *they* make it back here."

"I'm sorry, I guess you didn't need me adding to it."

Douglas muttered, "Too right."

Glaring at him, Rebekah said quietly, "What we didn't bet on is that there's a shockwave if they pass by close. The faster they are travelling, the more forceful the backdraft. I got knocked out."

"Are you okay? How long were you out for?" Douglas abruptly oozed concern.

Thinking back to Connor's words, Rebekah said, "Only a few minutes, I think. But there were too many vampires around for me to make it to the safe house. I had to lay low for a while. Too long, sorry."

"But, you must have found transport to get across country this quick?" Douglas scoured Rebekah's face until she blushed.

"I'm not useless. I checked out the valet parking at the big hotels by the river. I got lucky, until I ran out of gas."

"You must be more careful. An abandoned car will be noticed." Douglas' hard features underlined his real feelings.

"There's no pleasing some people," she muttered. "I pulled over in a village, it would be fine once the engine's cold. I even threw dirt on it." Rebekah bit her tongue as her mind shrieked 'keep it simple'. Liars always trip themselves up, her mother used to say, and she was beginning to see why.

"Well, let's just hope you're right. But you're here, and that's what counts." Douglas smiled, but it didn't reach his eyes. He slipped an arm around Rebekah's shoulders.

The urge to shrug him off and run back up the hill to where she left Connor was hard to resist. She glanced back towards the tree line, dragging her feet, but she couldn't see him, and tears blurred her vision once more. She turned back, seeking out Uncle Harry.

"Rebekah?" Harry's concern was genuine. "Are you all right?"

"It's just the sun, Uncle Harry. Of course I'm all right. I'm home," she said quietly and the lump in her throat threatened to choke her.

Douglas pulled her into step beside him and marched towards the eco-town. His suffocating presence settled over her like a mask, her lungs ached with the effort of breathing and suddenly she wished she was dead. *Dead like Connor.*

The walk across the gentle rise in the meadow ended abruptly at the foot of a sharp escarpment where part of the eroded hillside had fallen away. The avalanche had opened up a deep wound in the wall of rock and clay, creating the perfect site for the *manmade* entryway to Station Four. It artfully mimicked a natural fissure. The weeds trailing from the overgrown pasture up above added an extra layer to the disguise.

Douglas' determined step did not falter when the thick grass underfoot gave way to the clumps of silt which were dumped on the threshold each time heavy rainfall washed topsoil down over the cliff.

Pausing before the gaping crevice, and without losing contact, Douglas maneuvered Rebekah ahead of him into the tunnel entrance. As she stepped from the meadow onto the polished earth floor inside the concealed cavern, Douglas followed so closely behind she could smell the cloud of stale sweat clinging to his flesh.

His six foot tall bulky frame blocked the doorway and cast the reception cavern into darkness. Waiting for her eyes to adjust, Rebekah slipped back further into the gloom and leant against the wall. Her fingers folded around the familiar lumps of tightly packed rocks, and the cold, rough masonry at her back chased the sun's warmth from her heart.

Pulling a flashlight from his utility belt, Douglas flicked the switch, and played the dim beam deliberately over Rebekah's face.

She stared defiantly ahead.

When the dancing rays swept over the mud-covered chrome of the motorcycles parked in the alcove carved into one wall, Rebekah had the urge to leap onto one, mow Douglas down, and race headlong back out over the rough meadow. *But it's too late now.*

Douglas finally moved, making room for Uncle Harry at his side.

"Careful with the flashlight, Douglas. It may not be dark yet, but they'll see it."

"Hardly likely, Harry, although with the stunt Rebekah pulled, she might have been spotted. If they start the searches again, we'll know who to blame." Douglas threw a disgusted glance in her direction, before flicking the torch off and plunging them all into shadow.

Harry said firmly, "Let it go. At least we know the beta-blockers and suppressant spray work. Not a test we would have tried on purpose, but Rebekah pulled it off and that's all that matters." Harry reached out, fumbling in the half-light until he squeezed Rebekah's fingers, and added quietly, "You kept your head. I'm proud of you."

Rebekah's cheeks burned as she pushed away from the wall and muttered, "Thanks, Uncle Harry. But still, we need to take care. It might have been a fluke."

Turning her back on the parked motorcycles, Rebekah headed for the access tunnel leading into the heart of the hillside, stepping over the gulley which took rainwater from the cavern back out into the meadow. The floor beyond was worn smooth, and when Douglas' fingers closed on her arm, Rebekah recoiled and slipped on the slick surface. She could feel her pulse throbbing beneath his tight grip and her heart lodged in her throat.

"Mind out, we've got you back in one piece. It would be a pity if you took a tumble now," he said, as he propelled her forward into the descending darkness. "Let's get you inside."

There was no lighting in the first section, but Rebekah could almost see the spite on Douglas' face, and the tunnel seemed darker and more oppressive than she remembered. The feeling of returning home, of being able to relax as the threat of the vampire world melted away, had flipped on an axis, and every muffled footfall tightened the knot in her stomach. Knowing Connor would already be miles away filled her with panic. Guilt overwhelmed her as she admitted to herself that, given the time all over again, she would have chosen Connor.

After thirty yards, they slipped behind the heavy sackcloth curtain which prevented light traveling up the tunnel and being detected by keen vampire eyes.

The methods of lighting from here on in depended on the oxygen levels provided by ventilation holes, and were like milestones on a map. Dancing flames of wall-mounted torches burned in the first section, but deeper underground, they gave way to the weak glow of bulkhead lamps.

Along with her sight, Rebekah regained self-control and shrugged off Douglas' hand.

The main access tunnel connected to each of the large communal caverns, and when they reached the fork which led to the living quarters, Rebekah grabbed her opportunity of escape.

"I think I'll take a bath," she said firmly.

Douglas stared in silence, his narrowed gaze looking closer than Rebekah wanted.

She walked away with a considered unhurried stride, until she turned the corner and could heave a sigh of relief.

She took the descending tunnel path to the kitchen. The babbling lullaby of rushing water should have eased the knots from her shoulders, but it just made listening for following footsteps more of a strain.

As she walked into the laundry room, a large bear-like grip landed on her shoulder, and she gasped.

"Sorry, pet," said a gruff voice, and Rebekah's alarm was swallowed in a bear hug that matched the hand.

Rebekah wrapped her arms around Oscar's solid torso and hugged him back. Laying her cheek on the soft padding of his chest, she squeezed her eyes shut. Tears ached in her throat as she said, "Hey, Oscar."

His voice rumbled beneath her ear. "You had us all worried there for a bit. It's good to have you back."

Moving his hands to her shoulders, Oscar leaned back, looking down into her face. His graying hair was awry and, as always, he looked as though he had just finished laughing, until he met her eyes and amusement melted.

Silence stretched until Rebekah shuffled under his intent gaze and said, “It’s okay, Oscar, I’m safe and sound.”

With his eyes still scouring her face, he said slowly, “I guess you’re here to hijack my laundry session, hmm?”

“It’s okay, I can wait.”

“You’ll do no such thing. Just add bubble bath instead of detergent and you’re good to go.” He chuckled. “Go take that bath, lass. I’ll make sure you don’t get disturbed.”

She gave him a weak smile and nodded. She wanted to be alone, but she felt cold when his comforting bulk deserted her.

Rebekah turned away and walked the half dozen steps from the laundry room into the washroom, and the soft echoes of Oscar busying himself in his kitchen finally eased her tight muscles.

Grabbing a warm towel from where it draped over a hot water pipe, she ducked behind the heavy curtain, stripped off her clothes, and stepped gratefully down into the sunken Jacuzzi of warm water. A hot bath was a luxury reserved for foraging days. They were a reward to be earned. Douglas’ method heated the water in an inventive process involving the harnessing of the rushing tide of an underground spring. This powered a water wheel, which generated the electricity to warm tanks of water.

Rebekah sank below the surface and wished she could stay there.

She had lived in the eco-town for over a decade, and it was all she knew. Her memories of ‘normal’ human life were dreamlike sequences which might as well have happened to someone else.

Uncle Harry had moved into Rebekah’s family home in the early days, when the pandemic first started. With no memory of her father, who died when she was still a baby, her mother’s death left them both reeling. Harry had returned from the hospital, taken Rebekah into his arms, and held her until she had no more tears left. He had no idea how to cope with a ghostly-white six-year-old girl who followed him everywhere he went, in case he too died.

She woke up one morning and finally noticed the house had filled up with boxes. She didn’t know it then, but Uncle Harry already realized that things would never be the same, not just for them, but for any human being.

The Centre for Disease Control officially declared the pandemic a global event of catastrophic proportions, eight months later. By this time, in the City of London, too many of the sick died each day to plan individual funeral services; mass cremations became compulsory. Churches held weekly memorials where the names of the dead were read out, with the lists getting longer as each week passed. The services were held daily, near the end, and Uncle Harry stopped attending, concentrating instead on gathering the supplies needed to make their escape. The house eventually resembled a warehouse of supplies and equipment.

Rebekah could still remember falling asleep to the low rumble of the hushed conversations lasting long into the night.

Harry's foresight saved twelve men and four women when they took the decision to move out. Rebekah, three-year-old Leizle, and two-year-old Thomas were the only children. Harry had taken some persuading on that, but Leizle and Thomas' father was a structural engineer. He convinced Harry that building a long-term underground habitat relied on his expertise, but then early on in the construction work, he died suddenly of a burst appendix.

As a result, Rebekah found she had others who needed her. Rebekah and Leizle explored their strange new existence together and became surrogate sisters, sharing the responsibility of tag-along baby Thomas.

Relationships evolved; each community member rose to the top and carved their place in the order of things. Greg's military background took him outside the eco-town more than the others, and he became their eyes and ears, impressing upon them the dangers they all faced. The challenge of keeping the children quiet fell upon the shoulders of George, the oldest man the childhood Rebekah had ever seen. But he could spin a demon tale and had the children in the palm of his hand for hours at a time; his eyes, embedded in a walnut-like complexion, would light up as he wove a world of fantasy. Even now, thinking about George brought a glow to Rebekah's heart.

She could remember the buzz of excitement when Uncle Harry brought a box of old library books into the meeting cavern, and an evening reading routine quickly evolved. *For all of us, adults included, it was glorious escapism.* Uncle Harry regularly read from one book, 'The Day of the Triffids' by John Wyndham. No one could accuse Uncle Harry of being an optimist. The message was clear; do not think for one moment that the human race will ever be in ascendance again. *Vampires are here to stay, and the best we can hope for is to survive.* As depressing as the warnings sounded, over a decade later, Harry had been proven right, leaving Rebekah better equipped to deal with the new order as a result. *Until now.*

Now, meeting her first vampire had upended her preconceptions. As she reluctantly rose from the bath. The water she sluiced from her hair ran down her neck, and the downpour in the meadow replayed in her mind, bringing with it an image of Connor's face.

Stepping out onto the tiled floor of the bathing area, Rebekah inspected the rose-tinted marks on her skin. Taking a deep breath, she savored the feeling of tenderness inside her belly, the soreness between her thighs a tangible reminder of what her heart already knew, she was Connor's woman.

Rebekah had always thought of the eco-town as home, but now, she felt something she had never felt before, the hollow ache of defeat. She missed Connor.

Feeling as though she was walking the plank, an hour later, she entered the spacious dining cavern, the second largest in the eco-town's chain of caves, which had slowly grown longer over the years. Now, it was all about maintenance.

She waved at three men seated at the far table and made her way over to Leizle. The sight of the younger girl's hunched shoulders stabbed guilt through Rebekah. *She's been waiting.* Rebekah had eaten in her den, and she ruefully acknowledged the pain in her chest was indigestion. Even though it was her personal space, Douglas was not beyond paying her a visit. *Eating on a stomach knotted with tension was a bad idea.* There was safety in numbers, and she realized that eating here, with Leizle, might have saved them both some anxiety.

Rebekah slipped onto the polished wooden bench opposite Leizle and waited for the interrogation to begin.

"You're back." Leizle beamed, bouncing in her seat as she pushed away her plate. "What happened? I was so worried. We all were. Tell me what happened."

Rebekah stared at the cavern wall, pretending to study the mosaic of rocks covering its surface which, like keystones in an arch, gave the structure incredible strength. "Is that a damp patch there?" she teased. "What do *you* think?"

Leizle snorted and said, "You're not going anywhere until you tell me. So, you might as well spill."

As she digested the 'not going anywhere' notion, Rebekah's pretense at being cheerful dimmed, and the faint buzz of the electricity generator irritated her for the first time. Although, the glow cast by the flickering bulkhead lamp picked out cheerful copper-bright threads in Leizle's long chestnut hair, and the aura of happiness surrounding the younger girl was hard to resist. Some of Leizle's warmth penetrated. *So, I'm happy to see Leizle, at least.* Rebekah indulgently watched the girl plant her elbows on the table and lean closer.

Her green eyes were keen as she said, "I'm glad you're back, but look at this. I'd stopped too, but now, down to the quick again." Leizle scowled, holding out chewed fingernails for Rebekah to see. "I blame you. Don't ever scare me like that again." She held on to a cross face for a moment, and then her frown gave way to a luminous smile she couldn't suppress.

"I promise I'll be more careful in future." Rebekah could tell by the look in Leizle's eyes that her own smile was not convincing.

Before the questions she saw forming in Leizle's mind found a voice, Rebekah quickly launched into her tale. *A version of it, at least.* She repeated the details she had already shared, but, even from Leizle, she kept Connor a secret.

"So, that was a stroke of luck, finding a car with some gas." Leizle's tone was flat. Hungry for drama, she could not hide her disappointment that Rebekah's adventure was woefully dull.

Rebekah pasted a wry grin on her face. “Sitting here, running out of gas may not seem very dramatic, but it certainly felt like the end of *my* world.”

“Of course.” Leizle reached across the table and squeezed Rebekah’s shoulders. “It must have been terrifying out there alone. But you made it, and that’s all that matters,” she said firmly.

Rebekah swallowed a sigh. *It’s* not *all that matters, not any more.* Saying his name out loud felt like admitting she would never see him again and she was not ready to let that thought in. She set her chin. *Maybe, our paths are destined to cross once more. Who knows?*

“Leizle, leave Rebekah in peace, I’m sure she must be tired.” Douglas’ voice oozed practiced concern, and ice filled Rebekah’s belly.

He had crept up on them, he was good at that.

Leizle’s encouraging smile melted as she rose quickly and left.

Rebekah felt relieved. *I’m glad she sees through him, too.* Both girls had talked about Douglas, of course, but knowing and feeling were different things. It was *feeling* that would keep Leizle safe. It was the sixth sense thing where a woman detected danger before it was too late. If you didn’t have it, you couldn’t learn it. *Thank goodness, Leizle has it.*

Douglas sat down on the empty bench opposite Rebekah and settled his oppressive, ash-gray gaze on her face. Her skin prickled when she realized they were alone. Lifting her chin, she met his stare head-on with a look of blank inquiry. She could not help but notice the yellowed light which brought warmth to Leizle, made Douglas’ doughy complexion appear jaundiced.

Hooking a strand of damp hair behind her ear, Rebekah folded her hands on the table and waited. Though she had bathed and eaten, instead of feeling back to her old self, she felt abandoned. She scolded herself for that thought. *He may have woken up my heart, but Connor is not to blame for this.* Douglas’ face melted out of focus as her mind wandered, and when he reached across the table and gripped her fingers she registered it too late.

A frown folded his slack features as Douglas pulled her hand closer, pushing up her sleeve to inspect the purpling bruises on her arm.

"What's this?" he asked quietly.

She tugged her arm away. "It's nothing. I fell, stumbling across the fields. It was nothing."

"Mmm." Douglas looked into her eyes, narrowing his gaze. "They look like fingerprints to me. Well, Rebekah?" He jerked to his feet, stepping out around the table and pulling her up with him. His hand spanned her back, cutting off her retreat. He jerked her closer. "Are there any other *marks* hiding under this?" he asked, grabbing a fistful of her sweater and yanking at it.

Fighting to hold the fabric in place, Rebekah glared. Connor's 'love bites' on her skin seemed larger and more succulent when the sudden surge of anxiety made them throb. Fighting back her panic, she pulled away, and flushed with anger, she muttered, "Leave me alone."

The moment Douglas' glance over her shoulder locked onto the cavern doorway, Rebekah instantly knew why. His breath hissed sharply through his teeth and his hands fell away.

Chapter 10

Connor remained in the shade of the trees long after Rebekah disappeared, contemplating the undulating swells of the South Downs of Kent which appeared to be untouched by human hand. When Connor had watched her progress through the grass, even from hundreds of yards out, he noticed her worried frown. He almost pleaded with her to stay with him, but to what avail? *The danger is too great. But I wouldn't change a moment of the journey that led us here, to this.*

In their final embrace, when he took in a final deep draft of her scent, it grated over his throat, desiccating it one moment and choking him with venom the next. But he enjoyed suffering it. *It reminded me I'm not as dead as I always thought.*

He did not say half the things he had wanted to. *It would only have made letting her go harder.* She could not stay unless he turned her, and watching her suffer an eternity of regret, missing the family she left behind, *that* he would never do. But now, after seeing the 'reunion', he wished he could turn back the clock.

An older man, 'Uncle Harry' she called him, appeared from what, at first glance, seemed to be a gash in the hillside, and walked forward to greet her. He had been followed by a younger man, but still a good fifteen years older than Rebekah, by Connor's thinking.

Uncle Harry seemed harmless enough, but the other man... The scene left Connor feeling uneasy. Hundreds of yards away, across the meadow, he had gathered each word and each expression on the younger man's face like a collection of poison darts. *Douglas.*

The possessive cast on the man's features ate into Connor's brain like a maggot into an apple. He easily picked up on Douglas' tightly clawed grip around Rebekah, exerting control rather than comfort. *Maybe, I should be grateful. She clearly can't stand him.* But, the man's hold seemed sinister. *Or is my imagination in overdrive? Just jealousy.*

But then, Rebekah did the one thing he could not ignore. She glanced back towards the tree line, as if she felt him there, and the crawling distaste on her pinched face tore his heart out. Then the hillside had swallowed her up.

Intense loathing curled Connor's lip and rumbled an impending thunderstorm inside his chest. "Ah, damn," he muttered. *I knew this was going to be tough, but hell, I can't leave now.*

Like a sentinel in the woods, he hunkered down to wait. Listening to the hum of voices, he stared at the blackened gash which looked like an angry mouth on the face of his green-eyed monster. He concentrated on locating her, and finally, he isolated her scent and tuned in to the intonation of her speech. He eased the tension from his shoulders, reassured by the faint sound of her voice, a low subdued note, but her voice nonetheless.

Marking time went against the grain for Connor, and when the sudden waft of her anxiety-ridden scent reached him, he needed no further excuse to cross the meadow and enter her world. It was his invitation to throw caution to the wind.

Pausing long enough to dry wash his face in the sun-baked soil at the edge of the forest, staining his hard white skin with a human tint, Connor took flight across the meadow. Blending in had been easy when humans did not know vampires existed, even under close scrutiny they only saw what they wanted to see. But now, he needed the makeshift camouflage and some careful acting, when becoming a pretend human.

He moved with determined grace towards the entrance to the human habitat. Entering the tunnel mouth, he walked along the pitch-black passageway at a human pace, and slipped behind the sack cloth curtain. Connor filled his lungs with the medley of human aromas, and made his way with the unerring accuracy of a predator, to the arched doorway of the dining cavern.

Connor's eyes swept over the two standing figures, taking in Rebekah, recoiling, caught in Douglas' white-knuckled grip as he pulled on her sweater. Her face was pinched with disgust. As the flint-hardened spite in Douglas' eyes turned in his direction, Connor considered his options. His quick assessment of the heat signatures scattered throughout the tunnels confirmed that for now, at least, only this man knew he was here.

How do I play this? Connor considered tearing Douglas' throat out. He had many shades of anger fighting for his attention at the thought of the man's hands on *his* Rebekah.

"Who the hell are you?" Douglas croaked.

Connor breathed in the thick cloud of human nervous sweat.

He has guessed then, that I'm not just another guy. Connor was six feet and three inches of hard muscle, his deceptively casual demeanor ruined by a ferocious calculating glare. The dim artificial light played shadows across his uncompromising features and pretense slipped away as his brittle smile thickened the air inside the cavern with menace.

"I'm a *friend* of Rebekah's," he murmured as he advanced smoothly into the room. He read the concern for his safety on her face and smiled.

Connor stopped five yards away and locked eyes with Douglas, waiting for his next move. *I came here to warn him off, but now, it's tempting to just kill him.*

"Ah, we have company." Connor's tone lilted with the conversational subtext of 'saved by the bell'. *Things are getting interesting.*

Minutes slipped by in which no one moved, before eventually human ears also detected the approaching footsteps. Uncle Harry stepped into the room, his stride faltered and he stopped short and surveyed the unexpected scene. Some of the tension dissipated as Douglas clearly chose to believe there was safety in numbers.

"Rebekah's *friend.*" Douglas' confidence grew and he addressed Connor at last. His tone became calculating as he looked down, and his fingers stroked over Rebekah's wrist.

"I looked out for Rebekah at the safe house. I have a place in London..." He let Douglas fill in the blanks in his half-truths, and he enjoyed the moment when Douglas' eyes sparked in understanding and he came up with a rival.

"Funny, she never mentioned you." Douglas' knuckles blanched when his grip tightened. "Well, *I* am Douglas. Rebekah's *fiancé.*" Extending his arm in a dramatic manner which would have made Shakespeare proud, he said, "And this is Harry, Rebekah's uncle."

The word fiancé buried itself like a dagger in Connor's chest. His eyes darted to Rebekah for confirmation. *Not in her mind.* But, Douglas' smug expression still stung. Connor flexed his diaphragm and took the measure of the man. *Undercooked dough. Okay, we both know he knows, so let's see how big a fool he really is.*

"Nice place you've got here, Rebekah," Connor said, faking idle curiosity. Even though he was struggling to ignore Douglas' firm hold on her wrist, and the urge to snap Douglas' fingers like twigs was hard to contain, Connor exuded relaxation. He had no doubt how the game would play out.

"Maybe, we can give you the tour. I'm sure you must be curious about how the other half lives." Douglas pointedly met Harry's surprised look.

Communication passed between the two, and Connor's confidence grew. *This Douglas is a lone wolf, and Harry is too weak to fight him.* The encounter would remain their secret.

Rebekah started to speak, and Harry cut in. Waggling his eyebrows in an 'I know what I'm doing, follow my lead' gesture, Harry said, "Rebekah, now that you're refreshed, we must do the debriefing. We can't risk another mistake like that one." Turning to Connor and avoiding eye contact, focusing his stare on a point three feet to Connor's left, Harry added, "I'll leave you in Douglas' capable hands, for now." He jerked his head towards the doorway. "Rebekah?"

Connor almost smiled at the painful acting. *A stranger must be unsettling, especially one who makes his flesh crawl because somewhere deep inside he knows he's scared.*

Rebekah slowly followed Harry out of the room, and glancing at Connor's deliberately casual expression did not dim the anxiety in her gaze.

He wished he could tell her Douglas' ploy was transparent; his odor of excitement stank like stale beer, and Connor could almost hear his hatred fermenting.

"Looks like it is just us, then." Douglas' face froze in a comical grin.

Connor mimicked the gesture, but then he spoiled it by licking his lips.

Douglas swallowed loudly, and, committed to making his play, he moved out of the dining cavern and into the fluctuating light levels ranging along the length of the tunnel.

They set off down the painstakingly excavated passageways, and Connor enjoyed stalking Douglas, flanking his shoulder. His deathly silent progress made Douglas nervous and spawned a satisfyingly fear-drenched pheromone cloud.

"Very clever, Douglas, how you have provided the ventilation to use naked flames for light this far underground."

"Plastic pipes through the hillside, with filters on the top," said Douglas quietly.

Connor doubted he would find them, even if he did a fingertip search on hands and knees through the lush meadow overhead. "And the generator for the electric lights, how does that work?"

"Um, it's based on flywheel technology, using magnets. A battery spins the wheel, and then magnets switching on and off keep it rotating at the right speed for the generator." Douglas threw his words over his shoulder. He rushed onward.

"You seem in a hurry, Douglas. Are we going somewhere in particular?" Connor asked casually, as they passed a succession of tunnel entrances.

"I'm just starting at the lower levels. We'll work our way back to the exit," said Douglas and the decline into cooler air covered his twitching face in a layer of sweat.

"I see," Connor said, mildly. Surveying the surroundings, he was impressed by the sturdy construction. He used the echo of Douglas' footfalls as a form of sonar to map the tunnels and calculate the sizes of the caverns they fed into. He could smell the copper water tanks when they passed the kitchen cavern and his quick eyes caught a glimpse of a large Jacuzzi-shaped pool beyond, in what looked like a laundry room. *They've clearly been here for years.*

"Not much further now," said Douglas. "We'll start at the storage caverns. We have valuable artefacts and personal effects stretching back to before the bloo-"

Connor grinned. "Bloodsuckers? Think we can call a spade a spade, Douglas. It is just us two, after all."

Douglas' chin went up as he said, "Harry will be along in a minute."

"Sure, he will." Connor nodded slowly, smiling when Douglas increased his pace and finally darted into a tunnel which ended at a roughly-hewn cavern.

As they emerged from the tunnel mouth, Douglas stepped aside and pressed his back in to the rock-lined wall, saying, "Here we are."

Connor inspected the archway just up ahead.

He would have to dip his head to pass under it. On his left, a large boulder sat, cradled between parallel rails which crossed the threshold. Behind it, a coiled industrial-strength spring was held back by a lever, which, when released, would shove the boulder along the tramlines and seal the archway. *Ah, a prison cave.* Connor darted a glance at Douglas' sweating face. *Does he think it will trap a vampire?*

Connor assessed the weight of the boulder, the tensile strength of the spring, and calculated the speed at which the trap would close. He suppressed his amusement and said, "After you, Douglas."

"Oh no, please." Douglas reluctantly released his grip on the wall and extended an arm. "After you."

Connor grinned. I'll bite, he thought drily. He obligingly stepped over the threshold, and listened to the shriek of metal as Douglas pulled the rusty lever. The rumble of rock grating over stone filled the air and the boulder raced across the opening. Dirt plumed into the air as it crashed into the opposite wall and ground to a halt.

Relieved to escape Harry's probing questions, at last, Rebekah pushed aside the hanging tapestry which served as the door to her uncle's private cavern, and stepped out into the deserted corridor. *I'd better hurry.* She could hear Harry struggling into his boots, and if she was going to track down Douglas before Harry got his old bones moving, then it was now or never.

Visitors were half-expected in the early days, but now, Connor, even if he was human, would be met with hostility and be locked up and interrogated until Harry and Douglas were satisfied. And that was where Harry would go now, to find out if Connor was a threat. *And what if Douglas is dead?* Rebekah tamped down the flare of tentative happiness at the thought. *What if Douglas tried a Taser, or the cattle prod he found at the agricultural center? Perhaps it's Connor who's in trouble.*

She peered along the curved face of the tunnel wall and listened. *Better to just find out.* Taking a deep breath, she walked forward.

Suddenly, a sandbag-nudge of cold weight knocked her off her feet. Rebekah squeezed her eyes shut as the rushing air inside the tunnels snatched at her clothes and chilled her face, but left her unafraid. *I must be getting used to Connor's unannounced arrivals.*

They emerged from the tunnel and into the refreshing damp evening air. The scent of dewy grass filled Rebekah's nostrils as Connor beat a path across the meadow and headed back into the woodland. Slowing abruptly, his embrace eased and he lowered her gently to her feet. Dizziness hung on for a moment, the scenery still moving as if she was in the eye of a hurricane. *A hurricane, indeed.*

She opened her mouth to complain, and he kissed her. His citrus scent slicked her palate, and her words not so much died-on-her-lips as drowned in the tidal wave of relief. She pressed into the sculpted edifice of his body. Running her hands up over his shoulders as though discovering the texture of skin for the first time, she pushed her fingers through the hair at his nape.

Breaking the kiss and drawing back at last, he said, "Your *fiancé*, Douglas, is an idiot."

"He's not my fiancé," Rebekah said urgently. She had been in a world of agony thinking Connor might believe the lie.

"I know that. I would have smelled him on you." Connor raised his brow, and amusement danced in his eyes. "His odor is rank, by the way."

"I'm just glad you're safe." Rebekah breathed a sigh of apology. "What happened?"

"How you have survived this long is a mystery to me." He shook his head. "Did you know about the trap? The vampire cave?"

She looked sheepish. "I know Douglas thinks we can capture a vampire for research, and the one thing he's good at is plotting. That's why I didn't want you to come too close. He's dangerous. But the rest, no. He has a vampire cave?"

"Indeed, he does."

"Well, he kept that close to his chest. But then he would." Rebekah met Connor's gaze head on. "Greg would blow his top if he knew. His hatred of stupidity comes second only to his hatred of vampires. No way Douglas would let on."

Connor dropped down onto the grass and drew Rebekah down to sit beside him. He nestled her into his side, and when she realized they were in their glade, the thought warmed her. '*Their* glade' had a nice ring to it.

"He should listen to this Greg. As far as the vampire cave went, the man's an idiot."

"I'm getting the idiot part," grumbled Rebekah, trying to wriggle free, but Connor refused to budge, so she gave up. "Well, what happened?"

"I took the tour. 'Know your enemy', as they say. A good look around was on offer, so how could I refuse?" He looked at Rebekah's bemused expression.

"What?" he asked, suddenly becoming serious.

"Why did you come? I was so scared for you," she whispered.

"Oh honey, I came *because* you were scared. Your heart rate went berserk and your voice was shaking. How could I stay away?" he asked.

"How did you know? You were in London."

Connor grinned ruefully. "I never left." He rested his palm over her chest. "We are connected, I guess..." His smile reflected in his eyes. "You echo inside me somewhere." He paused, and then murmured conversationally, "I nearly ripped his throat out, by the way, for laying his hands on you." He bared his teeth in a brief reflection of wish fulfilment before smoothing his features again. "Anyway, the tour began at the vampire cave."

"So, how did you get out?" she asked.

"It was pathetic, the 'after you, this is our community treasury'." Connor laughed. "The man thinks vampires are magpies. I pretended to fall for it. Once I was inside, he pulled the lever and sprung the trap." His expression sobered. "I could have ended his life at any point, but he's genuinely too stupid to see that. He thinks I'm still in there."

Rebekah raised her eyebrows. *Stupid indeed, if Douglas had seen him fight; well I didn't exactly see it, just heard it, and that was enough.*

"I have to say, you humans have got a lot to learn about speed. Two dozen vampires could have walked out of the cave before the rock lumbered into place. The man's an idiot." Connor lay back onto the grass, taking Rebekah with him. Turning onto his side, resting his chin on his hand, he plucked at her sweater and said, "So, where is my reward for rescuing my damsel in distress?"

Giving up on the neckline, he peeled up the hem and spread his hand over her trembling stomach. "Ah, this is where it all began." His fingers flexed, and he breathed in her scent. "That warmed concoction that filled my stomach." He growled gently. "I can't be without you, you do know that?"

Rebekah grinned. "I was hoping your concern was more than just brotherly."

Connor's grin was a blend of mischief and regret. "I guess Douglas has his uses. My backside is still sore from the kicking I gave it." He plucked at the neckline of her sweater again as he met her eyes. "But seriously, Rebekah?"

"Yes?" She knew everything rested on whatever he said next.

"You have to live here. I have to know that you are not in danger from Serge." He put his fingertip to her lips when she tried to protest. "I have given this some thought."

"I'll watch over you. You will be twenty-four in three years. That gives us three years to make sure Uncle Harry - whose acting is superb by the way - is safe." He stopped and the look he gave her said, 'are you following this so far?'

Rebekah experienced a Cinderella moment, glimpsing a future where nothing would ever be the same. His cool chuckle against her lips trailed goosebumps over her skin, and his fingers stroking her stomach scrambled her wits. Rebekah swallowed loudly and nodded.

He whispered against her soft mouth, "Three years, and I *will* turn you. I'll spend an eternity making you happy, but on this, you have no choice. Three years, and then you are *mine*." He pulled back and examined her face. "Say, 'yes Connor', and then I can make love to you."

His eyes locked on hers while he unzipped her jeans. Rebekah knew her thundering heartbeat would be resounding inside him too, as he slid his hand down over her belly and dipped inside her moist warm center.

"Yes, Connor," she groaned, opening her thighs to let him in.

A while later, Rebekah lay resting on his chest, and when he inhaled deeply, ruffling her hair, the sigh passing through him made her smile.

He stirred purposefully. "You know I'm bluffing, hmm?"

She looked up into his serious face.

"You have as many years as you need. Nothing will happen unless you want it too. You do know that, right?"

"I want it too," she said simply.

His smile was assured. "I know you do."

An hour of contentment slipped past before he stirred again. "We'd better get you inside, it's getting late and I'm not much good as a hot water bottle."

"Do you have to go?" Rebekah knew the answer, but hope was hard to suppress.

"Hey." Connor arched a suggestive eyebrow and growled playfully. "I promise you, this is just the beginning. You're stuck with me, and I can be very demanding." His expression melted to serious. "I have to go back and cover our tracks, but when I have done that, I *will* come back."

"Good." she smiled.

"All I need you to do is stay safe. And that means no more wandering until I return, promise?"

"Yes, Sir."

Connor started to groan but then he caught sight of her tense features and knew she *was* taking him seriously. The cold air became bitter, and with Rebekah's skin feeling almost as cold as Connor, he enfolded her in one last embrace, before finally releasing her.

"C'mon, we better get you home," Connor said. When Rebekah refused to move, he added, "I'll be back soon, I promise."

He rolled up to his feet and pulled on her hand, and Rebekah had no choice but to go with him and stand at his side. With one last squeeze on his fingers, she let go and left the woods. Glancing back, she saw Connor watching her pick her way across the moonlit meadow, but the despair she felt only a few hours before no longer weighed her down.

Chapter 11

After Rebekah left, Connor did a lot of thinking while sitting alone in the tree line, listening to the slumbering heartbeats of the human inhabitants.

If he did not know they were there, the signs would have been disrupted by the thermal currents rising from the sun-warmed fields, by the warm blood of rabbits, badgers, voles, and all the other white noise vampires habitually tuned out. But, he *did* know, and tantalized himself, using their heat signatures to track them beneath the ground. Mapping out the meeting areas, he kept track of what represented, for him, a potential meal. He would always be a hunter.

What harnessed his hunger, what he had not been prepared for, was compassion. Because of Rebekah, the rest of the group were also off limits. Of course, Douglas also shared the eco-town with Rebekah. He could do nothing to change it, for now, and that frustrated Connor. He battled his demons. He *could* have let alpha-male instincts get the better of him and killed Douglas. *No one would ever know*. But Rebekah would, and he feared Douglas' ghost would not let her rest easy in his arms.

Douglas is a complication I can do without, but for now, Serge is the bigger threat.

Connor focused on the task ahead, first returning to the farmhouse, burying the fallen bodies, and removing traces of the battle inside. *Let Serge do his worst.* Business as usual remained the best plan of action for Connor; that meant performing his scheduled duties at Storage Facility Eight, where vampires served the sentences handed down by the vampire council. *All* the sentences were of death, but inmates moved through three distinct stages. In the first stage, dehydration hardened their bodies to granite. In the second, which lasted decades, their brains were kept lubricated by just enough blood to allow offenders to think about their crimes. The third stage, by council decree, was the deliverance of having their skulls crushed.

As the Doctor of the London Hive, Connor oversaw stage-three executions.

He whipped across country from the farmhouse to the outskirts of London. In an abrupt change of course, he headed north, until the granite gray beacon of Storage Facility Eight glowered on the horizon. The blood-streaked glow of early dawn draped the sky in an inferno, which softened the harsh rectangular silhouette to molten steel.

Unlike the human farm facility, no wardens waited to grant access. The padlock on the gates was a token deterrent, giving passing vampires the hint that visitors were not welcome.

The usual routine required Connor to punch in his access code, wait for the gates to disengage, and enter. In a moment of impatient rebellion, he scaled the perimeter fence and landed soundlessly on the other side. Circling the building, he checked his watch. *High tide, good.* His gaze swept over the swollen turbulent surface of the River Thames. Frothy white horses rode the waves, crashing into the towering concrete wall which held back the river and formed the plinth upon which the storage facility had been built.

Turning the last corner, Connor arrived at the main entrance and combed his fingers through spray-soaked hair before thumping on the door three times. The musk of an Egyptian tomb plumed into the air when the steel door was eased open by an invisible hand, and Connor stepped inside.

The atmosphere closed around him like a moist blanket, and he stopped breathing.

The retreat of the vampire doorkeeper barely registered as Connor collected a flashlight from an alcove in the stone wall and moved off along the carved granite hallway, accompanied only by the wraithlike whispers of his own skimming footsteps.

He flicked on the flashlight and swung it loosely at his side in time with each stride, the dim beam tracing an erratic arc over the flagstone floor. Its yellow glow barely disturbed the darkness, but scattered enough light to allow vampire eyes to see hundreds of yards with crystal clarity.

When he emerged from the passageway and stepped over the threshold into the first level reception area, the warden materialized from nowhere, like an actor compelled to step into a spotlight.

"Hello, Doctor Connor," he said, as if it was yesterday, and not three months, since they last spoke. "I hope you are keeping well, Sir."

Connor's eyes twinkled when the warden's right hand flapped in an abandoned salute.

Human habits were like 'tells' in poker. If you paid attention, a vampire revealed his life story in five minutes or less. Connor guessed the warden was born human in 1920, turned in 1950, and had served in the armed forces. *An officer and a gentleman, then.* Connor afforded him that courtesy.

"Warden James, it's nice to see you. What have we today? I understand there are stage-threes to pronounce?" Connor replied.

"Indeed, Sir. The stage-two chamber has forty-seven offenders locked-in. The stage-threes have received a maintenance dose of blood, and their state of consciousness is intact."

Connor nodded. "Are many stage-two inmates up for progression in the next hearing?"

The warden shook his head. "Most have a few more years remaining." His voice grew stronger as speaking lubricated the disuse from his vocal chords. "Only three are eligible for termination in the next hearing,"

There was no chance of reprieve for vampires in Storage Facility Eight. During the twenty-four hours in stage-one inmates were immobilized with a dose of muscle relaxant. Once the council passed sentence, there *was* no going back. Vampire dehydration became irreversible once it hit fifteen percent, and the penalty of locked-in syndrome - a fully conscious mind residing inside a granite hard body - spanned however many decades Principal Julian considered appropriate.

"And, how is The Butcher?" asked Connor lightly.

Something of a celebrity, and used by the council as a deterrent, The Butcher was first imprisoned in the mausoleum in London's Kensal Green Cemetery in 1919. His sentence of an eternity of locked-in syndrome gave him all the time in the world to repent his crimes *and* put an end to his killing spree, which threatened to bring vampires to the notice of the blinkered human population.

The warden smiled. "I doubt we will ever see another 'eternity offender'. He has another sixty years before Principal Julian will even consider pronouncing him ready for skull crushing."

"A hundred and fifty years in which to ponder your crimes. You'd have to be a fool to risk that." Connor shook his head at the chilling reminder. "Has he been fed today?"

The warden's head snapped up. "Not yet."

"Would you mind if I accompany you? Perform his annual check a month early?" Connor said idly.

"But, of course."

The warden headed at speed down the sharp decline which led to the bowels of the building. Akin to an iceberg constructed in steel, eighty percent of the facility was buried underground, with the lowest level housing the stage-three offenders and, since the rise of vampires, The Butcher.

At the bottom of the slope, the warden pushed through a rubber-edged steel door. It marked the boundary of the death chamber wing. The polished stainless-steel walls glistened with condensed moisture, and the rushing current of the River Thames could be heard through them.

The Butcher's cell was through a door on the left. Petrification of his body had occurred within a year, but the tablespoon of human blood drizzled into his throat each day preserved his consciousness, as his sentence demanded.

Connor followed the warden inside and clenched his hands behind his back, closely observing the ritual. The warden wheeled an aluminum trolley from its resting place against the wall across to the open, stainless-steel lined, coffin shell.

Peering into The Butcher's wizened petrified features, Warden James pushed back an eyelid and watched the contraction of the jet black bead of his pupil. "You have served 90 years," he muttered conversationally as he filled a metal pipette with blood, inserted it between the cracked dry lips, and discharged it into the vampire's mouth.

The blood stained his lip line red, but the desiccated features remained rigid. The warden studied the pupil reaction once more before nodding decisively. "He's ready for you, doctor." Turning away, Warden James trundled the trolley back to its station.

"Thank you," said Connor, stepping forward.

He cradled the aged vampire's skull in his hands. Settling his thumbs firmly onto the temples, and closing his eyes, Connor tapped into the hypersensitivity of his vampire enhanced nerve endings.

His hands tingled as blood red visions crowded his mind. Connor grimaced when bloodlust raged through his body, saliva flooded his mouth, and he *became* The Butcher.

Ice cold calculation chilled Connor; He followed a young couple through the thick fog of a 1900's London night. They stumbled into an alleyway. The Butcher watched them, his own groin swelling as the young man pulled the girl's skirts up, exposing her pale thighs and his own naked backside. The musk of sex plumed into the air as the young man's hard body eased into her soft wet flesh. She moaned when he began moving inside her, driving the sighing breath from her lungs. He rocked his hips into hers, pushing her breasts up into his hands.

Connor could feel the tenderness radiating from them, and he knew they were making love. *This is not lust*. Sadness weighed him down because he knew the couple were doomed. *I wouldn't be 'seeing' them, otherwise.*

At the moment of climax, just when the youth's body clenched tight, The Butcher's face appeared, leering over her lover's shoulder into the girl's flushed face. As his ardent body pumped into hers, fear crushed her chest. Her soft flesh clamped around his erection as panic rattled through her, and the youth groaned with pleasure. The Butcher yanked the boy's head back and buried his teeth in the pulsing carotid artery.

The girl's scream became a drowning gargle as, smiling, The Butcher reached forward and jabbed his thumbnail into her neck, severing her vocal chords and filling her throat with her own blood.

Connor had seen enough. He brought the shutters down inside his head. The blood red images faded to pink and the tension drained from his body.

"The neurotransmitters are functioning in the temporal lobe and his emotional responses are intact. The central cortex is at fifty percent hydration." Connor opened his eyes and withdrew. "I'll report to the council that our friend is still giving his actions serious thought." *Or enjoying them. I'm not sure he's suffering.*

When he left The Butcher's confinement cell, the stagnant atmosphere beyond the room was a relief.

In the chamber opposite, four vampires awaited the release of stage-three; the violent end of having their skulls crushed which brought release from the torment of their thoughts. Connor was not obliged to look into their minds like he had with The Butcher. Julian had changed the protocol which required Connor to give a condemned vampire the opportunity to express regret and make amends.

Julian had quickly realized that the vampires may be achieving 'closure', but it was at the expense of Doctor Connor, who, as their confessor, carried the vivid images they shared for weeks before finally being able to file them away where they could not haunt him.

Connor opened the death chamber door and walked in.

The bodies were laid out on a row of waist high stone plinths, and a metal C-clamp framed each vampire's head.

Connor walked along the line, ensuring that the six-inch diameter plates welded to each side of the clamp were correctly fitted at the temples. The metal arch passed over the crown of their heads, allowing the condemned an unobstructed view of the polished steel ceiling.

On one side, a thick screw protruded through a threaded hole in the frame. This was the free-running side where an adept twist of the T-shaped handle tightened the vice. Vampire strength made mechanization unnecessary.

Connor would give the command, pronounce the deaths as the doctor of record, and report back to the council.

He held his hand aloft, waited until the attendant at each execution bed grasped the metal T-bar, and then closed his fingers in a fist.

Driven by the hands of vampire executioners, the screws in each of the clamps accelerated into a fast rotation and slammed the steel plates together. The swish of oiled-metal was overwhelmed by the shriek of grinding bone, and then, with a loud crack, the skulls exploded and fragments spat into the air.

As crushed bone dust drifted across the chamber, Connor wondered how painless the process could really be, and, what last thought went through their minds.

The attendants removed the clamps, placed them in a crate marked 'used', and disappeared through a side door.

Pulling a key from his belt, the warden stowed the filled crate inside a walk-in storage room. Once cleaned and checked for damage, each clamp would be placed on one of the hooks which lined the walls, until they were needed again.

Connor waited for the warden to return and they left the steel lined chamber together, via the main entrance.

As they walked away, the metal shutter dropped into place with a groan, sealing the death chamber. The rumble of rushing water vibrated through the walls indicated the sluice gateway had opened. Like an airlock in a spaceship regulates oxygen, it allowed an avalanche of thousands of gallons of the River Thames to thunder through the death chamber, sweeping the vampire remains out into the fast-flowing current of the estuary. Low tide would drain away the remaining few inches of water and leave the room ready for its next set of inhabitants.

Raising his voice above the turbulent sounds of the cleaning process, Connor said, "Warden James." He inclined his head in farewell, and moved swiftly back up through the levels. In a matter of seconds, the main door loomed in front of him.

"Doctor Connor, Sir."

Recognizing the voice, Connor whipped around, lifting an eyebrow in inquiry as the warden rushed into view.

"A guardsman delivered a message from Principal Julian. You are required to attend the council, directly."

"Thank you, Warden," said Connor.

"I'm not sure you'll make it tonight, though, Sir. You are, of course, welcome to stay here until sunset."

Connor looked at his watch. "Thank you, but I'm not sure Principal Julian would appreciate the delay. I better get moving."

As he exited the building and whisked through the metal gates in the perimeter fence this time, he speculated. *Serge must have the bit between his teeth to move this fast.*

Setting off towards the city, Connor, staying barely one step ahead of the breaking dawn, was reduced to shadow hopping for the final approach. *Just typical, a sunny day.* He came to an abrupt halt outside the council building. Connor raked his hands through gray hair, reviving its black luster as the final stubborn dust particles of crushed skulls scudded into the air, drifting towards the heavens.

The smell of airborne calcium, a grim reminder of his own possible fate, focused Connor's mind on the cut and thrust of what lay ahead. *Serge will be setting out his case.* He set his jaw and mounted the steps. *Rebekah is safely hidden away, so, bring it on.*

He pushed through the oak doors and was met by a vampire dressed in the livery of the court. "Doctor Connor, they are waiting for you, if you'd follow me."

Connor nodded, adopted a meek demeanor, and fell into step.

Moments later, he stood in the dock of the opulently theatrical vampire council chamber. His alabaster complexion glowed in the ambient light, and the stark contrast of his raven black hair captured the drama of the occasion. The composure of his striking features reflected a respectful attitude. He was every inch the attentive, circumspect vampire; *I know how to play this game.*

Connor flexed his ribcage to fill his lungs, and, using the vampire function of speech, his throat vibrated gently as he inhaled and tasted the air at the same time. The atmosphere was heavy with the pleasant fragrance of burnished oak paneling and the beeswax polish used to maintain its glossy finish.

Waiting, he wondered how convincing Councilor Serge's story would be, and how hard he would have to work to wriggle off the hook. *I have the respect of the jurors, but will it be enough?*

The vampire council jury of three commanded the court from the elevated vantage point of a marble dais. Seated behind an imposing antique oak bench, each was dressed in black, but wore a color of cravat which indicated their decades of service. The jurors surveyed the surroundings like birds of prey.

Connor glanced through hooded lashes, looking for clues in their hard expressions.

The golden-toned presence of Principal Julian, head of the London Hive Vampire Council, was flanked by his two jurors.

Connor assessed the youngest Juror, Alexander, a vampire with hair the color of wet sand, and noticed the lively cast to his eyes was dull today. *He looks bored, that's a good sign.*

Juror Marius, he wasted little time on. The vampire was an enigmatic shadow. His cap of seal-black hair swept back from a strong brow and an aquiline nose brought intensity to his dark gaze. Like a black hole, his eyes were hungry for information, constantly scanning, but his face gave nothing away.

Finally, Connor met Julian's eye.

The principal inclined his head and said shortly, "Doctor Connor, good of you to make an appearance at such short notice."

"I try to please, Principal Julian."

Connor absorbed the full force of a scathing look, and he took the hint. *He's in no mood for levity.* He dutifully set his eyes front and center, and squared his shoulders.

The courtroom gallery was motionless; no rustling of fabric or involuntary movement. The vampires were at rest. Connor's gaze passed over the sea of immobile faces... *like a mill pond, but who knows what goes on beneath the surface.* Despite the varying skin complexions, which were five shades paler than when they were mortals, there was an eerie similarity in the glazed expressions.

They had endured decades of time, stretching back into centuries for some, so anything to fill it was a welcome distraction.

Connor wondered how long they had been waiting for this performance to begin.

It was shaping up to be an autumn day of more sun than cloud, and shadow-chasing was not to every vampire's taste, although the gallery would certainly thin as dusk drew in. The siren call of promenade was strong; to walk unfettered through London and feel the damp evening air balmy on their skin, and to feel human, even for a moment, without the fear of cloud cover breaking and the glare of sunlight desiccating their flesh.

The fifteen years following the pandemic had seen changes to these court sessions. The vampire code of conduct became redundant - 'foolish disposal of human remains' no longer threatened them with exposure. The hearings were often boring, dealing with in house fighting, and stirred little interest in the hive.

But today was different. This was the respected Doctor Connor being called to account. Vampires enjoyed a spectacle, so the gallery was packed. Connor's fleeting smile glimpsed out from behind his dead-pan facade.

"Doctor Connor," said Principal Julian, sharply, "I trust the stage-three sentences have been delivered?" His crisp diction filled the courtroom. His generic principal garb did nothing to disguise the ramrod straight posture of his 19th century origins.

Connor linked his hands behind his back and met the interrogation head on. "It all went smoothly," he agreed.

"And, The Butcher? I understand you examined him?" Principal Julian's youthful brow creased in speculation. "He's not lying in state for another month. You were a little premature."

"True." Connor inclined his head. "But, I was at the facility in any case. His blood dose has not required an adjustment for the last few years, so I decided that an early examination would not matter. Everything is now in order for the viewing. His hydration is good and he's still conscious. I'm sure the horror of his sentence will have lost none of its impact on the hive members."

"I would hope not. I expect it to *curb* reckless behavior."

Connor cast a sharp glance the principal's way. *Was that a warning shot?*

The circumstances which brought vampire wrath down upon the heads of Jack the Ripper and The Butcher no longer existed. Staying under the humans' radar and not revealing vampires as *real* monsters, and not myth, had become a redundant notion.

However, vampires living in a society led to conflict, and injuring a member of the hive by failing to seek confinement during grave sleep had attained the equivalence of first degree murder in this courtroom. Those who appeared in the dock rarely escaped unscathed.

'Threatening the food supply', whether by accident or design, foolishness or determination, carried the sentence of locked-in syndrome in the storage facility. The Butcher's fate provided a forceful reminder of what became of those who stepped out of line; the sentence of *eternity* awaited them.

Thanks to Principal Julian's hard-line approach, the hive ran smoothly, most of the time.

Connor said, "I'm certain The Butcher will be with us for a long while. Warden James takes his care very seriously. He considers him one of a kind."

"If Vampire Jack had not forced our hand, there would have been two," said the principal, soberly.

"One is enough. Being paraded past The Butcher should petrify even the most rebellious hive members," said Connor. *It certainly chilled me to the bone.*

"Perhaps. Which is why I'm surprised you're here to answer an accusation which calls that into question. I am mystified, as are the jurors."

Connor scanned the blank faces of Jurors Marius and Alexander. *They don't look mystified.*

"We are used to hearing cases of physical harm, but we thought charges of 'threatening the food supply' were a thing of the past. Surely, you would not risk ending up in Storage Facility Eight?" Principal Julian flicked a gaze to his left and beckoned. "Councilor Serge."

The silence in the courtroom was broken by the rustling of fabric as Councilor Serge rose to his feet.

"Now we have Doctor Connor here to answer your accusation, we can continue. But I repeat, for his benefit, you will need more than guesswork, councilor." Principal Julian smooth facade masked his obvious annoyance. "Doctor Connor is our most respected physician, one of the few who can function inside the human farm and this-" He waved a dismissive hand in Serge's direction. "The concerns you have voiced so far, do not constitute a case."

The councilor drew near, and the principal wrinkled his nose at the stench which always accompanied Serge.

"Principal Julian, you must agree it is strange that Doctor Connor's medical assessment of...?" Serge glanced at Connor, determined to make him jump through hoops, it would seem.

"Annabelle." Connor supplied, smiling sweetly, or as sweetly as six-foot three-inches of mildly irritated vampire could smile without breathing in too much of Serge's rotting aroma.

Serge's gaze sharpened, and Connor's smirk became fixed. *We both know I'm lying, but Serge must prove it.* Better yet, Connor knew the principal would not be lending Serge his support. Maybe when Serge qualified as a phlebotomist and surgeon, and had more than fifteen years of vampire sense under his belt, he would have a chance.

"Annabelle, just so," Serge repeated, his bony fingers framing his chin. "His medical assessment of *Annabelle* was advanced graveling, and yet, she did not report for farm duty, as Doctor Connor said she would."

Serge crossed the courtroom and looked Connor in the eye. "I wonder, can you reveal which cluster you returned her to? It would settle things, do you not think?" He tried to act casual, but satisfaction at closing a trap made him tremble.

Connor's eyes dulled to iron-gray and he muttered, "I'm sorry, Councilor Serge, I can't remember the cluster house location." His worried frown was convincing. "And sadly, medical advice is exactly that, *advice*. I assumed she would turn up at the farm." He rubbed the back of his neck, every inch the regretful physician as he looked across at the jurors. "I did not think the councilor would expect me to frog-march her there myself."

Principal Julian's green stare said 'don't push it' as he suppressed a twitch of amusement.

"Councilor Serge, the death sentence is irreversible, and you will need more than two missing guardsmen and a lost youngling to invoke it."

Serge opened his mouth and spluttered.

Julian plowed on. "A lost *youngling*. You have no proof she is human." His eyes flickered briefly as he added, "This is a very serious, and frankly, baffling accusation." He had no need to look to his fellow jurors for agreement, the stony silence of Marius and Alexander said enough.

Undisguised frustration glistening in his reptilian gaze, Serge locked eyes with Julian and inclined his head. "I shall present my case again when I have more evidence." His brittle tone implied criticism. "If you feel it is really necessary."

Principal Julian inhaled sharply.

"Need I remind you of council protocol? You will remove yourself from my court. And consider this carefully." Julian stared Serge down. "There is a difference between *evidence* and wishful thinking. You owe Doctor Connor an apology."

A smile lit Connor's eyes, but his smooth, porcelain face remained impassive. *This should be fun. Challenging Julian in public is not the smartest thing Serge could have done.*

After the council adjourned, Julian took Connor aside. "Well, Doctor Connor, it seems Councilor Serge is baying for your blood." His eyes narrowed, his youthful appearance belying many decades of experience. "What did you do, hmm?"

Connor met the probing stare. "It's better if you don't ask, Julian." He had no intention of compromising the principal. *Its better he doesn't know that there is no 'Annabelle'. Sparring with Serge is only the beginning, but, this is* my *fight.*

"This has the stink of a personal vendetta. I suggest you tread very carefully." His expression stern, Julian said, "I do hope you know what you're doing."

Connor nodded gravely, hovering indecisively.

"Is there something else?"

"Julian, when I made the trip to the storage facility, I killed a feral. I think a sweep of the woods is needed."

"I thought we'd seen the last of them, it's been three years." Julian swore beneath his breath. "I'll get Captain Laurence to sweep the fields around the human farm, although, you've probably done the job already. Where did you find him?"

"Heading along the North Downs, south of London."

Julian raised a brow. "I won't ask how it was that you were going in entirely the wrong direction. It's probably best I do not know."

Connor felt a little easier as he left. Julian was right, of course. *Ferals are a minor irritant to us, but it isn't us I'm worried about.*

Chapter 12

How can three days feel like a lifetime? Rebekah pushed her plate away, the food untouched. She knew not eating would not help her situation. *But honestly? The waiting is killing me.* Her appetite had been the first casualty of the conflict playing out inside her head.

The dining cavern had emptied out, but that would not last. A constant trickle of humanity would flow through it until the evening reading session drew them all to the meeting cavern.

The atmosphere was rustic and homely. The spotless wooden tables were a basic construction and the rustic benches had been polished slick by the accumulation of more than ten years of backsides sliding over their surface. Rebekah discovered the benches also numbed *her* backside when she sat there too long, daydreaming.

Rebekah immersed herself in a fragile world where Connor worshipped her body, well, her soul, really. Her body, he tried very hard to worship, and she still had the bruises to show for it. But he'd been gone for days now, and her impatience became tinged with doubt.

The new relationship argument echoed in her head. *Now he has gone, is he having second thoughts? Perhaps he won't come back? But, he promised.* She planted her chin in her hand. *He has a lot to do, for heaven's sake.*

Covering their tracks meant disposing of vampire bodies, checking out the danger, and, from what Connor had said, she knew Councilor Serge would not be easily put off the scent.

Rebekah grinned as she recalled the recent cluster of fingerprints trailing across her skin; being with Connor resembled a battle of good and evil. Her body simmered when excitement flared at his touch, but even as he chased a hot pulse under her skin, the cool touch of his fingers snatched her breath away.

She shivered, rubbing her arms briskly when certainty of his return rose as a warming tide inside her. *He'll come back.*

Thanks to Leizle, no one missed her the night of her meeting with Harry. Leizle had told Douglas that Rebekah was exhausted and gone to bed. Redirecting his attention formed part of an unwritten pact between the two girls, and, on this occasion, her help had served Rebekah particularly well. *I wish I could tell her about Connor, but, for now, its best no one knows he exists.*

After his encounter with Connor, Douglas had been in the mood to celebrate and drink a little, and Oscar had made sure Douglas was well-fed and too comfortable to consider leaving. A deliberate kindness by Oscar, she was certain. *He knows Douglas makes my skin crawl.* Everyone usually steered well clear of Douglas when he was in one of his manic moods, caused, this time, by the euphoria of 'capturing a vampire'. *Although, he would never have let others in on that secret.*

Rebekah got to her feet, deposited her loaded plate on top of a pile of dirty dishes and left the dining cavern.

The domed ceilings of the smaller tunnels leading off from the main artery were high enough for all but the tallest of the eco-town inhabitants to walk without stooping, but gloomier. Pulling her torch from the pocket of her combat pants, Rebekah was about to flick the switch when she heard the urgent hiss of whispered conversation. She stopped, dropping the torch back down to her side as the hairs on her nape went up. *Douglas.*

The voices echoed in the tunnel, and she strained to listen. She tuned in, to hear Douglas plotting. *There's no better word for it.*

"We've had him locked in there for three days. He won't have fed. That means he'll be weak, surely?" Douglas' tone had the jarring note of nervous excitement.

At least, he has the sense to know that he doesn't know anything.

Leaning over to one side, Rebekah brought part of Douglas' broad back into view, and could just make out Harry's white face beyond.

"Keep your mouth shut, Harry. Another day should do it. If they don't feed then they die. So, another day."

Tension gripped Rebekah's neck; fear was becoming a familiar companion. Douglas' determined enthusiasm had a sadistic edge to it, and she was relieved he was doomed to disappointment. She didn't really want to listen to more of his poisonous thoughts. *But, as Connor would say, 'know your enemy'.*

It was entertaining to think that while Douglas believed Connor was trapped inside his vampire cave, he had been with her, denouncing Douglas as an idiot. And listening to him now, Rebekah could only agree.

To think, Connor had insisted on waiting for her, and, for some reason, it seemed important he gave her that time. *But why would I want three years of* this?

When Douglas' arm had settled around her shoulders and he marched her into the tunnels away from Connor, she thought she had lost him, and her world felt as gray as his eyes. Thinking about him now, and of the way fierce concentration melted his earnest gaze to pewter whenever he touched her, it was all she would ever want. *So, why must I wait?*

Douglas' unrelenting advances loomed as her biggest threat. *He believes he has dealt with his rival, and after seven years of thinking of me as his wife-to-be, his delusions are unshakable.*

In the last couple of days, avoiding Douglas had been easier than she expected. *Too easy.* She had steeled herself for the confrontation over Connor, after all, he declared himself as her 'friend', so Douglas knew she had lied. Although she felt relieved Douglas appeared inclined to ignore the situation, deep inside, she feared it was a bad sign. *I'll breathe easier when he shows his hand.*

For now, Douglas seemed immersed in vengeful plotting. *But when that all falls apart, what then?* Until Connor confirmed the woods were safe, she couldn't sign up to go out on one of Greg's foraging expeditions, so she was stuck here. *When Greg gets back, I'll have to find a way of warning him about these demented vampires. Maybe I'll say I saw one.* While Douglas held his tongue, Rebekah would not mention Connor.

In the meantime, she would stay out of Douglas' way. *When Connor comes back, surely Douglas will accept defeat.*

Douglas turned away from Harry, and the light of a bulkhead lamp played across his features. The tight expression on his face filled Rebekah with foreboding.

She knew things would be tough, but he seemed different today, fired up and decisive. He was a man with a plan, and it did not bode well. She could feel the thunder clouds gathering.

Chapter 13

Harry paced the tiled floor of the hospital cavern. It was the only cavern they had taken the trouble to tile with precision. The manual preparation of the floor, using metal drums filled with concrete as rollers, had been back breaking, but worth it. *He ran his fingertips over the smooth, glass-like finish of the walls. Amazing what we managed to achieve with those bathroom tiles.* Harry's mind scuttled away down memory lane, clutching at the useful distraction from why he was *really* here.

A bird flu epidemic scare left humans unscathed. To counter scare mongering and manage mass hysteria, the panicked populace was prescribed an influenza vaccine – even though experts agreed it was no more effective than a placebo. When the big influenza pandemic hit, flu vaccine stocks were so low, it wiped out a crippling eighty percent of the human population.

He relived the early days, before the vampire clusters became hives, when London had yet to fill up. Going out on sorties, targeting the deserted shopping malls, had been less dangerous then. *We found these tiles in a hardware superstore that no longer had front doors, I seem to remember.* It gave them the means of creating a sterile environment.

Inevitably, his eyes were drawn to the reason he was sweating, and why, for the first time in as long as he could remember, he had a migraine.

Harry stared at Rebekah's restless form laid out in a hospital bed. The blonde hair at her temples was dark with perspiration, and there was a grayish sheen to her usually creamy complexion. The restraints running across her body were not tight, but they looked sinister.

"This isn't right, Douglas," Harry muttered.

"It's necessary. He made fools of us. She must have let him out."

"But she didn't know, I swear it." Uncle Harry's usual command gave way to impotent frustration. "You can't keep her sedated forever, and the others will ask questions."

"If this *friend* of Rebekah's escaped without her help, then can't you see that makes it worse?" Douglas clenched and unclenched his fist.

But Harry knew the truth. It suited Douglas to have Rebekah under his control, and he blamed himself for that.

"I'm damned if I'm going to let a bloodsucking leech lay a hand on one of the few eligible women we have, much less *my* woman." Douglas' eyes glinted with sickening fervor as he jerked his head in Rebekah's direction. "He has her in his power, so this is for her own good." Douglas looked Harry in the eye. "The sooner she is my wife, the better."

"It was never meant to be like this."

"Was I supposed to woo her, Harry? With hearts and flowers?" Douglas laughed. "Wake up, man."

Harry swallowed, and the guilt stuck in his throat.

Douglas arrival at the eco-town coincided with a low-point. They had *needed* his vision to survive, and the going price was a wife.

When he betrothed the fourteen-year-old Rebekah to Douglas without her consent, Harry knew he had let his sister down. *Margaret died thinking Rebekah was in safe hands.* His stomach swilled with disgust. *The danger of being caught by the vampires overshadowed everything else. But blood is still thicker than water and somewhere along the line, I lost sight of that.*

The bargain had seemed an abstract notion, after all, who knew what seven years would bring.

It was a little like promising your soul to the devil; you never really expect him to come knocking. But it was Rebekah's soul Harry promised. Douglas *had* honored his agreement to wait until she was twenty-one, but now, he was determined to collect.

One month ago, in Douglas' controlling mind, Rebekah went from being Harry's niece, to becoming *his* woman.

Harry could still see Rebekah's wounded expression when he told her what he had done, and that Douglas would not back down. But he promised to keep trying. He rubbed self-consciously at his throat, recalling the night Douglas made clear exactly how far he would go to force Harry's hand. The bruises Douglas inflicted had lasted a week.

His throat rasped, suffering from many hours of arguing with Douglas; pleading Rebekah's cause. *If only I was twenty years younger, or Douglas had a better nature to appeal to. The man has no conscience to prick.*

Harry's modified beta-blockers gave humans a critical edge in those early days. Gathering information on vampires was only ever a secondary consideration. *We were never foolish enough to believe the balance of power would shift back. 'They' are immortal, so, open and shut case. But, by suppressing our heart rate, we have a fighting chance. We can at least forage for fuel for the generators, renew supplies of blankets and clothes, and of course, raid 'their' crops.*

However, whichever way you looked at it, Harry had needed Douglas to overhaul the living conditions, or the real threat remained that humans would die of carbon monoxide poisoning, or worse yet, dysentery. While they *could* live without physical comforts, Douglas' expertise in rigging up the generators provided enough lighting to save their sanity and enabled warmed water to be piped around the caves in a crude form of heating. His mechanical knowhow made hot food and a warm bath a reality.

In this new world, Douglas held all the cards, and he knew it. Harry had never seen Douglas so furious. *I was right to fear him.* Rebekah had become the pound of flesh Douglas felt he was owed.

"You can't marry a woman in a coma," Harry snapped.

"But I *will* marry her. Surely you can't think her better off barren, being drained by a bloodsucker?"

"You don't know he *is* one, not for sure. You're letting jealousy cloud your judgement."

Douglas' face flushed to the shade of a rotting plum. "Have you seen the bruises on her body? It's disgusting," he spat. "She will marry me and have children. It is her duty to our community."

Harry recoiled under the tirade. *If he* is *a vampire, he shows more humanity than Douglas. I'm glad the trap failed.* But, he kept those thoughts to himself.

◇◇◇

Rebekah's subconscious registered the ebb and flow of voices around her, but she found concentrating on any one in particular too difficult. Although, she was aware that the voice she clung to was not there. She couldn't recall his name, or clearly define his face, and disappointment weighed her down.

She tried to move, but the blankets felt like lead.

"Uncle Harry?" Her voice scratched over a parched throat. She had lost track of time, but her head was clearing. As she stared at the meticulously tiled domed ceiling, she wondered, what am I doing in the hospital cavern?

She hated it here. It smelled of antiseptic and despair. No one ever ended up here for a good reason, and the isolation made the air of loneliness so thick you could taste it.

It was on the lowest level of the eco-town where a natural underground spring made it the ideal location for the hospital.

"Uncle Harry," she croaked again.

A hand lifted her head and another held a beaker of water to her lips. "Shh," Leizle hissed, "he'll hear you, and he's in a foul mood."

Fear iced her spine. She didn't need to ask who.

"What happened?" Rebekah whispered. She trusted Leizle, and she tried hard to focus and find some reassurance on her face. A curtain of vibrant chestnut hair covered her expression, but the green eye peeping out became clouded with worry.

"You were in the dining cavern and you fainted, spark out. You hit the floor like a sandbag and cracked your head on it. Douglas insisted that you needed rest." She scanned the cavern quickly, adding quietly, "It's been two days, and no one has been allowed to see you."

Rebekah frowned. She remembered sitting in the dining hall playing with her food, making patterns with it on her plate. Douglas appeared from nowhere and slid onto the seat beside her, and a sharp pinch in her thigh had made her leap to her feet with a yelp. The room tumbled, and when she turned to make her escape the floor rushed up at an alarming speed.

"*He* did this. Douglas." *He jabbed me with something, but why?* Even as she clutched at the memories, drowsiness dragged her eyelids closed, and a feeling of mourning shrouded her muddled thoughts. To sink into oblivion in her own bed was suddenly all she wanted.

She clawed her way back to consciousness and focused on Leizle's face, saying urgently, "When will I be allowed back to my den?" Rebekah liked her small cave. They had been dug out in rows and although you could hear the murmur of voices as companionship, you still had privacy. All her treasures were there.

"He's organizing a new den for you, near his." Leizle paused, looking into Rebekah's suddenly keen gaze. Her next words stung like a slap to the face. "He's planning the wedding."

Rebekah's body jack-knifed as she tried to sit up, and the band across her middle dug into her ribcage. The sudden pressure squeezed her heart tight. She croaked, "Wedding? No! Tell Uncle Harry, no he can't-"

"Shhh, he'll hear us. Harry tried to stop it, but, you know Douglas. I'm so sorry." Leizle laid a hand over Rebekah's, her chin emerging from behind the copper curtain on a mutinous slant. "We'll think of something, don't worry. We'll run away," she whispered, but they both knew that the trap was set to close.

Leizle's head shot around. She hissed, "He's coming. I'll come back." With a hard squeeze of Rebekah's fingers, she slipped silently away as heavy footsteps approached.

Rebekah subsided quickly and feigned sleep.

A warm, fleshy hand rested heavily over hers. Her heartbeat pounded in her ears when it moved to her thigh. The clammy heat creeping into her skin through the sheet disgusted her. She could almost feel his gaze crawling over her face, and just as panic began to grip her, his fingertips dug into her flesh and suddenly withdrew.

His footfall faded and left the room, and she listened until her neck ached with the effort of not moving.

Her relief was filled with a revelation. The elusive voice which had floated inside her head suddenly had a name. *Connor.* When *he* touched her, it had sparked entirely different feelings.

Douglas' touch swilled her stomach with bile. *God help me*. Adrenalin pumped, urging her to run, her left leg even twitched a little, but in the end, sleep seemed the more enticing means of escape.

Chapter 14

Julian's words of four days ago haunted Connor. *"This has the stink of a personal vendetta. I do hope you know what you're doing."*

Not really, thought Connor, as he whipped along the hospital hallway, his white coattails flapping in an agitated rhythm. But he *did* know he needed to see Rebekah again, and escaping Serge's attentions was proving impossible. *The damn man is everywhere I look.*

He entered a side ward and, from his pocket, pulled the vials containing his blood quota, both animal and human. *I don't have time to hunt today*. Pensively, he rolled the human blood vial between his fingertips, stirring a current which released a copper-tinged aroma that wrinkled his nose. He could not recall having an emotional response to it before. His reluctance to drink it surprised him. *It is what it is, a way of life, or death.*

The irony was not lost on him that a trusted facilitator of the farming process, charged with finding new ways of surviving the food shortage, was keeping humans out of the farm. *'Threatening the food supply' is where I am, about now, and Serge just needs to make the death sentence stick.*

Connor inspected the vials again. "Ah well, as the saying goes, needs must," he muttered. He had his other need to attend to also. Sleep. He quickly emptied the vials into his mouth and tossed them into the recycling cart.

With the desperation for Rebekah's safety clawing inside his skull, descent into rap-sleep would bring him the release of lucid dreams. *I can't go to Rebekah, but, I can feel closer to her.* For Connor, who never experienced the true oblivion of sleep, the last few days had seemed like years. The unrelenting hours of uncertainty resembled the constant grip of a vise.

Connor lay down on the examination table, closed his eyes, and prepared to enter Heaven through the gateway of Hell. He relaxed, even though a clenched fist twisted his insides, gripping his heart as rap-sleep overwhelmed him.

His cheeks hollowed with tension as he embraced the pain and his mind raced along the tunnel, chasing down the pinprick of light which exploded inside his brain and summoned a memory of his Rebekah. It was a pale imitation, but enough to save his sanity.

Crystal clarity pulled her image into sharp focus, and she appeared, sitting in their glade waiting for him. Walking through his mind, he sank down beside her, tucked a strand of silky blonde hair behind her ear, and kissed her. Connor smiled in his sleep as he stared into her chocolate-brown eyes and watched her face flush to rose. The agony of making love to her would forever stain his soul. As his body and hers found a rhythm, he held her and absorbed the waves of pleasure chasing up and down her fragile frame. *Everything I want, right here.*

He hung onto the euphoric feeling, until it suddenly turned to dust in his hands. He groaned in his sleep. The stone weight of his heart bore down and crushed him. The vision of Rebekah's pink flushed cheeks as she lay in his arms, faded to ashen gray. He gently shook her shoulders, but her head hung limp, and he could not wake her. Panic oozed through him. He shook her again, tightening his grip, until, like a statue sculpted in sand, she crumbled and slipped through his fingers.

His return to consciousness was the instant click of a hypnotist's fingers, but Connor opened his eyes slowly, waiting for the anxiety to subside. Sitting up and swinging his legs over the side of the bed, he muttered, "It means nothing." But his need to see the *real* Rebekah's smile, hear her heart and make sure she was okay, burned more urgently now.

Leaving the room, Connor collected his greatcoat and headed out of the hospital via the emergency exit. He felt rather than saw Serge's henchmen melt into shadows, staying out of sight.

He stepped out onto the sidewalk and swore, "Dammit. Promenade."

The sea of enraptured vampires wandered by. Connor searched the flowing crowd for dark-haired decoys and familiar faces, and found one of each. Waiting for the right moment, he left the sidewalk, joined the sluggish tide, and adjusted his stride to fit in.

He slotted himself in between a face he trusted and three dark strangers wearing long-sleeved dark shirts. *Not as tall as I'd like, but close enough, although, I'll need to lose the coat.*

"Charles," greeted Connor quietly, smiling when the young vampire faltered. Casting an eye over the fifteen abreast river of vampires, he added, "It's still busy, considering it's late."

Charles gathered himself, and nodded, "It's a nice night."

Despite the wintery nip in the evening air, its caress on vampire skin felt warm. Connor removed his heavy coat, slung it casually over one shoulder, and rolled up his shirt sleeves, welcoming the breeze through the thin cotton. *I might as well get some air exposure. Pity they don't care that moving faster increases the wind chill and speeds up the hardening process.*

Vampire tissue, like every other element of their existence, had conflicting needs. Tough surface tension relied upon air exposure; if covered too well, their skin softened over time and became vulnerable to injury. Yet another balancing act to manage, mused Connor.

Connor cocked his head. "Don't you ever wish they moved a little faster? It would make the walk more invigorating," said Connor, keeping an eye on the dark heads clustered over to one side.

Charles smiled. "You don't consider this snail's pace as exercise?"

"You need to ask?" replied Connor, laughing as he drifted out to where the throng thickened, his conversation drawing Charles with him.

Connor would normally have stirred the current himself. Looking after his human frame was second nature, and he was ever mindful that bursts of speed lubricated tendons and sinews. *Exercise is a good thing.* However, today, he wanted to remain invisible.

His dark-haired companions eased their way out to the edge of the procession, and Connor moved along with them. *This is it.*

He suddenly dropped his hand, and his coat slipped from his shoulder, landing with a muffled thump in the street. "Oh hell," muttered Connor, slapping his hand on his forehead in faked realization. "I have to see Principal Julian. Get my coat, would you, Charles?"

The smaller vampire, used to obeying orders, instantly dived for the coat.

Connor smoothly changed direction, arriving on the sidewalk at the same time as a dark-haired vampire who formed part of the fortuitous group. He blended in, staying with them for a distance of thirty yards, turning his face away as Charles, craning his neck, scanned the crowd, wearing a puzzled expression.

At the first opportunity, Connor entered a store, passed through the sales floor and exited by another door. He slowed to a casual walk and repeated the shopping maneuver twice more before, using the back alleys to make a U-turn, he headed south across the river and out of London.

Connor traveled southeast across the countryside, shadowing the same route taken by him and Rebekah, and keeping the narrow country road known as the 'A20' in sight. He didn't want to miss a human on a motorcycle headed up to London. *Things are tough enough already.* He finally settled on a vantage point of the hilltop just outside Swanley; less than ten miles from the eco-town location and within vampire surveillance range, if you knew what you were looking for.

Hunkering down, he turned up his shirt collar and folded his arms. The sweep of his black hair covered his brow, and he became all but invisible, even to vampire eyes.

Midnight crept in, and Connor remained still for so long a dusting of frost covered his cold skin. In the distance behind him the dead buildings of London cluttered the horizon like outcrops of coal, with a snowfall of stars as a backdrop.

He stared intently ahead, wishing he could summon the power of X-ray vision to burrow through the packed clay earth. It took all his skill to zero in on the distant eco-community, and, using the acute vampire senses he *did* have, he picked out the subtle blend of odors drifting on the breeze. *Fourteen humans are there today.* But, the only one who interested him was Rebekah. It should have been easier to single out her rhythm. When he tasted her blood, she had imprinted on him. As surely as ink would tattoo his skin, the colors and notes of her body had swelled the empty chambers of his heart and given him reason to exist.

But, he could not get a fix on her, and he was worried. *I finally give Serge the slip and get my moment outside London, and now what? Where the hell is she?* Annoyance grated like a bone saw inside his head and wringing Serge's scrawny neck blossomed as a perfect solution.

Connor heard movement in the woods, and the thickening of shadows told him he had company. He tuned into a muted heavy heartbeat and admiration rattled through him. *A human, and a smart one at that. He must know the terrain to have picked out my shape.*

Rising smoothly to his feet, still staring out over the landscape, Connor invited him in closer. He heard the whistling flight of the weapon launched at his head. He whipped around, and his hand darted out and closed around the handle of a blacksmith's mallet, halting the six inch lump of metal two inches from his face.

"Impressive," he murmured.

He scanned the deep shadow, and before the human he saw crouched there could move, Connor darted forward and pinned him to a tree by the throat. He stared into a mud-caked face, taking in the combat gear with a sweeping glance. "Military? Fancy your chances, hmm?"

The man jabbed a knife into Connor's stomach. The blade tore through his shirt, but skidded harmlessly across his hard flesh. Connor's brows shot up in surprise.

Curious about what the fool might do next, Connor released him.

The human reached into his combat belt, and in a jerking action, he smashed a glass vial on Connor's chest, and they both watched the acid burn its way through the black cotton fabric of his shirt and stain his vampire skin with a powdered residue.

Gripping the man by the front of his jacket, Connor growled, "What the hell is wrong with you? Have you got a death wish? Are you one of *them*? Rebekah's lot?"

The man's eyes widened.

"You are? Well, you're lucky I bothered to ask or you'd be a bag of bone dust about now. Start talking. What's your name?"

"Greg."

"Ah, the Royal Marine. So, why are you behaving like a prick?"

Greg sneered and spat at Connor. "I've seen you for what you are. Fucking cannibals."

Wiping the spittle from his face, Connor said calmly, "I've been nice up 'til now. You don't want to test me."

"Nah, 'cos you'll rip my fucking heart out, right?"

He had Connor's attention now, and his ice-gray stare burrowed into Greg's brain. "You've seen a feral?"

For the first time, Greg looked uncertain.

"Shit," said Connor. "Where? When?"

"Just over a week ago. He got Stan-"

Connor scoured the trees. "Where are the rest of your away team?"

Greg bristled, saying quietly, "Why?"

"You've been out in the field for weeks, Rebekah said, and I doubt you'd be out there alone. Go home, Greg. They need you back there. I already killed the feral." Connor tilted his head. "We're on the same side, *they* aren't us." Connor withdrew his hand. "Next time I see you, and there *will* be a next time because I'm watching out for Rebekah, don't throw acid on me, okay?"

The muscle in Greg's jaw twitched as he stood down.

Connor returned the blacksmith's mallet and smiled. "No hard feelings?" Checking his watch Connor swore gently. "I have a clinic waiting. Dig in here and wait until dawn, you stink of adrenalin. But do me a favor," Connor added casually, "go check on Rebekah, and tell her I said, 'Hi.'" He stopped short of voicing his anxieties, the man was nervous enough already.

With a sharp nod, Connor turned and disappeared, leaving Greg staring into empty space.

Making himself go back into the darkened streets of London rated high as the hardest thing he had done in a long time. With Serge sitting upon his shoulder, and not knowing Rebekah's whereabouts, 'acting natural' was almost unbearable.

His niggling doubts about her safety constantly came back to Douglas' smug smile. *Could the man be that stupid?* Connor feared the answer was 'yes'.

The clinic felt surreal in its normality. Connor called the next name on the list, and a patient wearing an eyepatch got up and followed him back into the consulting room.

Injecting animal blood into the vampire's eyeball in an attempt to hydrate it and restore the sight took Connor back to his Royal Eye Hospital days in 1910. Becoming a vampire had meant making tough decisions and saying goodbye to his human love, Lady Lavinia Cranham. It was a long time since that Pandora's Box had sprung open. *Dammit, I'm not losing Rebekah, I can't.*

Connor tossed the syringe at his surgical assistant, Anthony, knowing his lightning quick reflexes would catch it.

"Finish up here," said Connor as he swung out of the room, leaving Anthony gawping at the slammed door.

It's going to take Greg the best part of a day to get back to the eco-town. Dawn is still a way off. I can make it there and back before then. I'll face the consequences when I return.

Back out on the street, Connor rounded a corner, applied the brakes and stopped dead.

Serge stood six feet away, smiling. "Hello, Doctor Connor. We've come to take you before the council." His yellow eyes glinted with satisfaction.

"Again?" Although Connor's hackles rose, he disguised the sneer tugging at his lip with a blank expression. "Surely, there are other ways for you to satisfy your need for drama?" Connor's smile became ice cold and dangerously calm.

Serge shuffled his feet. "If you can just come with us."

The '*us*' turned out to be another pair of Serge's enthusiastic young guardsmen. Connor remembered how easily he had dispatched the first two. But *then*, Rebekah's safety resided in his hands. Now, her safety gnawed at his mind, and the feeling was just as urgent.

"Councilor Serge, when Principal Julian issues a summons, I will, of course, attend. Until that time, I think not." He took a step forward, almost touching his chest to Serge's. "Now, if you will get out of my way."

Connor sighed when vampire hands gripped his arms from behind. Escaping their clutches would be simple, but he felt annoyed at the inconvenience. Finding a fast way out of this was his only consideration; the rest was window dressing and he had no time to waste on niceties.

"Serge-"

"Principal Julian *has* issued a summons." Cutting Connor off, Serge grinned.

Problem solved. Julian's resolution would be fast and decisive. "Let's get this out of the way." Connor surged forward, slipping from the grasp of the surprised guardsmen, and leaving Councilor Serge to catch up.

In the council courtroom minutes later, Connor stood in the dock facing Principal Julian who was flanked again by jurors Marius and Alexander. The gallery was eerily empty this time. Even if the hive knew round two was about to commence, the hours of darkness were set aside to tend the crops which fed the humans. *For once, they have something better to do.*

"But there's always room for a good old-fashioned lynching mob." Connor scowled.

"So, Councilor Serge, what have you for us this time?" Julian asked wearily.

"I have the girl," Serge said.

The twitch in the facial muscles of the council jurors betrayed their surprise.

Connor, too, was startled into paying close attention. *He's lying. If Rebekah* was *here, I would know it.* But his gut churned until he knew for sure.

"Well, get on with it," Julian demanded, shooting Connor a quizzical glance.

At Serge's signal, a girl entered the courtroom.

Connor looked her over, and certainty returned. He deliberately expelled the insult of a laugh.

Undeterred, Serge turned to address the council, enjoying being their focus. "This girl's name is Annabelle. She has identified Doctor Connor as the vampire who helped her a week ago in the hospital." He paused for effect. "She has been living in a deserted basement and Doctor Connor has been bringing her food."

The accusation might be ridiculous, but it gave Connor reason to pause. In a truth-is-stranger-than-fiction moment, he recalled Rebekah asleep in her basement. Serge was nearer the mark than he knew. *Where is he going with this?* Turning his attention to the girl, Connor grimly registered the breath hitching in her swollen throat and wondered how long she had been crying.

Serge crossed the floor to stand beside the cringing Annabelle. His fingers tore away the fabric of her blouse, revealing shoulders covered with teeth marks and lesions staining her skin with red and purple blotches.

"Doctor Connor is keeping a human pet." Serge's eyes glittered in triumph. "This crime carries the death sentence."

"For goodness sake, Julian, where is the proof? It's a fairy tale." Connor knew that better than anyone because he had written the tale himself when he gave Serge the name 'Annabelle'. *I've never met an Annabelle, and I've certainly never seen this waif.* He could guess what Serge had promised in exchange for her lies. *Probably, release from a miserable existence as another vampire's pet. She certainly looks well snacked upon.*

"It is *Principal* Julian in council, please, Doctor Connor. As you say, this is not yet proven. However, I *am* obliged to detain you until the evidence can be assessed."

Connor's frustration moved from simmering point to boiling. "Very well, I'll submit to bite and blood tests, but for heaven's sake, Julian. Detention is not necessary, we can do it now."

Julian barked a reminder. "It's five in the morning, and crops come first, *Doctor* Connor."

Connor's dead expression conveyed it all. Wasting time locked in a cadaver drawer waiting for his innocence to be proven was a delay he could not tolerate. The indigestible sickness inside told him something was wrong with Rebekah.

Julian looked across at Serge. He was that rarity, a vampire who *looked* old. His skin was wrinkled and his hair was more gray than black. Rumor had it he begged a vampire to turn him, fearing he would die in the influenza pandemic. His thin, frail human frame meant he was cursed to being another rarity, a vampire without strength.

Julian's jaw clenched tight, and Connor relaxed, knowing which way this would go. Serge represented a thorn in the principal's side, and Connor was worth more than that as a friend, and a hell of a lot more as an honorable vampire.

"Very well, bite and blood tests in the morning. Without detention," said Julian. He glared at Serge, prepared for a protest, but not for the gloating smile which stretched the creped cheeks smooth for a fleeting second. Julian's eyes narrowed. "You better *hope* you are right, Councilor, otherwise it will be like Cinderella's slipper. If Doctor Connor's bite radius does not fit, then I'll be finding one that *does*."

Julian turned away from Serge's barely concealed satisfaction. "Connor- Doctor Connor," he said, hastily revising to the formal. "In my chambers, now." Calculation glittered behind Julian's eyes as he struck the bench with his gavel and declared, "Court dismissed."

He rose quickly and exited through the door behind the bench. Jurors' Marius and Alexander followed him in one fluid movement like a series of knots along the same length of string. The door closed behind them, and the silence was complete.

Inside his chamber, Julian removed his white cravat and hung his black robe inside the wardrobe, closing the solid wood door with the silent dexterity of a magician. He turned at the brisk rapping of knuckles, which rattled the door loudly in its frame.

"Come."

The door flipped open, and Connor materialized inside the room.

"What is going on?" Julian said slowly, projecting calm he did not feel. "Serge's reaction was not as I expected. So, are you going to tell me?"

Connor cast an appraising glance over Julian's mild features.

Julian's bronze-toned collar-length hair was immaculate, as always. He exuded the impressive bearing of a swan, serene and efficient; but under the surface a turbulent inquisitive brain and a good heart made him an astute and valued ally. However, he also had the suppressed emotional expression common to one born in the 19th century. London society might have changed a lot in two hundred years, but essentially, Julian had not.

"I'm not sure you'd understand, Julian. More to the point, I'm not sure you should become involved."

"I'll be the judge of that," said Julian firmly.

Connor sighed. "Okay, you win, but you may wish we never had this conversation."

"Clearly, this Annabelle is not the same girl as the one at the hospital," Julian said carefully. "Although, Serge thinks you have something to hide. Is he trying to flush you out? What's going on?" Julian's level stare demanded answers.

Connor said flatly, "It's not the same Annabelle. And yes, Serge is digging."

"So, what is it? He's raising the stakes in council, forcing you to *prove* the human girl he dragged into court is nothing to do with you, or face the death sentence. Why?"

"The stakes are already pretty high, Julian." Connor took a decisive breath and said, "I have found 'the one'."

"The one?" said Julian, and his confusion gave way to understanding. "Ah, so, there is *another* Annabelle, the one from the hospital. You're keeping her cluster location to yourself because you don't want Serge leering over her on the farm?"

"Not exactly," Connor said quietly. "Julian, how long have you known me?"

"About ninety-three years, give or take." Julian said, the laughter draining from his face at Connor's sober expression.

"Try, then, to imagine what it takes to say this. Her name is Rebekah, and she's human."

A sneer molded to Julian's features as he blurted, "What the hell, Connor. Are you insane?" He squared his shoulders, preparing for an argument, and felt confounded when Connor sank down into the battered leather armchair and became stone still.

The silence stretched. Julian could find nothing to say.

Finally, Connor said quietly, "For the first time in a hundred years, yes, I think I *am* insane. It certainly feels that way."

Connor's face remained blank while words poured out. His fears about Douglas hardened his tone to flint, but his voice cracked when he spoke about Rebekah. Finally, he concluded, "I have no idea what Serge has up his sleeve." He met Julian's pragmatic look head on. "But, I need to get moving, and fast."

Julian nodded. He registered Connor's lungs bellowing in agitation, as if holding her imagined scent at bay. *Even with this Rebekah miles away, he's suffering.* "So, it is love? Well, *that* I can understand, or did." Julian's mood became solemn. "I had a wife, of course, when I lived. Only for three years, but, nonetheless-" He paused. *I did not think vampire existence offered that depth of feeling, and I've been happy with that, but it seems I was wrong.* Julian straightened, and locking his memories back inside their box, he asked briskly, "So, what now?"

Connor rose to his feet and dropped a hand onto Julian's shoulder. "I need this business with Serge to go away," he said simply. "I just wish I could do the tests now and be done. You know now this Annabelle is a red herring?"

"I suspected as much. Though, it seemed a little theatrical, even by Serge's standards. He must *know* you will be cleared in the morning."

"Something does not add up," Connor muttered.

"Well, I'll help where I can, but Serge is out for blood, so tread carefully. The bite radius won't match, so I'll issue a summons and keep him occupied." Julian jerked his chin towards the door. "You go, and do whatever it is you've got to do. But Connor-" Julian waited until he had Connor's full attention.

"Don't do anything foolish. I would hate to see this 'Douglas' land you in the storage facility. I doubt he is worth that. Now, go."

Connor needed no second bidding. "Thank you, Julian."

Chapter 15

Connor left the council building and swept along the sidewalk, covering the ground at breakneck speed. Absorbing a chill factor which would have burned human skin, he shifted automatically up through the gears, until he detected the guardsmen.

Four. Damn. I don't have time for these fools. Vampires can stand as still and silent as stone, and be lethal in an ambush, unless, of course, they stink.

Stale air trapped inside their chests, and the rancid odor of their last feeds pervaded Connor's nostrils. *More of Serge's pet guardsmen, the stench is the same.* These vampires failed to understand that passing air through the lungs was not only part of speech, it was good hygiene.

The question is, what do they want? Connor suspicions inclined towards kill.

Harnessing the buzz of adrenalin rippling through his abdomen, Connor pinpointed the first opponent. He passed by the shadowed alcove and then, hitting reverse gear, swung back into it. He rotated quickly and the forceful uppercut Connor drove into the vampire's stomach punctured the diaphragm. The blow crushed his lungs, and he dropped to his knees. Connor cocked his head, considered the vampire's gaping mouth and leaned closer.

"Don't try to get up," he hissed. "I've cut off your blood supply. Your legs will harden to granite before you can cross the street."

Round two. He obligingly straightened, and an arm closed around his neck. Connor forced an elbow back in a two-handed shunt, dislodged the hold, and spun around. He grabbed the hapless vampire by the shirt-front and yanked him forward. With a manic grin, Connor's eyes narrowed. The vampire had the sense to register fear as Connor tightened his grip, jerked his arm back out in an explosive movement that ended abruptly. The vampire's head snapped backward and slammed into the wall behind. A crack appeared on the stunned face and crept down from the hair line, opening up a crevice in his forehead. A sharp repeat of the pounding movement crumbled the vampire's cranium, and Connor let him drop to the ground.

The two remaining vampires stepped into view.

"Well, what have we here?" whispered Connor.

The pair advanced in a synchronized pincer formation and Connor stood, arms relaxed at his side, waiting for their move.

He enjoyed being a doctor and embraced the prospect of using his knowledge to deadly advantage.

"You can still change your minds," Connor said casually.

"I've got the tall one." Julian's voice floated through the air, and the designated vampire disappeared. A blow hit him side-on and the momentum whipped him out of view.

The remaining vampire's head jerked around when his companion vanished, and Connor used the distraction. He shot forward and closed a vicious grip on to the vampire's face. He burrowed his thumb into the eye socket as he tightened his fingers and held him out at shoulder height, impaled, and dangling in midair.

"Councilor Serge?"

Connor felt the pressure of the vampire trying to nod.

"Kill?" he asked, and the vampire's skull rocked in the cradle of his hand again. Connor's fist closed in a vise-like grip. Forcing the vampire's chin up with a sharp twist of his wrist, he sliced his teeth across the exposed throat, growling in frustration. He dismissed the vampire before the body hit the sidewalk.

Pulling a linen handkerchief from his pants pocket, he wiped smears of blood from his mouth and hands. Cold congealed vampire blood was less gory than human. Unless the vampire was literally just fed and fully saturated, the tissue had little left to spare.

Julian strolled back into view. "Assassinate the character before the man," he said thoughtfully. "Serge did not want you detained."

"He could not have me killed if you locked me up. He played us both. He used the council hearing to undermine my reputation, nothing more."

"When you didn't turn up tomorrow for bite and blood work-" said Julian.

"It would look as though I'm guilty, and I ran. And he would have walked away from my murder." Connor's eyes narrowed with icy certainty. *Serge still plans to hunt Rebekah down.* "What brought you out here, tonight?"

Julian disappeared around a corner and returned holding Connor's coat.

"Unluckily for Serge, I had this in my closet. Charles said you'd left it with him." Julian's brows climbed in speculation. "I thought that if things are as urgent as you say, you'd need it. It's almost dawn, and even this time of year, you'll have some shadow dancing to do."

Julian indicated the three bodies and shrugged.

"I've got this. I'll have Serge hauled up in front of the council. But without witnesses it will only delay him for a short while. You'd better go." Julian's eyes glittered with exhilaration, before he nodded and melted away into the darkness.

Julian had taken pleasure from the kill. Something which made his sluggish juices flow faster was rare these days. He stood in the disused attic of his sparsely furnished Edwardian house. Careless of the cobwebs clinging to his clothes, he settled in his thinking place, where he looked out over the London skyline and watched the lilac halo of sunrise creep over the sky.

The city had changed so much in two hundred years. Fantastical inventions, for a time, made London a jewel of neon and sulphur-bright wonder, but now, she had plunged back into darkness. The buildings were in mourning, with walls shrouded in carbon-black and windows dressed in a cold glare. *Nothing much twinkles out there any longer.* The only light he could see, glinting like a gold tooth in a rotten smile, came from the hospital.

His London, 19th century *human* London, had been a different place. Full of the light, sounds and colors which his Eva had brought to his life. He understood Connor's conflict, and his pain, too. Julian focused on his reflection in the glass windowpane and allowed it to blur as two hundred immortal years melted away and took him back to 1812...

Julian smiled when he rounded the corner at the top of the wide oak staircase and looked down to see Eva teasing the curls of her honey-toned hair into place. As his eyes gathered every nuance and angle of her delightfully-delicate scowling features, he said softly, "You look beautiful, my dear."

He walked purposefully down the stairs, arriving at her side as she finally gave a satisfied murmur and smiled at his reflection in the mirror.

"As I said, beautiful." His hand settled on her waist when she turned to face him.

"You always say that. It is why I love you."

"Ah." His smile was wicked. "Surely not the only reason?"

Tracing an insistent path over her alluring curves, his hand slipped around to the small of her back. He drew her close, glancing down at the swell of her breasts. A tantalizing glimpse of satin skin flushed beneath his gaze as her heartbeat thundered visibly in the base of her throat.

"Julian," she whispered. A small frown of pretended disapproval framed the blue eyes she lifted to look into his, and he drowned in her turbulent emotions.

"Eva," he echoed, his breath warming her lips as he closed the space between them. His long fingers threaded sensually into the silken tresses of her hair. He paused, holding his breath and indulging the urge to press her trembling body to his.

Her skin warmed his palm through the thin muslin dress. The new fashion for ladies, thought daring and immodest by some, revealed such a charming expanse of creamy shoulder and delicate collarbone and had his whole-hearted approval. He did not miss the whale-bone corset his hold was accustomed to, although, unlacing it last thing at night was a chore he sorely missed.

"I like this new fashion. It suits you well, my love." He cleared the gravel from his throat and added impishly, "There is no crime in kissing my wife in my own hallway. I am the master here."

He smiled as Eva gasped in delightful surrender, and when he kissed her she welcomed him. Her softened mouth clung to his lips, and when the tip of her tongue danced over his, he growled in frustration.

"Temptress," he said hoarsely, releasing her and lowering his eyebrows in a playfully threatening gesture. The ruddy flush across his cheekbones and his tight jaw reflected the battle he fought to regain his composure.

Peeping up flirtatiously through long lashes, Eva smoothed her hands down over the soft fabric of her skirt, drawing his attention to her delicate frame and the slender length of her thighs.

"I think the fresh air of a walk will do us good, hmm?" Julian caught her fingertips in his and pressed a kiss into her lace-covered palm.

Eva smiled, her eyes alight with happiness that her husband of three years still found her alluring. She said lightly, "I'll wait outside. Oh, can you ask Bessie to bring my wrap?" She drifted away to the doorway, standing for a moment framed in the amber glow of sunlight before she gracefully descended the steps to the sidewalk.

Julian grinned ruefully and pulled on the cord, ringing the hall bell three times, knowing it would sound in the servants' quarters in the basement and summon Eva's maid. He also knew, that by the time Bessie received his instruction and traveled the length of the upstairs hallway and returned, another five minutes would in all likelihood have passed.

"I won't need my wrap after all, Julian." Eva's musical tone, alive with surprise, called out from where she waited outside. "It really is a beautiful evening,"

Julian lifted a sardonic brow as he took a pair of gloves from Garrett, his young footman. Frowning as he worked each finger inside the butter-soft leather, Julian murmured, "Garrett, apologize to Bessie for dragging her away from her smoothing iron. The mistress has changed her mind."

"Very good, Sir." Garrett nodded politely.

"Oh, and Garrett, can you inform Mrs. Warner, it is only eight for dinner this evening? Aunt Augusta is unwell. She has the stomach flu," Julian said absently, focused on tugging the second glove into place and securing the button at his wrist.

"Mrs. Warner will be pleased, Sir," said Garrett, adding hastily, "only 'cos it's even numbers, Sir. She likes even numbers."

"I know." Julian laughed. "Make sure you tell her, mind." Collecting his hat from Garrett's outstretched hand, Julian turned and moved eagerly forward. He was swinging into his second stride when Eva's agonized groan cut through the air, sounding as though a heavy weight barreled into her and forced the breath from her lungs.

Terror jolted up Julian's spine, the hat fell from his senseless fingers and, without thought, he was moving fast.

All that registered to his frantic gaze as he jumped the flight of steps and landed heavily on the sidewalk beside her, was not the man running away, but the shower of pearls, his anniversary gift to her, unraveling from the tidy row which had caressed Eva's throat. Cascading onto the ground, they ricocheted in lunatic disarray over the uneven flagstones, their luster enhanced to obscene beauty by the early evening light.

Stepping closer and grabbing Eva's arm, he pulled her into his body as her knees crumpled. Subsiding to the ground beneath her, Julian cushioned her fall until she lay against him like a broken doll.

His eyes locked onto the red stain devouring the delicate pink of her muslin dress. He bellowed, "No!"

With horrified fascination, Julian spread his hand over the blood-sodden fabric, molding his fingers desperately to her soft flesh and pressing down hard.

The biting pain of a knife blade was a myth; it was more like the bruising blow of a fist which, without the stiffened bone corset to protect her, had driven the breath from her body. It was only when her blood pressure plummeted, the sudden release of blood exploding sparks behind her eyes that realization dawned. Eva's gaze locked onto his, wide with puzzled shock.

Julian pressed his palm harder to the blossoming pool of red which stole the color from her face. "Eva, please, stay with me."

His whisper became a howl when he knew she had gone.

Julian had never noticed the stench of decaying vegetables which hung over London in summertime before that day, but, kneeling there in the gutter, trying not to gag at the smell of her blood, he did.

The vibration of footsteps pounding through the sidewalk beneath his knees signaled Garrett's return. The young man bent over double, fighting for breath as he gasped, "He's gone, Sir."

Julian's glazed stare watched Eva's blood meander along the gaps in the flagstones, transforming the horrific into almost beautiful intricate designs.

"He disappeared in the direction of the Old Kent Road. I left a copper chasing him, but I don't fancy *his* chances either, Sir."

Julian said with quiet determination, "No matter. I will find him."

Looking up, Julian's vacant green stare was cold and brittle in the fading light. Garrett's expression shifted from sorrow to dread at the look in his master's eyes, and Julian looked away.

"I'll help, Sir-" Garrett said slowly, stopping when his master shook his head.

This was something Julian needed to do alone, and the inexorable path which led to an encounter with a vampire was set. In the weeks which followed, he crossed into territory a man of his standing would never usually have entertained. Even his young footman, Garrett, being in service, with food and lodgings provided, considered the East End streets Julian rampaged along to be below his station.

And so, feeling invincible, or caring little if he was or not, Julian wandered the streets of London, a silent ghost aching for revenge. One night, frustration having transformed his attitude from gentleman to pugilist, and looking-for-a-fight etched into every line of his body, Julian thought he saw him, the man who ran through his nightmares.

He set off in pursuit, and when his lungs burned, and there were only shadows everywhere his eager gaze darted, he pulled up short and gave in to murderous rage. He punched out at the crumbling damp brick walls which closed in on him and felt nothing as he tore the skin from his tightly clenched knuckles. No longer thinking, just drowning in vicious intent, he strode along the cobbled back-alleys and shouted mindlessly for the bastard to show himself.

As he paused to draw breath, a savage blow shoved him sideways into the rough-hewn face of a tavern wall, and a cold vise closed around his neck.

The raucous amusement drifting out through the nearby open window of the bar mocked the pain slicing through his body. He could barely breathe, let alone laugh.

Julian's arm snapped with the force of the collision and he gritted his teeth, groaning. "Kill me," he ground the words out. "Do it now, I welcome it." He closed his eyes, wanting to die.

Moments passed, and still he waited, until his arm lost all feeling. Hot ash tingled in his fingertips and his grinding teeth ached. Finally, he opened his eyes and stared into a sculpted marble face.

The vampire's lip curled as he laughed. "So keen to die," he mocked. "You want to join her, hmm, your beloved Eva?"

The sound of her name galvanized Julian into action. He snarled, his legs jerking as he kicked out, trying to shove himself away from the wall. The grip on his throat tightened. The vampire dug his thumb into Julian's jugular, deliberately rolling black clouds through his brain until his body sagged, and the coarse brickwork bit into his scalp.

"Well, Julian," he spat. "Sadly for you, happy endings bore me. Suffering seems more fitting, for an eternity, if you are strong enough."

Julian's anger shifted to crippling alarm. The worst his imagination could conjure was a sadist, intent on making his death a long and painful one. His mind raced feverishly until he felt the razor-sharp pinch on his neck as his flesh was squeezed between two blades. Searing pain traveled up his carotid artery and paralyzing fear flooded in.

He had not seen the vampire move, and his blood starved brain fancied that glinting eyes in darkened sockets still bored into him. When the white face floated back into focus, its grin revealed darkened teeth, which appeared decayed, until a lap of his tongue wiped them clean. His slack jaw allowed Julian's blood to run down his chin.

I thought those were my last moments on earth; but I was wrong.

Julian folded the memories away, putting them back into the box inside his head. The safe place where all the treasures of Julian the man were protected from the bloodied vision of the day Eva died, and that now, ironically, stained every day of his continued existence as Julian the vampire.

Julian stroked his thumb over the leather-bound volume of 'Dr. Jekyll and Mr. Hyde' cradled in his palm. The story was hard to read, just as those revealing monsters are meant to be. Dr. Jekyll thought he was chasing a killer, unaware that the killer resided inside him.

Julian liked to think the vampire legend was true; in 1886, Robert Louis Stevenson saved a suicidal vampire from plummeting to his death in the highlands of Scotland, and the encounter inspired him to write the book. It was rumored he wrote the first draft in a three day frenzy, and was himself, like a man possessed. *Did the vampire bare his soul? No one will ever know. But, imagine doing battle with the killer inside for centuries.*

"I just hope Connor knows what he's doing." Julian raised a hand and dragged a fingernail down over the cold glass. The pane shrieked in protest as he scored a line into the surface. *Killing leaves a mark. I've not killed in anger for many decades, and I cannot see anything changing that.*

That thought sustained him; even ‘in love’, Connor would never cross that line. He had known the man for ninety-three years and never seen him out of control. *Surely, he won’t do anything foolish now.*

Chapter 16

The domed roof of the meeting cavern reverberated with the dying notes of a harmonica, and Rebekah caught sight of a glint of silver as the instrument disappeared into a breast pocket. A shock of sandy hair framed an unusually solemn expression on a familiar face, and she wondered what was wrong. As her lips formed the question, the tall man's name shifted in her mind like a jumbled anagram.

Ah, Sandy. The last harmonic note faded into silence, and her thread of concentration dissolved with it. *What was I going to say?*

The scraping sound of a shoe on hard-packed earth called her attention back to the front of the room. Turning her head caused a moment of giddiness when the room continued revolving.

Standing still required more effort than it should. Rebekah's legs trembled, and she stared at a patch of moss on the meeting cavern wall to help maintain her balance. She plucked absently at the skirt of the white dress; longer than any she had ever worn before.

Am I playing dress-up? How did I get here? Rebekah glanced down and saw a pair of clichéd white satin slippers. *Maybe it's a dream. I would never wear these.* Her head was filled with tightly-packed cotton-candy thoughts which whispered, "*This is not how it should be.*"

The half-a-dozen wooden benches creaked in unison as the congregation sat down. She focused on the man beside her and felt nothing. *Well, not exactly nothing.* A few dozen spiders scuttling around in her stomach made her feel queasy.

Her knees trembled and she longed to sit down, but fingers biting into her arm made moving impossible. A creaking voice began talking, and Rebekah felt a bubble of warmth swell inside her when she noticed George standing in front of her.

His tone was heavy as he read a long sequence of words which made no sense. She was suddenly four years old, and pouring the buttons from her grandmother's sewing box out onto the polished table until they cascaded over the edge. George's words felt like grandmother's buttons, the more she tried to catch them, the more they slipped through her fingers.

Their only burial service so far had been performed by George, when a young man, Adam, died of cancer. Getting the chemotherapy or radiotherapy treatment he needed had been beyond their power. However, Uncle Harry *could* offer morphine. The decision was Adam's to make. God's opinion aside, most here were just glad when he no longer suffered.

George was not ordained by the church, but it created a new tradition that the 'elder' of their community became the chosen one. *New world, new rules. But, this isn't a burial. So, a marriage, maybe?* Eligible men outnumbered the women four to one, and the eco-town had tiptoed around that one. *Until now, it seems.*

Got it. It's a wedding. A sense of achievement pierced the cloud cover in her brain like a ray of light, and she felt pleased with herself. *We've never had one of those before. A wedding. I must love him, then.*

Rebekah looked expectantly at Douglas, but his pasty complexion and bullish features left her cold, and a shudder rattled through her insides.

He put out a hand which swallowed hers. Looking down, all she could think was how fleshy and big it was, and the spiders in her belly scuttled faster. The recoil of disgust lay inside somewhere, but her dulled body couldn't summon the energy to act upon it. Even through the fog, fear clenched a fist around her heart. *This can't be right.*

All eyes were on her. Turning her head, she met Uncle Harry's rheumy, watery-eyed stare. He seemed older than she remembered. Standing beside him, Thomas clenched Leizle's hand in his, and her pinched face was paper white, except for the red-rimmed eyes. *Ah, poor Leizle, maybe this* is *a burial.*

George cleared his throat loudly. "I do," he prompted, when he had her attention.

"Oh." Her brow creased in concentration. *I do what?* "I do," she said, responding to George's frantic eyebrows.

Douglas grinned, and his meaty hand closed more firmly on her fingers. Rebekah looked up into his face. The smile he wore didn't reach his dull-gray eyes, and tears blurred his image as the caress of his hand became a spiteful squeeze.

His clammy heat made her long for an elusive arctic chill, the crystal clarity of cold.

Although the slack smile on Douglas' dough-padded face held her trapped in horrified fascination, another face nibbled at her consciousness, a face with a chiseled jaw-line and dramatic cheekbones. A face where a smile moved the muscles into an entrancing expression that took her breath away.

"You may now kiss the bride." George's voice was joyless.

A relentless tide of panic shoved bile into her throat as Douglas drew her in close beside him. His hot palm curled around her waist, and his face closed in.

The exhilaration left over from the battle with the guardsmen stretched sinew and muscle tight, and Connor unleashed the energy in a burst of devastating speed. He stayed within touching distance of the shade cast by the hedgerows and trees rushing past beside him as the weak rays of autumn sunshine struggled to break through the clouds.

The thick fabric of his greatcoat rubbed his cheekbones when he tucked his chin deep down inside the buttoned up collar, and his leather gloves creaked over hands he folded into fists.

Calculating what Serge's next step would have been once Connor was dead, boiled a bitter cauldron of hatred in his gut.

As he hit the top of the hill near Swanley, tuning into Rebekah's signature shouldered aside all other considerations. He accelerated hard, eating up the distance and descending into icy calm. *I will find her, and she will be all right.*

Connor arrived at the eco-town, reduced his speed abruptly, and stepped into the shadowed opening of the tunnel. He gathered his wits and walked down the pitch-black passageway at a sedate human pace. In silence, he slipped behind the heavy sackcloth curtain marking the boundary of the inhabited space, and the flames of wall-mounted torches spat in reproach as the condensation on his cold skin plumed clouds of vapor.

The congregation in the meeting cavern drew him, but he still couldn't feel Rebekah. His smooth features disguised the tension inside as he took an inventory and came up empty. Although, there was another heartbeat, a slower and less vibrant echo of the one he sought.

Sweeping his attention throughout the underground space, Connor did not detect any hotspots outside the cavernous room. *They are all assembled here, then. Some kind of ceremony?*

The moment he took to savor the cluster of heartbeats filled his mouth with venom. He advanced without care, knowing their dulled human senses made sneaking up on them unnecessary. In any case, their concentration was on the two figures standing at the far end of the cavern. Following their lead, his eyes narrowed when they locked onto Rebekah's back.

He pulled her altered scent across his palate, and when it stung his throat, his anger flared. S*he's been drugged.*

Seeing Douglas lay his hand on her jerked Connor forward, and Rebekah started as he materialized suddenly at her elbow. He searched her drained features, the glazed dilated pupils and deadened responses, and his anger shifted to cold rage.

There was no spark of recognition in her eyes, and he realized his fury scared her.

The draped white silk clinging to her curves became a shimmering waterfall with the trembling of her knees. Connor's anger became iced with guilt; his fingers itched to rip away the wedding dress and to turn back the clock.

"What have you done to her?" Connor glared into Douglas' suddenly flushed face.

Douglas' hand dropped away in surprise, leaving a sweaty stain on Rebekah's skin. A triumphant grin emerged. "Ah, Rebekah's *friend*, just in time to toast our happiness. Rebekah is my wife."

Connor visualized snapping Douglas' neck like a dry twig. *Problem solved.* He forced out a derisive laugh as he said, "Sad to say, Douglas, I hadn't finished with her, yet. I'm here to take what is already mine. I *might* return her when I'm done."

Connor hoped Douglas would lose his temper. He was wired and ready, and, as he had once told Rebekah, humans were ridiculously slow, so he would have enjoyed the moment to its fullest.

Studying Connor's set features, Douglas' satisfied expression struggled to stay in place and perspiration erupted on his skin. The fear-fermented odor stirred Connor's urge to hunt, and only Rebekah's eyes boring into him held him still. *Her* scent was more compelling, so for now, Douglas would survive another day.

"Is she worth dying for?" Connor asked quietly.

Grinning at Douglas, Connor sensed Rebekah's body heat plummeting as shock took over.

"I'm done here," he said dismissively, his eyes narrowing. "I'm taking what is mine."

Rebekah shivered when his arm closed around her, and the predator surged inside him. But, even though her fear saturated him in excitement, he clamped his jaw tight and suffered it.

Douglas' throat, however, was not so safe. So, with a firm grip holding what was precious to him close, he left. Connor heard the muttering voices of the stunned gathering trying to make sense of what they had seen. *I guess the cat is out of the bag.*

Connor rushed along the tunnels, shielding Rebekah's face with his hand to protect her from the chilled blast of gusting air. He recounted each of the horrified faces he had seen. *Greg hasn't made it back yet. I was right to come.*

As they broke out of the eco-tunnel entrance and into the meadow, Connor shielded his own face, too, dipping his chin until the raven's wing of his thick hair fell forward. Turning his head, he brushed his lips over Rebekah's forehead as she clutched at his neck. He frowned when an errant gust of air whipped his hair back, and a ray of sunshine broke through the early morning cloud cover. His skin tingled where the blood capillaries shrank in protest until, he buried his face deeper into Rebekah's hair.

Finally, Connor entered the woods and settled Rebekah into his chest, his speed easing from hair-raising to the soothing rhythm of a rocking cradle. When the stillness of the heavy air offered a blanket of warmth to Rebekah, he came to a careful halt.

Knowing Rebekah's legs would not yet support her, Connor lowered her gently onto the ground. His hands were reluctant to leave her skin, and it was hard to let his head rule his heart and smoothly retreat to a distance at which she would feel safe.

He ran his fingertips over the stinging skin on his brow, and, feeling the fretwork of hardened silvered-threads that glistened like veins in rose quartz, he grimaced. A warning shot. Physician, heal thyself, he thought ironically. *My next feed will repair the damage, but still...*

He shed his coat and gloves, not taking his eyes from Rebekah's face.

She settled on the soft bed of grass in their glade, hugging her knees and shooting nervous glances up at Connor, who stood a few yards away. He drew comfort from the blend of fear and sexual attraction in her scent, and the hormone-induced cardio workout pumping through her veins almost made him smile. *Will the feelings of apprehension and anticipation be familiar to her?* He hoped so.

Connor ran every opening line he composed through his head, but fear held him motionless. He could not yet let his relief swell into joy. *I've found her, but I don't have her back, yet.*

He knew his anger had terrified Douglas and he'd been blunt and callous. *But I came because she's* mine. My *Rebekah would know that. But, does this scared girl?*

Every time he moved, her head jerked, and she fastened her wide-eyed gaze on his feet as if he was a rattlesnake about to strike. And she wasn't far wrong. What he wanted to do was strip her bare and *make* her remember him, remember *them.*

It had been a long night. He wanted to be at the part where he could enfold her in his arms and love her, and make good on his promise to keep her safe. He knew it was only one of her agonizing heartbeats away. *But, how to get* her *to realize that? Where do I start?*

He plunged his hands through his hair, and when she flinched, he sighed. “Hey,” he called softly through the gloom, still ten feet away. “Do you remember me? Us? At all?”

Rebekah glanced up through damp lashes. Her thoughts were clearly written on her face, and Connor was encouraged by the conflict playing out across her features. Finally, she gave a half-hearted shrug.

“Okay, well, do you feel like you’ve been here before?”

A frown settled on her face, and she suddenly groaned.

Connor backed away. He saw the goosebumps on her skin, and the thought that her flesh crawled because of him, cut him open.

“It feels like I’ve been here before and it’s always cold.” She briskly rubbed her upper arms. “I just can’t remember it clearly.” She groaned again.

The wound closed a little as Connor laughed gently, and the scent of her frustration warmed his dead heart. *Frustration, now* that, *I can deal with.* “It is *me* that is always cold, and this is where we have been... together.”

Rebekah stared into space for a moment, and her skittering heartbeat gave him hope.

Connor stepped forward until diffused light illuminated his composed features. His body pretended relaxation as he resisted the urge to rush to her side.

“Hey,” he called again. “Do you trust me? Can I try something?”

She looked up, and he measured her start of surprise because he was a lot closer now, but she would not have seen him move. He locked onto her face, willing her to remember and to let him in.

Her voice was husky as she said, “Yes, you can try something.”

“Rebekah, close your eyes.”

She closed her eyes, and returned to hugging her knees tightly. She rested her chin on them, and, before her lashes had settled, his chilled breath fanned her cheek.

When his lips touched the corner of her mouth, he felt the rush of blood as her heart lurched, and he knew he was winning. The delicate scent he craved warmed from uncertainty to excitement. He moved to kiss the other corner.

"Hi, honey," he whispered.

"I *do* remember this." Her voice was heavy and thick, and as she sighed, his cool tongue tasted her.

More confident now, his fingers glided into her hair, and his lips tugged persuasively at hers, until she probed into his mouth and kissed him back.

Connor suffered the burn of her hot tongue. Her creamy scent stung his raw throat, and he loved it. He pushed himself deeper into revival sleep, gentling his touch, tightening the reins of control, and measuring every movement.

Settling beside her, he tentatively rolled her back onto the grass, and looked down into her flushed face. The moist cantering of her excited heart delighted him.

"Not feeling scared?" he asked, but he knew the answer. He knew her body better than she did.

"You smell like citrus." The words tumbled out as she stared into his face. A blush stained her cheeks, and her lashes quickly veiled the worried spark captured by the dim light. *Embarrassment is good.*

He reached out and tilted her chin so she could not hide from him, and chuckled. "You smell like a cocktail of all the human scents I hunger for, like a drug that melts my brain and rips me apart every time I look at you."

"Oh," she said. The stunned expression in her brown eyes sharpened with curiosity as her palms framed his face.

He stayed still while her hands rediscovered the rough velvet of his cheekbones, his jaw, and the contours of his mouth, and then she gripped his hair. "Connor," she whispered.

"Ah, you *do* remember." He growled with gentle satisfaction.

Resting on one elbow, he lay his palm on her hot cheek and persisted, "And Douglas? Do you feel that you are his?" He suppressed the disgust rearing inside him. "Or mine?"

"Yours," she whispered. "Connor, love me."

With a harsh sigh, he did what he had ached to do since he first saw her standing in the cavern. He moved down her body and, starting at the hem, he tore away the white dress.

Distaste curled his lip as, stroking the fabric aside, Connor revealed the triangle of scanty white lace panties.

Rebekah's cheeks burned and her hands moved to shield her body.

Regret flooded his gaze at her mortified expression. Stroking his hand down over her quivering belly, he nudged her hands aside and rested his hand at her groin. "No. Honey, you are beautiful, it was just the thought of *him* dressing you in this."

His throat worked to swallow as he twisted his fingers into the thin lace fabric and tore it away. Kissing her tummy, the flush of her excitement burned his lips and he smiled. "Better," he murmured.

Continuing up her trembling body, he trailed his fingertips up between her breasts.

Goosebumps sprinkled over her skin, and a shuddering sigh moved through her.

"Can I touch you?" he asked in whispered reverence.

She nodded, and he dipped his head, his lips plucking at each tight pink bud of her flushed breasts until she buried her hands in his hair. He drew one sweet tip into his mouth at last, and his fingers teased in a seductive rhythm until she pushed her other breast into his hand.

"Connor..." she sighed.

His tongue ran up her throat and he claimed her mouth in a soft kiss, resting his solid bulk carefully over her. Bracing his weight in a protective frame, he still gave her free will as her flushed skin infused him with the radiating warmth of her longing.

Every muscle in his body froze and he lost himself in her heat.

"Let me in, Rebekah," he said gently, pleading for her final surrender. "Please."

She explored the contours of his hard shoulders, her hands traveling down over the planes of his back, until finally, she reveled in the tight muscles of his buttocks.

A grumble rattled in his throat as she parted her thighs and his aroused body stroked into her slick heat.

On a quiet groan, he sank inside her, driving her breath in his wake. She wrapped her limbs around him, and he moved, a sensual rhythm stirring the lava flow of need inside her. His chest ached in a spasm of ecstasy as her scent filtered into his lungs.

Connor fought the one-hundred-year weight of the demons enticing him to tear holes in her flesh. He drowned in her growing excitement. He wanted to feel the furnace building inside her until his stone cold tissue glowed red, in his mind at least, before he left her. His own release burned like coal embers in his lap, tugging his velvet sheath tight, but he wanted to stay a little longer.

“Forgive me,” he whispered.

Rebekah gasped as he sank his teeth into the swell of her breast. Her flesh yielded. His jaws closed, massaging firmly until the craving inside him gentled its grip to an entrancing caress. Finally, taking a long hard draught of blood drenched in the rapture rushing through her, he lifted his head and reluctantly eased his body away before he lost control.

She gripped his biceps in frustration, and he murmured against her throat, “I’ve got you, honey, it’s okay.”

His fingertips found the sweet spot inside her. His hand on her hip stopped her escaping his persuasive touch as he drove her over the edge. He drowned in her whimpering cries when a climax rippled through her and a tide of spasms gripped his fingers.

Tenderness overwhelmed him. He held her trembling body against his and lost himself in the glittering shower of sparks which lit up her senses. Cradling her gently, molding her to his hard muscular frame, he arrived at the moment where he felt whole again. He enfolded her in his arms and kept her safe.

A long time later, he stroked his tongue along the bite wound marking her breast. “I’m sorry, I couldn’t help myself,” he murmured. Grinning sheepishly, he breathed through the soothing kiss he pressed to her flesh. “Vampires have needs too.”

“Connor, why can’t you stay, until the end?” she whispered, her tone heavy with regret.

He sighed. He knew she would ask. *But not now, not when I’ve only just got her back.* “I’m sorry honey, I won’t take the risk. I don't know what would happen, but one thing I *do* know is that I *can* father a child, in theory."

Rebekah looked at him in surprise. "Vampires, really?"

"Yes. Really." Laughter rumbled inside his chest. "I know you think of us as the walking dead, but, it is more accurate to say we are suspended in time. Blood hydrates us, and that applies to all our fluids." Connor lowered his chin to give her a hungry glance. "Believe me, if I could stay…"

He didn't tell her of his personal fear, that his icy chill could damage her soft, warm tissue. *None of us know.*

Rebekah's smile warmed her brown gaze. "All *I* know is this feels right. It is everything I should have felt standing next to Douglas-" Sudden realization hit home and she whispered, "Oh God. Connor, I'm married. What am I going to do?"

He rose up onto his elbow. "He won't touch you," he said softly. "I can't change what happened, but Rebekah-" Connor held her gaze. "You were *drugged*. You've not given him your body or your heart, and I'll tear his throat out if he tries anything." He shrugged. "You're not married in any way that counts."

His cool finger followed the curve of her cheek, and then trailed over the bite that marked her as his. "In every way that matters, you are mine." Connor looked up through thick lashes. "I could always remove him," he murmured, dressing it up with a playful growl which was a little too convincing.

"No." Rebekah quickly shook her head. "I hate him, but I won't have *that* on my conscience." A frown tugged her brows hard together. "He's not going to ruin this, us, and by not even being here. So, no. He *stays*, and I deal with it."

"You are far too good for me. I was thinking Douglas for breakfast, maybe Harry for dinner, and you, as dessert." Relief filled him as Rebekah thumped his chest and chuckled. *Can a vampire swell with happiness I wonder?* Connor began to think so.

Chapter 17

Connor and Rebekah could not stay in the dappled shade of their haven, suspended between worlds, forever. Finally, the day faded and afternoon lost the battle with the cold of an early dusk, and the time came to redefine their own reality.

As they walked across the grass, approaching the eco-town hand-in-hand, Connor glanced up at the clusters of dark gray clouds, and mused, “You know, there are barely seven hours of daylight to bother us on a winter’s day in England, it’s a vampire’s dream location.” As he took in Rebekah’s distracting, gentle smile, he added, “*My* dream location.”

Reluctant moments later, they slipped behind the heavy sackcloth curtain. The chilled atmosphere of the eco-town tunnels was warm to Connor. The naked flames lighting the way sprinkled hot spots over his skin while they walked in silence. *The pace of human-slow is a challenge I hope to meet often.* The torch light warmed his smile with an amber glow. *After all, there are only so many times a guy can whisk a girl off her feet.*

Even without Rebekah’s grip tightening on his hand, Connor sensed her apprehension. Her delicate features wore a pinched expression.

So beautiful, was all he could think.

He projected a soothing aura. Nothing scared him. His war-torn past existence meant he met adversity head on. *Douglas is weak, so, of course, I will win. The only question is, how long will I allow him to pollute Rebekah’s life?*

He squeezed her hand carefully, but still she winced. “Sorry,” he said. “Deep breaths, Rebekah, you’re distracting me.”

They entered the meeting cavern together. When Connor appeared, he estimated that it took two seconds for the twelve human heartbeats to accelerate from a stroll to a stampede. They clattered through his chest like runaway horses and made him salivate. *Grave sleep, my next priority.* He acknowledged the craving which lodged in his gullet like a hot stone. He wanted to begin with the fastest heartbeat, flood it with venom and savor the dying tempo until the blood thickened to syrup and coated his mouth. *Yep, I definitely need grave sleep.*

"Where's Douglas?" asked Connor, his tone vibrating through the cavern. He searched the fear-frozen faces and finally settled on Uncle Harry.

"I won't bite, I promise." A far from reassuring wolfish grin spread across his face.

"Behave," Rebekah mumbled, but his amusing quip had relaxed the cramped feeling in her stomach.

Connor caught her eye. "Better," he mouthed.

He had achieved his aim, portraying this confrontation as pure theater in which everyone has a part to play. *But, I have the final say in what gets cut from the script, and in my version, Dracula comes out on top.* With a fleeting fake frown, he curled his lip in a sneer, expressing the satire inside his head. "Rebekah, I'm a vampire, there is *no* contest."

Rebekah's own lip twitched, in spite of herself. However, the others in the cavern failed to get the joke. Their racing heart rates scratched harder at Connor's throat.

Let's get this done. "Douglas?" Upon hearing shoe leather scuffing the packed earth floor of the tunnel beyond, Connor said, "Ah, Douglas, you made it."

Making his entrance, Douglas sought out Rebekah, studiously dismissing all others.

Connor suppressed a leer. *Ignoring sharks when you're in at the deep end is never a good idea.*

"I'm sorry, Rebekah." Douglas looked into her face, his own reddened and regretful.

Bravo. Connor could smell Douglas' deception as if it were grease paint. Fear had an odor, and so did his oily malice. "I see you've decided to be reasonable," said Connor.

When Douglas finally glanced Connor's way, resentment and defiance flickered in his expression before the apologetic countenance slotted firmly back into place.

Connor's gray stare probed, and Douglas shuffled beneath its weight. *Incredible. He still thinks he can win.*

"Just so we are clear. Rebekah is home." Connor did his own piece of acting, smiling at Douglas. "But my claim still holds, and if *you* wish to continue living… here, you will honor it." Connor lifted Rebekah's hand and placed a deliberate kiss on the back of her fingers, still holding Douglas' gaze intently.

The pause after '*living*' sprouted sweat over Douglas' skin, and his hands folded into fists, unnoticed by all except Connor, who missed nothing. *Still defiant, unbelievable.*

"I shall visit, of course, and Rebekah will remain unharmed. Oh, and Douglas-" He paused to bore his meaning like a pile-driver deep into Douglas' brain. "You don't want to see me angry." Connor's tightened lips bared teeth which dripped with venom until he collected it with his tongue.

Douglas swallowed loudly, and hunger purred in Connor's throat. *Tempting though it is to end this, I need grave sleep. If I taste his blood now, I will not stop at one.*

The hush in the cavern was eerie, except to Connor who was tuned in to the thundering pulse rates gnawing at his concentration. *Human emotion is such an exciting array of scents and flavors.* It was ironic that vampires preferred their blood petrified. Historically, humans took care to humanely slaughter cattle because the adrenalin released if they were panicked ruined the delicate flavor of the meat. *Odd then that humans, once turned, like the blood to be pumped with adrenalin. Delicate is not something we yearn for as vampires.*

Connor focused on Douglas, who, although his alarm had risen to a satisfying level, still stank of determination. "I trust we understand one another, hmm?" Connor waited, and knew that whatever his reply, Douglas was still on the hunt.

"I guess I have no choice since our marriage was unconsummated." Douglas left the thought hanging and Connor's hackles rose.

"That's settled then."

Connor would have taken her away with him at once, but he judged he had about five minutes to find containment before his brain hit the survival button and shut down coherent thought. Connor himself was the biggest danger right now.

Drawing Rebekah with him into the tunnel outside the meeting cavern, Connor said softly, “I have to go. I need to rehydrate, to sleep. I’ll be in the vampire cave. Warn Harry that no one must go there until I return.” The words needed no further explanation. “And Rebekah, stay away from Douglas. I’m sorry, honey, but he has not given up.” Connor settled his hands onto Rebekah’s shoulders and gained her full attention. “Unless you have changed your mind? I can take him with me now. I would make it quick.”

A grumble rattled in his throat as shaking her head, she said, “I can’t, you can’t.”

“I know.” He released her, and with a sudden gust of air, she was left alone with his disgruntled words still hanging on the breeze.

Connor found his way down into the bowels of the eco-town and easily located the roughly hewn passageway leading to the entrance to the vampire cave. He took a moment to marvel again at what passed for the human concept of a trap.

This time, Connor pushed the lever, which moved with just a nudge of his hand. It activated the spring mechanism, propelling the boulder into lightning fast action to the human eye, and he went inside. Stepping over the rails which guided the huge rock, he waited for it to lumber, like a great gray elephant, into vampire view. Connor almost laughed aloud. As he had told Rebekah, twenty vampires, at least, could have escaped before the boulder settled into place.

As a trap, it was ridiculous, but it would serve Connor’s purpose. He would vary the depth of his sleep. In shallow grave sleep refreshment would take longer, but going deeper would release the sleepwalker and a boulder would not contain him.

He automatically laid out on the ground, the social vampire code as ingrained as any human habit. The white-hot blast of bloodlust raged through his tissue and the tight shrunken canvas of his skin carved a macabre smile into his features. His ribcage flexed as his body hunted for the blood in his stomach, the way human lungs hunt for oxygen when holding a breath beyond the limit that the body enjoys. Waves rolling onto a beach of splintered glass dashed pinpricks of pain over his skin.

Connor knew he had neglected his grave sleep control center for far too long. *How old am I? I fall in love, and half my brain cells appear to have died, or, at least, be so preoccupied with Rebekah that they are going to be the death of the rest of me.*

Connor's grin reflected sheer pleasure. The feeling of joy swelling inside took him back to his twenty-first human year, when holding a girl's hand without her chaperone seeing it, rampaged blood through his body to places which were definitely new and exciting. And back to when easing the fit of his pants around his flooded groin had made him feel like a man.

Thankfully, he had his draft of Rebekah's blood to draw upon, and a little of that would go a long way. With no airway to protect, ingested blood coated his lungs and stomach, which was a short hop away from every muscle and sinew in need of sustenance. But, more importantly, a step away from the express route up the carotid artery into his brain.

Akin to fire sizzling along the veins, the process was painful in the extreme, although, Connor projected calm. His resting hands lay linked over his stomach as if he were truly asleep. *If I had delayed a moment more, there may not have been a human colony; I could have dispatched them all in less than a minute.*

He closed his eyes and suffered; rehydration had its own rhythm. When his brain was refreshed he would feel a euphoric rush of energy, at which point, he would remove the boulder with little more effort required than pushing a child on a swing.

When the rush finally occurred, and his eyes snapped open, his body clock told him he had slept almost two hours, longer than his normal refreshment time. He rolled up to a sitting position, stretched to mobilize his lubricated tissue, and then, pressing his fingertips into his jugular arteries, he massaged along the length of his neck until swallowing no longer hurt.

His mind drifted briefly to Vampire Jack, or "Jack the Ripper" as humans knew him the first time around. When *he* delayed grave sleep beyond reason, the blood rush had dissolved his sanity.

The hungry synapses of Jack's brain had been drenched in a sudden surge of blood which compressed his spinal cord. Messages were barely detectable above the brainstem, with the frontal lobe and cerebral cortex no longer registering a personality. Jack had descended into vampire dementia, where the craving for blood became so overwhelming, he was compelled to eat the indigestible flesh. *At least he escaped The Butcher's fate. Even Julian considered Jack's suffering too great to perpetuate. I guess he was the first 'feral'.*

A grim smile settled on Connor's face as he sprang to his feet. *If I* had *lost it, there is a banquet waiting just the other side of that boulder.* "Much too close for comfort," Connor murmured. He had never had a closer call than the one today.

While the air in the tunnels still eddied in Connor's wake, Rebekah digested his words. Douglas' determination was not a shocking revelation. She had sensed it too. She briskly rubbed the goosebumps from her arms. *Douglas mustn't find out Connor is asleep. And for how long, I wonder?* "Dammit," Rebekah muttered, wanting to concentrate on his return. *I'm getting the hang of the vampire sleep thing, but knowing how long would be good, especially now.* She had learned from Connor, that to be gentle, he took revival sleep. *So, grave sleep must turn them into killers.*

"Okay, stay away from Douglas, that's all I have to do." *How hard can that be?* She automatically checked her watch, although it had little meaning. *I'm going crazy.* She went in search of Uncle Harry to deliver Connor's warning.

Rebekah sighed her relief when she found Uncle Harry alone in the meeting cavern. When he caught sight of her, he rushed forward and gathered her hands in his.

His sorrow was clear on his face, and his guilt descended into an outpouring that chilled her.

"He's not so bad. I'm sure he's sorry, too. He hates himself," Harry muttered, almost as though trying to convince himself.

A bitter weight settled in her chest. The 'absentminded professor' Uncle Harry was like an autistic child; reading people was beyond him. Rebekah sighed. *I can't do this today.*

"Uncle Harry, listen," she cut in gently.

Harry's mouth hung open in mid-sentence for far longer than was comfortable.

A warning shot of an impending migraine darted across Rebekah's vision, teasing her with dancing lights and hinting at the slice of pain she would suffer later.

"No one must go to the storage caverns. Not until Connor returns," she said quietly.

"Storage caverns?" Harry formed the words as if he had never heard them before.

"Douglas' cave in particular. Connor is resting, and no one must go there," she said, seeking eye contact and his understanding, and not certain that she achieved it. Nevertheless, she turned to go and make her getaway. *So close.*

She had not seen Douglas arrive, but she felt the cold discomfort of his eyes dragging across her skin. Without looking around, she crossed the meeting cavern and tried to slip away.

"Rebekah, please stay." Douglas oozed regret.

Her stomach rolled with greasy sickness at his approach, but she stopped, not sure what else to do.

"I *am* sorry. The wedding. God, please forgive me." His eyes skittered over her face. "I don't know what came over me. Really, I'm sorry."

Rebekah glanced anxiously at Harry, and his stooped posture and pleading look motivated her to stay. "Let's just move on. It's over, so let's forget it." She pushed the words through a dry throat and couldn't suppress the cringe when Douglas placed his hand on her arm.

When she shrank away, anger flashed in his eyes before he could arrange a thankful smile on his face. "So, no hard feelings?"

"Of course not," she said quietly. She slipped smoothly from his grasp, resisting the urge to snatch, and turned to go.

Leaving the meeting cavern behind did not bring the relief she expected. Rebekah's deep breathing kept time with her measured footfalls. It was not as effective as a paper bag, but it stopped the panic from running away inside her. Surging forward around the last bend in the tunnel, she entered her den, crossed quickly to the bed and sat down heavily. Toppling back, she stared at the roughly-tiled domed ceiling.

This was her own space. Rolling onto her side, her fingers closed on the scrap of Connor's shirt she kept hidden under her pillow, and she lay still, controlling the thunder that rocked her chest. *I'm scared. Douglas is dangerous, but surely he's not stupid.* Dread made her shrivel inside. Reaching down to the floor beside the bed, she grabbed hold of the smooth rock she kept close by and hugged it to her chest. "Connor, come back soon. Come back soon. Come back soon..." The mantra continued on in her head as she pressed her face into the citrus-scented fabric.

How long she lay there she had no idea, but it seemed an eternity. Then she heard footsteps and her breathing stopped. Connor, she thought, but she knew it was too soon.

Douglas sauntered into view, his broad shoulders filling the doorway as he leaned there. "Just talking to Harry." He grinned. "The vampire cave came in handy, then?"

Rebekah thought of Connor sleeping, and determination stiffened her resolve; she was not going to let Douglas win. *I'll die first.*

Swinging her legs over the side of the bed, she rolled smoothly to her feet and balanced her weight, clenching a white-knuckle grip on the stone she held behind her back.

"Get out," she spat.

Douglas pushed himself upright and moved forward, his eyes alight with malice and lust. "You can still change your mind, have a real man instead of a block of ice," he sneered, his voice hoarse with excitement. "If you're giving it away, then I think I'm entitled to a free sample." He sauntered closer.

Backing away, Rebekah drew him in and prepared to fight as, for the first time in her life, the acidic bile of hatred swilled in her gullet. Sweat seeped into her cotton shirt, and the damp fabric snatched at her skin as she shifted her shoulders, squaring up to Douglas. *C'mon, you bastard.*

"You know you owe me." Douglas was no longer grinning. "You made me look like a fool."

His expression slipped away to slack-mouthed arousal, and Rebekah's stomach filled with scuttling spiders again. Memories of his clammy hands, their spiteful grip, and the stink of his sweat stained her thoughts. *No way are you touching me, today.*

Without warning, she lunged forward, grunting as she swung her arm up in the flowing arc of a discus throw. Following through with all her bodyweight, she cracked the stone against the side of his head. The sickening thud juddered through her bones, and satisfaction spiked inside her as blood oozed from the graze on his temple.

Off balance, Douglas threw up an arm. Too late to ward off the blow, but his hand shot out and closed tightly around her wrist.

"You bitch!"

Rebekah screamed as his twisting grip shot pain up her arm and the stone fell onto the floor.

Anger galvanized him and he yanked her forward. She collided with the solid wall of his wide chest, and his arms pinned her tight. Rebekah's hackles rose. Disgust swallowed her breath as his wet mouth sucked at her face. Frantically shaking her head, avoiding his pressing tongue, she leaned away, struggling blindly. The terrifying heat of desperation swamped her as she tore an arm free of his smothering hold and slapped his face, hard.

His grip slackened for a moment, and she ripped away from his scrabbling grasp.

His bellowing rage rang around her den as Rebekah turned to face him again.

She fastened her eyes onto his face and backed away, pressing up against the wall. Her heartbeat pounded inside her head and scrambled her reflexes, and suddenly her arms felt like cast iron weights which would not move.

Douglas swayed in front of her, and the exit disappeared behind his terrifying bulk as he advanced with outstretched arms, hissing angrily between his teeth.

"You owe me, bitch," he said.

Choking on the fear inside her chest, with a strangled cry, she doubled over and drove forward. Ducking left as Douglas dived right, hope flared inside when her shoulder grazed past him, but his hand darted out and gripped her upper arm. He swung her in an arc, throwing her backwards into the wall. The impact knocked the breath from her lungs and cracked her head on the uneven tiles.

She sprawled there for a moment with her head shrieking, and Douglas pounced. His weight crushed her and an explosion of pain shot across her vision as the hard tiles bit into her shoulder blades. He grabbed at her hip, digging clawed fingers into her flesh. Groping her body, he tugged viciously at her shirt.

She gagged in desperation, crying out in pain when his clammy hand closed over her breast, squeezing hard. His mouth soaked her neck. He tightened his fist into her hair, yanked her chin up, and shoved his knee hard into her groin.

He pressed his face into hers as he said, "You like it rough. I saw the bruises."

Rebekah's mouth filled with bile and his panting breath fanned a cold breeze over the spittle soaking her neck. "No, no, no." Her voice cracked as panic gripped her throat. The roots of her hair screamed when she tried to pull her face away from his sweat-oozing pores and dripping saliva. She was drowning in him. Her scrabbling brain gave up on thinking and she thrashed wildly. *Just keep moving, keep moving. But, he's too close.* The heels of her hands kept slipping and she couldn't push him away.

His body smothered hers in moist heat and her lungs burned with stale air as terror locked it inside.

Douglas shoved an arm roughly around her waist, and the ground disappeared as he hoisted her into his chest. He grunted, stumbling forward. Her legs spun out of control, kicking out uselessly as she landed on her back on the bed. He pushed his leg in between her knees and pulled roughly at her pants. His weight cantered over her skin as he shifted onto knees and elbows and tore at her clothes. His body was heavy on top of her as he panted, his knuckles bruising her thighs when he fumbled with his fly.

"You ready for this." His breathing rasped in his throat.

Oh God. NO!

As her brain flooded with black clouds and she choked on terror, he disappeared.

A sudden breeze covered her in goosebumps as she gulped in fresh air and her lungs burned. A moment of shocked stillness was crushed by the desire to curl up and die. She pulled her shirt front together, drew up her knees, and rolled over onto her side, groaning.

'Oh God, oh God, oh God' rotated around inside her reeling mind. She curled into a ball and started rocking. The perpetual motion kept her thoughts from settling, and kept her from feeling the stinging abrasions left on her body.

Douglas found himself sucked into a time warp tunnel which whisked him through the air. The cold wind biting into his chest like a bed of nails took his open-mouthed scream and shoved it back down into his throat.

He came to an abrupt halt, and was spun around on his heel so quickly that the cavern walls kept turning. When the spinning sensation stopped, he was pinned against the roughly-hewn, stone-encrusted wall inside the sealed vampire cave.

Douglas stared into a chalk-white mask of fury, and choked on his own terror.

"Okay, you've got my attention, Douglas, you prick," Connor snarled. He could smell the musk of arousal still oozing from Douglas' pores, and, for the first time in his memory, he wanted to murder. *Not kill. Not feed. I want to murder the bastard.*

He sneered into Douglas' face from two inches away, clamped his hand onto the man's stiffened groin, and twisted. "I could snap this off and ram it down your throat," he growled. "You hurt her, you runt, and now, I'm going to kill you." Picturing Douglas' rapidly shrinking manhood mottling to purple plum under his vise-like grip gave Connor grim satisfaction. *Easy, just a little, enough to make him pee sitting down for a month. I'll see how I feel about snapping it off then.*

The image of Douglas' body crushing Rebekah, his neck red with lust and the musky stench of his depravity thick in the air, sizzled through Connor's brain. He stood on a cliff edge where blind fury demanded he step over into the abyss. *But, I can kill Douglas later in cold blood, and enjoy it more.*

Bracketing Douglas' jaw, Connor's hand applied inexorable pressure, tilting his head over to one side and exposing the artery pumping in his neck. "Better start praying," he muttered, as a purr rumbled through his throat.

Connor grinned as the sting of uric acid hit his sinuses long before Douglas knew he was about to wet himself. He closed his eyes and savored the moment as he bit down hard into Douglas' neck, drew out one mouthful of his terrified blood, and spat it out onto the floor in an explosion of disgust.

As always, Rebekah mattered more. Her breathless lungs, and her heart pushing adrenalin so hard that fibrillation seemed only a beat away, left him terrified he would lose her. Returning to her now was a compulsion he could not resist.

Connor moved to the door, releasing Douglas so fast that he staggered backward and crunched into the wall again. His outburst of expletives died on his lips as his pants soaked up the urine rushing down his leg.

Wrinkling his nose, Connor said, "You disgusting pig."

Flattening his palm over the rough pitted surface of the gray boulder still sealing the exit, Connor looked back over his shoulder. "You may never see daylight again, Douglas." He clenched his fingers and scored deep grooves into the rock face, enjoying Douglas' terror as an unnerving clatter of graveled debris hit the ground.

Suddenly, Douglas found himself alone inside the cave with the boulder firmly back in place.

◇◇◇

Connor paused at the doorway of Rebekah's cave. She still lay on the bed, curled up now as though hanging onto the throbbing of her tortured flesh. He could smell the bruising and the muscle in his jaw ticked as he fought to remain calm. She kept rocking until the chill of Connor's velvet-textured skin brushed against her back and molded to her thighs. "I've got you, honey," he whispered. His arm slipped around her waist and he hitched her closer into his body. "I've got you."

A sob caught in her swollen throat as she released the knot of tension inside and relaxed against him.

"I'm sorry. He won't touch you again, I swear it." Connor shifted up onto one elbow and turned her face to his.

Her eyes remained tightly closed. "I was so scared the nightmare would swallow me up."

Connor stroked her hair back from her face. "Rebekah, look at me."

Raising her damp lashes, the sunshine of his face released her, and then she gasped, reaching out and brushing her fingertips over Connor's lips. He passed his tongue over them, and when blood coated it, he spat it out. Connor doubted he would enjoy the taste of Douglas' blood, even if his own life depended upon it. He realized how it must look to her, and he shook his head. "No, he's still alive, unless I change my mind."

He scrubbed at his mouth with his shirt cuff until it was clean, and his eyes traveled down her body this time, hissing in a breath when he noticed the fist clutching her torn shirt front together. He rolled her onto her back and gently released her grip. Angry gouge marks framed her breast, and her face was red where Douglas' stubble had scraped over her skin.

"I've just changed my mind," he said darkly.

Rebekah gripped his arm urgently. "Connor, please, don't go, just hold me."

Connor sighed, his icy breath a soothing balm as he bent to kiss the marks on her breast, and then moved on to her grazed chin, cheeks, and swollen eyelids. “I’m not going anywhere.” He sank down onto his back, hugged her into his chest, and pulled her thigh over his stomach. Holding her close, he rocked her until she drifted off to sleep.

Connor wrestled his demons into submission and concentrated on finding a solution which would make Rebekah safe, truly safe.

During the hours she slept, he turned every conceived scenario over in his mind. As he inspected each one for flaws, in too many cases, like fossilized insects in amber, he found a fly in the ointment. *Or more specifically, a dough boy in the vampire cave, or a lizard on the council.*

Serge won’t let things lie. I’ll push Harry into moving the eco-town to a new location. And, who knows, maybe Douglas will get lost in the woods along the way. Connor grinned and allowed his mouth to fill with venom. A little wish-fulfilment painted a scene in which Douglas’ soft flesh was a mottled purple mass, and a certain appendage resided inside his stomach. The purr of satisfaction that vibrated Connor’s ribcage gently massaged his heart, and, for a moment, he almost felt alive.

Rebekah’s breathing, deep and still catching, tore at him. It seemed the only thing he was good at was letting her down. He felt in control and fearless in everything, except her. *If anything ever happens to her, I will gladly walk into the sunlight, burn, and die.*

While Connor waited for the shock of his sudden arrival to wear off, he scanned the weighty volumes of the chemistry, physics and biological engineering textbooks covering one wall of Harry’s personal cavern. He arranged a half-smile of apology on his face, aimed at calming Harry’s hyperventilating breathing, and reducing the older man’s heart rate before he passed out.

Harry had leapt up from his wing-backed armchair when Connor materialized in front of him.

Connor retreated to lean against the unfurnished wall of Harry’s cave, resisting the urge to unleash his impatience and dig his fingertips into the rocks that lined it. The purpose of the visit was to put phase one of his plan into action, and Connor hoped he could make good on the promises he was about to make. *Keeping my hands off Douglas showed restraint, and should gain Harry's trust.*

Connor watched Harry closely, feeling like a rattlesnake reassuring a mouse.

News of Stan's violent death had rattled the community, and even Connor felt it. He had not yet met Greg again, but it was clear Connor was adding to a burden Harry already found heavy. *It's a pity it was not Douglas who died at the feral's hand.*

"Harry." Connor sighed as the man started and fell back a pace. Patiently he tried again, "Harry, I know my presence is alarming, but I'm here to protect Rebekah. Do you understand that?"

Harry stared, and just when Connor was wondering if the man was comatose, he whispered, "You brought her back."

Connor's lip curled as he said, "Douglas is still alive as a show of good faith. I'm not a monster, I leave that to others, and I'm sorry you lost a man out there."

"Thank you." Harry swallowed loudly, and continued on a stronger voice, "And, I know you saved Rebekah from Douglas, something I should have done a long time ago. I thank you for that, too."

Connor nodded. They both knew Harry had much more to feel guilty about, and Connor wondered at the naiveté of a brilliant mind. Harry had been easy prey for a sociopath like Douglas to manipulate.

For Rebekah's sake, Connor buried the recriminations boiling inside him, inclined his head, and spoke slowly. "You, *all* of you, are no longer safe here. Rebekah attracted more interest than just mine. You will be discovered if you stay."

Harry's alarm was tempered by calculation. "We have survived this long, and we always knew this day might come. We know what we must do, we'll move out." Harry's chin rose. "Thank you for the warning, but we don't need your help. You told Greg you've killed the *monster*. We can look after ourselves."

Although Connor was impressed, his slate eyes were dull as he said, "You have no idea what you are up against. Make no mistake,

Harry, where Rebekah is concerned, my *help* is non-negotiable." Connor's menace thickened the air. "Now, all I need from you is your promise to keep Rebekah safe until I return."

Harry had the grace to look shamefaced as he croaked his agreement.

"There are things you need to know for your own protection." Connor took a measured breath. "Vampires *do* sleep."

Harry met Connor's eyes as curiosity got the better of him, "But not in coffins?"

Connor laughed softly. "Sometimes, yes."

Harry's surprise was tainted by satisfaction. "I knew it," he whispered.

"Not as you think, however. Imagine having three identities caged inside your head. When we take grave sleep, a door in our brain is unlocked, and we *are* mindless killers for a short time. Not ferals, but still dangerous," Connor said, marring his face for a moment with a manufactured fierce expression. "Now that we are no longer in hiding, we have other options. Cadaver drawers, abattoir cold stores, and bank vaults are all suitable places. Prisons."

"Grave sleep?" Harry frowned.

"Sleeping in coffins was just a joke that stuck. But, make no mistake, think of us as Jekyll and Hyde, and you will be close to the mark," said Connor earnestly. "Trust me, Harry, when you move out, you will need my help."

Harry nodded slowly as he digested this unexpected revelation.

"You will need to have enough beta-blockers and pheromone suppressant spray prepared for the entire group. Tell me what you need from the hospital, and consider it done," Connor said, leaving no room for argument. "You may be moving out faster than you think."

Harry's over-awed expression melted quickly to concentration as he seemed to flick on the professor switch inside his head. Seeking refuge in the familiar, he recounted quickly the list of pharmaceutical substances which appeared to be etched into his brain.

◇◇◇

Lying in bed beneath a heavy blanket, for a moment, the feeling of being unable to move overwhelmed Rebekah. But then, the hot, doughy flesh of Douglas was overlaid with the relief of Connor. She took a deep breath, savoring the delicious citrus scented aroma of Connor which still hung in the air inside the intimate space of her den, even though he had gone to see Harry. She opened her eyes, watching the drifting motes of dust dancing in a shaft of light.

Easing her stiff limbs, the bruising did not shriek as loudly as she expected. At moments during the night, Connor had rendered first aid in his own inimitable fashion. In the twilight world where waking thoughts tugged at slumber's blanket, the weight of his cold palms gently infused her angered flesh with the chill of his soothing touch.

The dappled light of dawn picking out her treasured possessions reassured her, and she found a cheerful note. This was *her* place, but, her little den now had a new significance. *Now, it is mine and Connor's.* The full gambit of emotions, from fear through to happiness, from despair through to hope, had rampaged through her over the last week. *But, the early hours of this morning fell into the happiness and hope category, for sure.*

"You're awake." Connor appeared from nowhere, wearing a self-deprecating grin, but the light in his eyes was euphoric. At least, so it seemed to Rebekah as his gaze stroked over her skin and chased prickled heat in its wake.

Being lost in watching him settled the smile of a simpleton on her face as he joined her in the bed.

"Hey, earth to Rebekah." Connor glowered, and that was entrancing too.

"Did you scare Uncle Harry?" Rebekah asked, meeting Connor's gaze at last.

"Only a little," he replied. "As always, I left London in a hurry. I have to catch up with Julian, and find out what Serge is up to."

"Is Serge still on your tail?"

Connor laughed. "He will always be on my tail. He digs, and gets frustrated when he comes up empty. He thinks your name is Annabelle, and that's as close as I want him to get. I won't underestimate him."

"Annabelle?"

"I had to give him something when he saw you at the hospital."

"I'm sorry." She stroked her fingers down over his strong jaw. "I am a nuisance to you, I know."

"Never that, honey. But for now, do you think you can stay out of trouble until I get back?" His locked gaze, granite gray in the dim light, was serious. But his fingers flirted with her skin and his lips softened with the distraction. "Say, yes Connor-"

'And I can make love to you'. Her memory supplied the punch-line. "Yes, Connor," she breathed, as Connor finally erased the remnants of Douglas' touch and laid a trail of delight through her senses. That was her last crystalline thought until Connor reluctantly stirred her from the blissful state of afterglow with a languorous kiss.

"I have to go, honey."

He slipped from the bed, his hard muscles moving beneath perfect skin as he dressed with smooth grace. Fully clothed, he leant over to kiss her again, saying with a rueful chuckle, "I've never liked playing Russian roulette. We must get a cover for that window funnel."

Left alone, Rebekah leaned up on one elbow and focused again on the fairy dust drifting lazily in weak sunlight. She leaned over the side of the bed to measure the lighter patch cut into the shadow on the floor. It was only a defused square foot. *But enough to make a vampire nervous, I'll get Oscar to fit a blind.*

Swinging her legs over the edge of the bed, Rebekah winced. "Stiff thighs. That's not really a surprise," she murmured with a smile, rolling back onto her side and nuzzling the scrap of citrus-scented fabric, a talisman that would bring Connor back to her.

Chapter 18

Continuing the search for Julian, Connor left the council buildings, and stepped down onto the sidewalk. Puddles of rainwater soaked the bottom three inches of his pants. The driving rain plastered his shirt to his chest as he eased into a run that took him along the north side of Hyde Park, heading towards Hammersmith and on to Kew Bridge. The eight-mile-long route to Julian's West London Richmond home was locked into Connor's autopilot, so he spent the journey cursing Julian's love of relaxing walks in Kew gardens.

"The man's a vampire, has no one told him that flowers look better in sunshine? And greenhouses are bad for his health?" muttered Connor as he rounded the last bend, vaulted the hedge bordering Julian's Edwardian property, and disappeared around the side of the house.

Connor arrived in a drop of air pressure and a gust of rain that soaked the carpet in Julian's study.

Julian glanced around, unfazed at the window bursting open. He remained standing with an elbow resting on the mantelpiece, and a thumb hitched in his belt loop, and waited. He had changed from his tailored principal's garb into a casual coffee-colored shirt, but he still exuded authority.

The rain-peppered wind whipped the curtains into frenzy as Connor swung his legs around in to the room, and said curtly, "Julian."

He watched Connor refasten the study window, took in his disheveled state, and said "I was going to say, gone are the days when vampires are reduced to entering through the window." Julian cocked his head to one side. "But, I guess it remains the most direct route when you're in a hurry."

He drew the heavy brocade curtains, muting the howling wind outside to a rumbling growl. All that was missing from the room's cozy atmosphere was the roaring fire which hadn't burned in the hearth for fifteen years, and it would never occur to Julian to light it.

Connor was drenched, but he didn't care. The cotton fabric of his pants and shirt creaked as his muscles rippled in dynamic movement, and his hair, sapphire filaments trapped within coal-black strands, dripped down his neck.

Cutting to the chase, Julian asked, "Is Douglas still alive?"

Connor nodded abruptly and continued pacing, his nostrils flaring with the air he bellowed in and out, and tight muscles propelled him around the room at a speed which was sure to irritate.

It was not a huge leap for Julian to make. "And how *is* Rebekah?"

"Let's just say, trying to keep her safe is killing me." Connor glanced at him sharply.

Julian grinned in sudden, genuine amusement, and the switch in his demeanor arrested Connor's pacing. *I'm hanging on by my fingertips, and he finds it amusing?* The back of Connor's neck burned, and he ground his fingers into the strung-out fibers.

Julian shook his head. "I wonder what Charles would have made of all this. I'm not at all sure he'd approve of us. Either that, or he would have lost himself in the fascination of it all."

"Charles?" Connor turned to face Julian. "You can't mean Dispensary Charles?"

Julian laughed. "Of course not."

"Who then? Have I met him?" Connor's hands dropped to his side and irritation died away to curiosity. *I'll bite. Julian's stories usually have a point.*

"Goodness, no. It was before you were born. I knew him for about fifty years, back in the 1800's." Julian's eyes sparkled. "Charles Darwin. You may have heard of him?"

"Hell, Julian." Connor said reverently. "You certainly got around."

"He is the only human I ever wanted to hang on to. He never knew it, of course." Julian's smile became wistful. "I met him at Cambridge University in 1828. He dropped out of medical school at age nineteen, and his father sent me to coax him back into academia." Julian appeared lost in the heart of the story. "He was a gentle man, and operations without anaesthetic were not something he could handle."

"Did you know him when he wrote the book?" Connor's brow creased, he knew the answer must be, 'No'. *After all, that was thirty years on from Cambridge, unless Charles Darwin was more enlightened than I thought.*

Julian met Connor's eyes. "No, he didn't know I was a vampire. It was Victorian England, but even with society being hampered by good manners, or the illusion of them, I could see he was something special. He had a hunger for, well, everything." Julian sank in to his leather armchair, melancholy running through every line of his body. "We were pen pals, if you will. I watched over him, I even got him off his backside to publish that damn book." Julian's voice lightened with rueful laughter. "That Wallace guy nearly beat him to it. I sent Charles a letter giving him a kick up the butt, telling him it was now or never, and the rest, as they say, is history. Thirty years of observations poured out onto the page in as many days to become 'On the Origin of the Species', and Charles became a household name."

"Is it wrong that I'm glad you resisted turning him?"

"You would disappoint me if you felt anything less. He loved his Emma, and put the book off for twenty years for fear of offending her religious sensibilities. She was the world to him, and you reminded me of that. The irony is that he proved the theory of natural selection, and here *we* are, the most unnatural of selections."

Connor joined in Julian's gentle laughter. "You'll have to tell me the whole story one day."

"One day, I will. From the HMS Beagle through to the billiard table I bought for him. What was it he said?" Julian looked at the ceiling, as though it was a page upon which he could read the words. "Ah yes, 'playing billiards does me a deal of good and drives the horrid species out of my head'. That always made me smile, would he consider me 'the most horrid of species'?"

"You're a good man, Julian. He was lucky to have you."

"Well, in the spirit of Charles' survival of the fittest and all that." Julian was serious now. His unnatural skin, smooth as the palest marble, had a fine network of veins. Connor's acute vision discerned them with ease; he watched them recede and swell again as Julian rubbed a firm hand over his jaw. "What are we going to do about Rebekah and you?"

"I need all the damn help I can get." Connor looked at the ceiling, too, retrieving the list that had swirled inside *his* head on the journey from the eco-town to here. "What Serge might be planning? How many guardsmen does he have? When he is likely to come after the humans? Anything, really." He cast an inquiring glance at Julian.

The bite and blood tests had put the Annabelle fiasco to rest, but, as they had already known it was a ruse, it didn't alter Serge's agenda to find Rebekah.

"I can delay Serge another day or two, at most. But, surely you're not asking me to spy on one of my own councilors?" Julian tried to hold on to his offended expression, but the sparkle in his eyes finally gave way to a grin. "Consider it done. Seriously, though, I think he'll commit numbers to a grid search, now he suspects there are humans to find."

Connor sighed in frustration. "How many guardsmen do you think? They are pretty young and easy to dispose of, but how many?"

"I think you're looking at half a dozen. He'll send them out in the same direction as the last patrol which mysteriously disappeared." Julian raised a sardonic brow. "And grid search from there."

"They'll find the eco-town for sure, and six is a big number for me to finish." Connor ramped up the pacing, as well as the panting; neither one had he ever done before Rebekah. "I'll have to hide them. I've already delivered the beta-blockers and the chemicals Harry needed, and he's stockpiling pheromone suppressant spray." Connor froze midstride and whisked around as his thoughts changed direction.

"Connor, please. Have pity on the carpet." Julian rubbed his neck, feeling the strain of keeping track of Connor's ever-increasing pace.

"I'll just have to break the news that moving out is not a safe option. Not right now." Connor was no longer talking to Julian. "I can hide them. Moving out will have to come later."

Julian reached out and grabbed Connor's arm, calling his attention back. "Charles always said, a grain of *balance* will decide who lives and who dies. So, is she worth dying for? That *is* what you're looking at here." It cut to the heart of the matter, and it had to be said.

Connor's sober gray eyes met Julian's speculation. "She's worth dying for."

Releasing Connor, Julian sighed. "Well, in that case, three guardsmen each aren't such bad odds, hmm?" His green eyes flashed and his pupils suddenly contracted to pinpricks. "I'll watch your back, on one condition." Julian threw a towel at Connor's head. "Stop soaking the damn carpet."

Chapter 19

At dusk the following night, Connor and Julian sat in the woods, and the cold earth tried in vain to steal heat, creaking under their weight. Connor had been back at the eco-town barely a day, preparing the humans for the upcoming conflict, when Julian arrived with bad news. Serge had already made his move.

They hunted together, and, after filling up on animal blood to prepare for the battle, they drank the vials of human blood Connor had taken when he did his last hospital round. They each kept one vial to tuck away as an emergency supply.

"I find it surreal that I can still go into London and work at the hospital, and no one notices I have changed," Connor mused. "I thought vampires were observant."

Julian laughed quietly. "Well, clearly not. They see what they expect to see."

"You're right. Just as I did when Rebekah turned up at the hospital." Connor shook his head. "I can't believe, even with beta-blockers and pheromone suppressant, that I was fooled." *But then again, I hadn't been. My body had known, it was just my brain that needed to catch up.*

"Well, let's hope the hunting guardsmen are easily fooled," Julian said grimly, and returned to surveying the terrain around them in silence.

The guardsmen were set to meet at the farmhouse about fifteen miles away, as expected, and the grid search would start there. *A calculated guess by Serge.* A harsh smile blanched Connor's skin. *I was thorough. I left no evidence of the kills.* He had crumbled them to quarry dust and buried the remains.

Ranging his glance over the North Downs of Kent, Connor could barely make out the eco-town entrance carved into the sloping fields. The fact the humans had lived there undetected, for years, was another example of vampire complacency, and the ridiculous assumption that everything was under their control.

Julian took a deep breath and opened a prickly topic. "You know the council is still waiting for you to join the human breeding project? If you continue to delay, it will look suspicious." He stared out across the fields while he waited for Connor to respond. The ten second rule of human conversation was a drop in the ocean. Vampires could wait unperturbed, indefinitely. Connor *would* reply, because he had no choice. Julian was speaking as the hive *principal*, and he expected an answer.

Eventually, Connor's battle face gave way to a vicious snarl of contempt. "They know I'm committed to modifying animal blood. I'm still working on that."

Julian appeared unfazed. He could also do scary when the situation demanded. "I don't like it any more than you, but the bottom line is, when all our humans die, we die. They won't breed-" Connor growled, and Julian raised his voice above it. "Pregnant women end their own lives rather than deliver a baby into our hands."

"Can you blame them?" Connor muttered.

Julian glanced at Connor's scowling profile. "We need to find a drug to calm them, one that will stop them hurting themselves, without harming their babies. Every month it gets harder to establish pregnancy; self-induced malnourishment will soon push us down the route of force-feeding the women with nutrients." Julian shook his head. "This will only get uglier."

Grinding his teeth, Connor whispered vehemently, "I can't look Rebekah in the eye and be involved in such a project. I understand the urgency, but I can't do it."

"We are running out of time, Connor. There *are* worse things. The Hybrid Breeding Project. If trials start on that, then you will have *real* conflict." Julian paused.

Connor eased the tension at the back of his neck. He hated being played, and he felt as though Julian's words were a fishing line hooked into his flesh and pulled tight.

"Some are warming to the idea of finding a way to impregnate humans with vampire sperm. Who knows where that will end?" Julian snorted. The 'some' were being 'warmed' by Serge, who was stirring a placebo of hope inside their bored chests.

Connor's fear of pregnancy colored every intimate moment he shared with Rebekah. "Have they thought about what happens if the human females all die? Does Serge even care?" Sarcasm bit into his tone.

The silence stretched in understanding of their shared conflict.

Julian stirred himself to say, "The autopsy you did on the girl who was raped by a vampire?" The tone implied the question 'do you remember that?'

Of course, I remember. Her face was carved into his mind, along with the blood-red anger he struggled to contain when he had cut open her dead flesh.

"Did it give us any clues?"

Julian's conversational tone irked Connor. They were discussing human life, not what color shirt to wear.

"Only that we can rule out freezer burn. She died of internal bleeding related to broken bones, not the act itself."

Connor was shocked at the buzz of satisfaction he felt when he uttered the words, and horrified that he found some comfort in them. He had been petrified that if he ever lost control with Rebekah, his icy temperature would cause soft-tissue damage. *But, no. Just the pregnancy thing to worry about, then.*

"How did it happen, anyway?" Connor cast a disapproving glance at Julian. "I thought they were better protected, being our lifeblood in every sense of the word."

"His cluster leader put him forward to clean out farm quarters. He passed the control tests, but, when he found himself alone with a sleeping human. Well, you know how their smell percolates when they are warm." Julian shrugged. "He was stupid. He needed rap-sleep but he didn't realize until it was too late."

Connor was stung by Julian's matter-of-fact attitude; he was a farmer discussing livestock, clinical and detached. *But then, my own attitude was the same, until Rebekah.*

"He's got an eternity to think it over, now. He's dehydrating in Storage Facility Eight." Aiming for persuasive and missing it by about a mile, frustration bit into his features, and Julian said, "Connor, please, think about the breeding program. We're running out of resources, and incidents like that one only make it more urgent."

"I can't promise anything." Connor gave himself a mental shake. *I should be grateful Julian's judgment is not clouded by obsession. I'm not sure I'd wish this hell on anyone.* "Let's leave it there, hmm?" Connor said, glancing again at the camouflaged entrance of the eco-town. "We have more urgent things to think about. When should I move them out into the burrows? The timing is crucial. They must have enough time to recover from the exertion of crossing the meadow." *But if they are in hiding too long and the oxygen becomes thin, their breathing will sound like an express train to vampire ears.*

Julian squinted up at the silver slice of the moon, and said, "Serge's attack is unsanctioned by the council, so he'll probably use a vampire cluster leaving London on crop harvesting duty as a decoy, and send the guardsmen out while there's a lot of vampire traffic."

Connor nodded. "That makes sense. The quiet period at the blood dispensary is around two a.m. Only the occasional hunting party goes out after that. There'll be a delivery from the farm about then, so there will be a lot of distractions."

"I think you should get them out of the eco-town and in place by two."

"That works. Human adrenalin levels are at their lowest around two a.m., and with the beta-blockers, too-" Connor rose smoothly to his feet. "I'll have them in place and meet you back here."

He frowned at Julian and took another breath to speak.

Julian laughed gently, executing a Boy Scout salute. "I promise to stay out of sight. They will not know I am here, not until afterwards. It won't do to scare the horses."

They were agreed that the sudden appearance of another vampire would make it impossible to keep the humans calm.

"I'll see you back here then, at two," Connor said, and loped away over the meadow and disappeared into the blemish on the hillside.

He was not surprised when he slipped behind the heavy sackcloth curtain and Rebekah barreled into his chest. He laughed, despite the tension coiled inside his belly, and, clasping his hands carefully behind her, he swung her around.

As her feet found the floor again, her grip around his waist tightened, and the worry in her eyes dimmed the glow of her smile.

"Just the easy bit to do now, honey," said Connor, dropping a kiss onto her upturned nose. "Getting George across the meadow without the old boy dislocating a hip."

Rebekah landed a punch on his arm and hurt her hand. "Ouch," she muttered as his cold fingers eased the pain, and he towed her slowly along the tunnels behind him.

"Are they in the meeting cavern?"

"Yes, all of them," whispered Rebekah.

Connor stopped and frowned, "All?"

"Yes. Greg went out and brought back the last of the away teams."

"Okay, better they are here than stumbling around out there like a herd of elephants, I guess," said Connor. *With a murder of crows looking to hunt them down.*

Connor stabbed his fingers through his hair and began walking again. "Twenty then, and they've all taken beta-blockers and used suppressant spray? And did Harry have enough pelts to go around?"

Rebekah threw an untidy salute into the air. "All present and correct. And you'll be pleased to know..." she wrinkled her nose. "The animal skins stink."

"Good," he said.

Connor entered the meeting cavern looking for Harry, to congratulate him.

Harry had impressed Connor once again. Even though his accelerated heart rate tap-danced over Connor's ribcage whenever Harry caught sight of him, he did everything Connor asked without question.

Connor surveyed the room, zeroing in on the group gathered at the farthest possible point in the cavern. He knew the meeting with the assembled eco-town inhabitants was going to test his skills of persuasion, and falling back on his somewhat rusty bedside manner, Connor smiled.

The plans had already been laid out for them. Hiding, staying quiet, and remaining calm was all they were required to do. Connor's grin was wry as the assembled heart rates thundered like stampeding buffalo. *A tall order, apparently.*

"Oscar, in case there is any doubt about Douglas." Connor took Rebekah's hand in his. "He stays in the vampire cave for this."

Connor expected some dissent, but, for once, Harry found a backbone and glared fiercely at the one person who dared to open his mouth in protest; the sound of teeth clattering when the man's jaw snapped hastily shut amused Connor.

Douglas was cowed, but he was still a distraction, and tonight was not a night for distractions. *So, Douglas can take his chances in the vampire cave. Sweet irony, no matter if we win or lose, his life expectancy is tenuous.*

"Let's get moving, Oscar." Connor's glance settled on the mountain of muscle in the form of a man, with a rock steady heartbeat. "Hello, Greg," Connor said.

Greg's face still wore a grim combat mask of dried mud and smudges of charcoal. "Connor." His short greeting was accompanied by an even shorter nod.

"Greg, you bring up the rear and make sure everyone gets outside safely, and I'll meet you in the woods." Connor checked his watch. "They have to be inside the burrows by oh-two-hundred hours. Oscar knows the way."

Connor made his way back to the eco-town entrance, listening for the ambling approach of humans trying to be quiet. He felt better for seeing Greg. *He knows the meaning of survival.*

He watched the yeti-like fur-dressed figures emerge and almost smiled.

Sending the first wave out across the meadow, he tugged fur hoods straight and told each one to keep their chin down and keep moving. As the last in the conga line of humans set out across the grass, Connor raced ahead to check the woods one last time. The night air was crisp and still, and, when Rebekah came into view holding onto George to keep him upright, Connor dared to believe things would go smoothly.

Deep inside the wood, where the stagnant atmosphere beneath the heavy canopy made breathing harder, Rebekah clung to Connor's hand as George descended into the hollowed out bunker Julian and Connor had prepared. His painfully slow pace was dictated by old bones, but Rebekah was glad for the extra precious moments with Connor.

"Rebekah," he said quietly, turning to face her. "You remember what I told you?"

As she went to answer, his cold finger settled on her lips. He shook his head. "Rule one, absolutely no talking." A tight smile softened the words. "The harmonic pitch of human voices carries. Promise me, no talking."

Rebekah nodded dutifully and, with her free hand, crossed her heart.

His flint-like gaze glittering, Connor stared long and hard into her face. Pulling her close, he snaked his arm around her waist as, seeking reassurance, he kissed her. Rebekah, needing it too, pushed her fingers into his hair and clung to his body.

Panting quietly, he reluctantly eased his embrace. "Please, stay safe, honey, that's all I ask. Do not move. Slow, calm breaths, and no matter what, under no circumstances come out until I come for you. Okay?"

Satisfied with her firm nod, he led her to the hole in the ground. As Connor steadied her path downward into the damp underground space, his urgent grip almost broke her fingers, until finally, he let her hand slip from his.

Rebekah turned away and, ducking her head, felt her way along the wall of wooden struts and gnarled tree roots overhead which gave the hideout strength.

Her sneakers sank into the newly excavated ground and darkness enveloped her. Eyes open or closed made no difference. Rebekah moved slowly forward in the narrow space, cringing when she trod on someone's toes and squeezing the anonymous shoulder in apology. For Rebekah, losing the sense of sight was tough, but of course, she had agreed to double jeopardy, not talking was her side of the bargain. Doing what she was told was never easy. It was in her nature to kick against that, but, she *had* won a small victory.

Connor had wanted all the females split up, muttering something about eggs in one basket, which sounded a little unnerving. However, Rebekah insisted she and Leizle stay together, and he had reluctantly agreed as long as the other four women were in other burrows.

Wondering how much farther she had left to go, Rebekah paused to listen to the quiet breathing of those sharing her interment. The fingers of a cold slender hand closed over hers, and she squeezed them in recognition. *Leizle.* As she settled beside her, Rebekah tightened her grip.

Scraping noises accompanied the gentle shower of disturbed earth, as Connor covered the burrow's entrance with a grid work of thin branches torn from trees far inside the woods and bound together with twine.

The shuffling sound of leaves being piled over the lattice of wood cramped Rebekah's chest in rational fear. In the blackness, the sensation of becoming entombed settled like a shroud when the nocturnal sounds she took for granted were all but extinguished. Rebekah nervously licked her lips, and, tasting the hint-of-lemon flavor of Connor's kiss once more, certainty filled her with quiet calm. She smiled in the darkness. *Everything will be all right, I know it.*

Still holding hands with Leizle on one side, Rebekah waved a hand in the air until she located Oscar's solid fur-clad shoulder and followed the trail down to take his hand, too. She occupied her mind with Connor's survival checklist, and the suffocating smell of the dank animal skins faded into the background. Joining hands and taking comfort from being part of the huddled group, she resisted the desperate urge to whisper. Connor had made the danger crystal clear.

Chapter 20

Connor turned over the mulched ground at the burrow entrance until the darker patina of disturbed leaves blended in. Pulling in a deep lungful of air and washing it across his palate, he could barely detect the humans. The result pleased him. They had been split into five groups, and the hiding part, at least, had been accomplished.

Connor still had mud under his fingernails from digging out the large burrows. The chambers extending under the tree roots had taken him and Julian less than an hour to excavate. He had embraced the physical release; shoring up the insides of the structures with tree branch supports had left his mind free to ramble and to plan the campaign. *I've done all I can.*

Minutes crept by until it was half past two, and, reluctant to leave Rebekah, but knowing that staying near her would bring the guardsmen in too close, Connor moved back into the darkest shadows in the woods.

He took up the position as lookout – standing still, listening, and waiting – and Julian set off to scout the farmhouse.

It won't be much of an early warning, but still...

Connor detected a change in the note of the breeze. He heard leaves rustle, and a scuttling of disturbed beetles. *Here they come.* An almost imperceptible plume of scent billowed as the guardsmen's approach compressed fresh damp moss underfoot.

Julian had been gone three minutes.

Much as he would have preferred to see the threat first-hand, and enjoy the adrenalin buzz of preparing for battle, Connor was more comfortable being here, waiting. *I would die for these humans, because of Rebekah. Julian is here only because of me.* Julian lacked emotional commitment. He couldn't feel compelled in the same way.

But, we are ready. Connor rocked on the balls of his feet, assessing the traction he would get on the loosely-packed woodland floor. Julian shared one passion with him, wholeheartedly; the enjoyment of the fight, especially when the enemy was Councilor Serge.

"They are on the move." Julian's tone was conversational as he appeared beside Connor. "Are the humans safely in the burrows?"

Connor nodded, scanning the woods and running his fingers over the vial of human blood resting inside his pocket. "How many?"

"Six, moving fast in an arrowhead formation."

The plan was to allow the guardsmen to come close; it was a grid search, they would be scanning and their minds would be occupied with that. The human smells, strongest in the eco-town, would be an irresistible beacon which would draw them in; the dank, pungent, mulch-covered ground of the woods should provide cover for both the cantering sound of heartbeats and the faint aroma of fear.

Draw them in and dispatch them one at a time. The plan is simple.

"Here they come," mouthed Julian.

Connor grinned with scathing satisfaction.

He knew vampire strength followed a predictable path. Being turned was the first step along the way; the congealed human blood in their veins gave new vampires great strength, but, with no control. When their own human blood decayed, they became weaker, and surviving conflict became more about cunning. Every decade that passed, transformed well-fed vampire cells into thirst pockets which, simply put, gave them devastating strength, and, by this time, they knew how to wield it.

Ice cold certainty that the approaching guardsmen were at the beginning of this path, with he and Julian at the end, lanced through his chest as Connor rehearsed the battle inside his mind.

The blanket of sound of fauna scurrying out of the way faded to an inhuman silence. The woodland seemed to hold its breath. *Time to go.*

Connor sought Julian's agreement, and, finding it, he moved out.

The first two guardsmen fell easily, silently, as Connor crushed their windpipes in his clenched fist.

Julian kept his eyes on the action. With his senses of smell and hearing scanning, he guarded Connor's back.

The woods hummed with the scuttling of disturbed insects and the whisper of foliage brushing over vampire skin. The faintest of human scents wafted on the breeze.

The third vampire emerged, but spun on his heel when he heard a noise.

If Connor had a beating heart, it would have stopped dead, because he heard it too. *Damn it.* Leaves rustling, agitated movement, and a sobbing human breath shrieked through Connor's skull. His thoughts came together into a plan of attack and he launched silently forward.

The attacking vampire took off fast in the direction of his prey. Connor went with him. The snarl breaking from his throat was drowned out by the sickening crunch as he barged into the vampire's back. Using his rival's explosive forward propulsion, with a shove, Connor forced him off course and slammed him into a tree trunk, crushing his nose and snapping both cheekbones.

The guardsman whipped around. His rage creased his shattered face into a comedic grin, which melted as gravity dragged at the detached bone structure. He gurgled, and a spray of glutinous blood speckled his chest when he flew at Connor, who sidestepped swiftly. Extending a lightning-quick arm, Connor grabbed a fistful of the vampire's hair and hauled him back. Hearing the bones grating under the skin, Connor decided to end it quickly. He pressed his stricken opponent face down into the mulched ground, applied a boot to his neck, and separated head from shoulders.

From his vantage point, Julian watched the action closely. With his back pressed against a tree trunk, he saw the first two kills and the third scuffle. He spared a moment to admire his friend's clinical precision before scanning around.

Deep inside the woods, Julian spotted the blurred trajectory of a fourth guardsman closing in fast on the flailing human.

Julian heaved a harsh sigh and shoved away from the tree, launching into his own pursuit. He had barely taken one step when a crushing blow to his spine deadened his legs, and he went down hard with the lead weight of an attacker pressing down on his shoulders. In a split second, pushing hard, he twisted on to his back, taking his assailant with him and pinning the vampire to the ground beneath.

Reaching back, Julian closed his hand around the guardsman's neck, but not in time. He felt fingernails gouging into his own throat, jabbing up into the soft space under his jaw.

"Not me, you idiot," Julian managed to grind out.

The vampire froze, but held firm.

"It's the doctor we're after," Julian hissed with quiet conviction, despite his disadvantage. "Do you know who I *am*?" Julian held up his left hand, and the pale moonlight glinted on the principal's seal adorning his middle finger as he folded it into a fist.

The spiked fingertips withdrew slowly and the vampire's frame beneath him sagged.

Rolling briskly away and regaining his feet, Julian glared at the figure rising more slowly.

Had he been human, the guard would have been sweating as he dipped his chin, lowering his gaze in groveling subservience. Killing a councilor would be an act of suicide, but to kill the principal was without precedence. *This vampire could have made history, in a bad way.*

Julian displayed venom-coated teeth in a show of strength. He said, "Well, what are you waiting for?"

A hundred yards away, Connor straightened and removed his boot from the vampire's neck. He heard the thump of solid vampire bodies colliding and a scuffle over to his left. But, keening sobs still cut through the night, to his right.

Julian, or the human?

Casting an intent gaze through the shadows, Connor stared in disbelief as he recognized the youth floundering on the ground. *Thomas.* The boy's hands framed his throat and frantic fingernails raised welted tracks across his skin. Connor registered the static charge of the panic attack sweeping through the youngster's brain at the same moment as he caught a flash of movement.

A guardsman hurtled in on his right flank.

Rushing forward, Connor grabbed the boy by the scruff of his fur pelt coat. He swung him around, and deposited the kid fifteen yards away in a winded heap. Tracking the vampire's charge, Connor darted into his path and, turning at the moment of impact, he shunted his elbow sharply back into the vampire's chest and shattered his sternum.

The vampire fell backwards, slammed into the ground by the force of the blow. Surging up again, he launched himself back into the fight, hissing and snarling. Connor stopped the manic forward propulsion dead with a blocking punch into the middle of the vampire's crumbling chest. The guard still pressed forward, his hands clawing their way up Connor's shoulders, and needle-sharp fingernails buried themselves into Connor's neck. As the claws dug in deeper, Connor drove a bruising uppercut into the soft part of his victim's belly, forcing a relentless path through the firm lung tissue until he closed his hand around the heart and twisted. He smiled reflexively into the smooth, shocked face, and the vampire dropped his hands to his stomach, cradling the innards slipping out through the hole. *So easy.* Relaxing his fist, Connor let the body hit the ground with a muffled thud.

Connor ran his fingertips over his neck where puncture wounds oozed pink fluid. *Well, that was number four.* Scanning the undergrowth, a frown creased his smooth brow when he pinpointed Thomas' quiet rasping breath. But, the hiss of vampire conversation wafted through the woods, and as he tried to make out the words, they reeled him in.

Primed for attack, Connor stealthily headed back towards Julian's lookout post. He wove a path between the tree trunks and spotted two figures standing together. *What the hell?* The arrogant angle of Julian's blond head gave Connor pause and kept him silent as he crept closer.

"You have a job to do. I suggest you focus on that," spat Julian.

His words drifted on the breeze, and his betrayal buried a hot needle of anger into Connor's brain.

Striding forward, Connor plowed through the undergrowth and stepped into the moonlight.

Julian towered over the guardsman, his hand resting firmly on the vampire's shoulder.

"My, this is cozy," Connor said flatly. "Going for the accolades after all, Julian? Such a pity." With a growl rumbling in his throat, Connor rocked his weight forward, his hand itching to close around Julian's neck.

Suddenly, the stutter of stumbling human footfalls rang through the trees, ricocheting from each leaf and wiping all other thoughts from vampire heads. Each one turned to peer at the spot in the darkness where two white faces made their jerky progress towards them.

Rebekah appeared with the fingers of vampire number six clamped tightly around her throat as he nudged her forward, holding her pressed into his body.

Connor's eyes narrowed and he took in her pale, stiff face. *What on earth do I have to do to keep her safe?*

Barely an hour before, Connor thought he had achieved that goal.

Rebekah had intended to keep her promise. *Lord knows I've caused him enough trouble. Stay still until Connor gets back, how hard can that be?*

How long they sat in the burrows, Rebekah could not say. The trance-like state of a sensory deprivation tank melted her thoughts t the point of semi-consciousness, where time meant nothing, until the ground overhead shook.

The scuffling sounds outside were intimidating. A number of sickening thuds, a snarl, and a heavy weight hitting the ground resolved into shocked silence as the huddled group held their breath.

A sickening thud ended in a groan, and then the whimpering started. Rebekah could almost feel the weight of the anxious glances darting around the bunker. The hitched breathing made it clear she was not the only one struggling to stay still. The faint broken sobs overhead tore at her heart. *It sounds human. Young, human, and hurt.*

Rebekah agonized; the voice of reason told her to sit tight, don't move, and Connor would help.

But in the end, she couldn't resist the wrench on her heart strings. She felt Leizle's fingers tighten around hers to make her stay. She squeezed back with reassurance she did not feel, and gently tugged free.

Running her fingertips back over the network of tree roots, she found the sturdy supports framing the entrance. She moved the wooden grate a few inches, cringing when the dislodged clumps of mud sounded like hand grenade explosions hitting the ground at her feet. She shrugged the weight of the deerskin from her shoulders, and, with breathless contortions, wriggled sideways. Anxiety ached in her chest as she squeezed through the smallest possible gap.

After the pitch-black interior of the burrow, the undergrowth seemed almost floodlit.

Thomas. Recognizing the writhing frame, Rebekah commando-crawled across to the boy, oblivious to the stones biting into her knees, and the moisture soaking into her shirt and chilling her stomach.

She grabbed his shoulders urgently and hissed, "Shhh."

A silent scream contorted her face when an iron grip closed over her hair, and she was yanked to her feet so fast her heart slammed into the floor of her stomach.

She folded both hands over the icy clenched fingers in an effort to ease the pain. She swallowed hard, trapping a yelp inside. Her only thought was that she mustn't endanger the others.

Pulled upright and arched back to fit into a cold hard frame, she had no doubt she was in the hands of a vampire.

Connor's directions to stay still taunted her. *Crap, he's going to bloody kill me.*

With a painful wrench which made her hair follicles burn, the vampire marched her forward. His knees bruised the backs of her thighs, and the pain kept her concentration sharp.

When the assembled figures came into view, Rebekah dared not look at Connor.

The moon seemed intent on picking out the fierce cast to his features. His anger emanated in waves and she knew some of it was directed at her. Her chin rose in defiance. *I'd do it all again. Thomas is alive, so it was worth it.*

Chapter 21

Connor's anger tightened sinew and pumped muscle. All he needed to do now was decide what to do with it. Julian had betrayed him, and Rebekah's fear-slicked sweat toasted his brain cells. His outrage at the reddening of her slender neck beneath the clasp of the vampire's fingers swelled anger to fury.

As Connor lunged forward, Julian suddenly blocked his path. The Principal's tight smile filled his vision. Grabbing Connor by the throat, Julian bracketed his jaw and levered it up, pressing a fingernail into the jugular vein.

Connor twisted, ready to counter, but hesitated at Julian's fierce growl. "Use your head, Doctor Connor, killing a member of the vampire council is never a good idea. Remember, a grain of *balance* will decide who lives and who dies. So, tell me..." Julian's eyes narrowed. He stared into Connor's crazed, gray gaze, maintaining a tight grip on his throat, until Connor finally dipped into their green depths and his purple rage began to cool.

"Is she worth dying for?" Julian asked quietly.

Connor held his ground, but stopped resisting.

Julian jerked his head, directing the vampire holding Rebekah. "Well, what are you waiting for? Get her to the farm. Go." He continued to stare Connor down, dousing his anger with the sanity of ice-green jade.

The vampire's grip on Rebekah's neck tightened, and Connor tasted the fumes of her horror-struck sweat as the creaking capillaries threatened to rupture. Connor's fist clenched in time with a knotted muscle ticking in his jaw, and he watched the vampire pushing her forward once more.

"Think, man. Think," Julian mouthed silently.

Connor blinked slowly, his eye-color changing from molten lead to steel gray, letting Julian know his unravelling thoughts were back under control and he understood the plan. Julian relaxed his grip and let his hand fall, knocking deliberately against the vial of human blood inside Connor's jacket pocket.

Julian turned away, his demeanor dismissive as he scanned the face of his erstwhile attacker. Judging how hard to push it, he barked, “Don’t just stand there. You came for the girl. I’m sure Councilor Serge will show his appreciation when you report back.” his glare indicated that the show was over and it was time to leave.

As the last guardsman moved away, Julian shot Connor a pointed look and followed the vampire out of sight. A dull thud was followed by a grunt and the sickening sound of compressed cartilage popping.

Connor took off through the wood.

Rebekah made her gait cumbersome, but the night’s events had chilled her brain. What began with skittering tension, had swelled to terror, visiting all the nerve-stripping stops along the way. Now, numbness set in as a babbling brook of thoughts, and, when she chased them down, only two thoughts broke the surface. *Julian is a traitor. Thomas is safe.*

And, Connor? She knew the sentence for killing a council member was death without trial. Her ears strained for sounds of reassurance. Silently, she begged him. *Please, don’t step over the line that will take you away from me forever.*

Bone cold fingers dug into her neck and her arm lost all feeling, pins and needles dancing in a fiery path down towards her fingertips. She focused on that pain as every footfall jarred her body and stirred dread in her stomach. Shadows thickened, the trees closed in, and the straggling creepers trailing around her ankles made stumbling easy.

The vampire tightened his spiteful grip when an unexpected stiff breeze snatched her breath away. It jerked her back to the present. He suddenly ramped up his speed, and her feet were no longer on firm ground.

Connor diverted through woods he knew better than the guardsman, choosing the setting for the showdown. The impact of each footfall rocked his heart in his chest, something he was disconcertingly aware of these days. Deliberately amplifying the noise of his approach, hissing loudly through clenched teeth and pounding his controlled stride through the undergrowth, he made sure the vampire heard him coming.

Whilst still running, Connor snagged the vial of human blood from his pocket and cradled it in his palm. As expected, the vampire picked up speed, but when he heard Connor closing in, he aborted his flight and whipped around.

Just when the arctic sting of rushing air numbed Rebekah's cheeks, she was jerked to a halt, and her head spun as she pirouetted about.

The vampire snarled over Rebekah's shoulder, and Connor's contemptuous grin pulled his features tight. Before the vampire could process his confusion at the doctor having the finesse of a galloping buffalo, Connor launched the vial of blood, smashing it open against the trunk of a nearby tree.

The splintering crack sent a shockwave through Rebekah as her captor's icy grip convulsed, constricting her throat in a painful spasm. The vampire sucked in the plume of scent, his pupils blew to jet black pools, and his head snapped around to taste the vapor-cloud of blood saturating the air.

Launching silently forward, Connor closed the distance between them in less than a second. He gripped the vampire's skull, and, as it turned to follow the bait, he carried it onwards and didn't stop until he heard the sharp crack of a snapping spine. The vibration juddered through Connor's arms and warmed him with satisfaction.

The deafening crack of fracturing bone exploded near Rebekah's ear just before the vampire's fingertips ripped away, unfurling four strands of blood-red scratches across her neck.

Before the decapitated body hit the ground, Connor reached out and pulled Rebekah into his arms.

She surrendered to the disorientation. Her head rocked back like a rag doll as her body was yanked forward, and she ran into an edifice of cold stone. A harsh sigh of lemon-iced breath gusted through her hair, and a fresh fragrance filled her lungs as the wall of muscle beneath her fingertips vibrated. *Connor.*

Holding her close and pressing his cheek to her hair, he took a deep breath, pulling her scent inside his aching chest until he exhaled it with a frustrated snarl. “Why the hell can’t you just do what I tell you?” He put his hands on her shoulders and looked down into her defiant white face.

“Thomas was hurt and I couldn’t bear it,” she said. “I’d do it again.” Rebekah faced his exasperation with strength he’d never seen in a human, her eyes ablaze as honey-scented adrenalin pumped through her bloodstream. Her rebellious chin jerked up and began to tremble, and the rest of her body took up the rhythm as shock set in.

“I know,” he grumbled and his lips closed over her open mouth, drawing her panting breath from her lungs. He soothed her agitation. He molded his tongue to hers and undulated a melting rhythm along its length. He wanted to taste her distressed pulse, but resisted. *It would calm her.* A persuasive whisper drifted through his mind, but Connor knew better than to listen. *The taste of her blood, heavy with adrenalin... I would not stop.*

Rebekah’s heart slowed, but when his citrus-spiced excitement mingled with hers, it picked up speed again. The cadence of it was intoxicating, and, pressing closer, Connor absorbed the beats as if they were his own. Her fingers clenched into fists and she tugged on his hair, pulling his face down. A tide of male satisfaction rose inside him at her efforts, for, without his cooperation, she would never move him. But, he wanted it too, wanted to immerse his body in the clustered desire of hers.

Visualizing the bruises he felt blossoming underneath his fingertips, he clutched her buttocks and lifted her to him, flattening his palms when she winced. But he was not sorry, he was past sorry. He wanted surrender. *She drives me insane, dammit.*

The heat of her thighs framed his aching body, and his frustration leapt the divide between them. Rebekah dug her nails into his back, and Connor froze. The sensation ignited the memory of a desire he had buried inside.

“What?” she whispered, wondering at the exhilaration lurking in his gaze.

"Ah, just a fantasy I've had since we met." He had thought about this since the day in the basement when the sound of her thighs brushing together had tantalized him, and curiosity had crawled under his skin. He wanted to taste the excitement of her nails dragging over his vampire flesh. His fingers molded to her nape as he lifted her jaw with his thumb and deepened his kiss, losing himself in her heat.

Rebekah could not be sure how it happened, but his nimble cold fingers moved over her skin, her clothing barely twitched as it was tugged away, and a bed of soft grass was suddenly cooling her naked back.

Connor gazed down into her pink face. His aroused body lay between her thighs, their bodies unclothed this time. He closed his eyes, and savored the satin of her skin warming the velvet of his. When he opened them again, the mercurial currents of molten silver in his gaze mesmerized her and his lips curved into a smile of faked innocence. "What?"

"You're a fast worker," she breathed, holding onto her frown for three seconds as his fingers teased her flushed breast. He tugged the hard bud of her nipple and a dart of pleasure moved her hips into him.

"Not too fast, I'm waiting for you to catch up," he chuckled hoarsely and, with a playful nudge, brushed his hard stomach enticingly over hers, tormenting the fiery heat between her thighs.

"Oh, I think I'm right there with you," she said as she welcomed him in, captivated as he ascended inside her, driving the breath from her lungs in an aching sigh.

"I love you," he whispered. His amusement melted and his body sought the enchanting warmth of hers. His tight abdomen smoldered with the effort of not crushing her fragile frame. He fought to contain the acid-burn of hunger tearing at his throat, begging for her blood to wash it down again.

"I love you, too," Rebekah whispered, with a mischievous glint in her eye as she dragged her nails purposefully down over his back, as hard as she could.

His steely gaze sharpened, framing coal-black pupils with intense silver rims. "God, Rebekah," he muttered, and she knew she had him, and nothing would ever take him from her.

He dipped his face to the swell of her breast, his lips playing over her nipple with painful care. He smiled as a blush of heat devoured the cool draft of his breath.

The fire inside her raged. She tightened around him, stirring an unbearable molten tide over the velvet steel of his swollen desire. He trailed kisses to her mouth, his body rejoicing in her shuddering climax, and he savored her galloping heartbeat riding roughshod over his.

He couldn't stay, the demon of that final taboo still living inside his head, but he held her cradled to his chest until she floated back to him. His cool fingers traveled the length of her spine and molded her body to his. Every time her sigh warmed the granite of his flesh, it took longer for the chill to return, as though she was breathing life into him, in his mind at least.

He whispered into her hair, "You infuriate, and scare the shit out of me, at every turn." As she chuckled, he groaned, "Please, Rebekah, take pity on me."

Chapter 22

When Connor and Rebekah arrived back at the battlefield, Julian had already uncovered the burrows, and the humans were climbing out, grubby, agitated, and shell-shocked. The fight had taken only an instant, but the waiting seemed endless to a human brain. Having their sense of sight stolen, the sense of hearing deadened by tight-packed earth, and their nasal linings clogged by dirt while they fought for oxygen in the gradually rarefying atmosphere, stretched every minute into ten.

Rebekah clung to Connor's carefully relaxed grip. Even in the dim moonlight, her eyes were drawn to the commanding presence of Julian; his golden tones contrasting dramatically with the blue-black shadowed hue of Connor's appearance.

At ease in the middle of the subdued mayhem, Julian watched their approach.

Rebekah glanced up at Connor's tight jaw, trying to measure his response. *Does he trust him?*

Julian met her gaze as though he could read her thoughts, his assessment laser-sharp. He raised a speculative brow, and her cheeks stung with embarrassment.

Turning to Connor, his expression a blend of amusement and apology, he said, "*Doctor* Connor. Good to see you, again."

"Principal," Connor said with a smile.

"And, you must be Rebekah." A half-smile curved his lips. "So, we meet at last."

Rebekah tried to feel grateful, but the hard expression Julian's features wore before was still fresh in her mind. The warmth of his current appraisal filled her with confusion.

Feeling her fingers gripping his, Connor drew Rebekah in closer to his side. "You've got some ground to make up, Julian." Connor slapped his friend on the shoulder with a force which would have broken human bones. "You've caused a bigger stir than we intended."

Julian smiled widely. Cocking his head and faking puppy dog eyes, he said, "I won't bite, I promise."

Rebekah chuckled, releasing the last remnants of nervousness inside. *I can remember Connor saying exactly those words, and he obviously trusts him.*

As Connor and Julian talked in hushed tones, too fast for Rebekah to follow, she absorbed the fact that, for tonight, at least, the danger had passed.

Rebekah scanned the shadowy figures moving through the woods. Uncle Harry and Greg were making an attempt to cover over the burrows again, until Connor caught their eye and gestured they should leave it to him and Julian. Harry raised a weary hand and moved away, carving an exhausted meandering path over the rough terrain. Greg dusted off his hands and started rounding up the stragglers who had sunk to the ground in a huddled mass.

Rebekah searched the grimy faces and was relieved to see Thomas being helped along by Oscar, with an anguished Leizle moving alongside.

Her green eyes had dark smudges underneath and her chestnut-brown hair was tangled and threaded with twigs and leaves. Rebekah waved to attract Leizle's attention, smiling widely when surprise wiped all expression from her face, and then it filled with joy.

Struggling forward on cramped legs, Leizle threw her arms around Rebekah. "Thank the Lord. We were so worried."

When Connor and Julian suddenly stopped talking, Leizle's hug stiffened. She darted a nervous glance at Connor as she quickly withdrew, moving away with a half wave and a smile. She was still skittish around Connor, but more so now with another vampire present.

Catching Connor's eye, Rebekah jerked her head in Leizle's direction and gave him a 'see you later' wave, before running after the younger girl and linking arms while they followed the others back over the meadow.

◇◇◇

In the aftermath of the battle, Connor and Julian settled at the tree line, looking out over the fields. Connor sat on his haunches, finely balanced on the balls of his feet, and Julian rested one knee on the ground. They had nowhere to be until dusk closed its gray fist over the sun and dragged it out of view.

The humans were safely inside the eco-town, and the hazy glow of dawn heralded a day of sunshine.

In the heavy shade of the trees, Connor thought of Rebekah and sighed. *To lay with her in the sunshine would be heaven. Instead, I draw her into my chilled world, and give nothing back.* If he could walk away, he would, but he knew he was not that noble.

After a long silence, during which Connor decided Rebekah would not thank him for a noble sacrifice, either, he took in Julian's clean-cut profile and grinned. "You had me going there for a while. It was a close call. You know I nearly lost it?" Connor raised a quizzical eyebrow when Julian remained silent, preoccupied with his own thoughts.

Julian finally found focus and replied, "I'm sorry about that. I guess the dead leg thing pricked my pride. I thought there was time to have a little fun." A wry grin folded his cheeks. "A fall came *before* my pride in this case. Although, faced with you, *and her,* arriving at the same time, my fun options went out of the window."

Connor replayed the uncomfortable moment. "It could have played out very differently. You took a risk."

"I thought you had him, number six." Julian tried to look apologetic, but excitement glittered in the green depths of his eyes. "I had some fast thinking to do, and your Rebekah certainly made life interesting." His sardonic grin tugged wider.

"I'd forgotten you two had not met. She's feisty, no shrinking violet that's for sure."

"Even though I'd never seen her before, the look on your face was enough." Julian shot a glance at Connor. "'Risk her life at your peril', came through loud and clear. I needed to come up with something, and I knew you'd pull it together."

Sarcasm dripped as Connor said, "Well, that's all right then, as long as one of us had a plan."

Julian's chuckle was spiced with relief. "You'd better believe it."

Each indulged his own thoughts and silence descended again. Connor felt as though he was on a rollercoaster ride. *I have trouble knowing which way is up these days.* But, like an adrenalin junkie, he loved it, and judging by the frozen smile folding creases into Julian's face, *he* loved it, too.

Connor pushed his hair back from his eyes. "We've bought a little time, but I think moving them out to a new location is still the only way to go. It won't take long for Serge to round up more recruits, and come at them again."

"I'll keep tabs on him in council, and you keep your ear to the ground in the hospital." Julian's eyes narrowed and he grinned as a kestrel dropped from the sky like a feather-clad stone and came up empty-handed.

A good omen maybe? Connor liked to think so.

"You're right, he'll not give up now," Julian said thoughtfully. "While you were *missing* with Rebekah." He raised a suggestive eyebrow. "I visited the farmhouse and made sure our tracks were covered. But it's only a matter of time."

"So, it's business as usual? Pull a double shift at the hospital and keep the enemy close, hmm?" He cast a speculative glance at Julian. "I'll talk to Rebekah, and get the plans for the move underway. Can I count on you?"

"As cover, certainly. As for the rest, I'm yet to be convinced they are worth the risk." Julian's look was apologetic. "I know you disagree, and I understand why you are drawn to Rebekah, but the others are-" He broke off as Connor's attention was snatched away.

Connor sprang to his feet, and looking out over the meadow, he braced as if the wind had picked up and threatened his balance.

Curious, Julian followed the direction of his gaze and saw the figure of Rebekah. Sunlight on her blond hair, her chin raised and a hand shading her eyes, as she walked in their direction. Catching sight of Connor, she smiled and lengthened her stride.

He stepped as close to the shadow's edge as he dared and waited, Julian forgotten. Laughter transformed his face when she threw herself at him at a full run, and he caught her easily.

Ah, thought Julian, I'd better make myself scarce, and he rose to his feet, too. He took another look at Rebekah, and suddenly, from nowhere, a pair of smudged-green eyes, almost a mirror of his own, appeared in his mind. Chestnut hair and a snub nose in a pale drawn face completed the vision and his fist clenched at his side.

Hunting in the woods was looking good; he was suddenly ravenous.

Chapter 23

Unwittingly observed by the keen eye of a lone vampire, Councilor Serge mounted the stone steps of his Georgian terraced house in London's Eaton Place. He pushed on the large brass doorknob, stepped inside, and closed the door.

The vampire smiled. He admired Serge's choice of architecture. The 18th century brickwork was in good repair, as were the cream-painted majestic pillars supporting the portico above the door. *A house built to last, then, fitting to a vampire's lifespan.* Smiling at the thought, he took off down the street. After making two left turns, he vaulted the six-foot high fence into the garden, and landed soundlessly on the soft grass at the rear of the house.

Settling in the thick shadow of an elm tree, he stared through the ground floor window and watched Councilor Serge taking a seat behind his desk. Serge's pallid complexion glowed in the beams of moonlight which penetrated the dirty panes of glass. Shadows clustered in the deep crevasses in his aged skin and dressed his face in a hideous mask.

The dark intruder reveled in the councilor's attitude of defeat. He had haunted the corridors of the council building maintaining an unremarkable presence. New hive members were not allowed inside the courtroom, and resentment burned inside his gut. *I'm expected to wait three more years, ridiculous.*

He was never one for following rules. After all, breaking them had landed him in London in the first place. Here, he had them all fooled, but, his anger at being shut out in the cold burned brighter, and he was in danger of falling into his old ways. *I had fun killing that guy out in the woods.* He had enjoyed stalking the group of men through the trees, but the injured guy they left buried beneath the earth under a tree was a lure too fragrant to resist. *His flesh was indigestible, but the taste of terror made it sweet. We all have our vises.* Pretending to be a feral was not a huge step for him. His sadistic tendencies lurked barely below the surface.

He timed this visit to the councilor's home with care. He smiled with malice, recognizing the impotent anger vibrating through

Serge. *Time has ticked by, and he still has no news of his mission. How frustrating.* By keeping company with Serge's guardsmen, the dark vampire knew more than anyone should. *The councilor has a great deal to learn about stealth, and how to launch an attack.* The vampire knew the coordinated grid search of the surrounding countryside hinged on a personal vendetta with Doctor Connor.

The only thing he did not know *before* it happened, was *when* the guardsmen planned to move out. *That part, Serge managed to conceal.* But the guardsmen had been gone for five hours now, and it seemed unlikely they would return. *My time to strike*.

His youthful air invited underestimation, and he played to that strength. Examining both vampires in this arena of conflict, he found his preferred benefactor to be a closed book. Doctor Connor spent most of his time inside the hospital, and with so many exits to cover, finding out anything useful about him proved difficult. *Tracking the doctor's movements has been impossible.*

Councilor Serge's routine, however, was laughably predictable. And so, the ambitious young vampire often followed him home, and knew exactly what to say to get the councilor's attention.

Reversing his circumnavigation of the house, he boldly arrived on the front step and knocked on the glossy black door.

Serge's face appeared. The arrival of a visitor gave him hope, and his breathing crackled in his dry chest with anticipation. Staring up into an unfamiliar face, his optimism melted into a sour grimace.

No, I'm not a returning guardsman, so sorry to disappoint you. The vampire suppressed a grin at Serge's crestfallen expression.

Clearly, taken aback at the sudden appearance of a dark stranger, Serge's bony fingers gripped the edge of the door. His thin shoulders blocked the entrance. "Can I help you?"

Wavy black hair fell forward, veiling his amusement as the vampire inclined his head in mock deference. "Councilor Serge, I'm here to offer my services, if I may."

"How so?" Frowning, Serge pursed dry lips.

"I'm new to London. But I am very good at listening, and I believe you have a problem I can help you with."

Serge looked around the stranger's shoulder to survey the empty street, and when the vampire brazenly stepped closer, Serge fell back into the murky hallway, pulling open the front door as though he had no will of his own.

"May I come in?" His guest's smile was encouraging.

Following Serge along the passageway, and watching his jacket flap against his thin body, the vampire cocked his head. *My Lord, he's older than I thought, weak, desperate, perfect.*

The study bore evidence of Serge having lived here his entire life, throughout his mortal and immortal years. Bleached squares on the walls marked the places where mirrors or portraits had once hung. It seemed he wanted no reminders of the miserable reality becoming a vampire proved to be for him.

Serge's steps stirred dust from the carpet into a cloud of silt, and his obvious frustration trembled inside his aged frame.

The vampire hung on to an open boyish expression despite the mildewed atmosphere in the room coating his throat. He resisted the urge to cough and shatter the moment. The smell of human sweat puzzled him, until he realized it emanated from Serge's ancient jacket.

His nose wrinkled at the thought. *Serge still wears his human clothes? Disgusting.* Although, he draped his features in eager confidence when Serge finally turned to face him.

"Who are you?"

"What's in a name?" The young vampire smiled. "People call me the General."

"You don't look like a military man." Serge's skin crackled when he frowned.

"I'm not, but I excel at getting things done."

"And, what makes you think I need your help with anything?" asked Serge, indignation rattling in his throat as he puffed out his chest.

The vampire's narrowed eyes were needle-sharp in the gloom. He already had what he came for. He had taken the measure of the man. Smug satisfaction was almost his undoing when, for a second, the mask slipped and calculation hardened his features.

"I'll make a deal with you, councilor. If the information I uncover gives you an upper hand in your feud with Doctor Connor, you will champion my entrance into the courtroom, and then the council." He assessed Serge's sun-deprived face. "What do you say?"

"I think you presume too much." Serge's affront came too late to cover the nervous glance he sliced across the room.

"The stakes are high, for both of us," the vampire murmured quietly.

Seconds ticked by in which Serge pretended disinterest, and his visitor's attention wandered around the room, allowing him to gather more information to add to his arsenal.

Serge's desk was cluttered with the legal books he used to help his feeble mind make sense of being a vampire. 'Vampire Law and Council Etiquette' was a well-thumbed edition. It caused amusement when the youth paused to think that there were rules he was supposed to abide by. *I'll never make a good vampire.*

Drifting across the room, waiting patiently for Serge to bite, he ran his fingers through fibrous cobwebs which clung to the expensive furniture. Underneath the dust lurked opulence. The high ceiling was dripping in gold leaf, and the elaborate cornices were intricate in design.

He had never seen anything quite like it. *Not since that night in 1964…*

As a youth of nineteen, he enjoyed the free love on offer in the 1960's. But, when the girl was not giving it away, he took it anyway.

It was the height of summer, and he had been lying in the meadow, feeling the earth shake beneath him with the thumping bass of the live music a band was playing on the distant stage. He opened his eyes when a shadow drifted across his closed eyelids and watched the girl lower herself gracefully down onto the grass and rest her chin on a folded knee.

His groin tightened instantly at the glimpse of powder-blue panties.

She hid her face behind a curtain of silky hair and blushed delicately at his approach. He soon discovered the girlfriend she came with had met up with an old flame and, for now, she was alone.

He masked his flush of lust behind a soft voiced stammer and nervous gestures before he pulled her to her feet, begging her to go with him for a walk.

He couldn't remember what she said, but he remembered smothering her screams when he pushed her down onto the gritty ground in the dank shadowed woodland. She was bra-less beneath the thin cotton dress, and his pleasure spiked when her tight body refused his probing fingers entry.

Fuck, a virgin.

His clamped hand bruised her face when he spread her thighs and buried himself inside her. His own juices lubricating a body locked tight around his in terror, he rammed his lust home until, in his moment of climax, he covered her mouth with his, and plunged roughly inside that too.

He used the panties to wipe the blood from his penis, smiling as he gently straightened her clothes and kissed her sweat soaked temple.

He had been a gentleman, and dropped her off at home afterwards, releasing her from the car to stumble to her door clutching torn clothes together over grazed skin.

He drove away from the house, but the gates at the bottom of the gravel driveway slammed shut at his approach. He opened his mouth to curse, and saw stars as his collar yanked tightly around his throat and he was ripped from the car. The stars imploded as he blacked out.

When he came to again, he was lying on the floor staring at just such a gold-dripping ceiling as the one in Serge's study, and his throat was so swollen he could not swallow. A man strolled into view, swirling claret in his goblet, but even in a dazed state, the youth knew something was wrong. The sluggish red liquid clung obscenely to the glass.

The man had slick black hair, and there was not one wrinkle on his face. *He's far too young to be the girl's father.* He took heart.

Rolling himself up from the floor and putting out a hand to support his weight, the boy recoiled as it sank into a cold wet patch on the carpet. Lifting his hand and looking at his blood-soaked palm was a brain-numbing moment when, for a bright young man, he was very slow on the uptake.

Gentle laughter drew the youth's attention. The generous mouthful the well-dressed man took from his glass stained his lips bright red and he nodded slowly at the horror spreading over his guest's face. "Yes, this is your blood." Jerking his chin towards the soaked carpet, he said conversationally, "And, so is that."

As the boy stared blindly, the man vanished, blasting a chilled breeze over his bloodstained skin, and the youth finally got it. Clasping a hand over his torn, stinging throat, he whispered, "I'm going to die."

"Oh no." The words slithered through his head. "Dying is too good for you."

His nape prickled as a cold sweat held him locked tight.

"You will leave Newbury, of course. In fact, you will leave the county of Royal Berkshire, altogether. And-" The boy suddenly found himself shoved up against a wall, his toes barely brushing the floor as the man's chalk-white face filled his vision. "If I see your face again, you will die." The man's ivory-clad fingers tucked a blood-smudged sheet of notepaper into the boy's pocket, and he grinned. "I'm giving you a fighting chance, which is more than you gave my daughter."

"Why?" he croaked.

The father laughed. "Because, I know you will suffer more as an immortal. You are a weak, spineless bastard. You'll get it wrong, and you will die a painfully slow, dehydrating death."

Well, I had the last laugh. He was wrong. I'm a fast learner, and almost fifty years later, I'm still here, older and wiser. Although, he still considered Royal Berkshire a no-go area; he had sense enough to know his luck could run out.

Focusing back onto Serge as the stale atmosphere in the room began to settle into his chest, the general coughed politely, commanding Serge's attention once more.

"What have you to lose? If I turn up nothing, you owe me nothing. It is not a difficult decision," he said mildly.

"Very well." Serge stared long and hard into the gentle features, missing the glee glittering in the mud-colored eyes. "My guardsmen were searching the woodlands south of London. That should be your focal point."

"I'll surprise you, Councilor Serge. Of that, I am sure," he purred, and with a wave of farewell, he left the house, grateful to fill his lungs with the damp night air.

His latest plan to ascend to power glowed like fire inside his belly, and he set off to begin his own grid search of the woods. Serge was right that the best place to start was to find out why his guardsmen never returned. *The old man is hampered by secrecy. He can hardly shout about it when he's breaking council rules by sending them out. But I have deniability, and walking in the woods is not a crime.*

He liked that word. *Deniability.* It was what his own father had said as he wrote the check to pay off his third rape victim.

When he had tried to offer excuses, his father silenced him with an upheld hand, and said, "I don't want to know. If the police come banging on my door, I want deniability."

Chapter 24

Just as he and Julian agreed, it was business as usual, and keeping eyes and ears open. Connor completed his surgical list at the hospital for the afternoon, and now his time was his own. He could have laid claim to the penthouse suite of the London Hilton Hotel as his home, when the spoils of London were up for grabs. However, the view from the twenty-seventh floor, taking in the majestic vista of Hyde Park and Buckingham Palace, was no longer breathtaking to him. The palace was an empty shell with a moss stained facade. Royal blood had proven to be no better at fighting off the ravaging disease of the pandemic than that of the commoner. It made a mockery of the splendid golden-hued Queen Victoria Memorial which graced the Palace doorstep; it stood for victory.

In any case, Connor did not have much time to spare, and he headed unerringly towards the bowels of the hospital and his intellectual home; the laboratory.

He left the waxed corridors of the surgical wing behind, slipped through a door marked “Biological Hazard. NO ADMITTANCE”, and glided down the worn stone stairwell, his shoes barely grazing over the gray quartz glittering underfoot.

The airlock doors leading to the specimen laboratory sighed as Connor pushed through them. The thick stagnant air in the stark clinical space never bothered him, but he activated the ventilation system for the sake of his blood samples.

Pulling on a white coat, he scanned the white ceramic-tiled laboratory and pushed back the feeling of disappointment.

Vials of blood, some stored in glass fronted cabinets and more in racks spread out across the ice white counter-tops, glittered ruby-red in the stark lighting. In the ‘human zone’, Connor rearranged the organized clutter, unpacking vials from racks, checking labels, and filing away the test results. It was a never-ending task generated by the unrelenting flow of the blood samples from the farm. Human samples underwent screening; full blood count tests, the status of antibodies and immune systems all regularly checked.

Satisfied he was on-top of the daily chores, Connor walked around the peninsular counter-top into the ‘vampire zone’. He turned his back on the platelet agitators, thawing baths, and the incubator cabinet filled with petri dishes growing dubious looking clusters of cultured cells.

Leaning back against the workbench and folding his arms, Connor stared at the twelve square yards of whiteboard mounted on the wall, upon which the progression of his thought process on replacing human blood in the vampire diet was carefully written.

The blood stored on this side of the divide was simian, and more than half the test tubes in the cabinets looked empty at first glance. But they were filled with the crystal-clear fluid of the blood substitute he hoped would provide the answer which would liberate both species.

Frowning, he studied the vector diagram illustrating the relationship between the antigens from the human ABO blood group system, and that of chimpanzees and gorillas. It was no surprise they shared characteristics, but isolating the formula which would allow animal blood to pass through the locked gateway of the vampire brainstem and hydrate the gray matter, in the same way human blood did, was like completing a jigsaw puzzle blindfolded... while wearing mittens.

The simian connection was an obvious one to explore, after all, the Rhesus system was the result of experiments which showed that rabbits, when immunized with Rhesus monkey red cells, produce an antibody which also bonds with the red blood cells of many humans.

Even before the pandemic, during his time performing surgery in field hospitals, Connor’s clinical curiosity led to him reading the Lancet articles on the results of early trials in the use of perfluorochemicals in the treatment of battlefield injuries. The particles of the blood substitutes were barely 1/40th the diameter of a human blood cell. They could carry oxygen to blood-starved tissue using crushed capillaries along which blood cells could no longer pass.

Opening the door to the walk-in refrigerator, Connor pulled out a tray of test tubes filled with simian blood and set it on the counter. He dipped a pipette into a glass jar and filled it with the clear liquid of perfluorocarbon particles suspended in water, and added twelve drops of the solution to each test tube. Connor hoped that when emulsified with primate blood, these minuscule molecules would be capable of finding a way in to hydrate vampire brain tissue.

"It's worth a shot."

Connor crossed the lab, zeroed in on the orbital vortexer sitting on the polished granite counter, and transferred the test tubes into the Perspex holding box, clipping each glass vessel into an upright position.

The shrieking lament of the warning siren penetrated into his basement domain as a mere whisper vibrating through the bricks and mortar. But it pierced Connor's concentration like a red-hot needle and, he froze.

"The farm."

The emergency siren meant only one thing, a human was about to die.

Connor's chin jerked up, and, experiments forgotten, he shed the doctor's whites, grabbed his great coat, and disappeared out of the door. He mounted the stairs in an effortless flourish and took the shortest route out of the hospital, emerging into the dull afternoon sunshine. His face stung for a moment until, yanking his collar up and burying his face behind the shield of thick fabric, he sidestepped into the shade.

The siren's scream was unrelenting, reverberating inside his skull as he headed west out of London. Passing by Julian's Richmond home, shadow-hopping instinctively, he covered the miles to the human farm complex at the vampire rate of Lord-knows-how-many miles per second.

"Supervisor Matthew better have a cast-iron excuse for this one," he muttered at the waiting guard who opened the gate in the perimeter fence and cleared out of his way.

Connor wasted no time in getting to the last siphoning shed in the row, which housed the human surgical wing and medical ward.

He shoved through the door and strode along the corridors, welcoming the sting of antiseptic inside his nose which sharpened his concentration. Bursting through a third set of doors, he came face to face with Supervisor Matthew.

"Well?" Connor barked, "And shut that damn noise off. I'm here now."

"It's a gynecological bleed. We've moved her into an operating theater. You'll need to scrub in."

"Shit," said Connor, bursting into movement.

Stripping his coat from his shoulders while he moved, he barged through the door into the sluice room, stopped at the steel sink, and scrubbed ferociously at his hands. He stabbed his arms into the sterile gown held out by an attending vampire, and pushed his hands into latex gloves in a continuous flow of movement. He backed out of the room and into the anteroom where three sets of theater doors faced him.

At the doorway of operating theater number two a clutch of vampire interns jittered from one foot to the other in disconcerted uncontrolled movements. Their shocked expressions were locked in place by the grip of their molded plastic masks, and the black beads of their pupils sparkled in the light when they all turned to look at Connor.

Connor was relieved to see Anthony, his surgical assistant, already there, standing with his back to the closed door. His sturdy physique made an effective barrier, guarding Doctor Connor's domain, but his stiff face was paler than its usual shade of chalk-white, belying the stress he labored under. He croaked, "She's bleeding out."

Connor frowned and nodded tersely. "We'd better get in there, then."

He quickly scanned the nervous faces crowding the space between him and the doors.

"Just you, Anthony, and get *them* out of here."

He surged forward, bowled the interns aside, and entered his theater.

Stepping over the threshold was like walking into a room filled with water. The thick sweet sticky odor of blood flooded into his lungs. A harsh bark of anger cleared the smell from his sinuses and flipped the twinge of hunger over into cold rage.

His bleak gray gaze raked over the limp, pale girl lying on his operating table. He ground his teeth as the implication of the river of blood staining her bulging abdomen and thighs in the luster of macabre crimson hit home.

"Gynecological bleed? It's a fucking bloodbath."

His shoulders hunched with regret, Connor crossed the room and reached for the scalpel to finish the butchery she had started. He heard Anthony enter the theater.

"I can't suture this mess up. It's too late to do anything other than lengthen the incision and deliver the baby," he said grimly, shooting a glance over his shoulder.

Connor's penetrating glance became a driving, spiraling turn when a growl tore from Anthony's throat and he dragged his plastic mask away to unveil a bloodlust-crazed stare.

Pinning his surgical assistant to the wall by the neck, it took all of Connor's self-control not to crush Anthony's windpipe as he battled his own demon, anger, borne of useless frustration. *Another life lies wasted on my table. Dammit.*

He lifted Anthony bodily. Scuffing his feet across the floor, he threw him against the operating room doors. Anthony's colliding weight swung open an aperture that swallowed him as he fell out of the room and sprawled on the floor outside.

Watching the door swing shut again, Connor forced his words through clenched teeth. "Get out and stay out." *I'm going to have to do this alone.*

Turning swiftly back into the room, Connor picked up the blade once more. The human girl's head hung limply. He stared down at the relaxed muscles clinging to her bone structure; the raw ingredients which needed human emotions to give them meaning. To say she *looked* dead was simplistic, but truth often is. Connor's features settled into a stillness which became every bit as eerie.

Her ruptured swollen abdomen oozed her life out onto the floor. He picked up a blunt edged C-section scalpel and sawed through the uterine wall. All he thought about was saving the baby.

"Dammit, how did she do this?" he rasped as he plunged his hands into a basin of boiling water, taking their temperature from icy to human warm.

The smell of her blood coated his throat, and even though hunger sliced a burning path through his gut, he slipped his hands inside her belly. Grimly, he lifted the wrinkled, red body from her and laid it in the cradle of the infant resuscitation table. He automatically went through the actions needed to bring a parent joy, or thicken their joy to grief. *In this case, it matters only to the dead; the council members will shrug and move on, and* she *can't even do that.*

His touch was sure, even when faced with the minute musculature and the fragile bones which were a delicate honeycombed masterpiece of nature. He inserted a bare inch of the finest catheter, using suction to clear the tubes, and then massaged the tiny chest. Resignation settled inside him as he tried to warm the baby's limbs, rubbing the waxy, reddened skin. *Nothing.*

First-hand proof that the human breeding program was failing miserably slapped him in the face, and for the third time, all his brain could offer was, "*Dammit.*" Two girls had reached their third trimester, and the council had been tentatively hopeful. *Eclampsia took one, and now, this.*

Connor wiped blood-soaked hands down his green surgical gown. *Being sterile no longer matters, it's too late.* The baby and the girl were both dead.

It was not the first time he realized that, in some, becoming a vampire eradicated empathy. Connor had never been sure if it was jealousy that humans had something they still yearned for, or the contempt of the suddenly superior. *Either way, it doesn't make for the caring bedside manners needed to reassure an expectant mother.* Connor grinned wryly. *As if we could ever fool them.* But, this was a clear case of vampire complacency in believing the girl accepted her own and her baby's fate. *But how the hell did she get hold of a knife.*

The blue tinge of cyanosis enhanced her skin with a disconcerting ethereal beauty, dressing her features in lilac-tinted lace. Her expression was peaceful. "Well, you won," Connor whispered as he passed his fingers over her face, gently pressing her eyelids closed.

Connor's throat slammed shut. The lure of congealing blood was no less potent, and just a lick would course through him like a shot of heroin, but he thought of Rebekah, his warm, pliant, beautiful Rebekah, and walked away, seeking refuge in the welcome burn of anger.

A snarl escaped him as he yanked his gown away, tugged off his mask and surgical cap, and cast them savagely aside. His raven-black hair clumped around his face, and the toughened-steel blade of his stare flashed as, bursting through the theater doors, his stride devoured the yards of the antiseptic-white painted corridor.

If Anthony has any sense, he'll be back at the hospital sleeping inside a mortuary drawer by now. Though, even that might not be enough to redirect the blast of the rage burning through Connor.

"Anthony," Connor roared as his lengthened stride skimmed the waxed floor. Concentrating on the measured extending and flexing of his muscles, he hung on to his sanity as he beat his way through doors, bouncing them off the walls and scattering plasterboard dust onto the ground.

"What the hell happened in there?" he shouted into Anthony's face. The fluorescent light cast Connor's expression in ice-sculpted fury and his black hair was comically disheveled, but no one was laughing. His wrathful glare was the most terrifying thing Anthony had ever seen.

"We didn't see it," stammered Anthony.

"For God's sake, it was a routine ultrasound scan. There shouldn't even have been a scalpel tray in the examination room," Connor ground out, shoving clawed fingers into his hair to keep them from closing around Anthony's neck again. "These people are morons."

Anthony cowered. The rippling muscles of his solid bulk strained the fabric of his white coat as he crossed arms, protecting his diaphragm, and for a moment, Connor felt shame. He was angry, but driving Anthony into adopting a vampire posture of attack-survival? *Not a good feeling.*

Anthony had been a boxer for ten of his thirty mortal years, and it was his misfortune that, unlike Connor, whose exposure to blood as a human surgeon strengthened his resistance, in Anthony the opposite occurred. Connor had his own views on that. He knew Anthony's boxing career was fueled by the anger of a bullied and beaten child. Now, Anthony, the vampire of sixty years, was indestructible. His anger had evaporated and the gentle nature he protected, re-emerged. It was bad timing for him. *Now, more than ever, he needs to be tough to resist the very thing he craves, human blood.* Connor liked Anthony and was not about to give up on him.

He looked into Anthony's stricken face, turned abruptly, and strode away.

Connor didn't want to be involved in this situation. Human surgery was one thing, but not this. *If she hadn't stabbed herself in the stomach, I could pretend it's not my concern.* It killed him that the human breeding project existed. *And now, it will turn me into a liar.* He loathed keeping his involvement from Rebekah. *But, it's being run by short-sighted idiots, and I have no choice. Will she understand that?*

Connor's frustrated rage demanded a scapegoat. Someone to unleash his resentment upon, and he knew just the person. He left the compound, kicking up a trail of spray as he crossed the slick, wet meadows of grass. Keeping his anger warm, he took the shortest route through the sidewalks of London. When it came to finding a target for his wrath, he considered Julian as good a bet as any. *He may be the principal of the vampire council, but he's also the closest thing to a friend I've got, and better yet, I can shout at him.*

Connor burst into Julian's chambers, shrugged out of his coat and flung it down on the leather armchair.

Before he could speak, Julian stopped him. "I heard," he said, with quiet authority.

They had not seen each other since the battle in the woods, and their unresolved differences thickened the air. They stood toe-to-toe, comparable in height, with Julian's bronze-toned determination squaring up to Connor's menacing dark presence. Julian's jade-green regard was unflinching. The shared physicality of an alpha-male was only a small part of their bond. They would never stand shoulder to shoulder on this issue, but, they understood each other, at least. The residue of human integrity struck a chord between the two.

Shaking his head, Julian said, "I'm struggling to understand what has happened to your detachment. I could do with *Doctor* Connor, the analytical surgeon, showing up about now. With Rebekah... Well, I've avoided pressing it, but I *need* your help with the breeding program." Julian's words weighed heavy with exasperation. "If only to keep Serge's dangerous ambitions in check." He crossed to his favorite spot in the room. The compressed patch on the thickly-piled carpet told the tale as he rested an elbow up on the mantelpiece and adopted a relaxed posture. "Connor, I'm waiting for you to arrive at the same conclusion; we have no choice."

Julian was not fooling Connor. Relaxation did not pull every tendon tight and fill the air with the hum of a tuning fork. Connor ground his teeth. He knew his expectation of Julian letting him off the hook was unfair. *Julian's help in saving the eco-town community was more than I had a right to expect.*

Connor's first priority centered on developing a synthetic blood substitute, but he knew each set of tests which failed increased the pressure upon him to commit to the human breeding program. *But now, with Rebekah, perpetuating human existence as cattle is unthinkable.*

"I *can't* be directly involved, you know that."

Julian's look said otherwise. "In the ideal world, I wouldn't ask you to, but this is *not* the ideal world Connor."

Connor struggled under the weight of Julian's assessment. "But dammit, Julian, they don't know what they're doing. How can they work on the farm and not understand that humans long for freedom?" He glared. "It may have been a hundred years ago, but I still remember it. Surgery was brutal. There were men who would have a leg amputated without anaesthetic to hang onto life, but if you locked them up, they gave up hope and died."

"Connor, as principal, *I* have no choice." His eyes were somber as he sought understanding. "Bottom line, we need the human population to thrive. If inseminated pregnancies and nursery farms can increase the population, then I will have a blood riot on my hands if I *don't* support it... And I need you," he added quietly. "If we can't find a way to calm them, make them accepting, this will keep happening."

"Drug them, you mean? But not harm their babies? A very honorable exercise," said Connor tightly. He knew the other baby's death had been avoidable, too. The mother concealed the symptoms of pre-eclampsia until it was too late; they had both found a way of escape.

"Well, honor is a luxury we can't afford." The pendulum swung back as *Principal* Julian squared his shoulders, abandoning relaxed in favor of courtroom hauteur. "I know you don't like it, but only you have the control to be near a bleeding human and *not* rip their throat out. Look at what happened to Anthony today."

Neither spoke in a stand-off they both knew had only one outcome.

Finally, Connor growled as the truth pressed down upon him. *I could have prevented what happened today. I would have known the girl's cooperation was a ploy.* "Rebekah will never forgive me."

Julian leveled a pragmatic stare and said, "Then don't tell her. More will die without your help."

Connor knew he had no choice, but he was not ready to roll over yet. "I'll think about it, that's all I can promise."

"Well, it's a start. But, don't think too long. Serge is stirring up support in the council for the hybrid breeding program." At Connor's sharp glance, he said, "Things are becoming desperate."

"The man disgusts me," Connor spat. "Surely, even he can see we can't risk more human females in a sadistic cause." Connor swallowed the venom filling his mouth at the thought of biting into

Serge's scrawny neck. Even the knowledge he would taste rank could not stop satisfaction flooding in. "It's a pity deliberately wasting human life in experimentation doesn't carry the death penalty. After all, he's still threatening the food supply."

"At least, while his focus is elsewhere he won't be recruiting guardsmen to replace the ones we culled." Julian's lip curled. "You will have time to organize the escape of your humans."

"Don't tell me you're regretting helping us, Julian? Turn them in, and there are six female feathers in your cap." The dead girl's features filled Connor's mind. Her slackened muscles tightened and transformed into Rebekah. "But remember, Julian. One of those is my Rebekah, and I would have to kill you," he breathed conversationally.

Julian's eyes flashed. "I'm not your enemy. I have no wish to see Rebekah on the farm, but I can still wish we were ignorant of their existence. Life would be simpler."

"You're right. Keeping tabs on Serge is a headache. And killing a dozen of his guardsmen in as many days still only buys us time." Connor sighed. "Simple is no longer an option, I'm sorry."

He focused on Julian's white face, inhaling and tasting the concentration of copper in his scent which indicated dehydration. Doctor Connor emerged as the dominant force in the room as he said, "You need revival sleep, Julian. You look wired. Don't let this get on top of you."

Turning briskly, Connor headed for the door.

Julian stared at the space Connor had left. The door was closed and the breeze of its movement whisked across Julian's skin, but he was lost in his own thoughts by then, cataloguing his tight tendons and grating tissue.

"Damn it, he's right." Wired didn't even come close. He needed revival sleep, and he was irritated Connor had to point it out.

If my stress levels spiral out of control, it calls my competence into question and lays us open to attack. That would be a gift for Serge.

Julian crossed the room, took two vials of human blood from the cooler and rolled them absently between his palms. *This is no time for stupidity.* Tension hummed through Julian's body like a simulated rush of adrenalin, and he grinned. *On the battlefield, at least, Connor and I know the score.*

Serge easily recruited juveniles, knowing they were very strong, but desperate for a mentor to make their existence more comfortable, but they were no match for Connor's and Julian's maturity. *They are, however, still lethal to humans.* The thought weighed on his mind, and not only because of his allegiance to Connor.

Julian downed the vials of blood without tasting them. Pressure was like an aneurysm building inside his skull as though his thoughts caused friction-burns inside the tightening space. He had not been the same since the night of the battle. His flashbacks always resolved into the same face, with green eyes and tangled chestnut hair. It was not only Rebekah who had piqued his interest. *I don't like it.*

For Julian, the rioting relaxation of revival sleep was a siren call of welcome release.

Chapter 25

Rebekah walked along the hallway of the safe house, shrouded in darkness. The effort of being furtive cramped her muscles, and even her bones seemed to ache.

Connor had now laid rubber flooring, and she wore the expensive sneakers he had pressed into her arms when he agreed she could *visit* in London. "You have no concept of quiet," he had said, "believe me."

Well, she did believe him. *And it scares the shit out of me.*

She sometimes wondered how they managed to survive before Connor. *A lot of luck, it would seem.* Smiling, she remembered other revelations which never occurred to them. "And, Rebekah..." He had waited until she won the battle with the distraction of his stunning features, and her brown eyes locked onto his. "No nylon, rayon or wool. You might as well announce your presence with a firework display. Vampires can smell the electricity of static sparks."

Rebekah checked her watch. *Time to go down into the basement.* She didn't give a thought to lights anymore, vampires embraced darkness, and so did she. She ran her fingers around the door frame to check it was properly closed. Another trick learned from Connor, do not move anything you do not need to move. *And don't take anything for granted, always check.* She did not bother to lock the door. Metal was as soft as butter in a vampire fist, which Connor had shown the day he had first come here to find her.

When she passed the hallway mirrors, her reflection reached out and pulled her back for a closer inspection. *I'm still a girl, after all.* Rocking back and forth, Rebekah played the moonbeams over her features. Her eyes glittered as they collected the light they needed to see. She fluffed up her blonde hair and pinched her pale cheeks until the word 'ouch' almost escaped. She scraped her teeth across her full bottom lip, making that red, too.

Deep breaths. She had no idea when, but she knew he would come.

Rebekah smiled, stepping back until her reflection sank into shadow. It felt as though Connor had always been hers. His passion in everything ran deep, and even though his hunger for her was alarming at times, his latent ferocity excited her. *Basement. Now. What happens if he gets here and I'm wandering around with a heart hammering like a dinner gong?*

Looking down at her sneakers, Rebekah negotiated the narrow, wooden open-tread stairway down into the basement. "What I'd give for heels to make my legs look a mile long, and drive him nuts." Rebekah muttered. Thinking of him, yearning spiraled inside her, tightening seductively until merely breathing made her tingle.

With both feet planted safely on the floor, she surveyed the basement.

The grime coating the skylight glass hid the worst of the debris, filtering the light and deepening the shadows. Evidence of the others who had shared the house trailed across the room like morsels fallen from a buffet table. *Okay, we wouldn't have been able to talk, not now night has fallen.* But she missed seeing their faces. The craving for company was hard to suppress. She retrieved an empty orange juice carton and rubbed her thumb over its waxy surface as though, like Aladdin's lamp, it could bring them all back.

The rest of the group had headed off on the motorcycles two hours ago, taking low risk routes back to the eco-town plotted out for them by Connor. It remained their best option when moving around. For humans, there were still only two choices if they crossed a vampire's path. One was to move motorcycle-fast and the other was to stand stock-still and hope.

That one worked out well for me. She grinned. It had proved the theory at least, that for vampires the scenery whips past like the view through an express train window. *The vampire certainly had not registered my presence. I just didn't figure on the backwash.*

The motorcycle panniers were filled with medical supplies delivered by Connor to the safe house. He had vetoed backpacks as being very un-vampire-like. Beta-blockers and the drugs Uncle Harry needed were more easily available with Connor's help, and they no longer needed to go inside the derelict London hospitals to find them.

Normally, it would be unthinkable to leave someone behind, but in her case, it no longer applied. *Uncle Harry still worries of course, but now, I have Connor.*

Leizle would worry, too, but as all women in love would know, when weighed against a night with her man, there was no contest. *She'll understand one day.*

Rebekah's hands refused to settle, so she refolded the blankets left from sleeping six in here last night. Her thoughts turned to the reason they were feverishly stocking up on supplies. The close escape in the woods had them rattled. After fifteen years burrowed into the rolling hills of the North Downs of Kent, their time was up. It was still home, but no longer safe. *We have to move out, and, thank God for Connor.* Her joy was iced with guilt. *He hasn't mentioned Julian lately. It can't be easy for him. I guess the principal has to appear uninvolved.*

It was going to take a lot of planning, and it looked like it was all down to Connor.

Connor stood on the sidewalk outside the safe house, once again wearing his charcoal greatcoat. The garment was authentic. He had some sentimental bones in his body. 1968 was not long ago for him, and his memory held a crystal-clear image of the Hungarian refugee who gave it to him. The Soviet invasion had clubbed his countrymen into submission, and when Connor came across his emaciated form, it did not promise to be a satisfying snack, even if Connor had been tempted. In the end, like Hansel and Gretel's tale with a twist, Connor fattened him up and let him go.

The greatcoat had been his reward, and he hung onto it as a square in the patch worked cloth of his humanity. *My thirst is always there, but I can still choose. I don't have to act on it.*

And so, with his collar pulled up, Connor's bulk was a blend of jet-black and charcoal, with the moonlight picking out indigo strands in the raven's wing of his black hair and stirring mercury into his gray eyes. His bone structure invited moonbeams and bent them to his will, casting ink-black pools beneath his cheekbones and accenting a brow line which gave his face intensity.

Bram Stoker would have been proud.

Connor grinned wryly. The fact Julian displayed signs of stress proved one thing. *He's not as detached as he pretends. But I can't argue with Julian; life would be simpler without Rebekah.* He had spent a lot of his day worrying about her. She was stubborn and he would feel easier if she would stay in the eco-town. *But she's fearless, and that's why I love her.* She was tantalizingly close, now.

The sour taste of his meeting with Julian lingered until he breathed in the warmed-syrup of Rebekah's scent, and, like casting sawdust on an oil slick, it calmed him.

He had not agreed to Julian's request. *Not out loud, at any rate. I'm not lying to her, not yet.* Connor grimaced. *It's just semantics, but after the day I've had...* He fancied he could still feel the waxy residue of the vernix-coated fetus clinging to his fingertips. He was feeling every one of his hundred plus twenty-four human years, and what he needed now, was to lose himself in Rebekah.

Drawing in a deep breath, he wiped the day's events from his brain. He immersed himself in the faint honeysweet scent of her skin, and hunger stirred in his gut. *Her heart rate is a little high. Does she know I'm here?*

He took the stairs three at a time, and, without conscious thought, he was where he wanted to be.

As he had done once before, Connor stood four feet behind Rebekah watching the denim-coated curves of her shapely body swaying enticingly, as she folded blankets, this time. He had fed at the hospital on vials of blood which didn't offer the excitement of the hunt, but a flavor of that excitement burned white-hot inside his chest now.

He inhaled her scent and a blade of need sliced open his windpipe. The tearing sensation no longer caught him off guard; he knew loving her would always be an assault on his senses. *But damn, the pleasure is worth everything.* The grazing of her thighs as she rocked her hips sang in his ears as a tuning fork of perfection, and he wanted to pull her back into his body.

Her fear never failed to saturate him in satisfaction. Even though his hunting instinct pounded on the walls of his chest, he held firm, preventing the hunger rampaging through him from unleashing a feeding frenzy. While he didn't terrify her anymore, he could enjoy an echo of it, by surprising her. She didn't know he was there, and her vulnerability mesmerized him as he stepped silently forward and closed his chilled fingers around her midriff.

And there it was, a brief moment to her, but a long cool draught to him. Her heart jolted in her chest as alarm raced along her spine. Every tendon tugged short while her body prepared to launch mindlessly forward. Connor smiled when her rush of fear drenched his mouth in venom.

He knew the moment she realized it was him. She turned towards him in greeting, the momentary alarm still tumbling her over a cliff of apprehension, but she knew, now, he was there to catch her.

Her palms imprinted onto his hard body, and his chilled nerve endings swelled to welcome the heat, flirting with pain and ecstasy. His playful growl vibrated beneath her fingertips when Connor chuckled, and he held her firmly as her knees shook.

As always, he wondered at mankind ever dominating the planet. *Evolution is clearly a comedian.* The human body was hindered by the tangled ball of survival reflexes called 'flight or fight'. They tightened reactions into knots and made useful action impossible. Connor's ironic musing hit a wall when Rebekah's eyes locked onto his, and the intense, fathom-deep, pools of warm chocolate swallowed him whole.

She gasped in protest at his creeping up on her, he inhaled the yelp of shock into his cool mouth, and it stung the back of his throat when he swallowed it down. Holding her close, his fingers tugged at buttons and zips, stroking over her skin as if a message written in Braille required his urgent attention.

She smiled into his mouth. "Hey, slow. I mean human slow, not vampire slow."

Lifting his head, he ran a finger slowly down over her delicate features. Drifting his touch across her cheek, he looped a silky blonde rope behind her ear, and the twitch of his lips became a rueful smile as he said, “Oops, too late.”

Her jeans hugged her thighs for a moment longer before falling to the floor.

She sighed in amused exasperation, and he whispered against her lips, “I’m sorry, maybe next time?” His hands smoothed over her backside as he lifted her effortlessly to frame his hips.

Her eyes widened in surprise. “You too. Or did you just come in here naked?”

“What can I say? I just find you too delicious to resist.”

He strode across the floor, skillfully avoiding the manmade trap of discarded cartons, magazines, and zip-locked bags of laundry. He sank urgently into revival sleep, until his dulled senses resembled wading through floodwaters. They arrived at the bed.

Rolling her gently down onto the mattress, smiling, he muttered, “How about I take *this* part slow?”

The dusting of blond hair over her skin glinted as the moonlight glanced off her trembling frame. The elusive display of pearly fragments, caught easily by his keen vampire sight, dressed her body in a robe of glittering splendor.

Revival sleep made him fearless. Laying her back, he moved down her body. The merest brush of his tongue stirred excitement, and the caress of his lips lay a tingling path down over her stomach. When he finally parted her thighs and closed his mouth over her, he wound the thread of his sanity tight. He had never dared risk tasting her, and his throat felt ragged with hunger as he held back the urge to bite.

Holding her hips, he dipped into her heat, drowning in the pulsing softness closing around his probing tongue, feeling the inferno of her climax tingling beneath his caress.

Her lungs clutched at the air in breathless sighs. Desire rushed through her bloodstream, her pounding heart stirring a raging current inside her, and the honeyed fragrance of it filled him.

Connor savored each moment. When her scent burned with satisfaction, he drove her body over the edge, his tongue stroking in a sensuous rhythm, tasting her ecstasy until she shuddered beneath him, and her whimpered breath told him she was spent.

As she lay there, abandoning her senses to the lethargy sweeping through her body, he moved reverently up over her, running his fingers over the swell of her hips, her quivering belly and ribcage. She was so delicate, and, as usual, the sight of the dusky pink marks, and an older rainbow of bruising, made him feel guilty, but only for a moment.

Connor pressed his lips to her throat, covering her carotid pulse. The turbulent flow thundering under her skin stirred the cocktail of rubies and diamonds. *Blood cells. Such a boring word for something so exquisite.*

“Am I forgiven?” He breathed, as the pulse in her throat became slow and thick.

Seeing the wisps of heat in her hooded gaze was all he needed, to know how much she enjoyed him. For now, it was enough. He pushed himself deeper into revival sleep and folded Rebekah’s body into his. He smiled as he absorbed the micro-tremors still sparking through her nervous system, tiny pulses that fluttered against his skin. Everything about her fascinated him.

She slept, and so did he. Not human sleep, of course. Laying with her now needed all his control. The wet shushing sound of her heart echoed in his chest and hunger pangs tore holes in the lining of his stomach. But in revival sleep he could be this close and suffer it.

He had still to decide what to tell her about the breeding project, and he was more than happy to put it off for a while longer.

Chapter 26

It was not just the oxygen-starved atmosphere inside the 'vampire' cave making Douglas feel sick, it was the cesspool of fear, anger and disgust swilling in his gut.

The smell of sweat and stale urine still clung to his skin, but Douglas had persuaded Harry to bring him clean clothes, at least; the blood splatters on his shirt from Connor's bite had begun to haunt him and invade his sleep.

Using a fork to move the congealing chicken and potatoes around his plate, bile burned the back of his throat. He rubbed a clammy hand over his neck and touching the scabbed over crescents Connor's teeth had tattooed into his flesh focused his mind. *Escape.*

"This food is delicious, Oscar." Douglas flicked a glance upwards, a grin smeared across his face when the chef got up and moved out of sight.

So easy. Douglas knew how to use the disgust he could feel emanating from Oscar. The tight expression on Oscar's face said he would rather be anywhere else than there, guarding the prisoner while he ate. Douglas smiled. *Let him hide from me. I can get to work.*

The obstruction of the boulder sat back on its haunches like a rearing circus elephant, waiting to roll forward onto all fours again at Oscar's command.

Douglas waited until Oscar took up a remote position, standing in the yellow glow of a bulkhead lamp about ten feet away. Leaning against the wall, Oscar gazed up the tunnel along which he would return to his kitchen, once this chore was done.

Moving nearer to the entrance of the cave, Douglas squatted and took deep breaths of air which had more oxygen than he could get when locked inside his prison.

Forcing down the nausea, he picked up a rock and, turning it in his hands, decided which way up to put it, before he moved.

Determination, faith, and cunning. Douglas grimaced. *That's all I need.* He had been chipping away at the interior walls when he was alone, excavating lumps of rock with the blunt knife he managed to steal. Oscar had bought the lie that it had fallen into a crevice. *I wasn't sure he would, and he'll be kicking himself when he realizes.* Douglas could almost taste Oscar's anger when the day came that he discovered the cave empty. *It's humiliating, being fed like a dog.*

Each time the rock was pushed back at mealtimes, Douglas placed another stone on the rockery he was building. Each one held the boulder back a little more, and, as the gap grew, the chink of hope inside Douglas glowed brighter.

He silently moved across to the entrance, his feet treading along an invisible tightrope. Leaning forward, he could see Oscar's boots and the back of one broad shoulder where, as Douglas expected, his jailer leaned against the tunnel wall. Douglas fitted the rock in its chosen crevice, and then, holding his breath, he switched his tightrope walk into reverse.

He surveyed the arrangement of bricks in his wall. *The gap is what? Almost a foot? Maybe three more days.*

Douglas grimaced in silent mirth as he played out the escape in his mind, making it look easy. *The last week has been the worst of my life, and they will pay*. The need for revenge was like a vein of gold running through his black heart.

The sound of footsteps pounding down the tunnel towards Oscar interrupted Douglas' daydreaming. The echoes of feet grew louder, and were joined by a chorus of agitated voices; their words spilling into a jumble of confusion. Douglas grinned when he recognized signs of alarm. *This might be easier than I thought.*

Oscar shouted, "Get everyone into the meeting hall."

A screech wailed through the air when Oscar pulled the lever, and the boulder grated forward to seal his prison. As the retreating footfalls faded, Douglas, in the act of adding to his growing barricade, shot forward and lifted a rock larger than any he had tried to handle before. The weight of it almost pulled his arms out of their sockets as, crouching like a sumo wrestler and grunting, he launched the rock in a last ditch effort. It landed, rocking precariously before, with a desperate shove, it came to rest in the doorway, cradled between the rails running across the threshold.

The huge fast-moving boulder closed the space, grinding along the rails until it drove Douglas' rock into the wall opposite. The rock crumbled, but the compressed core of it held firm.

The boulder groaned, settled into its new position, and silence descended inside and outside the vampire cave.

The hole is big, but, is it big enough?

Douglas sidled up to it and, in a vertical limbo dance, pushed into the gap. The rough rock face embedded shards of gravel into his fat, scoring deep scratches into his stomach and decorating his skin with blood-beaded grazes. He sucked in his gut and pressed harder. The sandblasted surface caressed his cheek, dragging the flesh back and refusing to let it go. His eyes watered and salty tears stung the torn skin as he pushed through the pain. His cheekbone creaked, and there was a moment when he thought it might snap, but he was wedged. Panic fluttered inside him and a sob cramped his throat. Squeezing his eyes shut, he shoved his weight forward, hissing between his teeth when his flesh burned. Pure determination scraped his carcass through the tight space. *The rest is easy.*

Scuttling along tunnels he had helped to build, he followed a route which avoided the meeting hall, and his first lungful of crisp night air was laced with the heady exhilaration of success.

It was dark and cold in the woods, but he didn't care. *I'm free.* Douglas' knot of hatred kept him warm, and it also kept him moving. *Seven years, destroyed. They didn't like me, but I had their respect, and now that's gone thanks to that leech.* His face twisted with disgust. *I even had Rebekah...* But, this last week, locked inside the vampire cave, his humiliation became complete. Douglas forced a bitter laugh through clenched teeth. *Who the hell does Harry think he is? Telling me to be grateful? That I should thank my lucky stars I had a safe place to hide when the bloodsucker was in town?*

Douglas' cold gray eyes glinted. "If you can't beat 'em, join 'em," he breathed.

Barely an hour after escaping, he pushed through the woods, headed towards London, he hoped, but not entirely sure. He was the one sweating now. He could make better progress once the sun came up. His biggest fear was he would end up circling back in the thickening gloom.

Even if he had been a Boy Scout, the foliage overhead made navigating by the North Star a non-starter. As the temperature dropped, the pluming vapor of his breath told him he should dig in for the night. He remembered the survival tale of a polar explorer who killed a bear, cut it open and slept inside the carcass to keep warm. A snicker tugged briefly at his lips. A rabbit carcass and his bulk were not a good match.

Scuffing the ground with the toe of his boot, he found a drift of dead leaves and bark between aged tree roots and used the blunt end of a rotten branch to dig around. He laid back in the hollow he made, wishing it was deeper, but deeper also meant damper. He pulled dried out leaves over him as a buffer against the cold, and resigned himself to a long, tough night.

Chapter 27

It was still pitch black when the sound of a motorcycle arriving outside shattered the silence. Connor pulled on pants, left the basement, and descended the wide stone steps from the safe house to the sidewalk before the engine was cut. His cold fingers plucked the key from the ignition, and he smoothly palmed it. The rider found himself inside the hallway, pinned up against a wall before he could draw breath.

Glaring into his victim's white, shocked face, Connor hissed, "Are you mad?" Annoyance rattled in his chest as he said quietly, "Vampires can see in the dark, and if we *were* out joyriding at night, what we would never need is a *headlight*."

Added to that, most vampires out and about at this hour were delivering harvested crops to the human farm. *This fool almost committed suicide.*

"At least, you didn't wear a crash helmet." *Human watermelon verses vampire medicine ball, we definitely don't need one.*

Vampires no longer needed to worry about the vulnerability of the *living* human brain, which had the consistency of jelly. *Mother Nature provided a nice thick skull, but the impact of a motorcycle accident would be like a wooden spoon stirring custard in a sturdy bowl. And to coin a phrase, 'game over'.*

The familiar waft of human adolescence clinging to the boy did nothing to lessen Connor's exasperation. Thomas was a long way from the potent strength of manhood, and his face crumpled. He retreated as far from Connor's frustration as he could.

"What on earth are you playing at?" Connor sighed harshly. He could hear the kid's heart thumping. When he finally focused on the boyish face, Connor's irritation was tempered by the terror on the cotton-white features. "Thomas. You again."

"Thomas?" Rebekah repeated, as she appeared in the hallway.

Connor released his grip on the boy's shirt and settled for a disapproving frown. *Rebekah risked her life to save him in the woods, and, like a bad penny, here he is again.*

Thomas gulped, shying away from Connor and locking onto Rebekah's reassuring face.

Connor set a careful hand on Thomas' shoulder and said gruffly, "It's okay, Thomas. No harm done."

"Why are you here?" asked Rebekah. "Has something happened?"

"Leizle and Douglas have gone." His voice was high and panicked.

"Gone? Where?" Rebekah blurted.

Holding up his hand, Connor said quietly, "Deep breath, Thomas. Now, tell us what you know."

"Leizle got cut off out in the field." Thomas shrugged. "Douglas is just gone."

Connor's nostrils flared. "Okay, buddy, you've done well." Stepping back and making room for Rebekah to put her arms around the boy's shoulders, Connor said, "Take him down below."

"Okay."

"Thomas. You won't be able to keep up with my motorcycle. Take beta-blockers and stay in here 'til dawn. Rebekah and I have got to get going. Do you understand?"

"Sure. You can trust me." Thomas jutted out his rounded young chin.

"Good lad." Looking at Rebekah, Connor said, "I'll see you outside in five minutes."

He strode out of the door, buttoning his shirt and pulling on the greatcoat he collected from the basement without Rebekah or Thomas seeing he had moved. He smirked when Rebekah shook her head and muttered, "Damn, that man is fast."

As promised, five minutes later, Rebekah made it down onto the sidewalk and gave Connor and the motorcycle a worried look.

Dewy moisture glistened on the tarmac as if it was perspiring, and Rebekah certainly was. Connor wanted to taste the damp sheen on her top lip, but there was not time.

He sat astride a Triumph 1200 Daytona. The bulbous gas tank, sprayed matt black, and black skeletal bones did not glint in the moonlight and blended into the shadows. But the one hundred and forty-seven horse power engine screaming would be a dead giveaway, once they got moving. What interested Connor, however, was that it had a top speed of bat-out-of-hell.

"C'mon Honey," he said calmly. He leaned over and, reaching across, he caught Rebekah's fingers in his. Rising to his feet, he effortlessly overcame her startled resistance. He pulled her up onto the pillion seat behind him, subsiding smoothly back down and gently fitting her thighs in snugly to his.

"We have to go." His grin sprouted more perspiration over her body as his eyes glittered with exhilaration. She swallowed down the dry pill of nerves as he said, "Don't worry, honey, show-boating is for idiots. No wheelies, I promise."

Rebekah clung to Connor's solid bulk. His riding style, like everything else about him, was forceful. His thighs twitched with every bump in the road. Black shadows hurtled towards them at terrifying speeds, and Rebekah squeezed her eyes tightly shut against the wind chill scalding her cheeks.

Connor could have moved faster on foot, but carrying Rebekah would have shouted *human* louder than the screaming motorcycle engine did. Their dash coincided with peak farming time, but Connor figured that working vampires were distracted vampires, and the motorcycle *was* moving insanely fast.

His foot tapped up through six gears in three seconds. *Careful, I don't want to break anything.* He flirted with the urge to be reckless. *If I were human, I'd downshift, wind open the throttle, and drop the clutch when the engine revs hit the sweet spot.* He would have enjoyed the rearing of the bike in a metal rodeo ride. The surge of speed would slam his stomach into his spinal cord, and unleash eerie weightlessness which his body would thrive on. *But I promised, Rebekah, no wheelies.*

He also knew that to get one hundred percent speed, you needed one hundred percent traction. So, every square millimeter of the tires rubber compound remained glued to the road and eighteen minutes into the journey the motorcycle's tires were already wearing. The manufacturers had not figured on the rider being a well-oiled machine in human form.

The scream of the engine at maximum speed was unabating, but his only thought was to return Rebekah to the eco-town. It would release him to search for Leizle. *Douglas can wait until Hell freezes over*. Thomas was safe for now, although the boy's thin frame and gangling limbs gave Connor pause. Thomas would ride his more sedate 250cc motorcycle back to the eco-town in the lull of cool early dawn. *I hope the kid can be trusted.*

When they neared the eco-town, they ran out of road.

"Hold tight," Connor said.

He swerved the motorcycle off the asphalt and they hurtled headlong across the field. He used his legs as stabilizers, providing forward propulsion every time the tires spun on wet grass and the engine note whined. Suddenly finding traction on the hard-packed earth inside the entrance of the eco-town, the motorcycle lurched forward. Connor skidded it to a halt, showering mud up the walls. He cut the engine and, reaching behind, swung Rebekah around onto his lap as he dismounted in a seamless fluid movement, and strode forward holding her close to his chest.

"I can walk." Embarrassment made her tone grumpy.

Connor laughed gently, and said, "Not this fast though, hmm?" And he surged forward, hugging the sweeping curves of the tunnels in an effortless parody of a toboggan run.

Seconds later, lowering her smoothly to her feet outside the meeting cavern, he raised a smug brow as he looked into her flushed face.

"You win. Show off," she muttered, tossing her head and stalking into the cavern.

Connor's amusement died when he stopped on the threshold and saw Harry.

Uncle Harry's pacing had worn a groove into the packed-earth floor of the cavern, and he ceased wringing his hands abruptly when he caught sight of Rebekah. He directed a fretful glance at Connor's carefully composed face.

"Harry." Connor nodded curtly. His set expression left no doubt he had little sympathy for the man. *Leizle, maybe.*

"Uncle Harry." Rebekah rushed to embrace him. "Where is she? What happened?"

Connor hung back, waiting. A muscle twitched in an iron-set jaw as he considered biting Harry's head off. Instead, he wet his lips and carefully swallowed his annoyance, along with the venom pooling in his throat.

"She went out with the group to raid the vampire crops."

Connor was impressed. *The joke's on us, not only are we feeding the farm, we feed free-range humans too.*

"And-?" Rebekah's face was very still.

"Greg took four of the guys and went to the lakes at Darenth to see how our fish reserves are doing. He left Leizle and the others within sight of the tunnel, getting back should have been a cinch." Harry dragged a hand down over his face, making his despair more hideous. "Sandy said she got separated and they couldn't use flashlights. The vampire farmers came across country so fast everyone had to take cover. All we know is they took Leizle towards London. God, what are we going to do?"

"Where's Greg, has he gone back out to look for her?" said Connor urgently.

"He doesn't know yet. He won't be back now, for about a week," said Rebekah quietly.

Connor raised a surprised brow. *He's seen the worst.* Greg knew the threat of ferals existed; one more obstacle in the war of survival. *He'll use his head.*

"We are stocking up for winter. He's on a long-range mission. When he has enough fish and root crops to last a month, he'll head back home. He gets cabin fever."

"Ah, so that's why he leads the away teams. And the others who went with him?"

Rebekah smiled gently, "Greg drafted a few of the guys. In his book, every man should know how to survive the elements, whether they like it or not."

"And Leizle is out there alone," Harry interrupted heavily.

"I'll find her," Connor said quietly. *If they took her towards London, they were not ferals or vampires in grave sleep. It gives me time to track her down.*

"Good. Okay, that's good," Harry muttered.

"And Douglas?" said Connor quietly, in an enticing whisper. "Can *he* survive the elements?" Comparing the pampered flesh of Douglas to Greg's flint-hard muscular mass, Connor knew who his money would be on.

Harry shook his head. "I don't know. Things were frantic here, and I guess he used the distraction..." Harry glanced across the cavern briefly, focusing on a point three feet to Connor's left.

He's getting vampires mixed up with Medusa. Reluctant amusement softened the harsh planes of Connor's face.

"We've never kept a prisoner before. We didn't think he could escape." Harry spluttered on his own saliva.

"Douglas is not stupid. I'm not surprised he ran," Connor said with a reassuring smile. "He knew, at any time, I could decide he'd lived long enough."

Connor moved quickly across the cavern, smothering a smile when Harry leapt back a pace. Turning to face Rebekah, and resting his cold hand over her cheek, Connor said, "I'll find Leizle." Adding, almost to himself, "Douglas can wait, for now." He dropped a kiss on her upturned lips. "All you have to do is stay safe."

The beseeching look he directed had a serious edge before he dragged himself away.

Chapter 28

Breaking out of the eco-shelter and into the moonlit night, the first thing Connor did was sweep the route leading across the meadow and through the forest to the fields of vampire crops. He grimly looked for remains, identifiable or not, since he had come so close to losing Rebekah to a feral. *Nothing here suggests a feral. So, I can rule that out.*

He took a crow's flight back through the countryside. The cold night air buffeted him and tree branches snatched at his coat as Connor used breakneck speed to ease the tension he felt inside. Although, a body that should have arrived back in London battered and bruised, instead, carved a brutal swathe of devastation through the woodland. Connor grinned. *When the time is right, I'll hunt Douglas down, and take my time in doing it. But first, Leizle.*

If she was *not* on the farm, then another chilling possibility was that she had become entertainment at a rap-sleep party.

Connor crossed the River Thames at Vauxhall Bridge and headed East towards Covent Garden. Number two Temple Place was an imposing Portland stone building, intricately sculpted in the 19th century, and it was also the primary venue for vampire rap-sleep parties.

He stood on the sidewalk listening to the rumbling growls of the vampire gathering seeping through the walls. *It sounds busy.* The lower gallery and the great hall could hold up to 300 guests in each room and tonight, it sounded as though they were at capacity. Connor's steely gaze dulled as he considered the consequences of that, for both Leizle, and himself. *At least, I can fight my way out.*

There were always rumors of humans being 'kept' at rap-sleep venues, and the popularity of Temple Place made this the most likely destination. The library which adjoined the great hall, via a concealed partition, provided a perfect place to hide contraband humans. *Time to find out.*

Inhaling deeply, he flirted with unlocking the cell door of the aggressive drunk and tapping into the belligerent mood he needed. But taking rap-sleep, and embracing the rioting sensuality was not something Connor wanted to do. Rebekah's scent was still locked inside his lungs, and he was convinced his skin still felt two degrees warmer. *It won't feel like cheating, it will feel like contamination.* But, he could only be sure Leizle was not inside by crashing the party. *I'll just have to fake it.*

He passed through the black wrought iron gate, walked up to the solid oak door and pushed it open. His forceful stride discouraged argument as he bowled aside the vampires loitering in the hallway, ran lightly up the staircase and entered the great hall.

On the threshold, he recoiled at the sight of a naked male vampire with a female bent over a chair in front of him. Her smile, despite the crushing grip he dug into her hips, instantly declared her a vampire, and the sneering mask of disdain her mate wore made the act lurid and degrading.

Connor turned away.

Upon the long table which ran down the center of the wood-paneled room, cut glass pitchers filled with human blood and crystal goblets winked in the myriad of twinkling light cast by huge chandeliers.

Walking past the fornicating couple, Connor drifted the length of the room, deftly side stepping the male posturing of vampires looking for a fight. He pretended the ruby-red lacquered nails of the few female vampires who had the luxury of choosing which male they wanted to couple with, were not dragging down over his hard chest.

A tall vampire blocked his path. "Lizbet has chosen you," he said with quiet authority.

Connor dropped his gaze to take in the elfin features of a vampiress who looked about twelve years of age and his stomach knotted with disgust.

"Lizbet." Connor bowed graciously. "I'm sure you can do better."

Spite glittered in her gaze, and Connor heaved a mental sigh. *Shit, she's got me in her sights.*

Vampires came to rap-sleep parties to satisfy one of two appetites, to have sex or to fight. With resignation, Connor looked Lizbet's escort up and down and allowed a snarl to fold his lip back.

"Are you here only for her?" As the words grated from his throat, Connor surged forward and pinned the tall vampire against the richly-carved paneling.

The vampire smirked. Connor allowed him enough room to shrug out of his coat. "If I win, Lizbet gets you afterwards. Agreed?"

"Agreed." Connor masked his disgust by shedding his own coat and shirt.

As if on cue, an attendant with a bowl cupped in his hands appeared beside them.

Connor dipped his fingers into the fragrant mix and smeared the oil over his chest and shoulders. He beckoned to his opponent. "What's your name? When I put you back together at the hospital, I'd like to know who I'm saving."

"My name's Hugo." Suddenly wary, the vampire murmured, "Hospital?"

Connor grinned maniacally. "It seems only fair." He stretched out his triceps and the edifice of muscle on his abdomen rippled. "I'm going to rip out your spleen. I think you can manage without that, provided I don't rupture your stomach."

Uncertainty clouded the tall vampire's eyes.

Connor almost laughed. "No? Shall *I* tell Lizbet, or will you?"

The delicate childlike vampiress suddenly shoved her escort. "Fight, damn you."

"I think, Lizbet, on this occasion, you are going to have to choose another mate." Connor's gray eyes hardened to flint. He pulled a rag from the shoulder of the fight attendant, wiped the oil from his torso, and tossed it onto the slickly polished banquet table. In deliberate slow movements, designed to press home his victory, Connor redressed, casually doing up each button of his shirt before tidying his collar. Choosing a glass of blood from a tray on the table, he downed it in one, and smiled. "My taste runs to sweeter pleasures than you can provide." Glancing at Hugo, Connor added,

"We are friends now, surely?" Grimacing at the cold blood dregs in his glass, he said invitingly, "Is there any fresh blood here tonight?"

Hugo smiled. "I see. Even a doctor finds human blood stored in bottles unappetizing. I understand."

Beckoning for Connor to follow, Hugo crossed the room, extracting from his pocket an ornate silver key which hung from a chain attached to his belt. Checking Connor was paying attention, Hugo inserted the key into a hole in an apparently flat oak panel. He pushed on it until it clicked, activating a spring-loaded mechanism, and a door sprang open. The smell of human fear-drenched sweat plumed into the air.

"I don't think you'll be disappointed," Hugo murmured, ushering Connor in ahead.

Connor stepped into the room and Hugo closed the panel behind them. "This is forbidden, you understand. You may drink, but do not kill, or I can't protect you. But I imagine you know that."

Connor nodded absently and scanned the room. The shadows were thick with cowering bodies. The clink of metal confirmed his suspicion it was not just fear keeping them glued to their seats.

The rows of books lining the walls made an incongruous backdrop to a vampire who had a human girl hanging in his arms. Her clothes were torn, red marks framed her breasts, and the vampire seemed to enjoy the pain stretched across her white face as he massaged her soft flesh, leaving pearls of blood in the wake of his hard fingernails.

Relief blossomed inside Connor when he discovered that none of the human girls in the room had the copper-toned coloring of Leizle, and he resigned himself to feeding before he could escape. Quickly, he crossed the room and pulled a thin girl to her feet. His arm around her waist drew her in close to his body, arched her back and exposed her throat. His nose brushed her pounding carotid artery and he licked salty sweat from her skin as he whispered in her ear, "Pretend, just go limp."

His jaws closed over her neck, and the razor sharp edge of his teeth bit in. She gasped and did what he said, letting her body hang slack in his grasp. Tears ran over her cheeks and dropped like splashes of hot wax onto the back of Connor's hand.

He took one mouthful of her blood, enough to stain his lips, and his wing of black hair hid his face while he pressed his muzzle into her thundering pulse. It took all his will power not to feed, but the despair tainting her blood turned his stomach. *I'll get Julian to raid this place. They'll be better off on the farm.* When Connor lifted his face and growled, as though replete, the tableaux of the other vampire still feeding filled his vision.

The vampire gripped the girl he tortured by the arm and, hearing the bone fibers creak, Connor lost his temper.

He released his own prey, letting her drop back down into her seat as he flew across the room. Prising the vampire's fingers from his victim's flesh, Connor bent them back until three of them snapped inside his palm.

Shock shuddered through the vampire and he stared into Connor's fierce white face.

With blood dripping from his lips, Connor ground out, "You've had enough. Go now, before I break every bone in your body."

Hugo appeared beside them, his gaze skittering from Connor's face to the other vampire. "Gentlemen, I think it is time you both left, don't you?"

Connor could not have agreed more. "After you," he snarled quietly as he withdrew, and the aggravated vampire disappeared without a word.

Casting a glance at the girl who had dropped to her knees on the floor, Connor resisted the urge to show he cared. "At least you won't have a body to dispose of hmm, Hugo? Better all round I think."

Hugo's narrowed gaze relaxed and he nodded. "Quite."

Minutes later, outside on the sidewalk, Connor shrugged back into his coat and set off for Hyde Park. Ignoring the route encouraged by the footpaths, he cut across the grass, through the trees, and across deserted roads until he saw the still, dark surface of the Serpentine, the body of water created in 1730 for the human enjoyment of boating and swimming.

In the vampire community, there would always be those who, as endless decades unfolded, considered immortality a punishment. *And they want to die. With the food supply getting low, who knows, they might get their wish. 'More blood to go around' would be Serge's take on it.*

Suicidal tendencies led to bizarre behavior, and over the last decade, vampires found a more sinister use for the Serpentine. They used it to simulate drowning, and the atmosphere around it seemed tainted by their desperation.

They could not drown, of course, but the water filling their lungs and stomachs took days to drain away, during which time they had no appetite. That was where they hoped for success. Suppressing their feeding instinct led to locked-in syndrome, and the first step along the road to the final release of a crushed skull, when the council decided they had suffered enough.

Standing on the bank of the Serpentine, Connor watched with grim fascination.

The inky moonlit depths resembled a sheet of black ice crying out to be broken. His eyes were drawn to the gliding form of a vampire slipping into the water. As he hit his stride, plowing in deeper, gray froth-crested ripples raced away as if trying to outrun him.

The atmosphere of despair anchored Connor there, surreal imaginings crowding his mind like an infection. Connor found the blackened glassy expanse compelling, and before the hypnotic spell could tempt him to join the ranks of the doomed, he dragged himself away. He forged onward across the grass until the smells of life, both flora and fauna, filled him and shouldered suicidal notions aside.

He grinned as a rabbit scrabbled in the undergrowth and his mouth watered. Normality felt good. He gained momentum when the glistening marble walls of the hospital building beckoned. Relaxing into his stride, moments later he propelled himself through the familiar corridors. His mood lifted, but although the blackened edges of depression dissipated, Leizle's fate was a dark shroud he still wore.

I've turned up nothing, yet. No rumor of a chestnut-haired, green-eyed addition to the farm inmates. Not a murmur. The blanks he had drawn frustrated him. *All that's left is to wait.*

He put on his white coat and prepared to go through the motions as *Doctor* Connor. He kept his eyes and ears open until the seemingly endless hours passed, dusk fell, and he was released to begin the search again.

Impatient to complete the last task on his list, he headed to the operating theater to perform surgery on a juvenile vampire who had sustained sun scorching. The dehydrated limb had hardened to granite and would need amputating. *I'll do the procedure, and then I'll put Julian in the picture.*

As he went through the final set of doors and into the surgical wing, a sudden cacophony set his eardrums ringing. "For goodness' sake," he growled, "What now?"

He swung into the operating room and confronted the chaos of the flailing patient knocking over trays of sterile instruments which clattered onto the floor. Anthony was flailing his arms around too, as he tried to catch hold of the agitated youngling.

"Anthony, get out of the way," Connor said, his low tone cutting through the pandemonium and ending his surgical assistant's frantic dance. Connor swiped a syringe from the instrument tray, stepped in close to the vampire, as if they were about to waltz, and smoothly buried the needle into the soft space framed by his jaw. Shoving it up into the carotid artery, he depressed the plunger, and the vampire hit the floor with a thump.

At his protégé's stunned expression, Connor raised a speculative brow and said, "Muscle relaxant."

Anthony scuttled forward and hoisted the crumpled figure up onto the table.

Connor collected the Mole grips and prepared to gnaw away at the graveled tissue, but he could feel Anthony's confusion filling the room. Wryly, he waited for the question.

Although reluctant to appear foolish, Anthony eventually braved it. "We don't feel pain, not in the human sense of the word, and, nothing at all in dead tissue, so why did he flip out?"

"Panic originates in the brain, and just thinking about the procedure would be enough. He probably needed rap-sleep and his aggression spiraled out of control once panic set in." Connor waited for Anthony to absorb this. He jerked his head towards the prone vampire. "He can still hear us, but his body is not under his own control at the moment. So, let's not keep him waiting, hmmm?"

Keeping her vigil at the mouth of the eco-town tunnel, Rebekah squinted across the meadow, shading her eyes from the glow painted across the sky by the rose-colored glove of dawn. She felt relief when the distant whine of a two-stroke engine gradually grew louder, and unfolding her cramped legs, she pushed up onto her feet.

Thomas, thank goodness. It had been a long night. When Rebekah watched Connor disappear, it unleashed anxiety to gnaw a hole in her chest. *But, at least one thing has gone right.*

Thomas trundled the motorcycle carefully across the clumps of grass on the final approach, and Rebekah hugged the boy tight when he dismounted. She knew how Connor must feel; his frame creaked under the pressure. At his soft grunt, she said, "Sorry." Though, she spoiled it with a beaming grin.

"*I'm* sorry," he muttered. "Harry told me not to go. But, I knew you'd want to know about Leizle."

"Hey, you were right." She placed a hand on his thin shoulder. It was tough being sixteen, and trying to prove he was a man. *His emotions keep getting the better of him.*

"Have they found her yet?" he asked lightly, but his eyes were flat.

"Not yet, but Connor won't stop looking. There's no sign of Douglas, either," said Rebekah.

Thomas glanced up at her and said quietly, "I think I saw him going through the woods. He was a long way up, towards the hilltop. But, I'm sure it was him."

"Never mind Douglas, he doesn't matter," she replied. Draping an arm over his shoulders, she drew him with her to walk down into the eco-town. She forced a feeble smile of reassurance, knowing the dim light would disguise her terrible acting. *I would feel safer knowing where Douglas is right now.*

When they slipped behind the heavy sackcloth curtain, the torch flames danced in welcome as she let the flap fall back into place.

"Connor will find Douglas, and he probably has Leizle safe and sound already. C'mon, you must be hungry. Connor killed a lamb, and Oscar is working his way through the culinary alphabet." Rebekah produced a wide grin to nudge aside the gloom on Thomas' face.

"He's only on C for casserole, so you're in luck, supper tonight will be a feast."

Chapter 29

Connor stared down at the relaxed vampire laid out on his operating table. The patient's naked torso glowed like pearl-dusted marble, with the exception of the gunmetal gray area staining one arm. Extending the damaged limb, Connor used a surgeon's black marker to outline the hardened tissue, and painstakingly injected the site with blood, turning the toughened hide pink and softening its surface.

The preparation done, Connor cut along the guideline and lifted the epidermis. He grunted. He was moderately successful, although the dried membrane still cracked in several places. Using Mole grips, Connor gnawed away the graveled tissue underneath. He packed the crater firmly with nylon gauze which would repel blood when the vampire next fed – no point wasting fuel, and absorbent cotton gauze would stink when the blood rotted. He laid the skin back over the top.

"Anthony." With a flick of his wrist, Connor tossed a tube of glue to his assistant. "We managed to avoid amputation. I'll leave you to glue the skin back in place, and make sure you fill all the cracks, okay?"

Anthony stepped up to the patient; he was alone before he had time to answer.

Determined not to waste time better spent looking for Leizle, Connor's intervention was faster and more clinical than usual. Bedside manners were less important when the patient feels no pain. *Anthony can handle this one, it will do him good.*

The moment he left the surgical wing, Connor dismissed the patient. He did not expect Julian to be able to shed any light on Leizle's fate, but he was clean out of inspiration, and waiting did not sit well with him. *I can't just do nothing.*

Connor pushed the hospital's toughened-glass front doors aside with barely the flex of a hand, leapt the flight of marble steps, and hit the sidewalk at an easy run which stirred the cauldron of unease simmering inside him. He ramped up to vampire top-speed instantly, his expression set in granite. *If she's in the hive, then my best bet is Julian.*

As always, the silvered face of the moon bathed the marble facades within London's square mile in an ethereal glow. The cold glare of darkened windows reflected Connor's progress with complete disinterest.

When he arrived at the council building, Connor took the steps three at a time. His momentum had transformed the damp night air into chips of ice, and the frozen fabric of his greatcoat barely moved when he stopped dead. As though conjured by the sweep of a magician's wand, he appeared in the council chambers' hallway like a black marble statue, the fierce frown on his face as rigid as the glittering frost on his coat.

In the same instant Connor appeared, Julian swept into view, dragging Marius and Alexander in his wake.

Hope flared, and then died for Connor as, staring straight ahead, Julian barked, "Doctor Connor, I need you in council, now."

"Julian, I need to talk-"

"It will have to wait." Julian's expression was unwavering, and, striding past, he said, "Councilor Serge."

Connor needed no further explanation. He wheeled around and matched the jurors' stride.

Taking a seat in the gallery, Connor resigned himself to the time wasting of Serge; the best he could hope was that the councilor's latest tirade of petty complaints would be short and to the point. Leizle's disappearance plagued Connor's concentration. *This better be quick.*

Connor focused on a spot on the wall four feet over Serge's head and breathed in the aroma of the freshly polished paneling before the aged vampire's halitosis took hold.

Serge rose to his feet, adjusting his jacket and clearing his throat in an effort to catch Connor's deliberately averted gaze. The ambient light cast a sallow glow over Serge's smug expression. His eyes gleamed, and his skin crackled over his bones as he smiled widely, revealing mustard colored teeth. Serge was less fortunate in his human raw material than practically every vampire on the planet.

Connor smothered his frustration with a condescending smile.

"Principal Julian." Serge waited until *every* pair of eyes reluctantly looked at him.

"Get on with it, Councilor." Julian blasted Serge with his irritation.

"Of course." Serge left a dramatic pause until Julian opened his mouth in warning. Rushing on, he said, smugly, "I have a new capture. She is young, fit, and has never been siphoned." He swung round to meet Connor's suddenly keen interest. "She has the strongest immune system and biological health of any specimen we have had."

Serge clicked his fingers, a door opened and a girl was marched into the court by a guardsman.

Before he saw her face, Connor recognized the unmistakable riot of copper-bright hair. *Leizle.* Though her eyes were murky green pools of dread, and Connor could hear the trembling of her knees, her chin jutted in defiance.

So, Serge is not time wasting, far from it. Connor's over-riding feeling was disbelief. *Where is he going with this?*

"She is a prime specimen, perfect for the hybrid breeding program," said Serge.

Meeting Serge's penetrating gaze head on, Connor's smile of faint amusement disguised the tension gripping the dry stone of his heart. He was a step closer to feeling out of control, and his lungs ached as he tried to suck in enough breath to speak. *Way to go Connor. Why the hell didn't I bring Julian up to speed on the Leizle thing?*

As the stunned silence in the chamber deepened, Connor glanced across the courtroom. *Does Julian recognize her?*

The Principal's white frozen face was not what Connor had hoped for.

As Connor prepared to say the words which would open the door, he wondered at Julian's extreme reaction. *So, he* does *remember her. Can I rely on him to follow the game plan I'm going to set out*? His jaw tightened as he tuned in to his friend's progressing state of anguish.

Julian's stress levels spiked like an electric charge blowing all the fuses, and his glazed stare of revival sleep was not encouraging.

He'd better snap out of it, and fast. Connor stepped up to the plate. "So, the hybrid breeding program has progressed through chambers?" he asked with convincing nonchalance. He did not look in Leizle's direction, but he detected the jolt of hope clenching her heart as *she* recognized *him.*

"Well, let's just say the capture of this girl will accelerate the process." Serge grinned at Connor.

"And this impressive list of healthy attributes, they have been confirmed?" asked Connor. *I hope not, because my plan depends upon it, and because if she's suffered a vampire health examination then her body will be screaming in pain about now.*

Serge's jaundiced gaze skittered around the courtroom, uncertainty slithering across his face as he said, "Well, not confirmed, no. But the indicators are good." He tried to recapture his previous confidence. "I'm sure you'd agree? I mean, look at her."

Connor gave a convincing impression of clinical objectivity when he turned and did as Serge demanded.

Although he did not have to battle the magnetic pull of his attraction to Rebekah, he could still appreciate Leizle's allure: her chestnut hair – striking even though dirty and tangled, her square chin, green eyes flashing with hope, and her youthful naiveté.

Her heartbeat remained strong and steady. Her faith in Connor made her stand taller and brought a glow to her cheeks as she bore the ordeal of Serge's scrutiny.

Connor finally met Leizle's gaze. Her relief at establishing a connection with him at last, relaxed her features, and his eyes narrowed in warning. *I need her guard up.* He drew in her aroma, passing it across his palate, and was encouraged by the healthy dose of fear. Connor prayed it would keep her focused and not let her betray them. *This has still to play out.*

Directing a glance at Julian's still thunderstruck blank mask, Connor's poker face threatened to fold as he wondered at Julian being bitten by an unexpected bug. *He* more *than just remembers her, then.*

"Surely, the girl's suitability for the breeding program is for Principal Julian to decide," said Connor, and the sharp gaze he bored into Julian spoke volumes. *Pull yourself together, and fast.*

Like an engine reacting to an ignition key, Julian began moving again.

"Councilor Serge, before we let our hopes run away with us, Doctor Connor will perform a complete physical on the girl. When I receive his report, we will talk again." Addressing Leizle's escort, Julian said, "Take her to the farm. Doctor Connor will join you shortly. Court dismissed."

Okay, a bit abrupt, but it does the trick. Connor avoided looking at Leizle as she was led away.

The heavy door of the courtroom thumped closed behind her, and Leizle kept her eyes lowered, hanging on to the hope glowing inside, even though vampire guardsmen surrounded her once more.

The broad back of the leading jailer became the anchor point she concentrated on, although her gut cramped when, passing over the threshold into a small holding room, Councilor Serge appeared beside her.

His cold grip, like an iron cuff around her upper arm, forced her to a stop while he stared at her.

She held her breath as his rank breath fanned her face. The cold glint in his eye made her breathing stutter.

"I'm sure we'll meet again," he said smoothly. "I look forward to it."

"Councilor Serge." A tall vampire wearing a dark uniform inclined his head. "I'm here to transport the patient."

"Of course." Releasing Leizle, his dragging nails leaving welts across her pale skin, Serge stepped back.

Leizle instinctively knew that she was a prize between two combatants. Councilor Serge may appear feeble, but her fear of him was real. *I need Doctor Connor to come for me.*

The transport turned out to be a sedan with a steel grid separating the driver from the prisoner on the back seat. Metal grills encased the internal door handles, and the seatbelt buckle was a padlock. *They take no chances.*

The car barely reached twenty miles an hour, so throwing herself out onto the road would be an ineffective way of committing suicide in any case.

The tinted windows and confined space of the darkened interior triggered claustrophobia in Leizle, and just breathing needed all her concentration. It was too dark to gather more than a vague image of the hulking siphoning sheds with their dull steel finish before the car pulled up outside a metal door.

Once inside, the vampire guided her along a narrow corridor past a row of cell doors. He swung one open and ushered her inside a windowless cell of ten feet square. The only item of furniture was a narrow bedframe bolted to the concrete floor.

Leizle dropped down onto the mattress, grateful for a dim bulb protected by a wire cover which burst into life when the door slammed shut. She began chewing her fingernails again. *I can't blame Rebekah this time.* When the skin became angry and inflamed, she sat on her hands, wincing when the rough denim of her pants rubbed against the sensitive skin. *If I carry on there will be blood, and that won't be good.*

She chose a rivet on a panel in the door and stared at it. Counting inside her head like a child playing hide and seek, she set a number at which she willed it to open and deliver Doctor Connor. After she had reached the number several times, she gave up and laid down on the bed.

Closing her eyes brought with it the chance of denial. She could be on her own bed in the eco town, if she tried hard enough to pretend.

She had no idea how long she slept.

A cold hand on her shoulder woke her with a jolt, and she shot to her feet so fast she almost fell over.

"The doctor will be here, soon. Come." The vampire standing in the cell wore the blank-faced expression of a lobotomy victim. No emotion colored the voice; it felt as though the words were a string of sounds which just happened to make sense.

The grip on her arm guiding her along the corridor was compelling as he marched her out into the night. The cold air bit into her stiff, sleep-cramped muscles, and she shivered, keeping her eyes on the ground in case she fell.

They headed toward the towering brick facade of a square building. When the vampire mounted a wide flight of sandstone steps without slowing down at all, Leizle had no choice but to look up or stumble. She noticed a rectangular copper sign beside the entrance doors stamped with black lettering, which she had no time to read. *It probably says 'torture chamber'.*

Leizle went through the doors and into a softly lit foyer, and faltered as her feet sank into plush sage-green carpet. *Torture of a different kind, then.* The familiar smell of leather emanating from plumply-stuffed brown armchairs stirred a long-forgotten memory of her father's study. With a little imagination, Leizle could have pulled the comfort of home around her shoulders like a warm blanket. But, as she expected, no such luck.

The frog marching continued on up a wide stairwell, along a corridor and into a small whitewashed room.

"Wait here." The vampire placed a folded white-cotton gown onto the examination couch. "Change into the gown."

He vanished from the room, and Leizle quickly checked inside the cupboards for any kind of weapon. Unless she planned on hanging herself with a crepe bandage, there was nothing useful.

Following the vampire's instruction seemed like her best bet. Being made to undress with them watching didn't bear thinking about. Stripping down to her underwear, she put on the white gown, wrapped it securely over at the front, and piled her clothes neatly on top of a cupboard.

There was no other furniture, so she hitched up onto the cold examination table and sat with her feet dangling in midair.

Trapping her hands under her thighs stopped her from grabbing her clothes and making a run for it. *Wait for Doctor Connor*. Anything else was just lunacy.

Chapter 30

Sebastian easily found the farmhouse from where, as Serge had told him, the guardsmen had begun their grid search. The years of gritty dust inside could be dismissed, but Sebastian dropped to one knee and tasted the pale gray powder concentrated in one part of the main room. He grinned. *Bone dust.* It wasn't much to go on, but a fight ending in death had all the signs of leading to something much bigger. *Why cover tracks, unless the stakes are high?*

Following the road south east, Sebastian found nothing else helpful and diverted into the woods to head back to London.

The lumbering sound penetrated first and without giving it a thought, Sebastian began tracking the creature he saw moving through the trees. He could smell human desperation and watched with a predator's amusement at the futility of his prey. *I wonder what he's doing here?*

Arranging his features into a sympathetic expression, concealed Sebastian's sadistic nature and used his benign nineteen-mortal-year-old face to best advantage. Pulling the wool over human eyes was a sport he never tired of. *Though, opportunities such as this are rare these days.* Sebastian smiled while he shadowed the blundering human's progress.

He filled his chest with the clean air of the Kentish woods. Sebastian had finally escaped the suffocating inner-city stench of Durham, a coal mining town in the Northeast of England, where he had left behind a trail of indiscretions. *I've been quite good since the '70s. But, it has been tough.* Coal-blackened skin acted as useful camouflage, and it was a time of chaos, when the poverty caused by the pit closures were beginning to bite. He had immersed himself in the beleaguered community, and did a little biting of his own.

Sadly, the blood he drank was not so much barbecued, as carbon-gritted. Sebastian firmly believed their blood tasted abrasive because coal dust permeated the miners' skin. It had been like swallowing low-grade sandpaper.

Now, the coalminers' wives were an entirely different experience. They were more succulent, and he became addicted to their lightly-smoked flavor. The soot-ingrained husbands mounted their wives; basting them with their tainted juices thickened the delicate cocktail of female blood to a full-bodied fortified wine.

Sebastian played Casanova's role to perfection. He flattered them until their dulled gazes glittered with the diamond chips of excitement. *Despite their pale gray complexions, they were passably good-looking, for the most part, and so grateful for my attention.*

But ultimately, he tired of the game of staining their skin with love bites, only pulling the blood to the surface until the burst capillaries bruised their skin and released an enticing odor which made his mouth water. Finally, his hunger won.

His lip curled with visceral pleasure. Sebastian relished those moments. When they draped their eager bodies over his, begging him to make love to them, and instead of playing the gentlemen and yet again protecting their virtue, he gave them what they craved. He drove himself inside them and swallowed their screams of pain with his kiss. Without their tongues, they drown in their own blood as he finally sucked them dry.

Whispering rumors afterwards, saying the women had abandoned their coarse husbands in favor of the heat of romance, Sebastian enjoyed turning the knife.

Okay, killing the boy was a step too far. The thin, grubby five-year-old had been his undoing.

The horror of running in through the doorway and seeing his mother's blood-drenched corpse hanging in Sebastian's arms had frozen the child stiff in those vital seconds when, if not escape, then a chance of raising the alarm was possible. The kid threw himself at the back door, grazing his hands on the rough wooden boards where the metal thumb latch rattled, but would not spring open. Sebastian had caught him in midflight and swung him around, tossing him across the room to smash into the stone fireplace. The boy's undernourished neck had snapped like a dry twig.

He had left the snack untouched, abandoning his usual clean up routine, and the perplexing disappearances of women within the community stepped over the line into the horror of butchered families.

And then, the tabloids began muttering about a serial killer. The vampire council demanded Sebastian appear before them, and they had shut him down. No second chances. Desist or be condemned to locked-in syndrome for eternity. *So, I have been good since then, mostly.*

Sebastian waited ten years for a space to come up in the London Hive. He was good at faking sincerity, and he had persuaded the principal of the Durham Hive to stamp his transfer papers. *He saw an opportunity to rid himself of me, and he took it. But hey, we both wanted the same thing.* Sebastian shed his reputation before the wax of the principal's seal had cooled, and was enjoying the luxury of his clean slate.

Soft expressions clung easily to his appealing features, and he harnessed the powers of smoke and mirrors. Sebastian was Houdini and Barnum rolled into one likeable package. But he found the glitter of spite in the murky brown/green depths of his eyes harder to disguise. Being good in London was never his intention. *But, not getting caught* is.

His bargain with Serge was a front. *If I find nothing that points the finger at Doctor Connor, then I'll make it up.* After all, the flawed Councilor Serge had been a soft target. *Flattering him was laughably easy*. The councilors' eyes had flashed with respect when Sebastian used the title 'the general'. The truth was, he was a chameleon, and a great judge of character, and the combination had never let him down. *What name would I have chosen if faced with Doctor Connor?* Even vampires hunger for attention, he thought with an acidic smile.

Councilor Serge's conviction that these woods held the key to secrets guarded by Doctor Connor was an idea worth exploring. *Maybe, I've struck it lucky?*

Sebastian's curiosity in the wandering mound of blubber-covered humanity became acute. He enjoyed the scent of hyperventilating anxiety. Expanding his ribcage and drawing it in, it stung like the sulphurous fumes of brimstone. He cocked his head and considered the possibility of life being that simple. *Could this be the evidence against the doctor I'm looking for? And if not, then, I can have a little fun.*

The man, sweating heavily, leaned back against a tree and began to slide towards the ground. Reaching around the thick trunk, Sebastian closed his fingers around the human's neck. He brought the man up short and absorbed the shot of fear sizzling along the synapses in the human brain.

Seconds passed, and the man's fear intensified. He tried to jerk his head, and croaked in a sudden burst of bravado, "Do it then. You want me dead and my blood disgusts you, so just do it."

"Tut tut," whispered Sebastian. "You really should be careful what you wish for." He flexed his icy fingers, briefly cutting the oxygen supply to the brain, and knowingly causing black clouds to trundle across the man's vision. "Now, my question is this, what are you doing out here in the middle of nowhere, alone and defenseless?"

Sebastian's riot of messy black hair suggested a playful and mischievous persona, until he rolled his top lip back and smeared cruelty across his features. Dripping menace from his gaze, he moved around into view and enjoyed etching terror on to the human face.

"I'm lost, I'm trying to get to London." The man wheezed as the fingers clamped around his vocal chords tightened.

"Ah, you are keen to join the farm, hmm?" purred Sebastian. "That's all that awaits you in London." His tone became bored. *I could drain him now and no one would know.* Playing with the rules was an undeniable thrill. *A final indulgence, before I become Councilor Serge's mild-mannered student.* Reaching this conclusion in less than a second, Sebastian's mouth opened as he went in for the kill.

The man started to cry.

"I want to be one of you," he said, forcing a strangled croak. "I *need* to be one of you."

Sebastian considered Douglas' clammy flesh, his nostrils flared at the musky odor, and venomous juice flowed into his mouth. He enjoyed the taste of anger and desperation, although his favorite flavor was terror, but he could wait for that. As he contemplated the fleshy face, gut instinct kicked in. *What was it he said? Ah, that was it, 'my blood disgusts you'.*

"Need?" Sebastian's curiosity piqued. "Why, *need*?"

"That bastard stole my wife. It's disgusting, the bruises. God knows what he does to her." The man dragged in a deep, sobbing breath.

"Which bastard would that be?" Sebastian's seductive tone invited a confidence.

"Connor," he spat.

"Ah." Sebastian sighed, his saintly smile more terrifying than the sneer. "Correct answer."

Holding the man in a viselike grip, Sebastian applied careless traction to his spine, lifting him until his toes barely brushed the ground. Before Douglas' anguished groan could fill the air, Sebastian was already propelling him through the woods.

How will Councilor Serge show his appreciation?

The man's yelps when the undergrowth whipped against his doughy skin went unheeded as Sebastian's mind raced ahead to London.

Chapter 31

That evening, Rebekah entered the meeting cavern to hear what news, if any, there was on Leizle, and Thomas was not there. She rubbed the back of her neck, her palm coming away damp with the cold sweat of apprehension. *Where is Thomas?* She cast a glance at the rows of intent profiles, all listening to Harry's heavy tone of regret. *There* is *no news on Leizle, I have to get out of here.* As she slipped from the cavern, chasing down her own thoughts, every one took her back to the same place. Each explanation began and ended with Thomas' words of this morning. "I saw Douglas in the woods." *Surely, he's not so foolish?*

Rebekah had not seen him since midday, and certainty sat like a stone in her chest. *Yes, he is that stupid.*

Before common sense could talk her out of it, she packed some vacuum sealed food pouches in her satchel for Thomas. *I'll find him, and he'll be fine. He's missed a couple of meals, that's all.* His thin frame haunted her.

The rhythmic scuff of her walking boots over the hard packed ground became a soundtrack to the argument racing inside her head. *I have to bring him back before Connor wrings his neck.*

"I don't suppose Connor was ever foolish, not even when he was a young human," Rebekah muttered.

She moved through the tunnels, glad that everyone remained together in the meeting cavern, drawing strength to ease their stunned grief. Harry's update told them little, except there was, as yet, no news at all. *Connor will find her. I just have to find Thomas.*

Worry made her angry. Rebekah's decision to shake some sense into Thomas lasted until she passed out from behind the sackcloth curtain. The cold blustering air took her breath away. *Crap, it's bloody freezing.* She was back to feeling sorry for him. *The woods, the motorcycle, and now*- She sighed heavily. *He's searching for Douglas. Shit, Thomas, strike three.*

The darkness of the tunnel gave way to the glow of moonlight. The night air smelled dank, and the cold ground chilled her feet even through the soles of her boots. The spiteful breeze spat icy air into her face; she pulled her woolen layers around her body, turned up the collar of her oilskin coat and zipped it all the way up.

She left the shelter of the entrance cavern, stepped out on to the oily surface of the dew-slicked meadow, and ran for the cover of the woods. *I hope Thomas wrapped up, too.* But somehow, she doubted it.

The moon played hide and seek behind the purple evening clouds, shredding her nerves whenever its silver light flooded the meadow. With a hundred yards of rough grass still left to cross, the rasping cold filling her lungs and numbing her lips made it harder than she could ever have imagined.

A tantalizing fifty yards remained between her and the woods, when a swell of moonbeams glittered over the meadow. Rebekah dived on to the ground and lay prone, giving her aching chest time to catch a breath. She focused on the blades of grass and waited until the clouds dragged a black shadow over the field again before easing up onto her knees and sprinting forward. *Nearly there.*

The irony of dodging moonlight as vampires did the sun was not lost on her.

As the shade of the trees closed overhead, she released a thankful sigh. For a second, Rebekah felt as if she had gone blind. The thick canopy cut out all the light. *And, that's good.* Like a child hiding under the bed, there was no getting to her now.

She froze and listened.

Animal noises were reassuring. Commonsense told her that in the presence of a predator, an eerie silence would descend. But when the hunter could wring a bird's neck before it could swallow its song. *Not so good.*

Stagnant air clawed its way into her chest, and a cough burned at her throat. Taking a carefully silent mouthful of water from her flask, she took another beta-blocker for good luck. She lifted her chin to swallow and the rush of cold air was like a metal collar around her neck. *God, it's cold.*

She crept forward a few dozen yards, finally pausing and pressing her back into a familiar tree. She recognized the cluster of silver birch trees which, in the gloom, resembled a picket fence erected by a giant's hand. *Does that make me Jack, hiding in his garden?* Rebekah shuddered. *Smelling blood is a big deal in my world, too.*

Tree-hugging her way carefully through the wood, the wintry chill gave way to bone-deep cold. The carpet of ice crystals numbed her feet. As she moved deeper into the undergrowth, heading towards the hilltop Thomas had talked about, the darkness became a thickly woven blanket.

Cold had been merely a word to Rebekah before tonight. Cold was not a shiver, her body was past that, and even three woolen layers and the oilskin did not keep the ache from reaching her bones. Her blood retreated into her core, searching for warmth and casting her clammy skin in a mottled blue shroud.

I bet even Connor would feel warm to me now. Her brain felt as stiff as her fingers and her sluggish attention fought to focus on Thomas. *He can't have had much of a head start. I should have found him by now.*

Tears of frustration decorated her lashes. *Damn, he's going to freeze.* The thought drove her on. Rebekah would never risk shouting, so she set off, using every stray beam of light to see in a landscape of charcoal and black pitch. Standing still every few minutes, she closed her eyes and prayed to hear something human.

After another half an hour, even her clattering teeth ached. She could no longer hear anything except the rattling inside as her body clung to survival. Standing still became impossible, and every time she tried, an undulating shiver almost pushed her over.

Rebekah gave up, or rather, she shut down. The possibility that Thomas may have already turned back taunted her. Retracing her steps would be easy, if she could stop the shuddering which blurred her vision.

I'll just sit down for a moment, just for a moment.

Before the tired thoughts could wade across her brain, Rebekah dropped down, feeling hard ground beneath her knees. She folded her arms and hugged the stone-cold weight sitting inside her, and tried not to topple over.

The frozen earth numbed her backside, and the pain in her chest subsided. *Is that tingle in my ribs heat?*

She rested her chin on her chest, tranquility settled into her bones and her eyelids drifted closed. And then, she heard it. A sob. *I should do something.* Minutes dragged by before she forced her eyelids open, focusing on the scenery of coal dust and gray ash as the sobbing noise scratched at her ears again.

The black thicket of tree trunks extended across in front of her, and a flash of pale gray flitting by beyond them jolted her mind to full attention. Holding her breath, Rebekah stared. *What was that? Thomas?* The knot in her chest told her she was wrong.

Rolling forward onto her hands and knees, pain screamed through every frozen muscle as she eased silently back up to her feet. Crouched over, she moved toward the quiet rasp of labored breathing. *Breathing is good. It can't be a vampire.*

Rebekah stubbed her toe on something softer than rock and her knees buckled. She landed heavily, and her startled outstretched hands collided with a bundle of ice-stiffened fabric. Her probing fingers discovered a face with features carved in cold cramped muscles and skin as firm as tanned leather.

"Thomas," she mouthed.

Her cold skin crawled when a flicker of white, closer this time, flashed between the trees. Resting her hands on the boy's eerily still form, she froze, held her breath, and waited.

A quiet rattling sound grew louder as the gray oval shape, floating in midair, drifted nearer. The black slit in the face became an oozing wound, and Rebekah heard something wet splattering the leaves of the undergrowth.

Shit. Vampire. Her hand crept forward to cover Thomas' mouth.

She tried to let the tension in her body go, knowing they could hear that too, tendons scraping. *So Connor said.*

Shit, shit, shit. Staring straight ahead, a shudder cramped her flesh.

A blood soaked hand appeared on a nearby tree trunk; the stained gray face rotated slowly, saliva bubbling in his throat as he scented the air.

The ink-black mass of his body obscured her sight in a shroud of darkness. She shrank away when he glided another step closer.

Forcing her eyes closed and bowing her head, Rebekah prayed. Her stiff face ached as she clamped her chattering teeth together, and remained motionless.

A drop of thin blood splattered onto her sleeve and dripped down her arm. The rancid stench from his coat almost made her gag when the fabric grazed her shoulder. Cold sweat crawled over her skin.

Please God, please God, please God...

Her flesh tingled as if it was trying to feel him, and the not knowing tore her gut open.

Finally, she prised her eyes open, and, slicing a glance left without moving her head, she kept his boots in sight. Her nerves screamed, she tried not to swallow, and she lost all feeling below the waist as the frost on the ground crept into her bones. The absurd thought that 'frozen meat doesn't smell' popped into her head.

A heavy droplet plopped onto the hood of her oilskin, and bile stung her throat as a stringy lump of flesh slithered down, hanging in front of her face for a moment, before the wet mass thumped into her lap.

Her throat burned, begging her to gulp in oxygen. Rolling black clouds oozed across her vision, each one becoming a monster in a shadow.

She strained her eyes left, and the boots were gone.

Her sluggish heart ached in her chest when a rustling sound beyond the trees gave her hope. *He's moving off.* Rebekah had no idea how many minutes she waited. She waited until the fear-cramped fibers of her muscles began to twitch. *Fuck... I have to move.* Gripping Thomas' coat in both hands, she pulled him steadily back, heaving at the bag of bones which seemed to be made of concrete. A few inches at a time, she dragged him deeper into the thick undergrowth until she couldn't see her hand in front of her face.

Rebekah collapsed over onto her side, and survival one-oh-one took control. She unzipped her oilskin and the fleecy inner jacket, pulled Thomas' body in close and drew the woolen layers around them both. She struggled to zip up the coat. The zipper took thirteen attempts, and counting them stopped her thinking about anything else. *I don't know what the fuck that was...*

"Thomas," she whispered his name, rubbing her hands briskly over their joint cocoon, until finally, he stirred, and the rubbing became a hug of relief.

His dry throat croaked, but it was enough.

"Shhh..." Her lips pressed to his ear, she said, "We have to wait 'til morning."

Rebekah hugged him again, trying to ignore the fact that this deep in the forest, even daylight would not penetrate. Morning might not save them. They huddled together. For now, just finding each other was enough.

Rebekah felt a tingle of heat again. She sank under a blanket of slumber; the numbness creeping in masquerading as a persuasive glow of welcome warmth. The icy fingers of frost stroked a path from brow to chin, dragging her eyelids down and her slack mouth open.

Chapter 32

Thank God Julian gathered his wits in time. Thinking back over it, Connor was impressed at how Julian sliced through the red tape. By conceding that perhaps Serge was correct, and expressing guarded enthusiasm, Julian took control away from the councilor. He decided that Leizle's suitability for the breeding program should be determined by the court, and Serge could not argue against it.

Connor admitted to enjoying the councilor's impotent rage. *Getting one up on Serge will always feel good.* When Julian insisted Connor perform the examination, Serge's complexion had blanched to tea-stained parchment.

By the time Connor left the council buildings and dashed across London, night had crept across the purple sky crushing the sun's resistance to streaks of blood on the horizon. The gathering cloud, transforming the face of the moon from its usual silver dollar bright smile into one of dull metal-gray, reflected his steely determination.

It felt good when he made the final run across the apron of grass surrounding the human farm factory. *I am on my way to examine Leizle, and there's nothing Serge can do about it.*

Following protocol, arriving at the perimeter, he stopped at the gates and waited to be allowed in. Connor's eyes skimmed the landscape on the other side of the fence, looking for the vampire sentry who would open the gate. Twelve yards away, on the boundary of no man's land, an area of coal black shadow moved and Connor swallowed his impatience.

He flirted with the idea of scaling the metal chain-linked barrier. It would have been quicker, but the silhouette of the vampire guard cut a swathe towards him and good manners prevailed.

"Ah, here we go," he breathed when the fast-flowing clump of shadow resolved into an unfamiliar face.

"Doctor Connor." The guard opened the gate and stepped back.

"Nice night," said Connor. Nodding briefly, he disappeared across the compound, knowing his escort would catch up. When the vampire materialized beside him, Connor asked, "No mailman tonight?" Connor missed the good natured banter he shared with the usual guard.

The vampire looked blank for a moment, and then said, "The mailman, of course. He's out hunting on Dartmoor. He'll be back tomorrow."

"Good for him," he muttered. Connor was pleased the vampire was off having fun. He liked him and his absence tonight could only be a good thing. *Things may get messy.*

The gate in the second perimeter fence was opened by a vampire intern.

Connor handed his new escort Julian's principal seal, his crest imprinted into a gold ingot. "Supervisor Matthew will be expecting me."

"Of course. This way, Doctor Connor, if you would follow me." The vampire dropped the ingot back into Connor's hand and set off briskly.

Connor fell obediently into step on the vampire's shoulder even though he knew the place like the back of his hand. He strode purposefully through the grounds, thinking ahead to his examination of Leizle. *It should not be hard.* He was, as always, untroubled by the thick scent of blood fumes hanging in the air as they moved past the siphoning annexes.

Leaving the sheds behind, the vampire skirted the fenced boundary of the accommodation zone. Connor cast a jaundiced eye over the rows of utilitarian barracks; sturdy ship lapped wooden constructions, capped with terracotta tiled roofs, and mounted on elevated platforms to stave off the dampness of the waterlogged landscape.

"More like hutches," muttered Connor.

At a glance, he could see fifty of the dreary dwellings and knew there were a dozen more rows stacked up behind. He felt fortunate that, so far, he was winning the battle with disease.

His concerns about disease made Connor ask, "Will Supervisor Matthew be joining us?"

"No. He sends his apologies."

"I'm sure he *does*," said Connor. *He has a lot to be sorry about.*

The constant stream of humanity trudging back and forth from the accommodation to the sheds had worn the grass away to a trail of compressed bare earth. Like dairy cattle, the humans were rounded up from their barracks, siphoned on rotation, and returned. Every detail was recorded. Not written down, of course. The accommodation wardens, chosen for their mental acuity, carried every human profile inside their heads.

Oddly, it helped to build a relationship of sorts with the inmates. *They feel better when a warden remembers their name, little do they know it is just regurgitated information. But, for some, it eased the path.* Duty-of-care was an illusion. The British welfare state curled up and died about the time the pandemic hit, and it was humans who had the duty to perform now, willingly or no.

"We have three new blood siphoning sheds, even though new arrivals are rare nowadays." The intern darted a smug look at Connor's profile. "We still siphon the more robust humans daily. It's still the best way to keep them in check. Escape is the last thing on their minds when just walking uses every ounce of effort." His conspiratorial chuckle struck Connor as obscene.

Connor flicked a glance up at the razor wire and said, "It's not escape you are managing in reality, though, is it? It's more a case of preventing the spilling of blood if they try." Connor bared his teeth in a simulated sadistic grin. "Don't want to waste the good stuff. I imagine you'd pay dearly for that, hmm?"

The vampire's laugh clattered with nerves this time.

Connor enjoyed an uncomfortable silence. "So, the robust inmates are siphoned daily. And the rest?" He already knew the rest, but questions would distract his escort.

"The rest we siphon weekly, except for those living in the new mixed gender compound. They have a bi-weekly regime and monthly medical examinations." The vampire puffed up again, on safer ground now. "I run the new medical center and make sure the breeders have a perfectly balanced diet, and that menstruation is regular and sperm counts are healthy."

"I see," said Connor.

"I'm taking you to the new medical block where we run the health checks. We even have a clinic up and running." The vampire tried to stay ahead of Connor's surging pace as he struggled to maintain his feeling of control. Preening and running was a cumbersome combination, and Connor swallowed the urge to laugh.

"And how is breeding progressing?" Connor asked.

A shadow passed across the vampire's features. "Not good. I move the females out of the dormitories; their comforts are pandered to, they have their own box, and vitamin/folic acid supplements, but still, the pregnancies fail. We lost two recently." He glanced at Connor with respect. "But, you know about that, of course."

Connor stared coldly. *Fail was one take on it.*

"So, the new female is certainly headed for the breeding compound?"

The vampire nodded as they reached a set of gates which bridged the gap in a ten-foot high stone wall. Turning his attention to an integral man-sized access door embedded within the larger iron-barred gate, he said, "The indicators are good, although that's for you to say." He swiped a security card which beeped. "The medical center is just the other side of this wall."

Entering the newer brick-built enclosure was like stepping into Utopia. The facades of *these* dormitories resembled 20th century terraced houses, and the flowerbeds out front splashed a frill of color around the grass lawn aprons.

Connor swiped and beeped too, thinking fast. *So, this physical examination is my best chance to get Leizle out.* Stepping through the gate, he faltered midstep. An image of Rebekah filtered into his head. Like a droplet of blood hitting a pool of clear water, it billowed and swirled long enough for him to absorb the detail. Discomfort plagued him and the words 'what's she up to now' solidified in his mind.

He pushed them firmly away. He had Leizle and his crazy rescue plan to attend to first. *But then...*

The clipped grass gave way to a polished quartz pathway which, like Dorothy's yellow brick road, drew Connor towards the brick built construction of the new medical block.

Ah, a little nostalgia to make them feel at home? It was certainly a mirage of the familiar in comparison to the granite-gray and steel siphoning sheds, and more welcoming than the bare wood of the human barracks.

Connor entered the new 'health center', as the plaque proclaimed it to be, and stopped within the inviting puddle of light projected by a honey-colored spot lamp onto the sage-green carpet. Connor's lightning assessment took in the tastefully decorated reception area. It showed the effort vampires were devoting to breeding humans.

Maybe a keen youngster studied fengshui, or was an interior designer when human. Either way, Connor found the end result pleasing. *Good God, and what have we here?* Beyond the cluster of comfy brown leather chairs was a vending machine bursting with healthy snacks and drinks and, the ultimate olive branch, a coffee dispenser.

Of course, wardens escorted the humans attending the clinic. Connor wondered if the males still wore handcuffs tethered to a chain around their ankles. Another practice used in concentration camps, it prevented prisoners raising their hands above shoulder level to garrote or cosh a guard. Vampires did not need the protection, but it made the boundaries crystal clear. *Stamping out hope is a bigger part of human acceptance than most realize.* He headed across the plush carpet. *But, this is a start.*

The fumes of fresh paint stung his nose, and he grinned at the idea of a vampire using a paintbrush. "The only thing funnier would be a ballerina operating a pneumatic drill," Connor muttered.

Stopping abruptly, he raised a brow at the vampire guide who still flanked his shoulder. "Second floor, and what room number? I think I can find it."

The vampire looked offended, seeing his opportunity to gloat disappearing. "Room 13."

"Thank you." Connor mounted the wide, polished wood stairway and did not look back. He traveled silently along the corridor until he reached Examination Room 13, hoping it was a good omen.

His plan centered on pretending to find cause for concern which required further tests at the hospital. *Hopefully, I can get Leizle to fake an anxiety attack. Human hysteria is always good for creating chaos. It will redirect their attention, and, somewhere between here and there, I'll return her home.* He would have to cover his tracks afterwards, but he had yet to think that part out.

Entering the room, Connor stopped inside the door, and waited for Leizle to register his arrival. *Was I ever that slow*? When she finally noticed him with a start, he minutely shook his head. They were alone, but he was under no illusions. Serge did not trust him and everything must appear as it should.

Leizle's face was a battlefield of confusion.

Connor intended the examination to be perfunctory, and he had no choice but to restrict conversation to instruction. *Leizle's a bright girl, but will she see it as an act?* The pheromone-cocktail she emanated clung to the roof of his mouth and he wryly acknowledged that fresh human blood was still his drug of choice. *Their emotions are such a colorful banquet, if only they knew how hard they make it.*

He acclimatized to her scent, and, like a deep-sea diver descending into murky depths, Connor sank into the tranquil waters of revival sleep. Once he had her measure, he stepped closer. *I'm not taking any chances.* Advancing slowly, he still arrived at her side without her seeing him move, and she leapt out of her skin, again.

Inwardly, Connor groaned, a rueful smile flitting over his face. "Lie down," he said, resisting the 'please' hovering on his lips.

He found it easy to control his feeding reactions to her scent. A cinnamon accent to her aroma made his nose sting, but nothing more. He was more concerned when her face drained of color and the glitter of jade in her eyes dimmed. *I need her to be ready for flight. What I need from her is a burst of adrenalin.*

Leizle lay back and folded her hands over her stomach, her gown trembling as her heart rate thundered.

Connor laid a professional palm on her forehead, taking her temperature more accurately than the mercury thread of a thermometer could. He inhaled slowly through his nostrils with his mouth open slightly, analyzing her scent as it washed over his palate. He measured the iron levels in her blood by how thick the scent was, and how heavy the metallic aftertaste. He gathered the information as part of the performance, in case questions were asked.

Connor picked up a wooden tongue depressor. "Open wide," he said abruptly.

Instead of inspecting her throat, he stared into her eyes, using the moment of proximity to plead silently for cooperation.

His voice and face were a comical mismatch, the icy edge in his clipped tone at odds with his brows, arched in apology.

"When did you last eat?"

"Last night."

"Do you consider your menstrual cycle to be normal?"

Leizle blushed, her answer becoming a strangled squawk of protest.

"Is your sleep pattern regular?"

'Yes," she said, huskily.

"Do you suffer with headaches?"

"Right now?"

His face became more serious, as though every answer she gave took them one step closer to an uncomfortable truth. Connor built the tension, leading her to the moment when he would tell her to scream. *I need her to just do it, with no questions asked.* He wanted the bloodcurdling variety. The scream had to make the ears of the vampire wardens vibrate with such ferocity that they would do just about anything to end it.

He opened his mouth, about to say 'scream as if you are dying and don't stop', when the door flipped open and deposited Anthony into the room. His face was locked into an earnest 'give me another chance' expression, and Connor would not have been surprised if he had whisked out a bouquet of flowers from behind his back. *He smells so sincere. Heck.*

The trolley Anthony towed across the room was loaded with the gynecological instruments required to perform a thorough human physical examination. His inquiring glance forced Connor to act natural.

Connor crossed to the basin, scrubbed in, and pulled on a sterile gown. It was routine when dealing with humans; risking cross infection within the herd was unthinkable.

Jerking his head, Connor indicated where he wanted the trolley placed, and then he faked a vacant frown. "Thank you, Anthony." Connor turned away, praying Leizle would not leap off the examination table. *She trusts me. That much is clear.* He knew by her apprehensive gaze, and by the firework display of electrical activity dancing inside her brain, how hard it was for her to stay still. *Anthony may get the scent of it too, but he'll assume it's the usual panic humans feel around vampires.*

"That'll be all." Connor pretended to focus on the patient and hoped his assistant would leave.

"May I stay?" Anthony asked. "You'll need someone to circulate the sterile field, you're scrubbed in." Anthony picked up the parcel containing plastic stents, one of which Connor should insert into Leizle's vein, along with the glass test tubes capped with non-return valves which he would fill with her blood. Anthony unfolded the package and laid it open without touching the sterile layers inside. His hand gesture said 'ta-dah', as he smiled hopefully.

Backed into a corner, Connor faced the prospect of examining a clearly terrified Leizle. He flicked a glance at her white face, and, turning his head so Anthony could not see, he mouthed, "It's okay." Relieved when she stayed lying down, he skimmed his hands down over her limbs in a quick assessment. Over his shoulder, Connor muttered remarks about calcium deposits and signs of old breaks in bones, mentoring Anthony as always, and distracting him in the process.

When Connor's cold hands framed Leizle's bare stomach, a bolt of electricity shot through him and light exploded inside his head.

The flash arcing behind his eyes printed an image of Rebekah's sleeping face on the walls inside his skull. Her eyes snapped open, and a filigree pattern of frosted lace crawled up her neck until it covered her features, finally decorating her eyelids and dragging them closed. But not before he saw her brown eyes die, the irises shriveling like autumn leaves drying out and crumbling to dust.

A knife thrust of dread stirred in the pit of his stomach. He knew Rebekah was *not* dead, but he was overwhelmed by her anxiety and the pull to find her escalated sharply.

I have to go, now.

There is always a moment, that *if only* moment, upon which the world turns. Recognizing it as though it was signposted in neon, Connor saw an escape route and took it.

As Anthony placed a speculum in Connor's outstretched hand to begin the internal part of the examination, and Leizle tensed, ready to jump from the bed this time, Connor hissed, "Sorry."

Blood samples were the next stage in the process. But, before Anthony even thought to put on the mask tucked inside his belt, Connor slipped a scalpel from his pocket. With a flick of the wrist, he pressed the blade to Leizle's arm. Her eyes watered with the shock of pain. The scent of blood filled the room as her anxious heart pumped at a satisfying rate.

The thick sweet odor of the blood, plump red cells oozing a red-berry aroma, bombarded Anthony's nostrils like a hit of cocaine. His brain activity fibrillated, his thought patterns crumbled, and he became crazed in an instant.

In less than three seconds, Connor pinned a snarling, out-of-control Anthony against the wall by his throat. Behind the hunger-driven gaze Anthony bored into Connor was a desperate question. He had seen Connor cut Leizle, and puzzled rage flavored his terrible thirst.

Connor bellowed, "Help. I need help. Now."

When the door to the room whipped open, Connor pushed a syringe of muscle relaxant into Anthony's neck, whispering into his slackening features, "I'm sorry, I *will* explain."

Anthony sagged, and Connor guided him down the wall. Anthony's solid bulk settled on the floor, and his slack hands flopped open, his fingers still jerking like upended spiders.

The vampire wardens rushed into the room. The smell of blood caused pandemonium. They circled like crows, flocking as if tethered together and incapable of independent thought.

Connor crossed the room and bandaged Leizle's bleeding wound. "Stay away." He held up a hand and interrupted the frantic circling formation. Their eyes skittered around the room, and, desperately trying to hold their own bloodlust in check, the wardens backed away, happy to comply.

"You need to contain him," Connor said, jerking his chin towards the prone form of Anthony. "And she is not safe until I stem the bleeding." While confusion still reigned, Connor lifted Leizle, and strode from the room.

Passing through the complex, Connor barked the orders which removed gates and allowed his speed to surge to a human run and then on to a horse's gallop.

The image printed on his retina of Rebekah's blue-tinged face was developing rapidly. Her lips were now cyanotic, and there was ash on her lashes. *No, not ash, frost.*

Anguish twisted Connor's face. He hurtled forward, heading out into the night.

Chapter 33

Sebastian's handling of Douglas was not kind, in fact, somewhere around the Vauxhall area of London, it became downright spiteful. Fed up of supporting the fleshy human carcass, Sebastian gripped the back of his collar, and, with a firm twist, he shifted from using Douglas like a windbreak held against his chest to dragging him along behind. Every flight of steps and curbstone along the way pecked at Douglas' heels and jarred his spine.

For Douglas, the flip gave him a head rush which crowded his vision with ink spots. The speed at which Sebastian towed him along never allowed him to properly catch his breath, and semi-consciousness became a blessing.

When the forward propulsion and cold wind stopped, Douglas found himself landed on the floor with all the care of a side of beef in an abattoir. As he lay in an awkward heap, the hot-ash sizzle of pins and needles brought with it awareness. He rolled over onto his back and stared at the ceiling. It was like nothing he had seen before. The ornate plaster casted rose which framed the light fitting overhead would have made Gaudi feel nauseated. Gold leaf clung to the impressive circular plaque like melted chocolate.

"Definitely not in Kansas anymore," he muttered.

A snort of derision made him realize he had spoken aloud. "Councilor Serge will be flattered to be thought of as a wizard," said Sebastian.

Douglas gathered his wits slowly, and Sebastian was not inclined to wait.

Sebastian whisked him bodily to his feet, holding onto Douglas' shirt-front until his legs decided they had a job to do and he snapped to attention.

He was a mere six inches from Douglas when he said, "Councilor Serge is waiting."

Douglas shuddered as Sebastian's cold finger touched the angry graze around his neck, where the edge of his collar had cut in like a cloth machete.

"Not having second thoughts, I hope?" Sebastian asked, his nail etching a blood-red necklace around Douglas' throat.

Douglas swallowed and shook his head.

Sebastian released him and circled away to reveal Councilor Serge, the oldest vampire Douglas had ever seen. A rotting aroma thickened the space between them when Serge grinned.

Douglas gagged.

"Well, is Sebastian correct, that you *need* to be one of us?" Serge locked his gaze onto Douglas' shiny skin. *The joke will be on him if he thinks being turned will make him virile and handsome. I certainly had. He's doomed to disappointment.* Serge assessed the white dough-like flabby body which would be exactly what Douglas would be blessed with for all eternity. *It's almost worth turning him, just to see the look on his face.*

Leaning in until his eyes filled Douglas' vision, Serge's deep breath sucked the oxygen from the air. He felt a burst of amusement when Douglas' throat worked, and he smelled the bile his victim fought to keep down.

Finally, Douglas gulped down the acidic cocktail, and his eyes watered as the cut on his throat burned. In the act of touching his neck, he stopped bare inches away when instinct told him he was better off not knowing. "I know where there are humans," said Douglas. Struggling for breath, he croaked, "But I need to be one of you."

"Ah, it is this *need* that intrigues us. Sebastian says it is a fight over a woman?" Serge's thin lashes veiled his eyes, and anticipation twitched his sagging cheeks. "And the name of your rival?"

"Connor," said Douglas.

Serge's smile deepened; he could almost taste Douglas' regret. *Too late now. He has chosen his side*. Serge sucked in a wet breath and pleasure trickled through him. "I think we can help each other out," he said. Looking over Douglas' shoulder, his eyes met Sebastian's. "You will be well rewarded."

Douglas swallowed hard. "Thank you."

Idiot, thought Serge, as Connor had done before him. *Sebastian will have fun when the time comes.* Even Serge found the prospect of making a meal of Douglas repulsive. He would gladly pass. Serge returned his attention to Douglas, focusing on his gray eyes. *Fish-scale eyes.* "I suggest you start talking, hmm?"

Chapter 34

In the leafy suburb humans used to call 'Richmond', majestic oaks cast an impressive canopy over the sidewalks and dusted the front of the houses in a fretwork of shadow. Julian's house, set back from the road beyond an uncluttered lawn apron and a gravel driveway, made sneaking up on the inhabitant impossible. And so, knowing the drop in air pressure warned of his fast approach, Connor was not surprised to see Julian framed in the doorway, intently watching Connor's silhouette resolve from a misshapen 'Hunchback of Notre Dame' shadow into a vampire carrying a girl.

Julian's eyes widened when Connor swept past into the house, holding a pale Leizle close to his chest, and moved quickly into the sitting room.

"Don't ask," said Connor, when Julian followed him. "I have to go, Rebekah's in trouble."

Connor lowered a bewildered Leizle onto the pristine, hardly-ever-sat-upon couch, before turning towards the door.

The premonition haunting Connor had progressed from a fragmented transparency of Rebekah's face to a fully-formed image of a mask of deathly pallor melted onto her skin.

"Something is wrong," he said, his pinched features easy to read.

"Wrong?" asked Julian, still venturing no further than the threshold. He lifted a brow and threw a pointed glance at Leizle. As it had in the courtroom, her sudden appearance clearly rocked Julian back on his heels.

Connor deflected the stab of guilt as he said shortly, "I'm sorry, but you're in this too. I'll be back as soon as I can." Wheeling around, he left, moving out of earshot before Julian could protest.

In a matter of minutes, less time than it took Julian to recover *his* balance, Connor stood in the woodland, barely a mile away from the eco-town, hunting for clues which would tell him where he should begin the search.

A hundred-year accumulation of emotion swelled inside him in one moment, and all the hysteria, fear, and panic he found so amusing in humans rendered him powerless. *Damn it, I can't hear anything except the panting of my own breath.* Clamping down on the knot of tension driving his lungs like bellows, he stopped breathing and listened in the newly reclaimed silence. *Still nothing.*

He halted near a clutch of silver birch when an image of their cream-colored, cracked bark leapt out at him. His jaw worked in tempo with his pumping fists until he lashed out and punched a hole in a nearby pearl-tinted trunk. As he crumbled the satisfying handful of wood to dust, he muttered, "I know you saw them, thought of them. Rebekah, help me out, here."

Unable to stand still any longer, he set off through the undergrowth doing the only thing he could think of; a grid search. He covered the ground at a speed which would register as a mere glimmer of shadow to the human eye. *I know she's here somewhere.* But, the further he went into the woods, the more the faint twitch of her heart – because that's all it was – seemed to reside deeper inside and all around him.

In the near pitch-black, he swept his eyes over every blade of grass, his night vision gathering the tapestry of textures.

His hurtling speed died when he heard a noise. He scanned in a 360degree arc, turning on one heel. The crackle of leaves drew his attention before a pale face appeared between the trees.

Shit.

The feral's head swung on a slack neck as he drifted through the wood. Inhaling noisily, he zeroed in on Connor's smell.

Connor frowned. *I've been on the human farm. I must reek.* He slipped the scalpel, still stained with Leizle's blood, from his pocket, and grinned. *Bring it on.*

The vampire accelerated, and a wave of turbulence whipped the undergrowth as he hit his stride.

Like a matador, Connor sidestepped and jabbed the scalpel into the feral's solid shoulder. The tip bent over as the blade tore a clump of fabric from the blood-stiffened coat.

Reeling around and barreling forward, the vampire's roar filled the air with a rotting stench.

Connor dug the scalpel in again.

The feral swung around and slapped his hand over the cut scored into his neck.

Without missing a beat, Connor darted forward and rammed the buckled scalpel blade into the enraged vampire's eye. He twisted the hook and scooped out the jelly-like eyeball, and thick fluid oozed down the shocked white face.

The vampire froze.

Grabbing a fistful of rancid hair, Connor shoved his victim's head down hard and drove his knee up into the feral's face, shattering his cheekbones. Stepping out of the way and shoving him to the floor, Connor stamped down on the base of the vampire's skull, crumbling the vertebrae to dust.

Without waiting, Connor refocused on the surrounding woodlands. The fight had scared the woodland creatures into silence, and he strained his senses, scanning for Rebekah once more. He set off again, confidence giving him strength as he honed in on the faint whisper of air grating through dry vocal chords. He just needed to get a bearing before the noise of nature's creatures chattering could drown it out.

He knew what skin and cloth would feel like if their image stroked across his mind, and still he almost passed them by. He continued on, until the frozen shapes registered in a 'hang on a minute, what was that' kind of way, and he returned to the spot with icy calm.

Pushing aside the foliage, not daring to look too closely, Connor gathered the huddled mass up into his arms, and settled them both into his chest. They were zipped into Rebekah's oilskin coat. Her arms were wrapped around Thomas' small frame and her blue-tinged cheek rested on the top of his head. Their silent bodies made Connor feel as though he was deaf. He was so used to filtering out the clamoring kaleidoscope of human scents and emotions that in the seconds it took to return to the eco-town, hearing nothing but his own fleeting footfalls and smelling nothing but ice, hope was hard to cling to.

When he reached the eco-town, he rushed into the tunnel entrance, and his deliberate stride reverberated in an echo off the rock-clad walls.

"Harry, Oscar," he bellowed.

Human footsteps came running, but to his vampire sense, they took forever to arrive.

If sunrise comes and she is gone, I will go too.

Rebekah was dreaming, and the bone-deep trembling, the ice in her veins, and the fear folded like a fist around her heart, became a dissipating memory. She sat, sleepy and relaxed, and hugged a giant hot water bottle. Molding her bare torso to its deliciously warm surface made the insides of her thighs and her belly simmer gently. She shifted in the cradled comfort of a lap, luxuriating in the warmth radiating through her seat, creeping into her bones and making her feel weightless. Every single nerve vibrated with the glow and she smiled.

Her memory stalled at the journey through the woods. Inhaling gently, she absorbed the clean masculine fragrance and the billowing specter of the monster in the woods faded. She remembered holding Thomas' frozen form in her arms, and feeling as though the cold weight of lead pressed her eyelids closed. *Am I dead? No, not dead. Dreaming?*

She lifted her head sleepily and as she turned it, her nose brushed skin. She warmed the other cheek on the smooth, hard, velvet-textured surface. As she shifted her weight, warm hands moved over her back, molding to her ribcage, and sure fingers caressed her skin. The movement pulled her closer and strong arms enfolded her body.

This isn't right. With a sudden jolt of confusion, a lightning strike sliced through the clouded comfort and startled her into instant awareness. The tingling heat in her body became the burn of ice as alarm trickled through her. *This can't be right.*

Rebekah's bruised heart lurched with a surge of adrenalin. She summoned the image of every male face she could remember, imagined how they might feel, and what struck terror in her heart was that none of them fit. *I don't know this man.* Suddenly, her body shriveled with the embarrassment of betrayal. *Who is this, and where is Connor?*

The powerful arms of this *naked* stranger – because she had worked that one out – held her trapped. She was wrapped around a hot body, a firm chest pressed to hers, and the back her fingers splayed over was silky smooth. Her hands curled into fists as she tensed, and when every muscle twitched, ready to take flight, he chuckled.

Rebekah's senses flipped like a tossed coin and disorientation scared the hell out of her. *Connor.* The chilled breath feathering the chuckle over her head belonged to him. The treacle-smooth tone of it was him, and even the way it rumbled inside his chest, all him.

But, he's hot.

Steeling herself to face her fears, she sought his face urgently. The soft pewter-gray of his eyes glinting in the dim light of her cave could barely contain his relief.

"It *is* you."

His being here proved her senses were better equipped than her brain, which now threatened to spoil the moment with a million questions. Connor was having none of it. As she opened her mouth to ask "How?", he lowered his head, dipped his tepid tongue into her mouth, and stole every thought she tried to capture.

"So, beautiful," he murmured, running a finger over her flushed cheeks.

Another chuckle rolled through him as his kiss opened the floodgates of relief and drowned out her voice of caution. Her body pressed to his, her hands clinging to his warmth in fascination, tracing every muscle rippling beneath her fingertips, and her mouth pulled him in as she molded her stroking tongue desperately to his.

For a moment, an alternative future blossomed, one they both ached for. A world where they could lay out in a meadow in sunlight and she could play shadows off his skin, watch the sun reflect like silver pools in his eyes, and see the stroke of his fingers scatter sapphire-tinted fragments through his black hair. A world where she and Connor were both alive.

Thinking was overrated, Rebekah decided. She moved closer, and his warm, hard stomach muscles braced as he shifted to support her. His reaction to her, the growl in his throat, was a powerful aphrodisiac. Her instinctive responses thrilled him, knotting the muscles beneath her demanding caress, as his body pressed insistently into hers.

"Ah, my Rebekah," he sighed against her lips.

Her hands framed his strong jaw as she tasted the excitement of his mouth. Being alive and, having been to Connor's frozen wasteland of desolation, having him here with her now, warm and feeling again, was enough. Love, a white-hot blaze of it, flushed her in perspiration. Threading her fingers into his hair, she pulled his face harder into hers.

"Easy honey, easy, I'm doing human slow today, don't test me," he whispered, smiling against her mouth.

Desperation whispered in her ear. *You'll never truly be happy. He can never be what you need him to be.* As she kissed him again, she moved her thighs higher to cradle his hips, and melted into him, wanting him to lose control, wanting him to want her too. "Love me, Connor. Please."

Connor exhaled sharply. His body became still, and Rebekah held her breath. The moment stretched into an age of heightened sensation, her pulse beating a tattoo she could feel humming through him too. Finally, she sighed as his caressing hands fitted her curves into his hard planes, and he rolled his hips into hers.

Sliding her palms up over his bunched shoulders, she whispered quietly, "I need you."

Tightening her grasp on his neck, she held her breath as an aching pulse tingled between her thighs. Arching her body, she sought out the tantalizing pressure of him beneath her.

His surrender was a mere glint in the jet pool of his gaze, a flame licked in their depths, and his chest moved as his resistance folded. Sliding his sure grasp down to span her buttocks, in a smooth driving stroke, he filled her. Gasping at the unexpected pressure surging up inside, she welcomed him and pulled him in deeper. She watched his face, fascinated by the shadows chasing across it. She absorbed every nuance of the battle etching white lines into his perfect features as he held himself in check, besieged by his demons.

His hand cupped her skull, holding her still, and he stared into her eyes as his desperate need of her undulated through his hips. A snarl trembled at his lip.

"Bite me," she breathed softly. She wanted him to feel her pleasure. *I want him to stay.* Anticipation trapped a breath inside her as the words struck a chord of almost unbearable desire through her, too.

The shudder running through him bunched his muscles from shoulders to thighs. His silver irises burned away to smoldering black coal as he froze.

"Bite me, Connor."

Her words released him. He buried his face in her neck, and with a knife sharp pinch, he pierced her. Biting down hard, he pulled her flesh into his mouth. His lips dragged over her skin as he buried his teeth a little deeper, clamped down and sank in to drink. Every muscle in her body hummed with each contraction of his jaws, his venom flowing like a citrus cream cocktail through her sluggish bloodstream. Tremors shook her and, as her blood filled his mouth and dulled the razor-edge of his desire, sparks exploded inside her head.

He clutched her tightly to him, satisfaction vibrating his throat. As the glittering shower inside her head subsided, and her muscles finally relaxed, the afterglow of her climax singing through them, every fiber in his body suddenly jolted, locking tight. He groaned, agony shredding the sound in his throat.

"Sorry, baby, I'm sorry." Alarm and regret sharpened his gaze when his eyes met hers.

Rebekah grabbed a handful of his mussed hair, making him look at her. As a tide of warmth flowed like lava inside her, she knew. He had tried to hold back, to move away, but, it was too late, and he had poured himself into her.

"I'm sorry." His breathing sawed in and out of flared nostrils. His body tensed again, in frustration this time.

Rebekah held him close, her hands stroking his hair until he relaxed. "It's okay." Her voice rang with quiet conviction. "Truly."

After another moment of stillness, a sigh moved through him as he nuzzled her neck, licking in firm strokes over her throat, coagulating the wound he had torn. He finally kissed her soft, open mouth again, stealing her panting breaths and running his hands over her still trembling body. "Still, I shouldn't have-"

Her fingertips were not so much placed on his lips, as slapped in place like a duct tape gag. Rebekah's stern look said *enough*, and Connor's lips twitched. Amusement lurked in the depths of his gaze as he allowed Rebekah to overpower him and push him back on the bed. She smiled when he kept her close into his side, not wanting to lose contact. She felt it too, the pull, as though their bodies were polarized with a magnetic attraction, two halves of a whole. *Happiness, that's the word.* Gazing at the curved ceiling of her cave, the glow of a lamp casting them both in a soothing light, Rebekah finally felt at home.

A long time later, with their bodies still entwined, he stirred, looking into her still-flushed cheeks. "I can't regret loving you at last, being with you, as I have always wanted."

"I know."

"I thought I'd lost you." His voice stayed low as he poured out his desperation.

Suddenly serious, she said quietly, "What *was* that, out in the woods?"

His sharp gaze scoured her face. "You saw him? I hoped you hadn't." He drifted his fingers down over her naked back. "He's gone now. It was one of the feral vampires I told you about. We flush them out and kill them if we see them. They're few and far between."

"But, he's gone?"

He frowned and nodded. "I found you, and that's the main thing. You're safe now." Relief whitened his skin to bone-white as his embrace tightened.

"Ouch." She smiled.

He softened his hold and laughed wryly. "Harry and Oscar thought *I* was demented, and for a while there, I was. I looked crazy, I think, bearing down on them, racing through the tunnels with you and Thomas in my arms." His face was grim. "Harry's face was whiter than mine when I barked at him to fill a bath with boiling water. I think he thought I was about to boil *you* alive, not me."

"What?" Rebekah's eyes widened. "*Boiling* water?"

"I warm my hands in hot water before surgery on humans." He shrugged uncomfortably. "I was desperate. I figured it would work for the rest of me. My tissue is denser than yours. Think of me as a man-sized storage heater. Granite warmed by the sun releases heat for hours after dusk," he explained. A rueful laugh erupted as he said, "It was worth the risk. I think I shocked a few people with my naked butt, but I couldn't care less about that."

The thought of Connor walking naked, the toned muscles of his taut buttocks and rock hard thighs, made Rebekah grin like an idiot.

Connor looked down at her and grinned back. Dropping a kiss onto her smiling lips, he said, "I got you back, and that's all that matters. And yes, Thomas made it too." He grinned again. "By more orthodox methods, you saved him, honey." His voice faded to a whisper as he placed his palm over her heart. "I thought I might never feel this again. I waited eighteen hours. Listened to every moth-wing flutter, because that's all it was." His eyes darkened. "I died every time a beat was missed, and when the deep breaths of natural sleep finally settled in, I prayed."

"If you thought you'd lost me, why didn't you turn me?" she asked seriously.

"I was too late. You were too cold, your heart had begun to shut down, and you were deeply unconscious, so feeding from me would have been beyond you." He met her gaze, looking for horror at the thought of drinking his blood.

Rebekah knew what he was thinking. She pressed a kiss to his chest and nipped the tightened flat disc of his nipple with her teeth. "When should I start practicing?" she teased.

His hissed sigh of relief turned into a chuckle. "I'm so glad I got you back. You do me so much good."

Dipping his head to kiss her, Rebekah savored his taste as citrus-syrup saliva flooded his mouth, before he resolutely swallowed it down. "Go to sleep," he whispered. Rubbing his chin over her hair, he tucked her into his side and trapped her hands in one of his. "Sleep, honey."

Chapter 35

The atmosphere inside Julian's house had become thick with fear and doubt. Leizle still sat upon the large couch. Ambient light picked out copper-bright threads in her chestnut hair and enhanced a complexion so pale she might easily be mistaken for a vampire.

Across the room, standing at the empty hearth, Julian was the epitome of an impressive English gentleman, with a world of uncertainty written upon his face. A Goliath to her David.

For a long time after Connor left the house, Leizle's shallow breathing was the only sound breaking the silence. Her fingers remained knotted in her lap and she darted glances at Julian. The stillness in his face offered no comfort.

Julian's nostrils flared as he appreciated the fragrance of the adrenalin pumping around her body. The nervous tremor humming through her frame resonated through him like the thundering approach of a stampeding herd.

An enlightened smile softened Julian's features. In addition to the trembling, he could read every expression that touched her face, no matter how fleeting. He could see easily into her mind. He wanted to move closer and reassure her, but the certainty she would scrabble away like a scared cat kept him at bay.

As she glanced at the bandaged arm she was nursing, he could almost taste her thoughts, and finally, her words tumbled out. "I'm going into shock. Blood loss, he cut me."

Julian tried for levity. "Do you think we're a tag team? Connor delivers you to me like meals on wheels, well, a takeaway- Oh, heck."

He shut up when he caught Leizle's startled glance. She shrank away. He could even smell the burning chestnut aroma of her clamoring dread.

"I was joking." He held up his hands as if she had a pistol aimed at his chest. *Stupid.* Julian looked at her and had no idea what to do.

He had *never* been at a loss in all his two hundred immortal years.

When chasing down the murderous bastard who killed his Eva, he invited his own death, and even then, he had been certain. *Kill or be killed. Of course, that didn't work out so well for me.* But, he made sense of immortality and used it to make him stronger, and to give his life, or rather his death, meaning. *I've always had a plan, until now.*

And now, as Leizle recoiled, he looked into her fear-frozen face, and impotence filled his cold heart. *How do I placate a girl who's been captured and terrified at the human farm? And, judging by the scent of blood and the bandage, has probably seen vampires at their most terrifying? Tough call.*

Okay, rewind to the beginning. "Do you remember me?' he asked gently, still holding his hands palms up. *She is certainly carved into* my *memory.* Since that night in the woods, his first sighting of her grubby face remained easy to recall. "I am Julian. Principal Julian."

"Yes." She swallowed loudly, and the noise flooded Julian's mouth with venom. *Dammit.*

"I won't hurt you, I have control," he murmured, talking to them both and issuing a *stern* reminder to himself.

Alarm flashed in her green eyes, and Julian knew he was right. *She's seen a vampire in blood rage. At a basic level, we're feeding, killing machines. Strip away the social veneer and we really* are *just bloodsuckers.*

"I'm sorry if you got scared, but I won't, *can't* hurt you. Doctor Connor would kick my butt."

Julian feigned amusement, and was encouraged when her crouched posture unfolded a little, although her knees were still jiggling as though the carpet repelled her heels.

At Connor's name, a spark of hope lit her gaze, and envy stirred in Julian's gut. *Easy, she's just grateful.*

"You look very pale. Are you okay?" When he had finished beating himself up and tuned back in to Leizle, he began to think she could be right. Her body heat was clustered in her core and her limbs were registering as cool to him now. *Maybe she* is *going into shock.* Concern anchored his green gaze on hers, and he suffered a world of pain as he fought the urge to cross the room and put an arm around her, comfort her, and maybe nibble, just a little.

The awkwardness stretched, while Leizle stared at him.

Going for reassurance, Julian fixed a half-smile on his face. He bore her scrutiny, and even though her gaze dragged discomfort over his skin, he projected tranquility.

Suddenly, his chin jerked up and his expression froze. "Someone is approaching the house. You'll have to hide."

"What? Who?"

Leizle did not see him move. She jumped when she was buffeted sideways. Her breath whooshed from her lungs as her feet left the floor and the chill of rushing air made her gasp.

Julian registered the burning heat of her body in his arms at the same time as he set her down once more in a different room. He still held her wrist in a cold grasp in case she stumbled.

Frowning, he said, "Don't move."

The words echoed in the air, but he was already gone.

Don't move. Leizle decided to take the warning literally, although sinking to her knees was unavoidable as her shaking legs made standing impossible.

She folded onto the floor, crushed by fear of the unknown. *Don't move, but for how long?* The rollercoaster ride of the past twenty-four hours seemed unrelenting as she relived her last moments of freedom out in the crop field. Being handed over to the reeking vampire with yellowed wrinkled skin stained her soul with terror, but the nightmare had ended here, with Julian.

When Doctor Connor ran his chilled hands over her body, embarrassment had been her overriding reaction. *What would Julian's touch be like?* Her heart raced, and fear had nothing to do with the tide of blood rushing up her neck and flushing her cheeks.

She was not yet safe, but in safe hands. Her fingers closed over the wrist Julian had touched and a warm feeling rippled up her arm. Naming it was difficult, but enjoying it was easy.

◇◇◇

The rustle of leaves and whisking of gravel outside the house gave Julian the warning he needed to prepare. Although, unceremoniously dumping Leizle in a room at the back of the house was not part of the plan. Annoyance glittered in his eyes for a moment. *She'll be back to being scared, and I'm back to square one. Still-*

His concentration returned to what was about to unfold; he entered his study and left the door open, allowing him a view of the hallway which led to the front door.

Julian's speciality as principal was intimidation, and he settled behind an imposing walnut Victorian desk. Julian enjoyed beautiful things. Staring ahead, he traced an idle finger along the intricately tooled edge of the leather-coated writing surface. The five-foot square area was clear of clutter. *Tidy mind and all that.* Julian grinned.

The neat stack of papers sitting upon the desk did not need to be there. He already had the information filed and collated inside his head. *However, suggesting weakness is useful.* Inviting underestimation was a weapon.

"Come." The word exploded from inside Julian as the intruding vampire's footfall reached the top step outside the front door. The visual and the odor arrived in concert, and Julian's eyes narrowed when his visitor entered the room. "Councilor Serge, to what do I owe this pleasure?" he said, with icy sarcasm.

"Principal Julian." Serge's head bobbed. His gray, lank hair slapped onto his forehead, only to be scraped back by bony fingers. "I beg your indulgence. I have an urgent matter to bring to your attention."

Julian's bored expression took in his uninvited guest. "This is very irregular, councilor. The jurors do not take kindly to private audiences, but you are here now-"

Examining his fingernails with nonchalance he did not feel, Julian took some satisfaction in hearing Serge's constricted gulp.

A thread of Julian's concentration detoured briefly to Leizle. He hoped she had heeded his warning. The human concept of quiet was on par with an elephant tap-dancing, to vampire ears, but he could hear nothing, yet. *So far, so good.*

With a frown, he studied Serge's pallid complexion. While his knee-jerk reaction was to tell him to go through the proper channels, he suspected the information in Serge's hands may mean the difference between life and death for Connor.

"I thought I should deliver the news in private." Serge oozed regretful concern. "Your colleague, Doctor Connor, has abducted my breeding program specimen."

"It is my understanding that Doctor Connor is performing her physical examination at the farm this evening, but go on."

"Indeed." Serge's eyebrows climbed in overblown surprise. "But it appears that there was a commotion, and Doctor Connor left. And he took the girl without permission, abducted her."

"I'm sure there will be an explanation," said Julian.

"Perhaps."

Julian sat back and waited, refusing to open any doors.

"And if there is no reasonable explanation? You must consider what action the council should take. Surely, Doctor Connor is threatening the food supply?"

So, that's it, he's seeking the death penalty for Connor, yet again. Meeting Serge's stare, Julian found the satisfaction he expected, but an undercurrent slithering in the depths of his yellow eyes caused Julian a prickle of unease.

Serge added meekly, "It may be a mistake, of course, but Supervisor Matthew assured me that he did not approve Doctor Connor's actions."

"Supervisor Matthew and Doctor Connor rarely see eye to eye. Perhaps he is overstating events."

"Perhaps," Serge agreed.

"I shall discuss your concerns with Jurors Alexander and Marius. If there is a case to answer, Doctor Connor will, of course, be called to account." Julian waited for Serge to come back at him. Demand the when, and how. *But, nothing.*

Serge dipped his chin. "I would be very grateful. She is *my* head of cattle, after all."

"Ah, come now, Councilor." Julian slipped the smooth glove of amusement over his rock hard features. "Once you brought the girl into court, she became community property." Julian's smile persisted, but his eyes glittered with green ice. "You know that."

"Of course, council protocol. Of course," Serge muttered. Wringing his hands and bobbing his head, he backed towards the doorway. "I look forward to the council's decision," he said, and, in a whisk of movement, departed.

Julian stared at the space left by Serge, tapping his foot in a staccato of unrest. *He accepted my half promises and fake gratitude too easily.* Julian paced the room. *He barely put up a fight. There's more to this.*

Julian shoved his arms into his jacket as he strode out through the front door. Skimming across the gravel and ramping up to cruising speed, he scanned for Serge. Hyde Park whipped by in a blur as he headed to the council building. "Loose lips," he muttered grimly. *Someone will let something slip.*

Suddenly, he groaned. Digging his heels into the sidewalk, the leather soles of his shoes creaked in protest and he stopped dead. His breath hissed between his teeth. "Leizle."

Within seconds, he was back inside his house stalking along the hallway and muttering under his breath, "I'll check on her, tell her to stay quiet, and I'll return as soon as I can."

Julian appeared in the room as slowly as his impatience would allow. He froze with his hand still on the doorknob when he saw she was lying on the floor. A quick assessment – slow breathing and silent muscle fibers – revealed she had fallen asleep. He told himself he was only there because he owed it to Connor. So, why then, looking down upon her folded frame, did he have difficulty not touching her sleeping face?

Returning to his study, in bold flowing script, Julian wrote, 'Make no noise. I will be back as soon as I can'.

"Damn, Connor," he murmured, as he folded the notepaper and slipped it under the hand laying palm down on the carpet where she lay on her side with her knees curled up. The silvered strands of moonlight straying across the carpet picked out the black crescents of her closed lashes and played shadows over her pale face. Asleep, she looked very young and vulnerable. Julian risked using a fingertip to move a tress of copper-colored silk from her cheek before laying a blanket over her. He couldn't trust himself to move her.

He left the house. Erasing the confusion from his mind, he closed in on the council buildings once more. *Serge won't still be there, but he enjoys gloating.*

He bounded up the steps and pushed through the heavy oak doors. Reducing his speed to his usual purposeful stride and straightening his jacket while he walked, he made his way to his chambers. Stripping his principal's robe from its wooden hanger, he settled it over his shoulders and tied his white cravat. He checked his reflection. Content that he did not look as rattled as he felt, with a final sweep of his hands to tidy his hair, he left and headed for the ante-rooms.

Once inside, he scanned the gathered vampires, recognizing the usual suspects. They fell into two categories, ambitious or boastful, and either one would suit his purpose tonight. *But, no Serge.*

Julian resisted the urge to check his watch. He could feel time pressing down upon him, with Leizle alone and likely to wake-up, but indolence would bring faster results.

He scoured the room for likely sources of gossip. Identifying a cluster of aspiring young vampires who were always hungry for attention, he drifted across the plush carpet, riding the wave of silence which accompanied the sighting of his face.

He was accustomed to being greeted by tension. Most vampires became nervous in their desire to impress. *When the principal of twelve decades speaks to them, they long to find something remarkable to say.* Using that fact, Julian prepared to cast his net and land an informant.

Julian chose to stand in the embrace of intricately-carved oak panels which framed a large bay window, pretending to study the moonlit gardens beyond. Conversations flowed around him, and he gathered the threads and drew them in. With winter approaching, crop yield and the renovation of greenhouses were causing concern.

Julian was pleased to overhear most vampires searched for solutions rather than wallowing in problems.

The recent death of the pregnant human girl featured as a recurring theme, and Julian began to think he was wasting time.

"I hope he's right. But I fear its wishful thinking on the councilor's part." Skepticism dulled the melodic tone of the disembodied voice which drifted across the room.

Interest piqued, Julian zeroed in on his target, and, fixing his eyes on the sandy-haired vampire, he smiled. "Just so." Julian inclined his head in agreement.

The vampire glided closer. "How could we have missed them? That's my thought."

"It seems unlikely, I agree. I suspect the councilor is clutching at straws," said Julian.

The vampire basked in Julian's ironic smile. "Councilor Serge says there is a nest. But if that was true, surely the *council* guard would lead the search, not Serge's household."

"You are a guardsman? Or aspiring-?" Julian waited to hear the vampire's name.

"Owen. Aspiring."

Julian's interest bored into the youngster.

Suddenly nervous, the vampire bobbed his head. "Sir. Principal."

"I wonder at Councilor Serge's optimism. It seems to me he has not thought this through." Julian waited, knowing that this vampire, with his lilting voice, would fill the silence with the information he needed.

The vampire shuffled under Julian's keen regard and began talking, revealing the number of fresh human captures promised by Serge. *So, now I know everything, except how Serge discovered the eco-town. He plans to capture the humans tonight.*

Serge's visit today was clearly intended to divert Julian's attention, assuming he would be drawn into investigating accusations against Connor. *But, it was a ruse.* He was launching an attack without the council's approval. *Presumably, he thinks the ends will justify the means, and he will not be punished.* But Julian knew there was more to it. Serge's vein of hatred for Connor ran through every action he took. *He's becoming reckless because he wants to see Connor dead.*

Julian shot along the dark, wet London streets, returning home. His jaw ticked as he faced the prospect that, having avoided touching Leizle, now, he had no choice.

Plowing a trench through the ordered sea of gravel on his driveway, Julian used the traction to brake before entering the house, skimming along the polished floorboards, and going to find Leizle.

He appeared in the room and found her still asleep. But this time there was no escaping it, he was there to collect her. He put a cold hand on her shoulder. Her eyes snapped open, and the cut on her arm throbbed as her heart rate peaked. The hypnotic cadence of her pumping blood drew Julian's eyes to the red stain on the bandage. The smell of blood filled his nostrils and his slack jaw snapped audibly shut. Fixing his attention on her white face, he held out his hand and said gruffly, "We have to go, now."

As Leizle sat up, unfolding stiff legs, the grating of her tendons vibrated inside his head like a chainsaw. But, it was nothing compared to the shock he got when she reached up and took his hand. A blade of hunger sliced through his windpipe, and every instinct screamed at him to pull her into his arms and bite into her carotid artery.

Unable to speak, Julian resorted to rudeness. He walked through the house, towing Leizle along behind, resolutely ignoring the sound of her heart scampering with confusion. In a seamless flow of movement, he collected a heavy black cape from a brass hook in the hallway, opened the front door, and stopped on the threshold.

Leizle shuffled her feet behind him, not sure why he was looking out into the night like a man waiting for rain to stop. She peeped around his shoulder, and he tugged her back into his shadow as he turned to face her.

"Okay, all's quiet," he whispered, looking stern. "Let's go."

Julian drew the cape around her shoulders, and, taking her hand, he swung her up onto his back. Pulling the cloak forward to cover his own shoulders, too, he stepped through the door, closed it behind them, and set off at a fast run.

He carried Leizle through the night at a face-numbing speed until even blinking required effort. Under the cover of the heavy black cloak, she hung on to Julian's uncompromising frame like a pillion passenger without a motorcycle. His cold hands gripped her thighs, supporting her weight and pulling her closely into his back. Her stranglehold on his neck was of no consequence; he was not breathing.

Julian was risking everything to get her back to the eco-town, but he had to find Connor, so he had no choice. He hoped to fool all but the keenest observer. *The cape is a little theatrical, but some vampires cling to clothing as a reminder of the era they lost in their turning, so-* He grinned as his theater-going days and sitting with Eva in their box at the Astoria came into his head. *It is* mine*, after all.*

Julian covered almost twenty-eight of the thirty miles without breaking stride, adjusting Leizle's weight while still running. Trying to ignore the burn where her breasts and stomach molded to his back, Julian filled his head with battle plans. *The hunt is on. Serge's guardsmen are on their way.*

He was relieved to see Connor standing inside the entrance cave when they arrived at the eco-town.

It eased him through the awkwardness of releasing his grip on Leizle and lowering her to the ground.

If he had lingered too long over the sensations of her warm body slipping from his shoulders, her flesh dragging a burning trail over his tight back, he would not have been able to stop himself biting into her soft skin. *I don't want to be yet another monster in her eyes.*

It gave him the excuse of being something he never would have been before, arrogant.

The moment her feet touched the ground, he cut her dead. Swallowing his hunger, he turned his back and launched into conversation with Connor. "I found out what Serge is planning, and we don't have much time. But first, judging by your face, you got here in time? Rebekah is okay?"

◇◇◇

Leizle's chilled flesh tingled with disconcerting heat as she strode away from Julian. Grateful for the cover of shadow, she hurried into the darkened tunnel. Her cramped leg muscles screamed, but she needed to get away from him before tears scalded her wind-chilled cheeks.

Striding mindlessly forward, she ignored the throbbing ache of the cut in her arm which mocked her pretense of calm. When she found Rebekah alone in the meeting cavern, relief opened the floodgates and a sob grated in her throat.

"Leizle. Thank God, thank God." Rebekah smothered her in a bear hug which would have made Oscar proud, and choked back her own tears. Holding on tight, neither girl moved. Finally, Rebekah whispered, "You're cold, let's find you a blanket."

Lifting her face from the damp patch she'd made on Rebekah's shoulder, Leizle said, "It's okay, I don't mind being cold."

"Really?" Rebekah asked with a knowing smile. "Principal Julian? I guess vampires are not so bad after all, hmm?"

Leizle swiped at the tears and laughed gently. "I guess not." Looking at Rebekah for the first time, she searched her pale features. "Are *you* okay? Connor said you were in trouble."

Rebekah rubbed her upper arms, a glint in her eyes as she said, "I'm okay, truly. It was nothing that a man-sized hot water bottle couldn't fix."

With a puzzled frown, Leizle opened her mouth, but nothing came out.

Rebekah laughed. "Never mind, I'll tell you all about it later."

Looking around the deserted cavern, Leizle said slowly, "And, what are you up to now?"

"Nothing terrible, I swear," she said, drawing a cross over her heart.

"Okay. So, what's going on?"

Rebekah was saved from answering by Oscar walking into the room hauling a canvas bag so heavy, it tightened every sinew in his body.

The bag hit the ground with a dull thud the moment he saw Leizle. With a cry of delight, he hurried over and gave her a firm squeeze. “Good to see you, lass, I knew Connor would see you right.”

“Hey, Oscar,” Leizle wheezed through her constricted chest. “Broken bones here.”

Oscar let her go, allowing Leizle to breathe again.

A few yards away, Rebekah grunted and flushed bright red when she tried to drag the bag across the floor.

Oscar laughed as he nudged her out of the way and hoisted it up onto a wooden bench. “Let’s see what we’ve got here.”

Keeping her eyes on the bag, Rebekah directed a distracted comment to Leizle. “Connor says it’s only a matter of time before the vampires come after us again, and I want to be prepared.”

“Prepared how?”

“To fight, if I have to.” Rebekah’s jaw muscle ticked. “Connor mustn’t know. I’d just feel easier knowing I have a better chance than the last time I had a run-in with a vampire.”

“What have you got in mind?”

Oscar unzipped the bag, and pulled out rolls of canvas which contained an assortment of knives, metal spikes, and hammers. Frowning, he went through his own filtering process. He gave Leizle’s and Rebekah’s feminine frames the once over. He returned most items to the bag until he was left with four sturdy short knives and a small switchblade.

Julian’s body had felt like velvet-clad steel to Leizle, so she was less sure about the whole knife thing. *But it can’t hurt, I guess.*

Rebekah picked up the switchblade and tested the action. She pressed the trigger, and the blade shot out at a speed that almost yanked it from her grasp. “Will it work? On them?” she asked Oscar.

“It has a toughened steel blade, so, maybe.” Oscar shrugged and said darkly, “But this is last resort stuff, right? Don’t go looking for trouble, Rebekah.”

Frowning, she said, “Oh don’t worry, Oscar, I don’t want any trouble. It just always seems to find me.”

Oscar took the knife, retracted the blade, and engaged the safety catch. "But this is life or death stuff, got it?" He waited until he had Rebekah's attention and then pressed the knife into her palm. "If Connor knew, he'd kill me."

"Of course," she said lightly, dropping it into her pocket. "I'll sew it inside my oilskin and forget all about it."

"Okay." Oscar nodded. Pushing his hand deep into his own pocket, he drew out a palm-sized kidney-shaped polished stone. Tossing it to Rebekah, he said, "Here, this is my lucky talisman. Maybe if things go bad, you could throw it at a vampire's head."

Folding her fingers around the stone, Rebekah's face reflected his serious smile.

"We should know soon how the land lies, and if we have time to move out, we will," said Rebekah quietly.

Leizle's flesh had thawed out at last, but Rebekah's words brought her out in a cold sweat. She murmured grimly, "If Julian's face is anything to go by, I think time may have just run out."

Chapter 36

Julian and Connor settled at the edge of the wood and looked down over the moonlit meadow. To their right, the tree line meandered away towards London, the direction from which the attack would come. The constantly moving shadows ambling across the face of the moon bode well for them. The darker it was, the better for hiding humans. They were waiting for the enemy to make a move.

"Does Serge suspect you made inquiries?" asked Connor, his tight lips suppressing a smile. He had never seen Julian look so alive. His hair was, by Julian's standard, a mess – thick blond strands of it brushed across his brow unheeded – and his eyes glittered with excitement.

"No, he was too busy *acting*, trying to put me off the scent." Julian smiled thinly at the memory. "But, my unwitting informant appeared to have Serge's measure. I assured him he would find the *council* guard more to his liking."

"Serge would never know they were here, unless someone gave him a grid reference," Connor said slowly.

"Discovering how he found out will have to wait," replied Julian.

"And no one saw you with Leizle?" Connor's smile twitched at the corners of his mouth, but the darkness saved him from Julian's irritation.

When Julian had arrived at the entrance of the eco-town and hastily shrugged Leizle from his shoulders, his agitation was obvious. Julian's abrupt dismissal of the young girl contradicted his usual good manners, and Connor had raised a mental eyebrow.

As she disappeared down into the tunnels, briskly rubbing her arms, Julian's narrow-eyed stare had tracked her progress, and now, Connor suspected he was no longer alone in his hell.

True, Julian's message was urgent, but Connor knew there was more to it. *Bitten by the love bug, maybe.*

"No one saw us," said Julian abruptly. The shutters came down as he groomed his hair with expert fingers and the veneer of authority smoothed his features.

Connor inhaled deeply, preparing to tease him a little more, when Julian changed the topic.

"Captain Laurence's sweep for ferals came up empty. So, the humans can rest easy on that score, in any case. Ferals don't have enough brain function to hide."

"Let's hope we have seen the last of them," said Connor. "Every vampire should understand by now that there is no way to survive without human blood rations."

"Well, at least now, we can concentrate on the threat of Serge."

A change of tempo in the nocturnal rustling inside the woodland made them both freeze.

"They are entering the wood on the northern boundary," Connor said calmly. "Are you ready?"

Julian raised a sardonic brow. "Are the humans ready?"

Connor grinned as he shot smoothly to his feet. "They will be, when I tell them the plan."

"Well, get it done. Their approach will be fast."

Connor's leaving generated a breeze that tugged at Julian's jacket.

The woodland creatures responded to the advancing guardsmen with a Mexican wave of silent surrender. However, Julian was satisfied that the woods remained a hive of unperturbed activity for a couple of miles around where he now sat. Badgers clawed the undergrowth half a mile away, and dung beetles bundled up pungent parcels a mile further out than that. Humans had only the lumbering of obvious creatures to draw upon to assess their surroundings. A vampire's spectrum was far more extensive, and the myriad of spiders and insects were the fine tuning on their environmental barometer.

Connor, too, listened to the cacophony of nature's concert as, plowing across the uncultivated meadow, his down-force snapped blades of grass. *So, we still have time.*

There were no trees. When the vampires were still doing grid searches, the unobstructed view offered an early warning system. But things were different now, and the humans would not be safe until the eco-town moved on. After the last battle, Connor and

Julian had excavated an emergency escape route through the hillside, which emerged on the edge of the wood.

When Connor entered the eco-town and whipped aside the sackcloth curtain, the thick smell of nervous human sweat registered as a wall of stagnant warmth. “They want to live, this will be easy,” he murmured.

Rebekah says they are drilled to move out fast. Connor made his way towards the dining cavern where the entire community waited. *Well, the evacuation procedures are about to be put to the test.*

He paused in the tunnel outside the dining cavern, where nineteen human hearts were beating, pumping nectar. The pheromone cloud of their sweat was guaranteed to draw in the guardsmen. Connor battened down his own hatches using revival sleep. Dragging a hand down over his face, he wiped the excited tension from his expression, and stepped slowly over the threshold. *Oh, hell.* They were still startled, and the canter of surprised heartbeats buffeted his senses.

All eyes turned his way as he said, “Okay, it’s time. We’re under attack.” He used words like a blunt instrument. “If you stay together, Julian and I can save you.”

Connor silenced the swell of muttering with an upheld hand. “It’s simple,” he said, “do exactly what I say, and survive. Or-” He shrugged and let the alternative sink in, absorbing the varying degrees of fright on white faces.

“Tell us what to do and we’ll do it,” Harry said with conviction.

Connor raised an impressed eyebrow. *Found a backbone, at last.*

“You all know, a few hours ago, Rebekah baited the trap.”

It had been nothing fancy. She merely walked a route from the eco-town, a mile into the woods, and back again. Connor could not risk tainting the trail, so he had settled for keeping her in his sights. *I was not going to lose her in the woods again. Now, I just need to get her safely through the night.* A sardonic grin bowed his lips.

“The vampires know the location of the eco-town, so they will be moving *fast*. They will follow the scent, and Julian and I will be ready for them.”

“What do you need us to do?” Harry asked.

“I need you to stay here in the dining cavern.”

“But-” Harry’s words died in his throat when Connor moved.

Crossing to the rear of the cavern, Connor clawed away a section of the rock-encrusted wall and broke through the final foot of hard earth to reveal the hidden passageway. The six-foot tall opening of the tunnel ascended into darkness. Every foot or so, wooden struts supported the chute carved through the packed soil.

Amused at the gawping human expressions, Connor said simply, “It brings you out near the woods. Julian will have unblocked the other end by now.” He indicated the bench seats nearest the tunnel mouth. “Stay together as a group, here.” He passed a glance over each nervous face. “At my signal, you will go into the exit tunnel, and run as fast as you can.”

“What’s the signal?” Oscar recovered first, and his expression was serious for once.

Connor raised a brow. “I was thinking, I shout, ‘RUN’.”

Oscar’s lips twitched. “Works for me,” he said.

Greg shifted from his resting place against the wall. Connor had felt his presence like an incandescent torch of energy. “And that’s it? Run?” Greg shook his head. “I’ll stay.”

“No, Marine. For this, *I’m* your commanding officer. You *will* run, and you’ll look after your charges out in the woods. Understood?”

Greg subsided back into his slouch, reluctant agreement filtering into his narrowed eyes. “Hooah,” he mumbled.

Connor nodded. “We have reopened the hiding burrows in the woods. Get inside, and stay inside.” His stern look pierced Rebekah. *She’d better listen this time; the hiding burrows work, but, it depends on her staying inside one.* Connor was beginning to think his plan to wait three years before turning her would age him by another hundred.

Rebekah met his gaze, and for him, the sun came out when she smiled. He crossed the cavern, pushed his fingers gently into her hair, and rested his forehead on hers. “Please, Rebekah, this one time. Do as I ask.” He tilted her chin and searched her dark eyes.

The warmth lurking in their depths eased the tension inside him. Placing a gentle kiss on her lips, he said, "Thank you, honey."

Turning back to face the others, he added, "And that's it.'

That's all they need to know anyway, he argued.

Connor checked his watch and glanced at Rebekah. "It's almost time." He landed a fleeting kiss as she opened her mouth to speak, and he smiled when it wiped her thoughts from her mind. "Julian won't let the guards sneak up on us. He's outside waiting."

Leaving the cavern, Connor jerked his head and Greg followed him out.

"Julian and I have everything inside the eco-town under control, Greg."

"But?" The marine folded his arms across his solid chest.

"But, *outside.*" Connor flicked his gaze upward. "I'm relying on you and Oscar to make sure they get into the burrows."

Connor handed over a nail gun, and Greg raised an eyebrow.

"I know what you saw when you watched Stan die. Take this. It's crude, but if you see one of those fuckers out in the forest, be my guest."

Greg grinned. "And how about these attacking vampires? Do I get a shot at them?"

"Not a chance. Stand down, soldier." Connor sighed. "Look, ferals barely have brain function. They are beyond reason and planning. You aim for the gaping mouth or the face, and it gives you the chance to run. You try it on one of us and the story will be very different, I promise you."

"Fair enough."

Connor laid a hand on Greg's shoulder. "I don't think you'll need it. The area was clean at the last sweep."

With a curt nod, Greg shoved the nail gun into his utility belt and went back into the dining cavern.

Everything Connor said was true. *But if giving Greg a purpose makes him sharper, then where's the harm?*

Connor took up his position outside the dining cavern, waiting for Julian's signal. He listened to the muted rustling sounds of humans doing their best to be silent. The waft of their scents fanned the banked embers of his thirst and his throat ached. Delaying his grave sleep was a crucial part of the plan, and as the hallucinations tugged at the threads of his sanity, the tightrope-line of control he walked became weaker.

The brush of shoe leather on the floor of the dining cavern roused Connor from his spot. Leaning onto one shoulder, he peered inside and shook his head firmly. Rebekah froze in mid-step. As much as it cut him open to see her pained expression, it was for her own good.

Returning to his vigil, Connor rested lightly against the wall and glanced at his watch. *C'mon Julian, where are they?*

Out in the woods, Julian blended into the shadow cast by a massive oak tree. He had not blinked for twenty minutes. *'Blink, and you'll miss it' is not a flippant remark right now, and I'm not about to let Connor lay that one at my door.* Ears, however, were always alert, so he need not have worried. He could not have missed Serge's guardsmen passing by. *Okay, not exactly elephants, but-* Some were so close it tested his power to resist the urge to reach out, grasp a head firmly, and, with a sharp twist, cut off all motor function.

But that would reveal our hand. There were eight guardsmen, and they knew nothing of Julian's involvement, although, Connor's presence they would probably expect.

Julian did not move until the pack picked up Rebekah's scent. He held back until they were mere smudges of ink in the distance, before unleashing a burst of speed in pursuit.

The thirst for battle was like a mouthful of dust he needed to slake with excitement. *But there's plenty of time for that.* He clamped his sights onto the fleeing shadows, and as he swerved around a thick tree trunk, he narrowly avoided crashing into the broad back of a straggler. This time, he did not resist. He dispatched the vampire like a drive-by mugger, grabbing the back of his flapping coat and swinging him around. The heel of Julian's hand crunched up under his victim's chin. The vampire's head rocked back and a satisfying snap resonated up the bones in Julian's arm. The shocked face continued its roll backwards and did not return.

Julian flexed his muscles like a victorious boxer, grinned, and moved on.

Keeping his distance this time, arriving at the tree line, Julian stopped and melted into the shadows. He watched the vampires flitting over the meadow, their paths crossing and clashing like a pack of hounds with too much information to process. *C'mon, pull it together guys. The scent is pretty strong.*

At last, one of the vampires lifted his head and whipped forward like an arrow shot from a bow, heading straight for the wound sliced into the hillside. The blackened opening swallowed him, and the other six clustered like magnets being towed along in his wake.

Game on. As the last one disappeared through the entrance, Julian darted across the grass and followed them inside. Pausing on the threshold, he reached up and closed his fingers around the keystone overhead. With a sharp tug, he yanked it out, stepping swiftly backwards into the tunnel as the rocks and earth tumbled down and sealed the exit. He turned to face the gathering darkness.

The cloud of debris rolled and billowed, plastering his clothes to his back, before Julian accelerated forward.

Even from deep inside the hillside, Connor felt a rush of air brush his cheek, although it would need to be entwined with a hundred others like it before the flame in the sconce beside him would flutter.

He stepped into the dining cavern and yelled, "Run."

The word echoed around the chamber, galvanizing every human into action. Then, the distant sound of the rumbling avalanche of earth reached Connor. *Julian is inside.*

The humans stampeded into the narrow opening, their clumsy shuffling adding to the cauldron of excitement. Their galloping hearts, terror sweats, and panic, bombarded Connor's senses, and he willed them to hurry, knowing they were drawing the focus of the vampires now moving through the eco-town. *The guardsmen won't be able to resist, even if they sensed the trap closing behind them.*

Connor herded the last human into the tunnel. In a moment of brief contact with Rebekah, he caught hold of her wrist, trailing his fingers over her palm as he released her. "Hide," he muttered.

He tracked the humans' progress until they disappeared up the chute, and, when he was sure they were all out of danger, he put clawed hands up to the tunnel roof, gouged holes in it, and collapsed it in a deluge of sodden earth, tree roots, and wooden struts.

Swinging into action, he traveled the passageways like a tornado, grinding the giant match heads of flaming torches to ash in a clenched fist or under a boot, and yanking bulkhead lamp fittings from the walls, extinguishing light sources by whatever means got the job done.

Seconds later, back in the dining cavern, he brushed the sawdust and ash from his hands and listened to the crumbling avalanche of rubble groan quietly as it settled into place.

Primed and ready, Connor sank into deathly stillness. He zeroed in on the whispering preternatural movements of the hunting guardsmen as they searched the network of caverns. The collapsed tunnels would not contain them; they were a diversion from the real threat. Connor.

Every step had been orchestrated to bring them to him; a formidable vampire with a century of raw power and cunning, descending into grave sleep. That was his last conscious thought before the gate keeper slept. Connor visualized the cell door of the asylum opening, and allowed his brainstem, the part that controls the reflexes in the body – whether human or vampire – to take over.

He unleashed the killer, and a white-hot blast furnace of insatiable bloodlust raged through his tissue.

Hunger boiled like a torrent of acid inside his gut and tingled along his lips. His tongue cleaved to the roof of his mouth as aching thirst shriveled his windpipe and insane craving ate into his brain. It was not a desire for water, rather, a raw chili-burn thirst that demanded a river of thick sweet blood.

Connor froze, savoring the eddies of air whisking over his skin; the first pair of guardsmen moving into range. His nostrils flared as he closed in on their moisture. Each vampire had a different flavor, and just the smell of their blood-drenched tissue filled his mouth with saliva. Their clustered heat signatures glowed like infrared hot spots, where their last meals had yet to chill to black inside their bellies.

Venom trickled unheeded down his chin. The cramped muscles of his face compressed his skull, baring his teeth. Snarls vibrated in his throat.

They did not sense him until it was too late. His hunger echoed in the darkness; a brittle snap of tendons was drowned out by the crunch of bone giving way under the relentless pressure of his jaws. Ecstasy spiked through him as blood-sluiced marrow filled his mouth and coated his vocal chords with thick coagulated nectar.

Wiping his hand down his face, he moved on. Connor struck the next victim in the chest, cracking his sternum, twisting the head as if undoing a bottle top and the vampire slid down the wall. The explosive crack of ruptured cartilage ricocheted a warning shot through the cavern.

Panic filled the air. The rainbow of scents shot darts of color into Connor's sensitized retina, and made hunting easy; he saw them all so clearly. He visualized a move, the snap of a ligament, a cold heart clenched in his fist, a thumb buried in the carotid pulse, and without effort, it happened. Depraved enjoyment peaked as he thrust his hand inside the abdominal cavity of a hapless opponent and delighted in gripping the spinal cord, feeling the discs between the vertebrae swell in his palm like compressed balloons, before they finally popped.

He was no longer hungry, he was having fun.

With each meal, his heart swelled, the pressure in his chest pushed against his ribcage, and his appetite sharpened to addiction, compelling him to find another kill.

A buzz of anticipation whipped him around to face yet another vampire. A familiar smell stung his nose and an alarm bell rang deep inside his brain, but it was diluted by the blood-soaked clouds of vapor staining his mind red. But, it *was* familiar. Even while trying to press the lid back on to Pandora's Box, and to think, he moved in for the kill.

"Sorry, Connor." Julian launched a huge rock at full pelt, hitting Connor square in the chest.

The jolt stopped him in his tracks, and, when Julian added a driving punch to the force of it, Connor fell backwards.

Connor's mind cleared as he wrestled the psychopath back into his cell, slammed the door shut, and found himself lying on the ground with Julian's boot clamped down onto his neck.

"Nice," Connor croaked.

"What can I say? I wasn't taking any chances." Julian grinned. "But hell, you're terrifyingly good. Six kills in twenty-eight seconds."

"Only six?" he croaked again, irritated.

Julian shrugged as he removed his boot. Or lose the leg, if Connor's searing look was anything to go by. "I stopped one outside, and the other went to run." He laughed. "Call it teamwork?"

Connor rolled up smoothly until he was sitting. Rubbing his fingertips in hard circles over his chest, he said, "I think you broke my sternum. Couldn't you find a bigger rock?"

"Hey, I came prepared. Rock has no heat signature. I knew you'd not see it coming."

Connor sprang to his feet. The explosion of movement was a blur, even to Julian. His eyes glittered in the gloom, and Julian fell back a pace, only relaxing when Connor chuckled, "Got you."

Julian chuckled in his turn. "As I said, I wasn't taking any chances." But he kept the bloodstained disheveled Connor firmly in his sights.

Chapter 37

When Connor collapsed the tunnel behind them, the avalanche filled the air inside the chute with clouds of dirt. The heavier grains landed in clumps on Rebekah's clothes, but the finer ones tasted like mud pie in her dry mouth. If the stuffy air in the tunnel made breathing difficult, then hyperventilating with anxiety made it almost impossible.

As dirt showered her face, the sounds of a snarling dog fight raging behind the bank of settled earth almost paralyzed her.

In her imagination, Connor was fighting a pack of crazed vampires and they were large bats with needles for teeth. *Ridiculous, I know.* But, fear did that, took commonsense, twisted it inside out, and then set it free to stumble about inside her head.

The weight of the switchblade resting along her forearm inside the sleeve of her coat taunted her with its absurdity. Digging a hand into her pocket and rubbing her fingers over Oscar's lucky stone seemed a far more potent force. *Praying and good luck, that's all we've got.* Her dust-clogged throat ached with the realization.

Thomas' hacking cough focused her attention. He croaked her name, and Rebekah turned away from her nightmare. Touching his elbow, she said, "Let's go."

As Thomas moved along in front of her, the gray light at the end of the tunnel encouraged her to pick up the pace. "Keep moving, Rebekah," she muttered, and pushed on up the slope of compressed mud.

Breaking out into the cool night air, Rebekah scanned her surroundings. Her eyes latched on to Thomas and then Leizle, and she almost laughed aloud at their grimy faces. Oscar beckoned urgently. The others were already scuttling into the depths of the woods. *Hide; I promised Connor I would be good.*

Greg crouched on the soft ground in front of a thick tree trunk, waving everyone past. A hiss of human pain came from inside the woods, and Greg's head snapped around. He flashed a thumbs-up signal to Oscar before diving out of sight, the oil black shadows swallowing him whole.

Gripping Thomas' hand, Rebekah set off in a half crouch, covering the ground quickly. The damp still air beneath the whispering canopy of leaves was eerie, and the chilled darkness settled like a suffocating blanket. She stretched her eyes wide, trying to distinguish Oscar's bulk from other shadows flitting through the trees. Flashes of pale gray winked – anxious faces glancing back over retreating shoulders – and Rebekah headed towards them.

She smiled in relief when a sound like a sandbag being tossed onto the ground was followed by a quickly smothered oath in Oscar's colorful tone. Imagining him sprawled out on his hands and knees made her smile.

At least I know which direction to go in now. Oscar foraged daily in the woods, so he knew instinctively where the burrows were. *Follow Greg or Oscar.* The instruction had been drilled into all of them.

Releasing Thomas and letting him race ahead, Rebekah paused, gazing quickly back at the tree line when she thought she heard footfalls behind her. *Could it be Connor? Already?* Her neck prickled, and she dismissed the elusive feeling of being watched. *Did Connor's plan work?*

Pulling the collar of her waxed fabric jacket tighter, she swung back to follow Thomas. A sudden breeze snatched at her hair. It whipped up to a stinging gale that plastered her clothes to her body, and Rebekah knew instantly. *A vampire is coming.*

Pushing hair out of her eyes, she searched for Thomas and felt relieved he had disappeared. *What if it's a feral?* Without thinking, she took off in the opposite direction. Running hard, she backtracked to the tree line, putting distance between herself and the others, knowing that they would still be scurrying into the hiding burrows. *They need more time.* Dodging the potholes, Rebekah put everything she had into outracing the torrent of wind snatching at her heels.

The unexpected explosion of movement made her cold muscles ache. She gritted her teeth, ignoring the voice in her head screaming, 'what the hell am I doing?'

She drove on blindly until her lungs were on fire. Her scalp burned too when she was yanked backward by the hair. A sick feeling of weightlessness filled her stomach as her feet swung out from under her. She yelped when her shoulder blades crunched into the rock face of padded stone suddenly standing behind her. The sound of saliva rattling in his throat turned her stomach. *Fuck, a feral.*

She leaned back into the vampire's cold chest, lifting her chin to ease the pull of his tight fist in her hair. Remembering the creature she saw in the woods that night, she knew this was not a feral. *I'd be dead already. I mustn't let him get a grip*. She shrugged inside her jacket and slipped one sleeve down until it covered her right hand. Scrabbling her fingers over the flap of the hidden pocket, she worked it open, choking on the heady rush of elation when the switchblade handle dropped down into her palm.

Struggling hard, and feeling the pain bite every time she collided with his solid shape, she fought harder until he did what she wanted.

Twisting her hair in his grasp, he turned her to face him and leered.

His grotesque venom-coated lips mesmerized Rebekah as his breath fanned her face, and the cloying smell of decayed blood made her gag.

The mess of black hair shadowing his brow could not hide the spite lurking in his mud-brown gaze.

His free hand laid a trail of disgust over her skin as it stroked around her waist, pinning her body against his, and crushing her knife arm between them. Fear kept her eyes locked onto the cold hard features, even when they moved in too close to focus on.

Trapped across her middle, her arm tingled where his cold vampire flesh pressed onto it. While she could still feel it, she gripped the knife tighter. With a jolt of self-preservation, she dug her other hand inside her jacket. The weight of Oscar's stone in her palm ignited a surge of rebellion inside. She pulled it from her pocket.

A predatory leer tightened his features, his hold on her hair gentled to a sickening caress, and a tide of panic clawed at her insides.

She could barely feel the switchblade hilt in her numb fingers. *It's now or never.* Staring up into his eyes, she turned her hand, aimed low into his abdomen, and hit the trigger button. The blade shot out at the same moment that she slammed the stone into the butt. The juddering impact darted pain up her arm as fear and hatred unleashed every ounce of strength she had.

His tormenting amusement disappeared, his eyes snapped open and he relaxed his embrace for a second.

Rebekah's feeling of triumph flared and died as her wrist twisted painfully, and the sound of grinding stone filled the air. The tip of the switchblade dug in for a moment before it skittered over his stomach, tearing his clothes and scoring a silvered line in the quartz-like surface of his skin, but nothing more.

Oily amusement returned and he tightened his hold. His fingers dug in as he captured her free arm, and her hand, starved of blood, tingled in an instant. Her ribcage creaked as he bent her backwards and needles of pain darted down her legs. Rebekah spat in his eye. Her scream of anger gusting into his face lifted the shadow of his hair from his brow and revealed an expression of cold calculation.

His hand covered her mouth and sealed the sound inside. His cold fingers pressed dents into her cheeks as he hissed, "I can smell you."

The cold metal vise of his embrace anchored her still, and his chilled breath fanned across her skin as his wraithlike whisper seeped into her mind. "So, *you* are the woman." His silky tone curdled her stomach; disgust churned inside her.

His nose pressed to her temple, a flush of perspiration crawled over her skin when his grinning lips brushed her flesh. "I can taste your fear. The clamoring of your heart is compelling. What's your name, I wonder?" His tone was conspiratorial as he relaxed his hand over her face, allowing air to rush in and clear the oxygen-starved clouds from her brain.

Who is he? Instinct told her he was Connor's enemy and she must keep quiet. *Serge? No, not old enough.*

His eyes bored into hers, demanding surrender. "Your name?" he coaxed gently.

"Annabelle," Rebekah said, her heart pounding so hard she wondered if it would crack ribs.

He chuckled. "I don't think so." Enjoying the wave of panic she tried to swallow down, he said, "Intriguing that you have enough fire in your belly to lie. It makes killing you such a waste." Closing his eyes, he dipped his head and rested his bared teeth on her wildly fluttering carotid pulse.

His cold finger traced a path down her neck from ear to shoulder and he eased the tight hold around her waist, unleashing waves of pain as the blood rushed back into her legs.

Rebekah squeezed her eyes closed, ready for the sharp pain of his bite. *I hope he chokes on it.*

The vampire's body suddenly jolted; a spike of metal glanced off his shoulder, tearing his shirt. He straightened abruptly, a harsh growl rippling through the hard wall of his body. Frustration tight on his face, he stared down, his eyes glowing with manic zeal. His hair writhed like black snakes in the sudden updraft of an approaching hurricane. "Connor is coming, such a pity."

Her last image was of his leering grin as his grip on her jugular cut off the oxygen to her brain, and she blacked-out. The dark clouds tumbled in. The smell of dirt assailed her nostrils as her legs buckled, but then a familiar citrus scent enveloped her, and strong arms swept her feet from the ground.

The clean-up took longer than the battle. They piled up the vampire bodies and their detached parts ready for transportation, and then, Connor and Julian set to work on resurrecting the collapsed tunnels.

Connor stripped off the blood-soaked 'horror-movie stained' shirt. He had washed, but his sculpted body soon became peppered with a sprinkling of soil as he worked alongside Julian. They worked in a companionable silence because neither one would enjoy eating the dirt still drifting in the air, so not breathing kept their airways clean.

The main entrance cavern needed more work, but it was passable, for now.

They were below ground once more, making short work of clearing the avalanche of debris from the tunnel in the dining cavern, Julian used his bulk to bulldoze a path through the loosely packed rubble and then pressed his back into one sidewall. Planting his hands on flexed thighs, he supported half of the sweeping archway, holding it in place while Connor used the heel of his hand to hammer a support strut into position.

"Done," said Connor, moving around to the other side.

Julian rotated quickly, his shoulders and back plowing an arc into the opposite wall, carving the same approximate shape, and, as before, he tightened every muscle and held it in place. Connor hand-hammered again, driving in six-inch long metal nails as though the wood was made of foam rubber.

With each pile-driving blow that rippled up his arm and dissipated into his chest, Connor became more distracted by Rebekah's heart rate. He recognized her adrenalin-pumped rhythm, and it made him itch to go. *But, it's okay, she's hiding, she's bound to be nervous.*

"Julian-" Connor was about to suggest they check on things in the wood. *Not* just *because of Rebekah.* Suddenly, her panic lanced through him, rolling thunder through his chest as her fibrillating heart clenched and terror starved it of oxygen, and he knew. *She's in danger.* His frustrated groan ricocheted around the cavern.

He muttered, simply, "Gotta go."

Before his words faded, he was gone, and Julian was quick to follow.

The spiked blades of meadow grass blurred into a green oil-slick as Connor accelerated up the hill and into the wood. He heard Rebekah gasp and wheeled in an arc, arriving beside her before the sigh of unconsciousness had left her. When the lights turned off inside her brain and her legs crumpled, he scooped her up into his arms.

He settled her into his chest, and an alien scent assailed his nostrils. He bent over her to trace the smell and, detecting the anticoagulant of venom – as unique in vampires as DNA in humans – his jaw snapped shut.

Julian arrived at that moment, his coat beating wildly against his thighs when he stopped dead, mere feet from Connor.

"What?" he asked.

"We missed one," said Connor sharply. "She stinks of his venom, but there's no bite mark." His instinct to hunt almost choked him.

Julian's brows rose. "Not a feral at any rate, or-"

Connor's harsh grunt cut him off. "Or I'd be scraping up her remains. But we still messed up, Julian." He knew he had missed any chance of pursuit. The vampire would be long gone.

He looked down into Rebekah's face. The black crescents of her lashes fluttered against her pale cheeks, and he said heavily, "I'll take her home."

Julian's glance encompassed the humans still scrabbling through the woods. "Let's get them back into the eco-shelter, and then I'll do a grid search. Make sure he's gone." Julian frowned. "He was not part of the attack, I made sure they were *all* inside. He must have been passing through, and was drawn to the scent Rebekah laid."

"Maybe." Connor's shrug rolled Rebekah gently in his arms and a groan sighed from her lips. "She's cold. I have to get moving."

Julian dipped forward to smell Rebekah's shoulder, and Connor's protective snarl tore through the night air. Withdrawing slowly, Julian rose to his full height and grinned. "If I'm going to sweep the woods for this vampire, I need to have his scent."

Connor's eyes warmed with unspoken apology.

Without warning, Julian dropped down and retrieved a long nail from the grass. "What's this?"

"Fuck," Connor breathed gently and shook his head, remembering the nail gun. "Greg. Find him Julian. I'm sure he's okay. And shake his hand for me."

Turning on his heel, Connor set off across the meadow.

He covered the seemingly endless yards of the subterranean passageways, cradling Rebekah's slack body to his chest. Her arm rested limply around his neck, and the chill in her limbs and her pale clammy complexion filled him with dread. *But she's strong, my Rebekah. It will take more than a rogue vampire to scare her to death.*

Moving quickly, he headed towards her den and each measured stride he took rocked her cheek against his shoulder. Touching his chin to the top of her head, he absorbed the juddering rhythm of her chattering teeth. Releasing her from his cold embrace and wrapping her in the warmth of blankets was all he could think of.

Inside the small space of Rebekah's haven, Connor lowered her gently onto the bed and her relaxed limbs rested where they fell. With painful care, he settled her on one side and wrapped the blankets around her.

Connor slid onto the bed behind her, fitted his contours to hers, and took her down-cocooned body into his arms.

Mental health may not be my speciality, but I've seen battle fatigue up close. A brittle smile settled on Connor's stiff features. There had been a variety of labels and buzzwords over the years. Post-traumatic stress was favored in the 1970's. *But, they all amount to the same thing, a brain that is overloaded. We take the brain for granted, until trauma throws a psychological spanner in the works.* Doctor Connor bitterly admitted that knowing how these things worked offered no comfort. His heart felt like lead.

Resting his cheek on her hair, he settled down to wait however long it took for Rebekah to awake. *Nothing else matters.*

Many hours later, his embrace tightened carefully when conscious thoughts began forming inside her head. The electrical impulses were like a shower of sighs, and he focused keenly as she stirred. He trapped a breath inside his chest, waiting for the moment when her eyes would open.

He was dreading seeing her lively gaze smothered by the mudslide of numbness; traumatic stress. *How much damage will there be?*

When Rebekah's eyelids fluttered open and she turned her head, her eyes lit up when she saw his face, and he smiled at last.

Her hand folded over his cheek as she said, "Connor." Turning his face, he buried his lips into her palm.

"Hi, honey," he whispered, and relief gripped him, locking his throat tight.

Chapter 38

Sebastian's fleeing stride devoured the miles. Heading north to where Douglas waited, he smothered his regrets, forming instead, a satisfying plan of revenge. Pandering to Serge and playing the role of his general had reaped its rewards.

The wind dragged the smile from his face as he hit cruising speed. *Doctor Connor's woman. I know his weakness now.* The death of the guardsmen played into Sebastian's hands. *I'm the only one who knows where the humans are.*

He closed in on his destination, and the odor of Douglas' fear-soaked sweat put the grin back on his face. *And then there's Douglas, of course.*

Respecting Douglas' role as their guide, Sebastian had handled him with more consideration on this trip, making the trek through the woodlands more comfortable, and even providing a warm coat to take the brunt of the wind chill.

Sebastian was playing nice.

The group of guardsmen had gathered in a copse of silver birch trees. A hole had been punched into the trunk of one, and that appealed to Sebastian's sense of drama. The regimented trunks, bleached by the moonlight, resembled bone-white fingers pointing skyward. Their eerie appearance made Douglas jittery, and Sebastian grinned. *Win, win.*

Sebastian had walked along the line of vampires, glared into each intent face, and decided 'this should be easy'. "We are here to *capture* the humans, *not* kill. They are undefended. Just go in and herd them out. Is that clear?"

Each guardsman had nodded.

"If you kill even *one*-" Sebastian's slicing gesture across his throat required no explanation.

Of course, he and Serge couldn't be sure Doctor Connor was *not* at the human nest, but the guardsmen did not need to know that.

When Sebastian abandoned a boringly terrified Douglas in the clearing to witness his triumph, he followed at a distance and shook his head at the lack of discipline. In Serge's opinion 'cannon fodder needs brawn, not brains'. *However, a brain cell between them might have been good.*

When the lone vampire emerged from the shadows, Sebastian's anger became reluctant fascination as the blond vampire took out a guardsman with ease and then collapsed the entrance to the human nest after disappearing inside.

I should have entered the fight when I saw him. Serge would have expected it, but Sebastian argued, 'what the councilor did not know'. *I'm glad I held back.* They had gambled on the possibility of Connor being there. *But, we didn't expect an accomplice.*

Sebastian had been about to slip away when the bluster of human scents wafting through the trees made him wait.

He saw them moving through the woods, and had honed in on the slender woman, his gut instinct telling him she was *Connor's* woman. Her odor was laced throughout the woods.

The fiery heat of her caramelized scent filled his nostrils, and she promised to be anything but 'boringly terrified'. When she sensed him coming, she took off towards the tree line.

He had enjoyed toying with her, letting hope clamber through her before he finally caught up. It thrilled him when she fought back, arousing an appetite suppressed for so long. It had been hard to find restraint.

Now, with his escape secured, he recalled the rebellion written on her face. His fingertips found the deep groove her blade had scored into his stomach and his dead blood quickened.

It had been so tempting to bite into her flesh and discover what Connor finds so compelling. Would her dead carcass have enraged the good doctor?

The impact of the metal spike bouncing off his back had snapped his attention back, and ironically, saved him. Sebastian might not have noticed the sudden change in air pressure otherwise. He was not a fool. He knew that only a vampire of formidable strength could generate such a shockwave, and so, he had left. *But, she'll be worth the wait, and I will scar her as she has me.*

Sebastian considered his retreat to be tactical, however, his thirst for revenge still grated through him. He halted in the wood and turned his attention to Douglas.

Materializing in the blink of an eye, which made Douglas jump, Sebastian cocked his head with the curiosity of a cat observing a mouse. *Ahh, my consolation prize.*

He studied Douglas' shiny, color-drained face.

"Well?" Douglas croaked, as nerves sucked the moisture from his mouth. Pressing back into the tree, the rough bark biting into his shoulder blades, Douglas slid down until the damp ground stopped him.

Sebastian wondered at how a human face could blend so well with the pale sheen of a silver birch. "You were right, of course. We found the human nest."

Sebastian grabbed the front of Douglas' coat, yanked him to his feet, and pinned him against the tree. Douglas's teeth snapped shut, grazing his tongue and filling his mouth with blood.

"The thing is, Douglas, it's time to decide."

"What?"

"The guardsmen are not coming back." Sebastian clucked in disapproval. "You forgot to tell us about the other vampire."

"There's only one. Connor." Douglas's eyes met the hazel-green mire of Sebastian's scorn.

"Well Douglas, it *is* decision time. Only you and I know this location." Sebastian's brows rose. "We could tell Councilor Serge the nest was deserted. We were ambushed and barely escaped with our lives." Sebastian watched the calculation playing out behind Douglas' fish-scale colored stare before reeling him in. "Of course, if I turn you now, then Serge's fury will roll off you, and you need not suffer broken bones." Sebastian shrugged as if to say 'your choice'. "And *we* will have the power."

Douglas managed a nod.

Sebastian pressed a thumb into the curve of Douglas' jaw, tilting his head and exposing his neck. As his cold breath transformed the sweat on Douglas' skin to a layer of frost, Sebastian said, "Unless I decide to kill you, of course."

Douglas' heart lurched as it shunted adrenalin up his carotid artery, and the synapses of his brain lit up. Sebastian felt the electrical charge like the pull of a magnet. *And there it is.* His smile became spiteful. *Terror. It tastes so much better.*

"You can do better than that, Douglas."

With a sharp jolt, Sebastian threw Douglas across the clearing, and watched the body bounce from a tree and thump to the ground. He whipped Douglas up by his throat, suspending him with his feet barely brushing the ground.

Groaning, Douglas stretched his eyes wide.

With cold detachment, Sebastian tore open Douglas' coat, baring his chest, and dragged a fingernail down over his stomach, opening up a gaping wound in the layer of fat.

Douglas' hands clutched frantically at his oozing flesh and came away covered in blood.

Sebastian's grip strangled the scream building in Douglas' throat. "Shhh. It won't do to let Connor know we are here."

Tears filled Douglas' eyes as Sebastian pushed his chin up and buried sharp teeth into his soft neck, not sweet and succulent, but doughy and damp. Only a burst of frustrated hunger prevented him spitting the fermenting draught of blood onto the ground. Douglas hung limply in Sebastian's grasp, compliant. *Maybe he still hopes his time has come, and it has.*

Sebastian's jaw worked in jerking, vicious strokes that ripped through flesh, and his grin faded as the delicious scent of Rebekah was overwhelmed by Douglas' stench.

His time to die.

When Sebastian released his hold, the dry tissue of Douglas' drained limbs creaked as they folded awkwardly beneath the rolling dead weight of his torso. The air sighed from Douglas' lungs as though death was a relief. Sebastian left the body where it fell, the glazed eyes staring up at the tree canopy and horror etched onto the face. The bland, biscuit-colored hair fluttered in the sudden flurry of air as Sebastian moved off towards London.

He would report the abortive attack to Councilor Serge, the ambush. *Sadly, Douglas died in the battle before they discovered the human nest.* He had all the power. He just needed to decide how to bring Connor to his knees, and, of course, to explore the pleasures of Annabelle. *Until I know her real name, that one will have to do.*

◇◇◇

Julian's grid search of the woods took in every blade of grass inside a four-mile radius of the eco-town. *That should turn up something, if there* is *anything.* He had an image of Leizle's grubby face pushed firmly to the back of his mind, but she was on his list of things-to-do. Every few seconds he huffed in a sample of woodland air, comparing the taste and smell to the scent of the rogue vampire locked inside his chest.

Spotting a heap of fabric lying on the ground, Julian altered course. He could see the gaping wound carved into the body from eighty yards out, and the congealed blood barely filled the crater in its torn neck. *Well-drained.*

Not a tossed uniform, then. Thinking the vampire may have shed a disguise, finding a shattered body threw him for a moment. Dropping to his knee, Julian leaned closer and compared the venom samples again. It was a match. *The guy stank.* Julian couldn't imagine the meal had been a satisfying one. He flipped the coat open and found the jagged tear down the flabby torso was more like an incision. *Not a feral in feeding frenzy. I wonder if Connor will think that's better or worse.*

Shrugging out of his jacket and folding it over a tree branch, Julian set about digging a grave, using his hands to break up earth and the dead man's shoe to clear it away. His diamond-hard nails cut through the sedimented layers with ease, and he stopped digging only when he could stand upright in the hole and not see out. *That should do it.*

Dropping the battered leather shoe at his feet, Julian jabbed a foothold into the wall of the trench with his boot, and boosted himself up and over the side.

He rolled the carcass into the pit and covered it over. Burying the body deep underground in the freezing temperature would preserve the venom in the tissue. Julian kicked over the traces of the grave. *If this vampire turns up, the body will put him away.*

His expression was hard as he returned through the woods. He *had* hoped to report back with better news, but, apart from the faint trace near the body, his quarry left nothing for Julian to track. *He's been gone too long.*

Minutes later, Julian strode down the rebuilt emergency exit tunnel, combing back his hair with his fingers and straightening his windswept jacket. Amusement played around his mouth. *Connor nearly ripped my head off when I sniffed Rebekah's neck.* His animosity had been a tangible force.

He's got it bad.

Shaking his head, Julian emerged inside the dining cavern like a glowering magician. He was tall and imposing, with his face set in concentration, and the six humans assembled there ran away. *Very funny.* He'd forgotten that Connor was the only vampire they expected to see. A wry smile chiseled into his features. *Fear is not the vibe I'm looking for.*

Julian went in search of Leizle, the next task on his list. Treading more carefully, he sank into the tranquil pool of revival sleep and the relaxation eased his movement to vampire slow-motion.

He found her sitting alone on a wooden stool in the meeting cavern. The glossy rope of her chestnut hair, guided by her shoulder blades, hung in a braid down her back. While Julian absorbed her image, her scent, and considered what to say, the breeze stirred by his arrival wafted over her skin and Leizle shivered. Julian's fingers flexed as he resisted the desire to rub her shoulders, and, as if she knew what he was thinking, Leizle chafed her arms briskly.

"Pull yourself together, girl," Leizle muttered.

Julian was arrested by her voice. Offloading her after their dash through the night was the last time he had touched her, and only now did he realize how much he yearned to see her face.

"Thinking about him will give you pneumonia if you're not careful," she whispered, rubbing her thighs as though his hands were still imprinted on her flesh.

Determined to avoid her and suppress his urge for more, even now, Julian lied to himself. *Connor doesn't want to leave Rebekah yet. That's the only reason I offered to find Leizle.* But now he *was* here, he admitted it was the only place he wanted to be.

"Hello, Leizle," he said gruffly. His long stride closed the space between them.

She jumped up and turned quickly. Her braid whipped through the air, and Julian's hand flashed out to catch it. As he closed his fingers around the copper-colored rope, a thrum of electricity shot up his arm as though the shock of her emotions surged along its length. She caught her breath, and he resisted the urge to touch her cheek.

"I didn't mean to startle you," he murmured.

A blush transformed her porcelain skin to a delicate shade of rose, and the enticing aroma of it wended its way over his palate.

With effort, Julian concentrated on the reason he came. He wound the silken strands of her hair slowly around his fist. "I've come for this." With a gentle tug, he lifted her chin and stared into her upturned face.

He flexed his ribcage and pulled in a deep breath, regretting the weakness instantly, when a flood of venom soothed the sting in his throat but not the ache in his chest, nor the cavernous craving for her blood.

He cleared his throat and swallowed, saying abruptly, "I've come for your hair."

"My hair?" Leizle had been studying his expression as if trying to read his thoughts. "My hair?" she said again, as though the words made no sense.

Gentler now, but still pretending detachment, Julian tried again. "Connor sent me to get your hair. We need it."

"Why?" she breathed.

"I can't explain. But it will cover your tracks. Stop them looking for you." Having said all he needed to, he retreated behind an emotionless facade.

"Take it," she said flatly. Not looking away from his veiled eyes, she pulled a penknife from her jeans pocket and held it out. "Take it."

Julian took the knife and sawed through the braid, wishing he could ignore the dull pain of confusion in her eyes as her face drained of expression. He did not cause physical pain, but he could see his rejection hurt.

"Thank you," he said. Turning on his heel, he disappeared from the meeting cavern.

Julian broke into a run, accelerating rapidly, pushing his body to the limit. Demons snapped at his heels. *Better for her, no good can come of getting too close.* "The sooner Connor moves them on, the better," he muttered, closing his fist around the silken rope and resisting the urge to bury his nose in the sleek strands.

He tucked away the last memory of her that cluttered his mind; Leizle fighting for balance, the ragged ends of her hair fluttering in the storm of his agitated departure. Her groaned words of 'pull yourself together' as she sank back down into her seat, were harder to fold away.

Chapter 39

Connor finally faced up to leaving Rebekah and made the journey to the hospital. *She's safe for now.* He burst in through the heavy glass doors, arriving in the emergency room in a pulse of pressure which spun the needle of the barometer on the wall. The whirlwind that was Doctor Connor, had arrived.

Powering his way along the slick polished floors, he entered the blood dispensary. Connor pushed aside the rubbery-plastic doors and paused inside the threshold as they clapped shut behind him. The perpetual motion of vampires rolling to the front of the queue reminded him of a conveyor belt.

He crossed the room and put his hand on the chest of the vampire stepping up to the dispensing counter. The vampire opened his mouth, saw Connor's uncompromising expression, and snapped his jaw shut again.

"Charles," Connor said, turning to address the familiar figure doling out blood rations.

"Doctor Connor. Are you trying to cause a stir?" Charles raised an ironic eyebrow and held out three vials of blood.

"I couldn't resist. Don't you wish more vampires were impulsive?"

With a half-smile, Charles said, "My job is easier if they aren't. And you provide me with quite enough color, Doctor."

"A good thing, I hope?" Connor said. He took the glass tubes and turned away, smiling when the silent conveyor belt of vampire movement resumed.

Barely even a ripple. His lips twitched while he considered the havoc he could wreak if he really tried. *One shove and they'd go down like dominoes.* He headed off to find a place to take rap-sleep. *I need to be on full alert.* He stepped into the examination room where he had first stumbled across Rebekah and shook his head drily at the pull he still felt to come here.

In a ruthlessly efficient execution of the hydrating process, Connor drank the blood and tossed two vials across the room into the recycling crate, and dropped a full one back into his pocket. He leapt up onto the bed, lying down in a fluid movement. His carotid arteries pumped the blood from his gullet into his brain, and the cell door swung open to welcome the flood. Connor relaxed into the pain and surrendered to the delirious tempest of desire. As always, his rap-sleep was saturated with Rebekah, but this time tinged with relief that she was safe within the confines of the eco-town. Douglas' death was something to celebrate.

When his eyes snapped open again, he sprang to his feet, collected his white coat from the back of the chair, and was on his way out of the door before he had finished raking his hands through his hair.

Setting a course for the mortuary, Connor speculated on Julian's obvious discomfort when he handed over Leizle's braid. All Julian said was, 'Tell Rebekah to explain the plan to Leizle'.

Connor expected him to say more, but Julian merely raised a brow and walked away, his part over with, for now.

They both had roles to play in the final act of freeing Leizle from the attentions of Serge. *Phase one; set the scene.*

Connor checked his watch. Julian would soon deliver the report to the council that Leizle had thrown herself out of a second-floor window in the hospital and sustained a fatal head injury. Leizle committing suicide rather than becoming a prisoner on the farm would ring true, and Connor would be ready to take the lead role in the play when summoned by the council to give his account of the tragedy.

Alone in the mortuary, Connor pulled open his white coat, registering the chilled air as a warm caress. A body draped in a sheet lay on a trolley, and he wondered at how the relaxation of death made the human form melt. *They all look so frail.*

He had been waiting for the newly transported female corpse; hoping she would die soon after admission to the medical center had made him feel uncomfortable. *But at least she succumbed without my help.*

Flipping back the linen sheet, he inspected her slack features. Laying a hand on her cheek, he calculated her temperature. *Good, she is almost cold.* Somehow, knowing she had had time to be peacefully at rest, mattered. He didn't believe in souls and afterlife, but if it was *her* belief, then he could be sure he was looking at an empty shell. He took a relieved breath.

She was older than Leizle, and the distinctive blue pattern of cyanosis staining her skin indicated oxygen starvation resulting from collapsed lungs. But only a doctor would detect the sign of something more than a head trauma.

He knew her from clinic rounds, and felt more regret than he expected when he pressed his hand onto her cold features. Applying pressure until the cheekbones snapped and the jaw crumbled, he rearranged the fractured bone structure into a broken jigsaw which bore little resemblance to a human face.

Connor tugged Leizle's braid from beneath his shirt, where it lay coiled around his waist, and loosened the strands. He clawed his nails over the shrinking scalp of the corpse and made enough congealed blood ooze from the wounds to help fix the distinctive chestnut mane in place. *It only has to pass a fleeting inspection.* He smeared the blood from the glass vial inside his pocket on to the clumped tresses in the final touch to perfect the disguise. Moving quickly through the check list of 'signs' to fake, he ran his hands down the length of her body, compressing tissue and crumbling bone in strategic places to fit the scenario of a fall from a height. Only a doctor would question the lack of pre-mortem bruising. Finally, with the nick of a blade, he added the infamous cut to her arm and the deception was complete.

Connor washed his hands, straightened his clothes, and eased the collar of his shirt which suddenly felt tight. Flicking the switch inside his head to 'Doctor Connor', he set off to work his shift, and to wait until the council called for his attendance. *Julian will have the final showdown in hand.*

After leaving the mortuary, he conducted a lightning fast tour the hospital corridors looking for Anthony, irritated that his surgical assistant was avoiding him. Connor would have preferred to have found him before the storm broke in the courtroom. *But, if he's gone to ground, at least he's out of the way.*

He kept an eye out, still hoping Anthony's anger would make him track Connor down and demand answers.

In the walk-in clinic, Connor discharged half a dozen vampires, after grinding away areas of dead sun-scorched tissue with modified pliers and delivering fear-of-God lectures.

The highlight of his shift proved to be saving a vampire from locked-in syndrome. While overseeing a blood delivery from the farm, Connor scanned the room, trying to appear busy. Standing in the queue, the vampire's eyes skittered around the walls, one hand clutching at the other as if he was miming the incy-wincy-spider rhyme he probably had never even heard.

Connor knew the signs instantly. *He's too agitated to feed. Revival sleep is long overdue.* Bedside manners would waste time, so he grabbed a vial of blood from a passing trolley. Closing in fast, Connor pulled a syringe of muscle relaxant from the pocket of his white coat and jabbed the needle into the vampire's windpipe, anesthetizing his gag reflex. In a seamless movement, he poured the blood down his patient's throat. Seconds later, the life blood the casualty needed slid down his gullet. *Extreme, but it got a feed inside him quickly enough to save him.*

Staring into the vampire's glazed expression, Connor grunted as the relaxation of revival sleep softened the tight lines of the vampire's features.

"Good," he muttered, and then moved on to his next task. As he left the blood assembly point, he wondered how Julian fared. *Will the summons come today?*

He rounded a corner, slamming a door into a wall with the force of his sweeping hand, and stopped dead. "Juror Marius." Connor bowed slowly. *So, this is it.*

"Doctor Connor." Marius' coal black eyes studied Connor with curiosity. "The council has convened to hear the circumstances leading to the death of the human girl. We expect your attendance."

"Of course," said Connor.

Marius disappeared, and Connor raised a brow. *Julian, or Serge, is surely in a hurry.* He peeled his white coat from his shoulders and tossed it into the nearest linen bin with a quick twist of the wrist. *The waiting is over.*

He set off for the council building. *I wonder why Marius played messenger.* Connor had never seen a juror at the hospital before. *But then, we've never before had a situation like this one.*

Pausing outside the courtroom door, Connor adopted an appropriate apologetic expression.

As he laid his hand on the polished wood, the door disappeared, pulled open by an unknown force, and Connor narrowly avoided being barged aside by Anthony exiting the court; the loose end that could unravel everything he and Julian had planned.

Anthony rocked back on his heels, indignation tightening his broad shoulders.

"Anthony." Connor greeted him carefully.

The brown eyes were hard in his tense face as he answered, "Doctor Connor."

With one last penetrating look, Anthony skirted around Connor, turned on his heel and disappeared from view.

Connor became grimly aware of Anthony's feelings when the heavy oak entrance doors slammed shut as he left the building. *What now? Did he tell the truth?*

Needing to work harder at arranging his features this time, Connor made his entrance. Taking the place in the dock, he fixed his gaze on the opposite wall, ready to speak only when spoken to. *And irritating Serge will be an added bonus.*

The epitome of impassive, Connor waited for the charade to unfold.

Doubts crept in, when Julian's blank expression gave nothing away. Connor sliced a look at the jurors, taking a snapshot of the demeanor of each. *They look bored. Anthony can't have voiced his suspicions.* Over the decades, Connor had come to understand their personalities. *They share the distaste for Serge and his time-wasting.* Connor hoped that would be enough.

Juror Marius did not suffer fools gladly, but he was a stickler for protocol, and he waited patiently for Serge to pause before saying, slowly, "Doctor Connor's reputation remains unimpeachable. I trust you have more to add?"

Connor relaxed a little. He felt certain Marius would not have seen anything over the last few weeks to change that view.

Juror Alexander appeared less indulgent of Serge, and glared at him as though it would speed up the process.

"Threatening the food supply is the charge I seek." Serge's sallow face wore a tentative grin. He could not even pretend to gloat.

Connor quickly veiled his amusement. *He expected to stand there with a group of human captives to parade before the council; instead he has eight missing guardsmen.*

"Have we not been here before, councilor? You had nothing then and have nothing now." Julian locked him in a disapproving glare. "Please, stop wasting the council's time." As Serge opened his mouth to protest, Julian raised his hand. "I know this girl lies in the mortuary, however, you cannot prove Doctor Connor is *responsible* for her death. Therefore, you have nothing."

"If I could just examine the body. She was my property, after all," Serge said weakly, making a last ditch attempt to persuade the jury.

"Last time I looked, *Councilor* Serge, you had not been elevated to juror status." Julian's rigid spine impressed his indignation on the court. "Are you suggesting the inspection of the girl's corpse by Doctor Connor and Juror Marius is not good enough?"

"That is certainly not my intention." Serge backtracked with reluctance. Still clinging to the prize, he added, "I just thought, with such a brief introduction to her in court, Juror Marius-"

"I have all my faculties, councilor." Marius stirred to answer. His dark eyes were dead pools as his lips condescended to smile. "I need no help from those of lower ranks."

"We have examined the body. We are satisfied." Julian looked to Alexander for agreement.

Alexander's inclined head closed the argument.

Julian addressed the assembled vampires, avoiding looking in Connor's direction. "Doctor Connor removed the girl from the farm. That much is true. Surgical Assistant Anthony's testified that it was for her protection. The wardens confirmed the attack in the examination room."

White faces in the gallery bobbed minutely in a ripple of agreement.

Julian met Connor's calculated candor. "Doctor Connor could not have predicted the girl would commit suicide; therefore, he is guilty only of ignorance." Julian resisted the twitch of amusement as Connor's eyes sparked at the patronizing comment. "And maybe, stupidity. Case dismissed," Julian pronounced.

The courtroom emptied quickly, and even Serge melted away.

Julian jerked his head, indicating Connor should join him in his chambers.

The jurors vacated the bench with fluid efficiency and the door thumped closed behind them, leaving Connor alone to enjoy the calm. *The storm has been weathered, for now.*

As he left the court, passing through the door and swinging left to join Julian in his chambers, the obstacle of Marius blocked his path.

"Juror Marius?" Connor raised an inquiring brow.

Marius tidied his slick dark hair and pinned Connor in his sights. "Every now and again, a vampire does something extraordinary," he said slowly, weighing his words.

Connor nodded, but held his tongue.

Marius' jet eyes gleamed with sober intent. "I wonder, Doctor Connor, are you such a vampire?"

"You flatter me, Juror Marius," said Connor. "There is nothing extraordinary about me. That is, unless you count my talent for riling Councilor Serge."

"You certainly have that." Marius smiled solemnly as he stepped aside. "Well I mustn't keep you, Principal Julian is waiting."

"Of course." Connor smiled in his turn, bowing his head as he walked past the juror and continued on along the hallway.

Stopping abruptly, he rapped his knuckles on the door and entered at Julian's familiar command of 'Come'.

"So, Anthony backed me up?" Connor asked quietly.

Julian's face was serious. He finished hanging his robes in the wardrobe before answering. "He did, yes. But knowing him as I do, he was clearly fighting some demons. I did not press him in court, but if I had? I don't know. You need to talk to him."

Connor smiled grimly. "Believe me, I tried. He was not at the hospital. When I bumped into him outside the courtroom, his mood was… uninviting, to put it mildly."

"Well, before he changes his testimony, find him."

Connor nodded slowly, turning a speculative glance on Julian. "Oh, by the way, I just had an interesting encounter with Marius."

Julian smiled. "He's astute. He misses the old life, and he envies your fervor. But, he knows nothing about the humans."

"Is he dangerous?"

"No, I think not. A minor complication, nothing more." Julian crossed to his favored spot by the hearth and landed a blow on Connor's shoulder as he swept past. "For now, it seems you are in the clear, so celebrate."

Connor shrugged the fist-shaped dent from the fabric of his coat and grinned, surprised when the astringency of alcohol stung his sinuses.

Replacing the crystal stopper in the decanter, Julian turned a hundred watt grin on Connor. "Cheers," he said with determined high spirits as he handed over a glass.

"Really?" Connor laughed. Swilling the brandy around the bowl, he raised a brow.

"Come, you've done this before, pretended to eat in front of humans." Julian laughed in his turn. "It's like eating beetles and worms, not good for you, but you can do it for a dare."

"We're not home free, you know. Serge will come back with something." Connor frowned. "And, that vampire in the woods is a concern. If he was one of Serge's, he would have been here today, and Serge would have made his case. I don't like it."

"I don't like it either, but I've got his scent. If he turns up, I have Douglas' body as evidence. We have a good shot at shutting him down. You are ready to move the humans out, in any case, so Serge will soon have nothing. Harry's made up enough beta-blockers and pheromone spray to last?"

"It's a two-day hike to the derelict church, but yes, they are ready to move. The catacombs underneath the chapel are easy to guard, so they will be safe. It will be too cold to stay for any length of time, but, as a halfway house, it will do."

"Well, in that case, honestly? I think we need to celebrate. If not the war, we won a battle today." Julian put the glass to his lips, tossed it back and swallowed the burn. "Mmm, it's not as bad as I remember," he spluttered.

"Okay." Connor, resigned to the ritual, threw his head back and emptied the glass. He tilted his head and screwed up one eye. "I agree, Rebekah's burn is far worse."

"Oh, get out of here," said Julian. He nudged Connor hard in the ribs. "I'm sure you can find a better way to celebrate, but, Connor?" Julian's voice arrested his friend's departure in midflight. "First, find Anthony."

Chapter 40

Connor did not need to be told twice. *First, find Anthony.* A swift detour through the blood dispensary at the hospital confirmed a sneaking suspicion. *Anthony went out with a hunting party, so he's definitely angry.* Not really surprising, but Connor felt irritation at the additional delay. The moment of his reunion with Rebekah scampered further into the distance.

He covered the two hundred miles to the gateway of the hunting park at Exeter in fifteen minutes; it provided a blissful release of the tension Connor had carried since he stepped into the morgue and dressed the dead woman in Leizle's hair.

As the thunderclouds in the dark sky cleared away, moonlight broke through and glinted on the metal strands of the eighteen foot tall chain-link barrier. The imposing perimeter fence meandered across the landscape from coast to coast, and even Connor's vampire vision could not see an end to it.

With the human ghost town of Exeter lying behind him, Connor reined in his speed and performed an emergency stop when he ran out of road.

The boundary of the vast expanse of Dartmoor scrubland was manned by vampire game wardens, supposedly to keep the big cats inside, but Connor knew better. The stocks here were as important to regulate as those of the human farm, and, a rotation of the hunting zones prevented the park being stripped of breeding pairs.

He stopped at the Exeter gate and waited until the warden ushered him inside and directed him to the brick built changing station. A vampire met him at the turnstile counter, and Connor recited his unique identification number.

"LH5839204."

As though he had the thousands of numbers tattooed inside his head, without batting an eyelid, the vampire said, "Ah, Doctor Connor. How are things at the London Hive?"

"Challenging, as always." Connor smiled and took the parcel of clothes tagged with his personalized number. In the act of turning away, he stopped as if a thought had just occurred to him. "Surgical

Assistant Anthony of the London Hive, did he make it down here today?"

"Yes, he did."

"And, are we in the same zone?" asked Connor, with a persuasive half-smile.

"I'm sure that can be arranged." The warden barely paused retrieving Anthony's information. "Zone B"

"Thank you."

Connor strode away, anxious to get changed and track Anthony down.

The moorland was three hundred and fifty square miles divided into three one-hundred-square-mile zones, with a fifty-square-mile nursery. There were other hunting grounds at Bodmin Moor, but each hive member had their favorite haunts.

Anthony and Connor were no different. They had their own habitual hunting paths within each zone, so Connor was hopeful this would not be too difficult.

He entered the cavernous changing barn. It resembled an old library with twelve foot tall double-sided shelving units dividing the internal space into rows. Instead of books, the shelves were loaded with wooden crates. Collecting a crate and crossing to a wooden bench, Connor stripped off his clothes, folded them roughly, and dropped them inside. Unashamedly naked, he returned the crate to its numbered slot. Limbering up rock hard muscle as he moved, Connor returned to the bench, unwrapped his hunting package, and stepped into a leather loincloth which fit his never-changing physique like a glove. Modesty flaps at back and front brushed his thighs when he moved.

He left the changing area by the rear door, pausing when a vampire warden appeared and filled Connor's outstretched palms with oil which he used to slick back his hair and rub over his torso. A daub of blue paint on his left shoulder blade allocated his hunting zone as B, and, when the gate into the moorland opened, Connor broke into a forceful run.

He covered ten miles, oblivious of the crosswind snatching at his body, and effortlessly scaled one of the large outcrops of granite where, in the height of summer, big cats laid out and sunned themselves. The artificial landscape provided stimulation for prey and hunting vampires alike. Offering caves, dens, and densely packed trees, both species had everything they needed to get the most out of their time here.

Right now, Connor just wanted to locate Anthony. From his vantage point, scanning the moonlit terrain, Connor watched hunting parties weaving through the trees. He hunkered down and waited for Anthony in what was their favorite resting place. *How long will he be?*

Distant flurries of movement, and the ebb and flow of snarls torn from vocal chords, punctuated the passing minutes. Connor honed in on each, hoping for a recognizable feature which would tell him it was Anthony.

Hearing movement thundering through the undergrowth, Connor's eyes narrowed as a Siberian tiger broke cover with Anthony loping after it. If any doubts remained about Anthony's mood, they were wiped out as, closing the gap, he launched forward and, in mid flight, wrapped his arms around the tiger's chest. He dragged the cat to its knees. Its paws still scrabbling as its brain yelled, 'keep running'. The tiger's roar stuttered into a bellow of pain when Anthony tightened his grip. The feline ribcage imploded with a sickening wet muffled crunch. Anthony, grimacing until the tendons in his neck bulged, filled the night air with his own ferocious growl.

Connor frowned and rose silently to his feet. *This should be a piece of cake.*

The moonlight glimmered over Connor's oiled body as he stood tall, and Anthony's head snapped around, every muscle in his hefty frame turning to stone. His brown eyes glittered as they bored into Connor's.

With a sharp nod, Connor sank back down on his haunches.

Moments later, Anthony dropped down beside him, dragging his hands down over his blood splattered face and wiping them on his loin cloth.

"Feeling better, I hope?" asked Connor, carefully. Tuning out the red smudges staining his skin, he measured Anthony's attitude, unflinching. *This is crunch time.*

Anthony's jaw muscle ticked as the glittering excitement of the hunt faded. His usual reverence skulked in the depths, but his affront at Connor's treatment of him surged forward. "Why?"

This was no time for shorthand, Connor needed to be clear. "Why? Why did I cut her? Why did I inject you with muscle relaxant?"

Anthony swallowed and flexed his fists. As a boxer, he would rather punch Connor than talk. As a vampire with aspirations to be as well respected as Connor, he had more sense. He nodded. "Both."

"I apologize for using you, Anthony. I had to think fast to save the female from Serge." Connor paused to make sure Anthony was listening. "The girl was going to be the first in the hybrid breeding program." Connor's lip curled with genuine disgust.

"Hybrid?" Anthony frowned. "Serge had the council's consent for that?"

Connor knew he was tap-dancing now, bending the truth. "He had applied for it, yes." Connor's oiled chest heaved with pretended indignation. "I couldn't let it happen. Serge is a deluded sadist." He let his words sink in. "I had to intervene."

Staring out, as though his concerns were written across the star-studded sky, Connor carefully chose words loaded with feeling. Anthony would know he meant every one. "It's a crime against nature. We are an *unnatural* species, and a hybrid is a step into the unknown. It cannot be allowed to happen." For a moment, Connor lost himself in his own passion. "Would a hybrid breed be an immortal food supply enabling the likes of Serge to live forever? Or would he magnanimously die, allowing them to become the new immortals who no longer depended upon humans to survive?" Connor's face tightened with a snarl. "The consequences are too horrific to contemplate."

Antagonism drained from Anthony's body. His shoulders relaxed as he shifted his weight, and Connor knew he had him.

Connor rubbed his hand over his face in real regret. “After the other girls’ deaths, I did hope to save her. I’m only sorry it turned out badly.” *Not everything is a lie.*

Anthony digested what his mentor had said, in silence.

Connor waited too. Having spent decades as a surgical intern, he hoped Anthony would not throw it all away.

“I understand your contempt for the hybrid scheme,” Anthony said at last. With an expression of understanding, he added firmly, “I guess we’ll just forget it?”

“That is what I hoped. I’ve known you a long time, I knew you would understand.” Connor dropped a hand onto Anthony’s solid shoulder. “And thank you, for trusting me enough to keep your doubts to yourself. Of course, the council may call upon you again…”

Anthony shrugged. “I have already told them the girl was startled and tried to run. The cut was an accident and I lost it. That about covers it, I’d say.”

Connor raised a brow as he said, “I’ll see you tomorrow, back at the hospital for rounds?”

Anthony nodded decisively.

Connor felt happy that, for now at least, Anthony was on board. It was enough. *Though, I’ll need to be around when the questions start eating at him, as they surely will. He’s not stupid.*

Surging to his feet, Connor reached out a hand and pulled Anthony up beside him. “I hope I haven’t ruined your night, but I didn’t want this to get in the way.”

“We haven’t hunted together for a while. Seeing as we’re here, why don’t you join me?”

Frustration cramped Connor’s chest as he swallowed his refusal and smiled. “Sure, I’ve got an hour to kill.”

Anthony laughed and landed a blow on Connor’s shoulder which was much harder than he expected.

Three hours later, the weather turned, and as always in England, when it rained, it poured.

After saying goodbye to Anthony, Connor changed back into his day clothes and cruised at top speed across the countryside. Closing in on the eco-town, he barely noticed the driving rain beating down. His body hummed with anticipation, and, easing back from a run to a prowling walk, he entered the eco-town tunnels.

Scraping wet hair out of his eyes, he sluiced away diamond-hued droplets which ran down his neck and lay shimmering on his skin. Moving purposefully along the dimly lit passageway, he arrived outside Rebekah's den. He leaned back against the wall and paused to listen, absorbing the scent and taste of her. Flattening his palms in a feline-like caress over the tunnel wall, his stroking fingertips carved grooves into the flint-hard surface. Connor was where he wanted to be, and all thoughts of Anthony melted away.

Sinking into revival sleep, he pushed away from the wall and stepped over the threshold. He laughed at her stunned expression as, for a moment, Rebekah's mouth fell open. But in the next, she rushed forward and threw herself into his arms, laughing too, when he whisked her around.

Setting her back on the ground, he held her away from him, and gazing into her flushed face burned pleasure through him.

"You're home," she whispered, and he suddenly realized that he was.

"I'm home, but I'm very grubby, and wet." He grinned.

Hanging firmly on to his shirt, Rebekah said urgently, "Did it all go okay? Leizle's hair worked?"

"Yes, it worked." His long fingers stabbed through his own greasy hair as he said, "But we have not tracked down the vampire that touched you."

Rebekah's grip slipped away as goosebumps crawled over her.

Connor caught her hand gently in his. "We will, Rebekah. He was not in court, but it's just a matter of time before he surfaces inside the hive, and Julian will be ready."

Folding her into his arms, he murmured, "We are moving out tomorrow night, in any case. And in the meantime, I'm not going anywhere. Julian has our back. This time tomorrow, everything this phantom vampire knows will be useless. You and the others will be safe."

"You're right." She met his eyes and the determined spark in their depths took him back to their first meeting.

"What?" he said darkly.

"I marked him."

"You did what?" Connor released her slowly, pinning her with an incredulous gaze.

"Well, I think I did." Rebekah lowered her lashes as his cold composure took him away from her.

Her sudden nervousness was all that held him in check as he said carefully, "Go on." But, he already knew he was not going to like it.

"When he caught me, I stabbed him," she whispered.

Connor frowned. "You can't have. We are tougher than that."

"Well, it marked him. I felt the blade judder, digging in to-" her words died in her throat, as Connor's gray eyes glinted menacingly.

"The blade?" The picture played out in his head and dread landed like a sledgehammer blow onto his chest. His hands moved to her shoulders as he said grimly, "He could have killed you. If he had lost his temper he could have snapped you like a twig."

Connor's own grasp tightened and fear-laced frustration pulled his features taut.

Even with the pain of his clamped fingers biting in, she said vehemently, "I can't sit here and do nothing." Tears of anger spilled over. "Don't expect me to. And if you do, you've got the wrong girl."

A rasp ripped from his throat as he growled at her. "Damn it, Rebekah."

She flinched, and for a moment, as he felt the bruises threatening to blossom beneath his fingertips, he was in hell, too. "I'm so sorry, honey." His icy touch gentled and stroked over the pressure points on her arms. "I scared you. I'm sorry."

"I'm sorry, too," she croaked. "But I can't be helpless. I won't be"

"I know." Connor's frustration melted. "It's why I love you. I *know*."

The remnants of his fear faded as his lips touched hers. He took everything he needed from her, molding her to his will until she surrendered and her body clung to his. His voice was rough as his fingers laced through her hair and he held her trapped. "If you get yourself killed, I will go insane. Do you want that?"

She shook her head, ignoring the pull on her hair. She framed his face with her hands.

"Just be careful, for me. Okay?" He searched her face until he found what he needed in her eyes. Dropping a kiss onto her lips, he said, "I really need to wash up. I'll be right back."

And as always, his instant departure left Rebekah feeling bereft, with her body still reeling. He disappeared before his voice faded.

Moving silently past the empty dining cavern, Connor made his way through to the kitchen and into the laundry room.

Shedding his clothes as he crossed the threshold, he peeled damp cloth from smooth hard muscles until he stood naked. He filled a bowl with warm water from the Jacuzzi. Connor frowned, running through Rebekah's words and shying away from how close he had come to losing her. Fighting the feelings of impotence, he soaked a washcloth and scrubbed at his skin, sluicing dried blood and oil residue from his hair and body.

His muscles twitched when a waft of her honeyed scent filled his nostrils, and he smiled. *Rebekah.* His skin, warmed by the water, tingled when he scrubbed harder. Her thundering heartbeat was playing havoc with his concentration, and, when she drew closer, he could hear her breathing.

When the curtain finally moved aside and she stepped into view, she smiled. The sight of her ignited the glow of a sunrise inside his chest. He could forgive her anything to see that smile.

Locking his body tight, holding back the need to cross the room and kiss her, he stood still and delighted in the racing of her pulse as the sight of him dusted her skin in perspiration.

Rebekah caught her breath. The magnificence of his naked body stole the words she had been about to say. A hot flush blossomed deep inside her when the muscles in his abdomen tightened beneath her gaze. With a shake of her head, she recovered her senses and said huskily, “Can we start over? I’ve missed you.”

Without lifting his head, his lashes unveiled the molten heat of his silver-gray eyes. His voice stroked over her skin, unfurling tendrils of desire inside her as he growled gently, “Hi Honey, I’m home.”

“So I see,” she said lightly. Grazing her eyes deliberately over his body, she said quietly, “I think you missed a bit.”

Her legs felt weak when she stepped forward. Reaching out to trail her fingers over his chest, she moved around to stand behind him. She took the washcloth from his slack fingers and ran it over his shoulder blades, mesmerized by the rivulets of water meandering over his taut muscles. She moved back around and stood in front of him, running the cloth over his chest and stomach. Her eyes met his.

He reached out and skimmed his hand lightly over her collarbone, his finger wandering down to dip into her damp cleavage. His gaze held her captive as he unbuttoned her dress and pushed it away.

“Not afraid of me anymore, then?” He smiled as revival sleep wrapped his raw hunger in cotton wool and deadened the pain, defusing the hot-wired current of desire touching her skin ignited.

Laying her hands on his hard chest, she leaned in to kiss his smile. “No, never afraid.”

Effortlessly, he lifted her to straddle his naked hips, fitting his hard body to her softness. Her hot skin warmed his bare chest and stomach, and contentment rumbled in his throat as his tongue teased her nipple. She moaned as he pulled the hard bud into his mouth and grazed it over his teeth.

“God, Rebekah,” he grumbled, his body trembling against hers.

As she clung to him, he buried his face in her neck. His thirsty tissue begged to be saturated in Rebekah’s essence, but he could endure it.

She sought his lips, and he lost himself in her heat. Her heartbeat echoed through him, her skin damp where her body ached for his.

He walked the tunnels back to her den, sat down onto the bed, and took her with him as he rolled onto his back.

"I've missed you, too, honey," he chuckled against her lips as she wriggled into his lap.

"Love me, Connor."

His response was instant and urgent. He licked the salt from her skin, absorbing the scent and taste of her, and when his hand brushed between her thighs, she groaned in welcome.

Goosebumps clustered over her body as, aligning her hips with his, she sat up and took him deep inside.

His slate-gray eyes registered surprise. "Definitely not scared of me anymore, then. Huh?" he said. His grin dropped away when she began to move.

"If I live forever, nothing will ever be better than this." He heaved a sigh. *Okay, for every ounce of pleasure, I have ten times that weight in pain, but she's worth every moment. Life will never be dull again.*

With their enemies closing in, how can Connor and Rebekah hope to survive?

Their battle continues in
Fire and Ice Book 2: Survival

Out on Amazon Kindle and in paperback, Summer 2018

Watch out for the Prequel to the Fire & Ice Series.

Death of Connor Sanderson

How did Doctor Connor become a vampire?

It all began in London, in 1910...

www.ingramcontent.com/pod-product-compliance
Ingram Content Group UK Ltd.
Pitfield, Milton Keynes, MK11 3LW, UK
UKHW041846200726
13854UKWH00005BA/2196

9 781999 661403